I0716152

ADVANCE PRAISE

Gray Matter is an emotional story that goes above and beyond what I hope for in a book. With hilarious banter, a heart-wrenching theme, and strong bonds of friendship, this book made it to my favorites list within the first few chapters.

— KIMBERLY PATTON, AUTHOR OF *THE KNOWING*

In *Gray Matter*, Avery Volz's vivid descriptions and immersive storytelling pull readers deep into the characters' lives, capturing the raw emotions of early adulthood. The narrative skillfully portrays the angst of navigating choices, opportunities, and the uncertain hopes that define this stage of life. It also delves into the power of first love, exploring what love truly means in a time of growth and self-discovery. Through its exploration of mental health, the book effectively advocates for awareness across the spectrum of suffering, offering an empathetic portrayal that resonates long after the final page.

— ASHLEY COURNOYER-SMITH, SCHOOL PSYCHOLOGIST AND AUTHOR OF *MY BODY KNOWS. DO I KNOW?*

Gray Matter offers readers fresh perspectives on the often emotional and challenging concepts of mental illness through vivid imagery and thoughtful comparisons interwoven with a mix of poetry, humor, and storytelling. It illustrates and enhances the reader's connection to the characters, their challenges, and how mental health struggles can complicate and deepen romantic connections.

Volz seeks to dismantle stigma through her characters' experiences. This approach not only fosters empathy but also builds awareness of the diverse ways mental illness can affect individuals. The support of friends is also portrayed with compassion, highlighting the crucial role of understanding and solidarity in navigating personal struggles.

— IONA CONLON, ALUMNI RELATIONS AND
STEWARDSHIP OFFICER AT PENN STATE,
YORK CAMPUS

GRAY MATTER

ALSO BY AVERY VOLZ

Broken Beautifully Series:

To The One I Love

To Now and Forever

GRAY MATTER

AVERY VOLZ

Edited by
DEBORAH KEVIN AND KRIS FAATZ

HIGHLANDER PRESS

GRAY MATTER. Copyright © 2024 by Avery Volz

All rights reserved.

This is a work of fiction. Names, characters, places, events, and incidents are either products of the author's imagination or used in a fictitious manner. Any resemblance to actual persons, living or deceased, or actual events is purely coincidental.

No part of this book may be reproduced in any form or by any electronic or mechanical means, including information storage and retrieval systems, without written permission from the author, except for the use of brief quotations in a book review.

ISBN: 978-1-956442-44-1
Ebook ISBN: 978-1-956442-45-8
Library of Congress Control Number: Applied For.

Published by Highlander Press
A division of Highlander Enterprises, LLC
501 W. University Pkwy, Ste. B2
Baltimore, MD 21210

Cover design: Patricia Creedon, Creedon Design
Managing Editor: Deborah Kevin
Editor: Kris Faatz
Author photo: Helen Kruml

For my favorite matrix glitch.
You know who you are.

AUTHOR'S NOTE

I got the idea for this book after taking an abnormal psychology class my freshman year in college. It was my favorite class I took in undergrad, because it deeply reflected my interests in the psychology field, namely, squashing the stigma around some of the more severe mental health disorders.

Struggling with a mental health disorder is no cake-walk. In fact, I struggle with severe anxiety and depression—and have, ever since the gray days of middle school. I understand what it is like to feel isolated and uncertain, to think that nothing will ever change and that no one will truly understand the lowness of the lows. But that is why I wrote this book: to educate others on what it means to love someone who struggles with a mental health condition. It takes patience, kindness, and listening ears. It takes a soft, understanding approach. It takes support and strength. Above all, if your own mental health is in shambles, you will not be able to help someone else. Take care of yourself first.

I have been on both sides of the coin in recent years—the one giving love and the one needing love. It is a tricky road to walk (a *gray matter*, if you will), but I believe that with kindness (toward us and others) that it is possible.

If you or someone you know is struggling with a mental health disorder and contemplating suicide, please know that you are not alone. Call 988 or 1-800-273-8255. Or, if you prefer texting, 741741. THERE IS LIGHT AT THE END OF THE TUNNEL. Don't give up. I'm rooting for you.

Love,

Avery

PROLOGUE

I am a freshman, and I know freshmen are supposed to be bright-eyed and bushy-tailed, but just now, in the dead silence of my very first English class at the University of Rhode Island, my stomach growled like a hormonal chihuahua. So, I am not feeling very lively and chipper at the moment. I am publicly embarrassed and hangry, which is a dangerous thing for the innocent students in a two-mile radius of me here in the dining hall.

The cook calls, "Grilled chicken sandwich with cheese!"

Before he finishes the announcement, my feet are moving. I am so hungry I don't even spot the other hand reaching for the sandwich until I snatch my meal off the counter and collide with a man who has dazzling blue eyes.

"Oh, sorry," the boy says.

It is a wonder my jaw does not shatter on the floor.

In fact, I'm suddenly afraid my eyes are going to dislodge from their optic nerves and pop right out of my head. I have had my fair share of exes—two to be exact, if we are only counting actual relationships and excluding meaningless flings. They were cute, but this guy is *hot*. Except, as I take in his light-golden waves of hair and his square jawline and his broad shoulders and strong arms, "hot" does not seem like the correct adjective. That doesn't feel respectful enough. This guy asks for respect without even opening his mouth. He's *handsome*. Like movie star, I'd-pay-to-have-your-heart handsome. Even Chris Hemsworth doesn't have hair like that.

Unfortunately, my addiction to sordid TV dramas like *Gossip Girl* and *Pretty Little Liars* informs me that guys *this* good-looking are douchebags. Nine times out of ten. 99.9 percent. Almost no room for error in that calculation.

"I think that's my order," the boy murmurs, gesturing to my sandwich. There's a splash of pink in his angular cheeks.

"I don't think so," I reply. My voice sounds three octaves higher than normal, and I know it is not just the hunger.

"Grilled chicken sandwich with cheese!" the cook calls again, placing another plate on the counter and eyeing me directly.

Shit.

"Gosh, I am *so* sorry." I hand the gorgeous guy his order and pick up my own.

"That's okay. No problem." He smiles, and I want to know how long he wore braces because his teeth are flawless and white. *Perfectly* white! Does he not drink tea with almost every meal?!

Note to self: pick up some more Crest 3D-Whitestrips.

"Great minds think alike," he adds and holds his plate up in a way that says *cheers!*

I blink at him. What douchebag says "great minds think alike" in a way that makes your heart melt into a puddle of rainbows? All I can do is smile. And wonder why he has not walked away from me yet.

"I'm Abel," he says in a tone that closely resembles sunshine. If sunshine could be heard.

"Carrington," I answer robotically.

"Carrington? What a cool name!"

"Thank you."

His smile deepens. "Want to come have lunch with me, Carrington?"

I blink at him again. What douchebag asks you to have lunch with him after you almost stole his food?

"Uh, sure." He can probably see my heart pounding. He definitely sees it. He has big, beautiful eyes.

That's when I remember Ethan, the guy I met this morning in English class. The hero who sat next to my roaring stomach and still asked me to lunch. I compromise.

"Can my friend Ethan come, too?"

"Of course!"

Right on cue, Ethan walks into the dining hall, winking his floppy black hair out of his eyes and texting someone with his thumb. Turns out, it is a text to me, asking where I am. I wave him over and introduce him to Abel.

"Hi!" Abel exclaims with another smile. I'm confused as to why he is so upbeat on a Monday morning in August at the start of the semester. I'm going to bet the culprit is five cups of coffee. That's my secret, anyway.

Ethan offers a swift nod. Not even a verbal greeting.

"We're seated right over here, guys," Abel continues, unperturbed.

I can feel Ethan's eyes burning my skull as we follow Abel through the crowd, but I'm not really sure what he is so upset about. A freshman's first week of classes is a social goldmine—even if it means gaining just one contact you can text later to confirm an assignment's due date. I am simply doing my job by accepting this cheerful man's invitation to lunch. Ethan will thank me later.

Abel leads us to a table in the far corner of the dining hall. Two people are already seated there, locked in conversation.

"Kelsey, Noah, this is my new friend, Carrington. Carrington, these are the friends I just met in calc class."

The girl—Kelsey—looks up first. Her fair face is outlined by caramel waves of hair, and her bright yellow eyeliner matches her sunflower J. Crew smocked dress. She looks at me like I have twelve heads.

"Did you say *Carrington?* What a cool name!"

"Isn't that a mortgage company?" the guy—Noah—asks. I hardly notice anything about him except for his stark green eyes that could be hired as traffic lights and his windswept brown hair.

"I'm not sure about that, but I go by Cari for short." I'm trying to be nice, but my stomach really is starting to get mean now, and it is seconds away from clawing through its cage.

"Oh, and this is, uh...." Abel snaps his fingers and grills Ethan with a concentrated stare.

"Ethan."

"Right!" Abel smiles and gives a thumbs-up.

"Yes, it's true," Noah says as we sit down. "Your eyes are not deceiving you. I am *the* most good-looking guy you will ever meet. Try not to fall in love with me."

We all laugh, except for Ethan.

My stomach could orgasm from this food. I realize I am eating like a deranged hound dog and lay off a little.

"So, anyway, my manager calls me up, and he's all like, 'Noah! If you and Taylor are gonna do it, save that for your own house, not the break room!' Except we were just making out during our lunch break. It didn't even mean anything."

"I bet it did later, though," Kelsey urged with a smirk.

"Oh, yeah, totally. I lost my virginity to her like a week later."

We all laugh again, and this time, I feel lighter since my stomach has transformed from Stripe the Gremlin back into Gizmo. Even Ethan cracks a smile now.

"Hey, I'm not one for body counts though," Noah says. "That's Abel's job."

"Oh, absolutely." Abel furrows his eyebrows and nods slowly.

"You could sleep with like, forty girls, and it wouldn't be a quarter of what this guy's had."

Ethan is suddenly interested now and is staring at Abel like he's a god. And I'm staring at him, too, 'cause here's the chink in the damn fence. He *is* a douchebag. *I knew it!*

"He's kidding," Abel clarifies quickly. "I'm a virgin."

Oh.

Oh.

Wait...for real?

Ethan's not much of an actor. He can't conceal his surprise, but I am not one to judge since I can't either. This confession doesn't even faze Abel. He just goes back to eating his sandwich and smiling like a happy little puppy.

"So, Carrington, what's your story?" Kelsey asks.

"What do you mean?"

"Where'd you grow up? Do you play any sports? What's your favorite color?" Noah suggests.

"Yeah, what's your address and credit card number?" Abel says, and I glance at him to confirm that he's kidding.

Kelsey reaches out and smacks his arm. He laughs.

"Well, I grew up in Newport, so I've been in Rhode Island my whole life. I have a younger brother. Uh, I love baking. I played softball in high school." I shrug. What else is there? "I'm obsessed with the brain, which is why I'm majoring in psychology."

"No way!" Abel leans forward and grills me with an excited stare that makes my heart race. "Me, too!"

"Really?"

"Oh, it's no surprise that he is," Kelsey intervenes.

I take a sip of my green tea and turn back to Abel. "Why not?"

For the first time, our table goes quiet. It only lasts five seconds, but something tells me I asked a question that was not meant to be asked. And now my soul is slapping a hand against its forehead in embarrassment.

"I have bipolar disorder," Abel answers matter-of-factly.

At first, my brain becomes a blank screen. Then, the initial gut instinct response filters in, and I almost say something corny like, "I'm sorry. I didn't know." But that doesn't sound too great, considering it might make him feel like this disorder limits him in some way. That would be the stigma talking.

"Okay," I say instead.

It is not a gold star response by any means, but when you have a clinical psychologist as a mother, you learn to train your voice to sound more positive and, in this case, accepting.

But...*what the hell universe!?* I have known Abel for all of twenty minutes, and from the way his smile slides higher on the right side down to the fact that he looks and sounds like rainbows, this guy does not deserve a condition that affects roughly one percent of people in their lifetime.

Even though I am eighteen, I have not yet perfected the art of shutting up, so I ask a question that is absolutely none of my business. "What type of bipolar?"

"One," Abel says. He offers a beautiful smile.

"What's that mean?" Noah asks.

"It means that I have more emotional highs."

Mania, I remember, from my mother's *Diagnostic and Statistical Manual of Mental Disorders* (DSM).

"Do you take medication?" I ask because I can't keep my mouth shut.

It sounds even more nosey than it's intended to, but ever since I was old enough to comprehend English, my mom has been working with clients who have mental health issues. You learn a little something growing up with a mother like that.

"A mood stabilizer, antipsychotic, and antidepressant," Abel answers, and thankfully, he doesn't seem opposed to talking about it, which is great. I'm an aspiring psychologist. I crave every little detail.

"Do you have to...?"

"Have my blood monitored every three months and go to weekly therapy? You betcha. But hey, it's all part of the fun."

His chill demeanor turns my brain into a pink slushie. He seems so unbothered about the disorder, about Ethan's scowl, about the silence constricting our table. It is like he exists with an impenetrable shield against all the negative bullshit in this world. I'm jealous...and brimming with respect for him.

He's not even *close* to a douchebag.

"What class do you have after this, Carrington?" Kelsey asks.

Okay, so we're done with the mental health talk. Got it.

I check my schedule. "Psych 1 1 3. General."

"Oh my gosh, same," Abel exclaims again. Having wolfed down his sandwich, he reaches for one of Kelsey's mozzarella sticks after she okays it. A string of cheese extends from his mouth.

My body is now well fed and overflowing with relief, which is a beautiful combination. I am relieved that I will know someone in my psych class, but also because Abel is the kind of attractive that makes me want to put my AirPods in, blast "Love on the Brain" by Rihanna, and curl up in a ball until I drown in my feelings. I want to spend more time with him. The universe is a hell of a businessman.

"What's that?" Noah asks, pointing to the checkered black and white composition journal peeking out of my backpack.

"That, sir, is a notebook," Abel deadpans. Kelsey smacks his arm again.

"Oh, I write poetry," I say, zipping my backpack all the way shut.

"Like, *poetry* poetry?" Noah sets his elbows on the table and pins me with a look of genuine curiosity. I'm surprised the same guy who just spilled the details of his first time has even heard of poetry.

I really need to stop judging books by their covers.

"Yeah. I just got into writing recently," I murmur. I have a big mouth until the conversation turns to my interests. Then I get pink-cheeked like a schoolgirl with a crush...which may not be that far off right now.

"Ooh! She's talented. I can already tell," Kelsey squeals.

"Can you read some of it?" Abel requests.

"Absolutely not."

His jaw drops. "Why not?"

"'Cause I'm a coward," I answer immediately, like the answer was just *waiting* on the tip of my tongue with a jetpack.

"I'm sure it's amazing. I'd love to hear it. Speaking of, what's your number?" Abel asks.

"Wait, no fair!" Kelsey cries. "If he's going to text you and ask for poems, then I want to, too."

"Yeah, what the hell?" Noah shrugs.

Suddenly, three phones are shoved in my face. Poor Ethan. He looks like he would rather be eating grass alongside a bunch of cows than sitting here with us.

I put my number in Abel's phone first. He leans back in his seat, and a grin slides across his lips. It is so handsome, I have to physically stop myself from saying, "Wow. I really like your face."

"You can send me poetry *any* time," he says in that positively golden tone. "You know what, Cari Carrington? I have a feeling."

"Which is?" *Please don't see my heart racing. Dammit, he defi-nitely sees it!*

"I think you and I are going to be friends for a long time."

1

———

SIX YEARS LATER

W ʜᴇɴ I sɪᴛ ᴅᴏᴡɴ ᴏɴ ᴀ ʙᴇɴᴄʜ ʙᴇsɪᴅᴇ ᴀ sɪɢɴ ᴛʜᴀᴛ sᴀʏs, *Kᴇᴇᴘ Maryland Beautiful,* the weight of my decision finally hits me like a freight train.

It is not that I regret moving nearly 400 miles south to find some peace and quiet; it is that I realize I'm finally going to *get* peace and quiet after nearly two years of nothing but noise. The noise of my agent's emails clogging my inbox. The sweet noise of people stopping me on the street back home in Newport and asking me to sign a copy of the poetry collection I wrote. The glaring noise of Kai's text message saying,

> Look, Cari. We had a good run, but I need to think about my future.

In other words, *I dated you for shits and giggles, but poetry is not a real job, and I need a woman with real interests.*

Screw Kai Bell. Seriously.

See, twenty-four is such a gloomy, glorious age. You are still fresh out of college, meeting new people, carving a slice of the juicy, sour apple pie that is the real world. And at the same time, you are carving a slice of the juicy, sour apple pie that is the real world. As a writer, that pie gets moldy real quick.

I don't mean writer as in—gingerly tuck your hair behind your ears and murmur, "Yeah, I...I write a little in my free time." I mean *writer*. Publication deals, agent, *New York Times* Best Seller.

When I released *Left or Right* toward the end of my senior year in college, word spread like the freaking flu virus. But in a good way. Who knew a poetry collection about choosing life over suicide could be so well received in a society that is literally choking on its own stigma? Life as a young poet looked so *beautiful!*

But then my boyfriend dumped me, and my agent was up my ass for another gold star manuscript, and my mother said I *might* want to reconsider not getting a master's degree—you know...for prestige and to continue the family tradition of becoming a clinical psychologist as if a hundred-fifteen-page poetry collection with Reese Witherspoon's Book Club sticker stamped to the cover isn't enough to make my mom proud of me.

That is why I am sitting on this park bench now. Because I said to hell with it and am chasing my own dreams instead.

I can hear Christie, my agent, so clearly in my ears: "Why Baltimore though?" Said like I'm sitting on a bench in Mordor and not nine miles from the National Aquarium.

"Because I need a change of scenery," I had said in that sugary tone of mine. *I literally can't write anything else until I'm in a new place.*

Call it writer's block. Call it impulsiveness. I stand by the decision. I also just assumed I'd end up in Baltimore after college anyway because my original plan *had* been graduate school.

Of course, my mother's response was "While you're down there, pop into UMBC to see if they'll take you for a doctoral program."

I didn't even respond to that text message.

It is fairly warm for the beginning of October, so I curl my hands around my journal, sit back, and people-watch—my favorite way to look for inspiration in Catonsville Community Park.

There's a girl with curly magenta hair and about fourteen piercings sunning herself in a swath of buttery sunshine. Ten feet away from her, a man is throwing a stick and applauding his wooly mammoth of a dog for fetching it. There is a frisbee game between four boys that might turn into bloodshed soon for the way they're trash-talking each other. A young girl and probably her mother are having a picnic on one of those predictable white and red checkered blankets. A lone jogger steals my attention, and I squint at him because he looks an awful lot like—

My heart slams into the brick wall of my ribcage. My mouth becomes the Sahara Desert in zero-point-three seconds. My brain screams, "THIS IS NOT A DRILL," and floods my synaptic gaps with dopamine. Not five feet away is Abel Harpen.

The Abel Harpen from my undergraduate years at the University of Rhode Island. *The* Abel Harpen in approximately 98 percent of my classes there. *The* Abel Harpen who was almost—and should have been—the love of my life.

I am so shocked that I don't even move to say hi to him. Miraculously, though, he looks at me.

He stops right in his tracks.

Vaguely, I'm a little annoyed with how the past two years have treated him physically because, oh my dear lord. The old him was built, sure, but *now*, his arms are next level brawny in the sleeveless Under Armour shirt. And his *face* for Pete's sake. No amount of memory recall can perfectly capture his knife-like jawline. In fact, I'm sure my skin is getting cut just *looking* at him. And his hair...those wavy rivulets of sunshine-toned hair.

Needless to say, my tongue is in a double knot.

Thankfully, he's not weird around people like me. His face lights up instantly and he waves. I wave back, but I don't remember lifting my hand to do so. All I notice is the sound of his sneakers hitting the ground as he approaches me.

"Carrington Daughtler," he declares in a voice that is so familiar it makes my right eye twitch. "I almost didn't recognize you with your hair. It looks awesome. How are you?"

I touch my newly dyed rose-gold hair and forget how to talk.

"I, uh...I'm good. I'm good."

"That's awesome!" He sits next to me, and I instantly smell a conglomeration of sweat and aftershave. It is hot in more ways than one. "What are you doin' here in Catonsville?"

Typically, I can answer questions on the dot (I have media training, for God's sake). But something about talking to Abel short-circuits those skills, and I have trouble forming sentences. Eventually, I manage, "I just moved here actually. Trying to...write something new, you know?"

His eyes flick down to my journal, and he jerks like the tectonic plates beneath our feet have just jolted him upright.

"Oh, right! Gosh, I should've known. How many times has your book sold out?"

"Three." I can't help the flirty crook in my smile. It's just a natural reflex around him.

"Yeah. See, I could never write a book."

"You would never write anything, *period*," I remind him, and he laughs.

A *real* laugh, like the deep in the belly, I-forgot-how-fun-it-is-to-joke-around-with-you kind of laugh. My blood pumps a little faster.

"So why are *you* in Catonsville?" I ask.

He exhales and runs a hand through his hair. That perfect for no reason hair. "I'm in my second year at the University of Maryland Baltimore County for my master's in psychology."

This time, the tectonic plates shift beneath *my* feet. "Wait! You're in their master's program?"

"Yep." His face beams with the smile I remember so vividly.

"Wow." That's all I can say.

Once upon a time, he and I had the same goal: finish our undergraduate years with psychology degrees and then travel to UMBC for a master's and a concentration in clinical work. And we would be in the program together right now if my writing career hadn't taken off. *Gosh, my mother would've loved you.*

"Wow," I say again. "Congratulations."

Abel shrugs. "What can I say? I've got a lot of drive."

"Still got that ego, too, I see."

"Don't worry. It never left."

We giggle together like two eighteen-year-olds.

I still remember the day I met him. Six years ago in the dining hall at URI, three days after freshman orientation. You'd think by now, I could get over the fact that I almost stole his lunch. But truthfully, I don't want to. That is one of the only instances that my hangriness led to something good.

"I can't believe this." I try hard not to sound too eager, to play it cool. "It's been so long. We have to catch up."

Catch up on the fact that we almost kissed the spring of senior year at the twilight barbeque and how I *almost* said the L word to him. Almost. Before I chickened out and escaped to Manhattan to be a poet.

Oh, and we would also have to talk about the fact that he suffers with bipolar disorder. A few weeks after we met, he explained that he'd inherited it from his mom.

"But it doesn't matter," he'd said at the time, the clementine sky accenting the hints of gold in his hair. "Because my dad never left her. He loves her. *Unconditionally.*" I remember how his eyes shimmered while saying that. "I know someone will love me like that, too, no matter what I go through or...what I put them through."

I swore to myself at that moment, as an eighteen-year-old in the middle of a courtyard on campus, feeling so small under that massive, breathtaking sky, that if I *ever* got the chance to be with him, I would *never* leave him.

"Heck *yeah*, we gotta catch up!" Abel agrees, snapping me back to the present moment. He taps away on his Apple watch. "I gotta finish my run, but if you're not doing anything tonight, I was planning to go out to dinner with Kelsey and Noah."

Another electric shock to the heart. "Kelsey and Noah are here?"

"Mhm. Noah just arrived last night, and Kelsey's here visiting her sister."

This was my college group: Kelsey, Noah, and Abel. The Core Four, as we once called ourselves. Sure, I had lots of other friends as well, but these people each hold a quarter of my heart in their hands...despite me moving away and not really talking to them for two years besides the occasional *happy birthday* and *merry Christmas*. A formal apology is in order.

"Do you mind if I tag along to dinner?" My heart climbs into my throat as I ask this.

"Not at all! Is seafood okay with you?"

"You act like you don't know me."

He flashes that million-dollar smile that makes me forget everything about everything. "We're going to Sea Legs. It's only about five minutes from here."

"Are you going to bring your girlfriend?" I swear my mind has a mind of its own because the question just slips out. Now my face is *definitely* a freckled strawberry. *Nice, Cari. Nice.*

"Nah, I'm single." My lungs constrict. "But you should tell your boyfriend to come along if he's game."

"Recently dumped." I flash a thumbs up and grimace.

Abel's eyes widen. "Oh, he was never worth it then if he couldn't see how amazing you are."

And suddenly, Kai Bell never existed.

"Thanks." I smile up at him. "I'll see you guys tonight then."

"Yep. Good luck with your new project."

What new proje—?

"Oh, thank you!" I hug my journal to my chest. "Bye, Abel."

"Bye, Cari Carrington." The nickname puts a lopsided hole in my heart.

I have missed him beyond words.

He jogs off. Just like that. I slump into the bench because, dammit, so much for peace and quiet. Of all the cities in the world, I choose the one that has him. This is either really good or really, really freaking cataclysmic. A small part of me is big time hoping it's the former, but I can't admit to myself why.

2

———————

My apartment in Catonsville, Maryland, is what my younger brother Tucker would call *easy on the arrogance*. A one bedroom, one-bathroom home with off-white walls, clamshell-gray flooring, and turquoise cabinets. Not something to brag about, according to Tucker. But Tucker doesn't know about the faint creaks in the floor or the especially squishy cushion on the end of the couch or the way the stove clicks three times before igniting a flame. It is an apartment that screams, *I have no idea where my life is going, but while I'm freaking out, I might as well smell the roses.*

I climb out of the shower and squeeze water from my newly rose-gold hair, which is currently tangled like the wires of an old pair of headphones.

The color of my hair was an on-the-spot decision at the salon back in Manhattan. I had been battling a nasty bout of writer's block and did the only thing I could think of that would distract my brain from its own stupidity: schedule a complete makeover. I'm talking long, dark walnut-colored hair to shoulder-length rose gold pink. Thankfully, the panic attack I had during the dyeing process was short-lived. This color suits me. When you know, you know.

My mother, on the other hand, had a heart attack. That was a rough Easter celebration, to say the least.

I am nearly done combing through clumps of tangles when my phone buzzes. It's my friend Katerine from the Big Apple. Her text shows a picture of a spotless white SUV tucked into a space in a parking garage with the caption *Not Kai Bell pulling up with his new bitch*, followed by the emoji with its eyes Xed out.

On any other day, in any other city, this would make me want to punch a wall. Screw Kai Bell. Seriously. But right now, my ex is the furthest thing from my mind. I text a quick middle finger emoji and go back to de-clumping my fuzzball of a hairdo.

I'M nervous when I pull into the parking lot at Sea Legs. Not quite sweating buckets, but close. I haven't seen Kelsey and Noah in ages, and I'm chowing down through my bottom lip just thinking about what they will say to me now. After I quote-unquote *chose the poetry*.

It takes approximately thirty seconds to spot Abel in the restaurant. He's wearing a tangerine crewneck with the words *Don't sweat it* scrawled in big white bubble letters. Plus, it's him. He is the most attractive guy in the building. Everyone else is mediocre at best. Poor things.

There is Kelsey in a baby blue wrap coat, white Gogo boots, and soft blue eyeliner. I haven't cried in two months, but my throat closes up at the sight of her. And Noah with his wind-swept bronze hair and evergreen-colored eyes. My lips start to quiver.

"Well, well, well," Noah says, rising from his seat to give me a hug. "If it isn't Miss New York City...now with pink hair!"

His hug makes my nostalgia bloom.

"My turn!" Kelsey shouts. She swats Noah away from me and gives me the biggest smile in the history of smiles. "Look at you! The hair! Ugh, I love it so much."

"Was this like a freak accident or something? The fact that we're all in Baltimore at the same time?" Noah asks.

"It's called fate, dumbass," Kelsey quips.

"Actually," I say, brushing hair out of my eyes, "I'm renting an apartment here. I've had writer's block for two months, and not even pizza from Chief's in Manhattan can cure that shit now."

"So, you settled on a big move instead," Kelsey clarifies.

"Exactly."

It feels nice to know they all so readily accept me back into the group. It makes me think maybe the isolation of the past couple of years was all in my head.

"Well, I'm here because Big Boss has me on another consultant trip," Noah states with his chest puffed out, unconsciously begging for our badges of approval.

"Oh, right. I forgot you work for that software company."

"How dare you," he hisses at me and then grins.

The waitress disrupts our reunion, and we are forced to sit down and read through the menu. I order a crab cake because I feel like it should be illegal to come here and *not* try them. Abel copies my order. Just by glancing over at me, he turns my heart into colorful dust.

After we order, and the waitress leaves us alone again, he leans forward and props his chin on his palm. "So, Cari, what's the Big Apple like?"

"Big," I answer, slightly breathless from his eye contact. "And pretty. Sometimes. But not when the family in the apartment above you lets their three kids run around at four in the morning."

"Jesus," Kelsey mutters.

"But I shouldn't complain. It's where I met Christie, my agent, and I've gotten to do a bunch of cool interviews in bookstores."

"Ah, yes," Noah says. "Today, local bookstores; tomorrow, Jimmy Fallon."

"I also had some worthwhile experiences while I was there. I dated an aspiring heart surgeon."

"Dated? As in past tense?" Kelsey pins me with a you-got-to-be-joking look. "Heart surgeons make bank, honey."

"It wasn't worth it, trust me. He always had to have things a certain way. One time, we went out for a picnic to celebrate his sister's engagement, and he told me not to wear blue because blue is *her* favorite color, and I wasn't supposed to outshine her."

Abel shrugs. "It might've been a compliment, in a weird way."

"Nah, more like he was secretly in love with his sister the whole time," Noah retorts. "I bet there was a whole incest deal he never told you about."

My face contorts, and Noah chuckles.

"Well, it doesn't really matter because we were together for a year, and then he left me for his medical degree and a blonde with huge tits."

"Oof." Kelsey's expression screams sympathy.

"Okay, but honestly, those are *the* girls though." Noah nods in agreement, and when I glare at him, he laughs harder.

I shush him and continue. "All in all, though, Manhattan is a great place."

"Noted," Abel says with a glowing grin.

It is embarrassing how his bare existence floods my brain with a neurotransmitter sugar rush. I'm thankful that Kelsey and Noah don't notice the massive blotches of red on my cheeks. And if they do, I'm glad they don't say anything.

I confessed my crush to them in December of our sophomore year at URI. I had expected them to slap their foreheads in shock, but they only stared at me with a couple of blasé expressions.

"Girl, we knew that," Kelsey had said, glancing back down at her Apple MacBook and sipping from her Vera Bradley water bottle.

"Wait, what?" My stomach dropped.

"We're not blind." Noah barked a laugh. "You defend Abel every time someone tries to say anything bad about him. And you blush like no one's business every time he shows up."

I sank my teeth into my lower lip. "Am I *that* transparent?"

"Yes," they had said at the same time.

"Oh God...do you think *he* knows?"

Kelsey and Noah had shared a squinted-eye glance.

"Hard to say," Noah answered.

Of course, at that time, Abel had already been talking with Camila Sanders and had asked her out a week later.

Kelsey pulls me out of the past and back into the restaurant. "Okay, let's get down to business. Meg's party is Friday night at eight."

"Isn't that a little late for a cocktail party?" Abel asks.

"If you're an old man, yes." She turns back to me and Noah. "Be sure to dress fancy."

"What's going on?" I reach for my glass and take a swig of lemonade.

"My sister got a promotion to be manager of her real estate company last week."

"That is definitely something to drink to," I agree.

"For sure. Can't wait to get flat-out drunk," Abel exclaims with a mile-wide smile, which is pretty funny because he, as far as I know, has never had a drop of alcohol in his entire life.

He stays away from it to protect his mental health. Smart move. Smart man.

In the six years that I've known him, I have witnessed Abel's mania very few times. When I did see it, it was pretty clear—like when he adamantly insisted that he did *not* need sleep. Or when he talked my ear off about concepts that didn't connect at all. Or when the smallest things set him off. But he typically disappeared before the mania got worse than that.

I didn't like to think of Abel in a hospital, but when he didn't answer texts or FaceTime calls for extended periods, it was difficult to assume he was anywhere else during those episodes. The hardest part was that he hardly acknowledged it. He would simply return to campus however many days later with his usual smile and matching spirits. All I could do in those situations was casually remind him I was there if he needed me and then proceed to change the subject.

The worst instance happened at the end of the second semester during our junior year.

Abel had been dating Camila Sanders for seventeen months at that point—not that I'd kept count or anything—and Remy Ausberg threw a party. Call me lame, but I'd wanted to stay home and pretend I was allergic to people so I could write instead. But by then, Kelsey had become overbearingly persistent, so she'd dragged me out anyway.

I hadn't been expecting to see Abel at the party at all. He never came to parties, period. In fact, he'd said many times that a party was *not* his scene. So, when I saw him on the staircase with his body pressed against Camila's and their lips moving like the kiss was life or death...forget the tequila in my cup. I was about to blackout from jealousy.

After he was done trying to swallow her, he turned toward the crowd, which was a maze of dancing bodies reeking of alcohol, sweat, and weed. Abel had shrieked, "TURN THE MUSIC UP!" and leapt off the staircase *into* the gaggle of bodies. Literally. People caught him, though just barely. If the music hadn't been blaring, his knee would have audibly *crunched* on the wood floor.

Two weeks later, Camila dumped him. She called him fucking insane to his face and then walked away.

I remember wanting so badly to sink my knuckles into her bronzer-caked cheek for that. She didn't understand—or even *try* to understand—what he was going through. She'd taken approximately one intro psych course in her entire college career, and only to cover a gen ed credit. Mental health was a non-issue for her. Part of me knew I should at least try to understand her side of the story (since, at the time, I planned to be a clinical psychologist), but a lovesick mindset makes you biased, and I'd had a fever for four years.

Here and now, seeing Abel again, that fever is still very much alive.

"Be at Meg's house at eight," Kelsey reiterates. "I'll send the address in a group chat."

"Ridiculous. I came to Baltimore on a business trip, then when I have free time, I get sucked into party mode again." Noah shakes his head. "What if I'm not in the mood?"

"Yeah, have fun sitting in your hotel room, writing emails about software products." Kelsey rolls her eyes.

Noah's lip curls into a smirk. "Touché."

"I, for one, think a party sounds great." I glance around the restaurant, wondering where the hell our waitress is.

"Abel, don't give us that look," Kelsey says.

My attention immediately snaps back. Abel smiles bashfully and shifts a little in his seat. "I'll just, uh...have to check my schedule."

Kelsey heaves a sigh. "Jesus, what *is* this? Have you all turned into a bunch of clowns? Abel, I haven't seen you in, like, two years, so don't even think about pulling your flaking bullshit on me now."

Abel tends to flake on plans a lot. He is here one moment and gone the next. Kelsey and Noah have always theorized that he secretly hates us all and that he has a whole other life he's not telling us about. That's a little abstract, though. I prefer to believe that he stays at home, daydreaming all the ways he can make me laugh.

Abel holds up his hands. "Okay, okay. I'll be there."

"You better," Kelsey warns, and then her eyes soften. "Who knows, maybe you'll even find the love of your life at this party."

Her statement makes me feel like someone just sank a knife into my large intestine and then squeezed lime juice on the incision. Jealousy's a bitch.

Abel shrugs. "Never say never, I guess."

The lime juice attacks me again.

Okay, I have it bad. Except maybe—*hopefully*—the universe is Cupid's cousin who gets off on rekindled relationships and second chances. Regardless, I'm going to that party on Friday.

3

Hi Carrington!

How's the weather down there in Catonsville? I hope it's inspiring some amazing poetry! I'm emailing to alert you that Polly&Pippy poetry sales are rising right now. They are projected to skyrocket in the next year. If you can get a manuscript in by late December/early January, we should have smooth sailing. Happy writing!

Best,

Christie Jayner

I STARE AT THE EMAIL WITH SHARK EYES.

Late December? It's already the middle of October, and I have written approximately three poems—all with lame metaphors and exhausted clichés. Basically, laughable at this point. Basically, an embarrassment. I toss a nervous glance at my composition notebook and sink my teeth into my lower lip. The poor thing is giving me puppy dog eyes, dammit.

I type a quick "Will do" and hit send.

The thing about poetry is that you need to take the normal clichés and hang them upside down over a dunk tank. In college, I'd taken a few creative writing classes. One semester, my professor had said, "Carrington, your work is too predictable. Add some oranges in there." That was an expression he used often. *Add an orange* meant do something the reader would never expect. And since then, I'd all but dedicated my life to picking those oranges and squeezing them into my work.

Except now the orange trees have stopped bearing fruit.

If I could, I would drown writer's block in the bay where it belongs. But since I can't do that, I secure my hair into a clip, don my sneakers, snatch my journal, and slam my apartment door behind me.

Inspiration can be everywhere and nowhere simultaneously. It's like that one best friend who is always around but never there when you actually need something. I must look pretty strange right now, driving down the main street in my Honda CR-V, craning my neck at every building around me, hoping *one* of them will spark something in my brain.

That's when I see it: a help wanted sign posted in the window of a place called Ruth's Bakery. Now, I'm a little iffy on the existence of God, but this seems pretty fatalistic somehow.

I parallel park on the busy street and walk inside.

A bell chimes overhead, and I have to look back out the window to make sure I'm not hallucinating. *Everything* in this bakery is purple. The tiled floor, the seats, the tables, the walls. There are even purple ribbons decorating the cases of pastries. And you guessed it, purple icing galore.

An older woman swings through a pair of purple doors, brushing silvery strands of hair out of her face. She's a little on the plump side, wears rectangular glasses, and has sun-kissed, wrinkled skin. But she moves like she's twenty, at the counter in an instant, pen poised on a piece of paper.

"Good morning! What'll ya have?"

I stare at her for a moment, my lips parted dumbly. "Uh, actually, I saw that you're hiring."

"Oh, of course!" She disappears into the back again, leaving me all alone on this quaint purple planet. "Here's an application form. What's your name?"

"Carrington," I answer, wondering if I'm supposed to fill out the form right in front of her.

"Nice to meet you. I'm Ruth. I'm guessin' you like to bake?"

"*Love* it."

Not everyone knows this, but baking is my second superpower after writing. When I was twelve, my mom pulled me into the kitchen, gave me a recipe for her homemade chocolate chip cookies, and told me to get to it. That was the day I discovered I'd inherited her magic touch, and I have ruled the kitchen ever since. Plus, it wouldn't be bad to have another job here in Catonsville. Royalties are always shifting, so I'm going to need some extra cash.

I fill out the personal information on the application and notice that Ruth is staring at me, like maybe I'm a secret serial killer.

"So, uh, I see that you're a massive fan of the color yellow," I say, trying to break the ice.

She blinks at me and then bursts into laughter. I don't think it's that funny until she starts wheezing and snorting like a pig, and then I'm howling because those types of laughs always take me out.

"Aw, gee-zooey," she says, panting. "That was a good one."

We both wipe our eyes. I finish filling out the form and hand it back to her. She scans it for a minute and then looks at me over the rim of her glasses.

"Carrington, have you ever been convicted of a felony?"

"No."

"Good. You're hired."

Wait, what?

"You start tomorrow."

"Just like that?" I squint at her, wondering if this is some kind of prank and if a guy in a clown suit is about to pop out and scare the living shit out of me.

Ruth shrugs. "I know exactly who you are. I read *Left or Right* when it first came out, and I loved it. You're hired."

Can somebody say *perks of being a best selling poet?*

"Thank you!" I'm beaming.

"There's one catch though." Ruth crosses her arms over her chest. "Since you're hired, you have to sign my copy."

I release a breath. "Pass me back that pen!"

If I were to drive up the road from Ruth's Bakery, I would come across the massive circle that is UMBC. The cluster of buildings and orange-gold trees where future psychologists walk around, the weight of their potential graduate degrees presumably crushing their shoulders. And yet, they are probably smiling anyway, feigning positivity because fake it 'til you make it, right? If I think about it, it is almost like we are breathing the same air.

It's never too late to apply for grad school. That was what my mom had texted me the night of my first public interview for *Left or Right.*

I stare into the distance—at the trees that block my view from the university's circle—and feel the hot urge to charge toward it, burst through the door of the first building I see and go ape shit on them. Embrace full Freudian regression. *You're the reason my mom's not proud of me!*

My parents are the epitome of polar opposites.

Dad adores the lax life: reclining on the couch, cracking open a can of Coke Zero, and binge watching some comedian who ruled the world back in the day. He does his fair share of housework—mostly to escape Mom's glare—and then returns to his spot on the recliner that *no one* is allowed to steal. He loves driving at sunset with the windows rolled down or snoring on a lounge chair beside our pool in the backyard. He's mellow. Quite possibly the most unbothered eighteen-year-old stuck in a fifty-six-year-old's body.

Believe it or not, he met Mom in the early '80s at a party. They bonded over Madonna's album, *Like a Virgin.* True story. But if Dad is Palm Springs, Mom is Alaska in the middle of January.

She is always tense and tight-lipped. Always sitting with one leg crossed over the other, hands clenched together in her lap, chest forward and chin up. The queen of intimidating stoic expressions. She is the type of clinical psychologist that will be brutally honest with you after an examination. Some people need that. Others can't take it. I know I can't. Especially since when I was really young, I wanted to be just like her.

"Carrington?"

I turn to see Abel walking up the sidewalk with another guy.

"Did your dog die? Is that why you look like you want to murder someone?"

I try to casually smooth my hair even though it's up in a clip. "No. I was just applying for a job at Ruth's Bakery."

"Did you get it?" The guy beside Abel asks.

I nod.

"Cari Carrington, I want you to meet Hunter." Abel steps aside.

Hunter is tall, and the first thing that comes to mind is *beanpole.* He looks like a shrimp standing next to Abel, but if Abel was not around, I suppose Hunter could be kind of attractive. His curly hair is the color of coal tar, and his eyes are green, so they remind me of summer leaves and neon nail polish and allergies. But he's got a nice jawline, too. And a nice smile. I mean, he's got nothing on Abel, but he looks nice enough.

"Hey," Hunter says. There is a boyish twinkle in his eyes.

I nod. "Hey, man."

"Hunter and I are in the same cohort together," Abel says. "This guy is a genius."

"No, no, no. *He's* the genius." Hunter tosses back.

My eyes flick between them and then I add, "I'm a genius, too. I just write things."

The boys look back at me—Abel with a perfect grin and Hunter with his eyebrows raised.

"Wait a second," Hunter says. His eyes widen. "I've seen you. You're that poet. I got my mom your book for Christmas last year. She loves poetry."

So, you put one picture in the back of a book and up on a website and you're famous. *Awesome.*

"I'm Carrington. Always nice to meet a fan."

He laughs and shakes my hand, and, for some reason, our eyes linger a little longer than they should. But it hardly means anything. Abel is standing approximately two feet away, hair glowing in the morning sunlight like a freaking angel's.

"What brings you to Baltimore?" Hunter asks.

"People-watching and inspiration." I shrug. "I have to write something else, or my good friends Polly and Pippy are going to drop me in the dirt."

"Who?" Abel asks.

"Polly and Pippy of Polly&Pippy Publishing."

"I've always wondered this," Hunter says. "Are Polly and Pippy real people?"

"Probably."

"You don't know?"

"All I know is that my agent's name is Christie. My editor is Pamela. And for publishing services, I talk to Candace. She's the company's president."

Hunter nods, and it looks like he's actually trying to sort through those names instead of just filing them into his short-term memory like a normal person.

"Has it always been your dream to get published?" he asks.

Before I answer, my eyes happen to slide to Abel. When I register the expression on his face, my mouth snaps shut. He's green. His handsome face is all twisted up and contorted like he's going to upchuck his guts right here on the concrete.

"Whoa, Abel." I touch his shoulder. "Are you okay?"

"Just feeling kinda nauseous," he mutters, pressing a hand to his stomach.

Hunter reaches into his backpack. "I think I have some Advil or TUMS in here."

"Was it something you ate?" I press.

Abel seems to be hurting. Abel seems to feel sick. My instinctual, protective side takes over. It's been like this ever since I met him. As long as I have a say in it, nothing bad will ever douse his light.

"No. It's the meds." He groans. "They make me feel sick and foggy a lot. Usually I'm all right, but today, they're kicking my butt."

"Or your gut," I joke with a cheesy smile, trying to lighten the mood.

He doesn't laugh. In fact, he looks greener.

"Let's get inside," Hunter suggests, pointing to the café three doors down. "We've got an hour before class. We can just chill out and take a breather."

I am happy to see Abel has made such a kind friend. Hunter even has his hand on Abel's shoulder as if to steady him. The concern in his eyes is genuine and clear as day.

"Well, feel better," I say, pouring as much enthusiasm as I can muster into my tone. If I didn't have some writing to do, I would go with them.

"Bye, Cari Carrington." The way that Abel smiles even when he feels like crap will never cease to amaze me. If I felt like that, I'd be flipping everyone off.

"Oh, wait!" I call, and the boys turn back. "I'll see you on Friday night, right?"

Abel holds a thumbs up. "Absolutely."

I can't tell if he is lying just so I'll shut up and leave him be or if he genuinely means it. I can never tell with Flakey Flakerson. That's what Kelsey and Noah used to call him in our days at URI.

I sigh, say a quick prayer to the universe, or the mothership, or God, or whoever's listening, that I will see Abel at the party, and climb into my car.

4
____

On Friday night, I FaceTime Katerine while curling my
hair for the party.

"So wait," she says. "They want that manuscript by *December*?"

"Yup."

"Have they no respect for the creative process?" Katerine is an
accountant and is the last person on this planet to pick up a book. She
bought mine to support me, but it has been collecting dust since her
purchase. Our firecracker personalities mesh so well together though.
If we didn't get along so well, our friendship would have ended after
"Hello."

"They just like me for the cash I bring in," I tell her, easing the
curling iron from another lock of hair.

"Freakin' gold diggers."

Okay, kidding aside. "I shouldn't complain. These people gave
me my life."

"It's not complaining," Katerine counters. "It is verbally
processing your emotions. Isn't that supposed to help people?"

"Probably." The definite answer is yes, but since I gave up
psychology, I don't go into specifics anymore.

"Anyway," Katerine says, "Why are you getting all dressed up?"

"My friend Kelsey's sister got a promotion, and Kelsey's throwing her a cocktail party."

"Please drink for me tonight, will you?"

Katerine gave up alcohol after she decided to start with that nutritionist. Now she is a plant-eater, and I don't know how she does it. I'm a carnivore down to my bones.

"Sure thing."

ALL OF THE townhouses in Meg's neighborhood look identical—same sand-colored vinyl and dark wood doors—but I would have to be an idiot to miss the balloons and CONGRATULATIONS, MEGGY banner on one of the porches, where there are also four dozen or so cars parked in the driveway. I basically have to park in Europe because Kelsey, unsurprisingly, seems to have invited everyone Meg knows and then some. When I finally get inside, I find Kelsey chatting it up with a redhead and swirling the drink in her glass with a lazy grin, which is her go-to flirty move.

I remember the exact day she told me she was bisexual. We'd been combing through the thongs in Victoria's Secret when her confession popped out like a champagne cork.

"Is that why you're not head over heels for Abel?" I'd asked.

"That and personally, he's just a little too picket-fence for me."

"What's that mean?"

"If I'm going to date a man, I need a *man*. Abel's a teddy bear."

I started to counter this, but Kelsey quickly changed the subject to whether a pair of panties with cherries on them would be too Gen-Z-ish.

I'm rooting for her now with this redhead. Kelsey would never admit it, but she hasn't had much luck in the romantic department. Then again, none of us have. I figure I will finally have luck when I'm pushing up daisies.

"Cari!" Noah waltzes toward me, clearly drunk already. "What are you doing without a drink?"

"Good question."

Kelsey went the whole nine yards with the beverage order. I grab a pink lemonade Smirnoff and turn back to Noah.

"Bets are on." He grins. "How much do you want to put on it?"

"For what?"

"To see if Abel actually shows."

I take three sips of my drink, considering. "What am I up against?"

"I have twenty bucks down that he won't show. Kelsey bet fifteen."

"What, no heart and lung, too?"

He glares at me and rolls his glassy eyes before tipping his head back and drinking some more.

"Twenty that he *does* show," I say.

"Bold claim. But it's already 8:40, so don't hold your—"

His eyes lock on something behind my shoulder, and I taste triumph before I even turn around. But when I do, I am struck totally and entirely speechless.

Abel.

What more is there to say?

He is wearing a navy-blue long-sleeve sweater and white jeans. His hair is *so* effortlessly styled; every other guy should be ashamed of himself by comparison. And that *face...*

"You're drooling," Noah slurs, pointing to my mouth.

I slap his hand away.

Kelsey spots Abel, squeals, and directs him toward the kitchen where there is a gallon of lemonade, cans of soda, and a few water bottles on the counter. It occurs to me that Abel will probably be the only person at this party not drinking, and my heart swells for him even more. In the meantime, I down my Smirnoff.

"Twenty bucks. Cough up."

Noah groans and fishes his wallet out of his jeans.

An uproar of giggles explodes from the corner of the living room. I recognize Meg in the middle of the group, her laugh easily the loudest.

I first met Meg when she came to cheer for Kelsey at our graduation from URI. Since that day, I have been following her on Instagram and trying desperately not to show that I am envious of her entire life. Who wouldn't be? She is smart, kind, and beautiful—all the keys to unlock everything she could ever want in life.

When she turns, I think she's looking at me, so I wave and say, "Congrats, Meg."

Her eyes shift slightly to my face. "Oh, hey! Thanks, Carrington!" And something calls her attention behind me again.

Or, not something, *someone.*

Then, like this is a corny-ass romance novel stolen from Wattpad, Meg stands up and struts right past me. She doesn't stop until she's in the kitchen with her fingers grazing Abel's bicep. He pulls her into a hug.

When the fuck did they get so close? I backspace the question from my brain and replace it with a solid answer. *Oh, right, duh! Abel is better looking than Adonis, and Meg just happens to have eyes.*

Noah's gaze sears a hole into my left cheek.

"What?" I mutter.

He leans against a chair, his green eyes more like lasers. "You're still in love with Abel."

"And?" There's no sense in denying it.

I am a wide-open book. I might as well tattoo it on my middle finger.

Noah clears his throat and cocks his head at me. "I don't know. I just thought you would've forgotten about him when you moved to Manhattan."

I look at him like he has feathers sprouting out of his hair. I almost tell him that's ridiculous; no man has ever compared to Abel Harpen, not even Kai, who managed to numb my brain with his meaningless romantic gestures. But then I peek back at Abel, and he's pouring himself a glass of lemonade and smiling at something Meg is squawking about. And my heart squeezes fondly.

That smile. The light caught in those eyes. The lone dimple in those angular cheeks. Those things are my world. They make everything else silent. Even my overworked muscle of a heart sighs with relief at the sight of him.

"The drool's back," Noah comments.

"I'm not over him," I confirm, raising one shoulder as a shrug. "Is that bad?"

Noah purses his lips. "It's bad in the sense that you met the guy when you were eighteen, and it's been six years, but you still haven't told him how you feel. I mean, correct me if I'm wrong," he adds quickly.

"Nope. You are correct."

"Well then, Miss Daughtler." Noah grills me with that intense gaze that makes me feel like I have centipedes tap-dancing down my spine. "What the hell are you waiting for?" He points to the kitchen.

"I can't go now!" I whisper-shout.

"Why not?"

"'Cause he's talking to Meg!"

Noah opens his mouth and rolls his eyes. It's his way of saying *Oh, for God's sake*. "Meg is thirty-three, Cari."

"And hot, and rich, and—"

"Not the one for Abel." Noah shakes his head vigorously. "Put on your game face and get in there."

He takes me by the shoulders and spins me around so I'm facing the kitchen again. I wish I could remember the karate moves I mastered in the third grade right now so that I could drop Noah's ass and run for my life. But unfortunately, I only made it to a yellow belt before I quit.

"Noah, stop!"

"What's wrong with you? Get in there and fight for the man!"

I successfully manage to wriggle out of his grasp, which I credit to the week of kickboxing I did last month. "I can't! I'm a coward. Plus, look at the way he's looking at Meg."

Noah glances over my shoulder. "He's literally just smiling at her. But yeah, definitely. I bet he's about to propose." He shakes his head. "I swear, it's like you make stuff up in your head just so you have a reason to avoid your feelings."

My jaw drops. "I don't—"

"What's it going to take?" Noah intercepts. He picks up his drink and tips it back.

A rewired brain and a lot of Vodka.

But then a miracle happens. Abel happens to look out of the kitchen, and his eyes land right on me. It's only for a split second, but to me, it feels like a hundred years, and I can consciously feel dopamine flowing in my brain now. I tug my dress a little lower on my boobs for good measure.

Noah notices. "Take it easy, tiger. You'll turn him off."

"Shush."

I toss my hair over my shoulder absentmindedly.

"Oh, now you've done it. He's coming over here. I know it's tough for you but try to act natural."

I don't have time to knee him in the nuts before Abel has approached us.

"Hey, guys!" He holds up his cup of lemonade. "Cool party."

"Hi, Abel!" My voice comes out high-pitched, so I clear my throat and lean back nonchalantly against the wall.

"Hey, dude," Noah says. "Fancy seeing you here."

"Back atcha." Abel grins, and now I think I might actually be drooling.

Half a second passes. Then Noah adds, "Well, I was just about to go make out with a girl, so you two should catch up."

There is no girl. He's a jackass. A smooth one, but a jackass nonetheless.

"Oh." The tiniest hint of pink creeps into Abel's cheeks. "Have fun."

"Plan to." Noah winks at him and shoots me a pointed look.

"Uh, are you feeling better?" I ask, once Noah is down the hall and around the corner.

Abel glances at me briefly before dropping his eyes to the hardwood floor. "I had a headache this morning, but yeah, I've mostly felt better today. Hey, do you want to go out to the balcony with me? It's crowded in here."

I'd go anywhere with you. "Sure."

We slip out of the crowd unnoticed. Kelsey is still too busy flirting with the redhead, and Meg has moved back to her group of girlfriends.

The October air has frosted fingers tonight. The balcony is empty except for the two of us. I shiver slightly in my long lace sleeves. Abel ditches his cup on the glass table and places his elbows on the railing instead. I wish I was an artist so I could paint his side profile against the dark navy sky and the sparkling buildings in the distance. His hair ruffles in the wind, and he gazes into the night like there's something waiting for him out there.

"What's on your mind?" I venture.

This is the thing about Abel. He's a people person until he's not. He's only extroverted because his looks demand it of him, and everyone thinks they know him. But in reality, he wears the most protective, impenetrable armor around his heart that no one—not even myself—has ever broken through completely. He has dropped little hints to me in the past about the man under the shell, but only on *his* terms and in very small doses. He is a man of many layers, and I'm just a puppy, wagging her tail and waiting for him to let me in.

"I can't get over this view!" he exclaims.

There it is, the hint that he's covering up from me. I learned his tactics back in college—how he disguises deeper thoughts with outward positivity.

It always makes me a little sad. No matter how many times I remind him that he can talk to me, he hides instead. But I get it. Boys don't cry, blah, blah, blah. I'd really love to sock it to whoever invented that stigma.

"I know," I reply, playing into his game. Because it feels safe for him, and I can respect that. "I love this place."

"Would you ever want to live here permanently?"

I twist my lips to one side. "I don't know. I always assumed I'd end up here after college, probably because of my original plan to go to graduate school. But I don't know about long term."

"Yeah, me either. I think I might want to move to Montana."

"Why?"

"Peace and quiet." He says it in his pleasant tone, but I know him well enough to understand that he's *actually* looking for peace and quiet.

So am I.

"Hey, I hear ya," I say. "Life can be so chaotic sometimes. It would be nice to just get away."

"Absolutely." He looks up at the string of bulb lights hanging above the balcony. "How's poetry going?"

I sigh. "Not well at the moment."

If anyone else had asked me, I would have lied right to their face. I guess I'm just like Abel that way: obsessed with keeping up a reputation. But this *is* Abel, and I want to spill my guts to him every waking moment of every day. I don't want to seem perfect to him; I want to seem *real*. I want him to understand that I bleed like him, struggle like him, so that he sees me as a human being and not some untouchable goddess. Because then he'd be motivated by his dick, not his heart. And I'm a hopeless romantic, so I crave something *authentic*.

He frowns. "Oh, no. I'm sorry to hear that. You're not finding inspiration here?" I admit I'm not. "What do you think the problem is?"

"I guess I'm distracted," I say.

"By anything in particular?" I know he genuinely cares because there's a crease pinching the skin between his eyebrows, and his eyes are warm with sympathy.

This is the one thing I can't be vulnerable about, though. We are such good friends. If I confess my feelings, it might shoot an arrow through our friendship, and I don't think I can live like that. Leaving for New York was hard enough. Learning how to live without him was downright hell.

"Just stuff." I shrug.

He nods. "I get it. School's stressin' me out. I have these intense classes and I'll start seeing actual clients next year. The material's a lot more intense compared to undergrad. It's overwhelming sometimes."

"I can imagine." He's looking at me with the bluest eyes I have ever seen. I often catch myself wondering what it would be like to climb inside of them and swim around. "I know you can do it though. You're Abel Harpen."

And that is more than enough.

"That is so sweet, Cari. Thank you." His smile is gentle. A splash of pink swells in his cheeks. It turns my heart inside out.

"How's your mom?" I ask.

The blush dissipates, and he looks back out into the bustling night. My stomach squeezes. Sometimes I feel like I'm treading water by asking these questions because I don't want to pry. But I love Abel's family almost as much as he loves them.

I met them for the first time over Christmas break during our freshman year. It was the first time Abel brought me to his house—a two-story giant that looks as sharp and clean-cut as the Harpens themselves. But on the inside is an organized disarray of knickknacks. Abel's dad is one of those Amazon junkies, purchasing something new almost every five seconds. So, there were mazes of miniature train tracks cutting every which way on the living room carpet and about twelve trains of all colors and sizes zipping around. In the center of the room was an enormous Christmas tree with silver and red globes for ornaments. Abel's younger sisters Charlotte and

Melanie were in the living room, too. Melanie was seated on the couch with a sketchbook while Charlotte was playing with a football.

We found Mr. Harpen in the L-shaped kitchen, whipping a whisk in a ceramic bowl, his apron shouting, *Dads can bake too, smartass!* He asked me about how my academics were going, and his voice was surprisingly mellow for a man with a tattoo on his bicep and a dark goatee. Then again, that tattoo is a list of his children's names, and I'd seen pictures of Melanie and Charlotte trying to twist his goatee into a short, pudgy braid. He is a family man through and through. That is one of the reasons Abel idolizes him so much.

Mrs. Harpen was seated at the oval-shaped oakwood table with a book in her hands. Come to think of it, all the times I've seen her, she's had a book with her. Abel explained that reading keeps her out of her head, keeps her nerves from catching fire. That Christmas, she glanced up at me and immediately wanted to know if I was dating her son.

"We're just friends, Mom," Abel had answered.

I remember how his response settled like a jagged rock in my stomach. We were *best* friends, actually. He'd forgotten the *best*. But it didn't seem to matter because then Mrs. Harpen fired questions at me like she was playing target practice. It had been the beginning of one of her manic episodes, Abel later explained two days after our massive New Years Eve party when she was arrested for flipping off a cop and speeding away despite already being pulled over.

I never quite knew if Mrs. Harpen was a fan of mine. I'd won her husband and daughters over just by saying I knew Abel's favorite color and favorite movie theater snack. But she was a locked door. It didn't matter how many times I tried to twist the knob, she never quite let me in. But I also knew that she was between psychologists at the time and had recently been fired from her job as a waitress. Her mental health—regardless of the medication—still fluctuated. From the way Abel described her at school, she seemed like the kindest woman on earth. I couldn't blame her for being suspicious of me, like, *who is this girl that just waltzes right in on our family and thinks she can take my son from me?* I didn't let that get to me. She is the mother of my favorite person on this whole planet. Whether she is experiencing mania or not, I love her just for birthing Abel.

"She's doing better now," Abel murmurs, roping me back to the balcony. "She checked herself into a hospital about two weeks ago. She didn't even lash out, she just said, 'I can feel it coming back,' and then packed her bags and left."

"Just like that?" There's nothing accusatory in my tone. In fact, I feel kind of hollow. It has been way too long since Abel and I talked like this—about the important and deep stuff.

"Just like that." Abel looks at me. A frown pinches the left corner of his lips. I hate it. "She's had to try a dozen different medications, but she doesn't stay on them. Part of me thinks she's getting to the point now where she knows how it affects the rest of the family." He shrugs. "You can't just go off and blow through your credit card on random things and say everything that pops into your head."

That last part makes me wonder if he's talking about himself. Rumor had it, he'd done the same thing while dating Camila. But that was just a rumor I'd heard from someone whose name I don't even remember.

"What about you?" I ask.

My tongue immediately turns to sandpaper. I should *not* steer the conversation in this direction. I should *not* ask him this question. Yet my brain is starving for an answer.

"What?" His eyes are on me again.

"Does mania make you feel invincible?"

Seconds pass and then he nods. "You feel like God, basically." His voice is louder and more casual now. I know he's trying to beat around the bush because it makes him uncomfortable. He would sooner do the Macarena in the middle of a freestyle circle at a massive party than explain the details of mania to anyone. "But then you crash and burn, and *that* part sucks." His back is to the city, and his arms are extended behind him, resting on the guardrail. His demeanor is consciously chill, pleading *I'm normal, I promise.*

I hate that he feels like he has to act like that. Like he has to justify it. A confession works its way into my throat—the confession that I adore him to my bones and that he never has to act for me.

But I try for a joke instead to put some ice on the tension between us. "I know the feeling. I get that way when I'm on my period."

His eyebrow quirks . "Really?"

"Nah. I just lay in bed and cry till the Advil kicks in."

"Wow, you're pretty tough."

"The toughest," I agree. "I eat bowls of nails for breakfast. Without milk."

He catches my *SpongeBob* reference and we're dying laughing in two seconds.

There we are! The old us. The Carrington and Abel that used to go out for pizza and milkshakes every Friday night. The Carrington and Abel that used to piss off the college librarian by seeing how far we could shoot paper airplanes while the people around us rolled their eyes and tried to study. The Carrington and Abel that tried to out-bench each other in the gym—I always lost—before hopping in the car and driving around, singing "Love Song" by The Cure at the top of our lungs. (It is his favorite song of all time despite being born in 2002.) It was the us that didn't have to worry about being adults yet.

I miss that so much, even my liver is aching.

"You know something," Abel says, "I haven't seen *SpongeBob* in a while. That feels like a crime."

"That hurts." I press my hand to my heart and try to conjure up some puppy dog eyes, but it fails because Abel hunches over laughing. "Hey," I whine, "you promised me we'd grow old together and watch *SpongeBob* marathons till we can't hear or see anymore."

"Oh my gosh. You're right, I did!" His face lights up.

Second semester of sophomore year, on the way to our research methods class. He'd said *we* so casually, and my heart demanded the memory be burned into my hippocampus.

I mull over our plans for a moment. "I don't think I can watch *SpongeBob* for that long anymore."

"Me either," he admits with a grin.

"Want to switch it out for an ice cream run sometime?"

"Whoa." His eyes widen and his mouth makes a little O shape. "You read my freakin' mind, Cari Carrington. I was just going to ask that."

5

———

I DON'T WRITE POEMS ABOUT THE GUYS IN MY LIFE.

It used to make Kai upset. He would hound me over and over for a poem, using tricky language like, "But, Cari, you're so talented, my angel. One poem, please?" Said with the sexy crook in his grin that originally glued me to his side. But over time, I realized he just wanted something to show off to his snooty country club friends so they could compare girlfriends.

Fuck that shit.

Writing about guys in general has always left a sour taste in my mouth. Like that abhorred, mildly pornographic movie disguised as a romance film where the girl's ass is out the whole time and they're having sex poolside. It is cringey and a waste of my time. So, if that's the case, then tell me why I'm churning glittery romantic metaphors over in my mind as I squeeze globs of cookie dough into little balls on this my fourth day at Ruth's Bakery.

Ruth sets her bowl under the electric mixer and puts it to work. I half expected her to be a Kitchen Chatterbox. That is what my mom used to call my brother Tucker when he was younger. He would talk her ear off while pretending to help make pumpkin pies for Thanksgiving dessert. But Ruth is totally silent as she moves between the oven, the mixer, the back room. It's not an uncomfortable silence. She has that firm line in her mouth and that determined glaze in her rain-gray eyes. I appreciate the silence, actually. It gives me space to think through all of these bubbly, flinch-worthy love metaphors that are invading my prefrontal cortex.

I try my absolute hardest not to relate them to Abel.

Around ten a.m., the phone rings. Ruth and I are painting the freshly baked cookies in a pastel purple frosting. She reaches over to grab the phone, pinches it between her cheek and shoulder, and continues frosting.

"Ruth's Bakery, how can I help ya on this fine morning?" Her frosting hand pauses for a fraction of a second, and her eyes dart to the left. She leans into the phone. "Well, tell her I said happy birth-day! Of course...Absolutely. Not a problem. We'll have those ready by noon." She slams the phone into the cradle and smears more frosting onto a cookie—aggressively this time, I might add.

"Big order?" I guess.

"Another bakery screwed up a woman's order, and her daughter turns six today. They need twenty cupcakes by noon."

I let out a whistle and set down my rubber spatula. "Well, it's a good thing she called the best of the best then! I can get those started."

Just as I grab the binder full of Ruth's five-star recipes, I catch the glint in her eye. It is only a flicker, but after you've spent years people-watching to make some orange juice with your poetry—as my college writing professor would've said—little flickers in someone's expression become massive neon signs on the highway.

"Are you okay?" I was going to be a psychologist once upon a time. Let's see how well I handle this.

Ruth looks at me quickly and glances away just as quickly. She continues frosting the cookies.

"Yeah, honey. I'm good."

I press my hip into the counter and cross my arms. We can be superheroes and get those cupcakes done in a few minutes. For now, though, my new benevolent grandma of a boss is upset.

She laughs at my expression, but her smile disappears. "It's just that it's...*my* daughter's birthday, too." Said with zero enthusiasm or excitement or thrill, but instead with a hint of sadness and a splash of dread.

"But?"

"She hasn't spoken to me in thirteen years." Ruth's eyes are glued to the cookies as she works.

I uncross my arms. "Geez, Ruth. I'm sorry."

She shrugs and scrapes the last of the frosting out of the bowl. Her expression is clear: *No more questions.*

Got it. Too far for today. But I'll keep cracking at it, because I was born with overwhelming amounts of empathy. I'm not going to stand by and bake cookies all day while Ruth bites back her problems. For today though...*good job, team!*

I smile at her and flip through the training binder for her famous cupcake recipe. "Do you like music, Ruth?"

"I love country," she answers, tossing the bowl into the sink. "I was born and raised in Chattanooga, Tennessee."

"Gosh, that makes so much sense because you're the only ten *I* see."

Finally, she smiles. "Honey, if that's how you flirt, you've got some serious work to do."

"What are we waiting for?" I exclaim, gesturing to the BlueTooth speaker. "Let's blast some good ole' Luke Combs!"

It is the staring contest of a lifetime: me versus a blank piece of paper. The pencil is the mediator, but I know it's biased toward the notebook, so I'm toast.

Screw. Writer's. Block! Screw it harder than stubbed toes and lost cell phones and Kai Bell! Five more minutes of this, and I'm going to have steam shooting out of my ears like a cartoon character.

I ditch my journal and push myself off the lumpy cushion on the couch. I retrieve my yoga mat, which has an ugly splotch in the center from when I spilled chocolate ice cream on it while lying on my belly and watching the *Hunger Games* marathon on TV. Today, I will use the mat for its actual purpose.

In Manhattan, Katerine and I had a strict workout schedule. When she was done being a superhero accountant for the day, and my brain was fried from Zoom interviews and the latest meeting with my agent, we'd hit up a Zumba class or a spin class. Mondays, Wednesdays, and Fridays were our lift days. Today is Sunday, so I'm pulling up a yoga video on YouTube.

Exercise is supposed to reduce stress and get your creative juices pumping. Yet, as I'm standing in Warrior Two pose—and shaking slightly—I feel nothing. No aha moment, no spine-tingling idea, no sudden urge to grab my journal and write for hours on end. Not even the corny lovey-dovey metaphors are helping me now.

The only thing that does occur to me is that I am losing my edge. The realization hits me as I'm transitioning to Downward Dog.

Maybe the collection of poems that came together for *Left or Right* was a once-in-a-lifetime event. The single shot in the dark that changed the entire course of my future. But it's like I drank a swimming pool of celebratory champagne after its release and got sick with Writer's Block Poisoning. Because right about now, I'm feeling like a fraud. A fraud with sore muscles, which becomes more obvious as I sink into *Chaturanga*.

Probably all writers feel like this at some point. That bedrock low where every blank page seems too long and every word looks disgusting and the only things that shimmer are a carton of ice cream and reruns of *Parks and Recreation*. I used to watch interviews of my favorite authors on YouTube and scroll right to the part where someone asked them how they deal with writer's block. Answers varied.

"Nature."

"Music."

"Scrolling through my husband's For You page."

After a while, the variety kind of pissed me off. I was looking for one clear-cut answer. One cure-all magic potion that would erase my doubts and frustration for good. News flash, kids: that doesn't exist.

My phone chimes. I sigh in relief. Thank you, stranger, for catching me with your grappling hook and yanking me from this thought spiral.

Turns out Stranger is Kelsey.

> Hey, I'll be in town for two more days.
> Wanna go to a bar tonight?

I'm already folding up my yoga mat as I respond,

> Is fire hot?

As soon as Kelsey and I were twenty-one—her birthday is exactly one month after mine—we made a pact to locate the best bars we could find, stretching as far as Providence and even Boston. We have quite the photo collection of us posing drunkenly beside and under glowing bar signs with our drinks hoisted in the air.

Tonight, it is no surprise that Kelsey sends our Uber driver to a place in Fells Point that, upon first glance, looks like an abandoned tattoo shop decorated in vandalism. Kelsey insists this is the coolest bar around town.

I have learned to trust her on that.

Two possibilities strike me as soon as we walk in: either the owners are Christmas freaks, or Santa himself got drunk here and projectile vomited. Rows and rows of green and red Christmas lights hang low on the ceiling. Then I spot the fake spiderwebs and the skulls perched on shelves under eerie chandeliers and think, okay.

Maybe Santa puked, rinsed with mouthwash, and then made out with Halloween. Either way, it's cool. The overhead lights are dimmed way down to give the effect that you just walked into a different dimension. One with live music, sweet-smelling alcohol, and a glow in the dark bar top. This is our type of dimension.

We settle for two seats at the bar that are closer to the door. Even on Sunday, there are enough people here that we have to lean in close to be able to hear each other. With the live music and ear-shattering guitar, I guess I'm about to master the art of lip reading. We order whiskey--a supposed house favorite—and get to talking. Shout-talking.

"You're not too famous to be in this dive bar with me, right?" she hollers in my ear. "There aren't gonna be paparazzi banging on the windows?"

"I'm not Miley Cyrus!" I call back, and she laughs.

It took me a while to warm up to Kelsey after we met in the dining hall at URI six years ago. The reason? Blatant jealousy. I'd figured that because she is female with eyes and a beating heart that she was falling for Abel just as hard as I was. For the majority of our freshman year, our interactions consisted of strained smiles and forced laughter—at least on my end. But then in April of that year, she spun the world on its axis and asked me if I wanted to go to Remy Ausberg's end of year party with her. (He was only a sophomore at the time and was already famous for his legendary mansion and access to alcohol.)

"Is Abel going?" I asked with a slight bite in my tone. Back then, I didn't know about his downright hatred for parties.

Kelsey's face crinkled. "Who cares?"

That night, we got drunk and lost ourselves in the throbbing music. As unbearably intoxicated as we were that next morning, she stuck by my side and held my hair while I spit my stomach up in the toilet. It was a disgusting way to start a friendship, but it worked.

Kelsey and Abel's relationship turned out to be PLATONIC in all caps anyway. Kelsey later confessed to being bisexual with a taste for bad boys when she's in the mood. That was the last time I let a man wrench himself between me and my potential friends. Kelsey and I have become SISTERS.

"How's your family?" I call over the roaring music.

She leans forward, nearly spilling whiskey on her turquoise bell bottoms. "*What?*"

"Your family!" I shriek. "How's your family!"

"Oh!" She giggles, takes another sip. "They're good! Layla is in her junior year at Massachusetts Amherst."

"Still for biomedical science?"

"Yeah, she's still the brains of our family!" Kelsey laughs. "Bryson is now a freshman at URI, and Chase is a senior in high school this year! Obviously, Meg is doing great!" Kelsey adds with a shrug.

Meg, Kelsey, Layla, Bryson, and Chase Wichett are the type of siblings that everyone wishes they could have. A tight-knit family with even tighter bonds. Sibling group chats full of memes and school pictures and hilarious selfies. FaceTime calls every Sunday. Raging support during Layla's ballet recitals and Bryson's basketball games and Chase's science fair projects. Best friends that get to share blood. Part of me wishes I could be a part of the family, too.

Mr. and Mrs. Wichett love kids. That's why they couldn't stop having them. But after Chase was born, Mrs. Wichett suffered a postpartum hemorrhage, and it scared Mr. Wichett so much that he got a vasectomy the following month. With the five kids they do have, they treat them like royalty. Summer trips to Italy, Mexico, Australia. Shopping trips in places with swaying palm trees. Bougie beverages on white sand with crystal waves ebbing and flowing. It does help that both Mr. and Mrs. Wichett work high up in the medical field.

"I can't believe Chase is a senior now!" I try to clear my head with a sip of whiskey.

"He also made homecoming court!" Kelsey exclaims, fist-pumping the air. "Baby Chasey's going to bring the crown home just like Bryson did!"

I have to laugh at that. Leave it to the Wichetts to dominate a popularity contest.

The door swings open, and a couple of muscle heads with beards and face piercings walk in alongside their sunbaked, bleach-blonde girlfriends. They head straight to the back corner where the band is playing, and one of the girls calls for a few shots of Tequila.

"While we're on the subject of siblings," Kelsey shouts. "How's Tucker?"

"He got his bachelor's in May and has a full teaching job now!"

"Eleventh-grade civics, right?"

"Yep!"

Kelsey straightens on the barstool. "I'll be damned. Maybe I should wow him with my knowledge on how a bill becomes a law, so we can fall in love!"

Yes, when Kelsey is in the mood, she adores bad boys. But my brother is the one exception. He's no teddy bear like Abel, but Tucker is still scared of spiders and needs to have his kitchen looking spotless and well-organized; otherwise, he will flip out with a panic attack. Kelsey doesn't care. She likes him for his charisma, taste in Marvel movies, and knowledge of government styles. I don't get it, but she's taken with him. At least he's a gym rat and makes a mean mojito. I'll give him that.

"He's not still dating Amara, right?" Kelsey asks.

I shake my head. "They broke up two years ago!"

And what a breakup it had been. I stopped studying for my college finals just to drag him out of his bed and insist he eat the ravioli I whipped up for him.

"Perfect!" Kelsey shouts. "Now I can make my move!"

"Don't get so excited. He's been dating the school nurse for a year now."

"The *school nurse?*" Kelsey demands. She smacks the bar top but almost slips off the stool, so we start giggling uncontrollably.

"Whatever," she calls after righting herself. "I don't think Mommy Dearest would like me anyway! What do you think?"

"Well, it could be different!" I wipe some whiskey off my lips. "She likes my brother more than me!"

"Damn!" Kelsey shakes her head. "You, me, Tucker, and Abel could've been something fierce!"

The whiskey stales on my tongue. "What did you say?"

"I said *you, me, Tucker, and—*"

"No, I know what you *said!* Why bring Abel into it?"

Her face somehow displays three emotions at once: surprise, annoyance, and a look I would title Do You Think I Was Born Yesterday?

"Don't play that game!" she warns, shaking a manicured finger in my face. "You were out on that balcony with Abel for like an hour at Meg's party!"

My cheeks must be smoking because they get so hot I have to press the chilled glass to my face for a second.

"I didn't know you caught that!"

"I'm a wizard, Cari! I know everything! I know you still like him!"

I'm tipsy but not drunk enough to scream my feelings from the rooftop. Kelsey waits, one hand glued to her hip, eyebrows arched, lips pursed. She knows she has me cornered.

Several heartbeats go past. Then I hear myself say, "Yes, I do!"

She releases a breath and shouts, "Thank God! I thought you were going to screw it up again!"

I frown. "Screw what up?"

"Fate!" She jiggles her glass in my face and somehow, I hear the ice clink together over booming applause for the band. "You and Abel are soulmates! It's time to face the facts! Just do us all a favor and tell him how you feel this time!"

6

————

Miraculously, my head is not spinning when I jolt awake the next morning with my duvet double-knotted around my legs and drool dribbling down my chin. Even though I am certain that my hair resembles a chicken coop and that my armpits need at least twelve swipes of deodorant, I will call this a win!

Alcohol, twenty. Cari, *one!*

It's almost too bad that Ruth's other assistant works today. I could have been in there, baking like a boss. I stretch my arm out to grab my phone from the bedside table and freeze when I see the screen.

Okay, so I may not be hungover, but Mercury definitely slipped into retrograde while I was asleep because there are two text messages on the screen: one from Abel. And one from Mom.

I don't remember the last time either of them texted me unprovoked. Abel, because we haven't seen each other in two years, and during those 730 days, his silence all but confirmed that our friendship no longer existed. I figured he had moved on after I left for Manhattan but that our chance meeting here in Baltimore is a wonderful glitch in the system.

Mom, on the other hand, because she is Joan Daughtler and

doesn't text me anything other than a quick uncapitalized happy birthday and merry Christmas. She was *really* pissed when I moved to New York. So, seeing as we are still two months from Christmas and my birthday already passed this year, I'm kind of scared.

> Hi sweetheart...

she writes. All right, I'm terrified. Something is definitely wrong here.

Although maybe...*just maybe*, she is finally accepting my decision to be a poet and wants to rebuild our bridge. Maybe she is finally dropping the baggage with two years' worth of disappointment and anger and uncomfortable holiday family meals. Maybe my mom is ready to be my mom again.

I sit up in bed and open the rest of her text. My skin is tingling. My soul is elevating. *Please, please, please let there be an apology in this message!* I don't think I can stomach any more offhand side-glances or eye rolls or, hell, any more lack of affection from my—

> Hi sweetheart! Just wanted to send you this application for a graduate program at the University of Cincinnati! Why not check it out?! ;)

I wish I was Ironman.

Or the Hulk.

Because I would *love* to crush this phone in my bare grasp and watch my mother's text message crinkle and explode. Fizzle out of existence like a bad dream after some chamomile tea. But since I'm not an Avenger, I whip my phone onto the floor and hear it ricochet off the corner of my bedside table. I snatch up my journal and throw it open to a blank page so I can write.

Your tongue
is an ice pick,

chipping at my choice
through your ChapStick.
My stomach's
upside down
in a mud slick.
You sip from your mug
while my blood kicks.
Floods quick—
Regrets, second-guess, shame.
I guess my fame
is only as strong
as your blame.

The pencil falls out of my hand. I'm breathless, not from writing a poem (I'm not *that* out of shape), but because of what I have just written. What kind of horrid, traumatized, sick cavity of my brain just spewed this...oddly gorgeous poem? Gorgeously *unnerving*.

I try to pick apart the words and place them back into the missing puzzle pieces in my head. To no avail. My eyes flick left to right, left to right, reading and rereading. I wasn't aware that I could unconsciously hold so much anger. College psych classes be damned; this is something different. There is a tightness in my chest I have not felt in a long time, like a fist has my heart in a chokehold. At the same time, the tingling in my soul is back. I tap into it, feed it, coax it out into the sunlight. It feels a little like newfound freedom. It tastes good. My tastebuds beg for more.

I stare at the poem and cock my head. I might have trained to be a psychologist a few years ago, but my own brain has bright yellow police tape zigzagging across every entrance. Off limits, even from myself. This is too much to process right now. All I know is that writing this fury-fueled poem feels a bit like...therapy.

When I write the title, I'm not even aware of my hand moving: "Think Before You Speak." I back away from my journal and feel for my phone on the ground. That's when I remember Abel's text, and it is a magnet for my heart.

It's a picture of him wearing one of his old URI sweatshirts. This one has a massive black smudge on the right elbow. Abel's smile is lopsided. The caption, with a crying laughing emoji, reads,

> I think I'm officially ready to forgive you
> for this

My laugh is breathy and emotional. I reply,

> I humbly apologize (for the 50th time) for
> accidentally setting your sweatshirt on fire
> the time you tried to teach me how to grill,

Not even a minute later, my phone buzzes.

> I humbly accept your apology :)

Abel Harpen. Capable of open-heart surgery without even touching me. I don't feel heavy anymore. The poem isn't pulling on my arm like a toddler, waving its arms and demanding attention. All that is left is healthy curiosity about it.

Dr. Harpen, you are a magician!

7

There is a certain finesse to people-watching that is often underrated. It's all in the presentation.

For example, it is better that I sit here at the table in a sandwich shop in Catonsville with a peach tea, cold-cut sandwich, and journal versus if I sit here with nothing and just stare wide-eyed at people as they pull their kids close and scurry out the door. This way, I look presentable. And normal. This way, the older woman at the table to my right won't notice that I overheard her whining about how sour the pickles are here. She won't notice that I now realize her voice arches up at the end of every sentence like she's asking a hundred questions. And this way, the grown man in the corner won't notice that I caught him picking his nose not five minutes before picking up his extremely saucy meatball sub and devouring it.

It is all in the presentation.

Katerine calls me a stalker, but I prefer the title Poetry Enhancer. People-watching gets my imagination going. My poems will be stronger from this. My metaphors will hit harder. Besides, I'm most likely never going to see these people again anyway, and if a small part of their everyday activities makes the final cut and spruces up my poetry, then good for them. They're lucky.

But one girl has caught on to my act. She's staring at me through narrowed slits for eyes. Her bottom lip fills out more than the top, and it could be pretty if it wasn't sinking into a disappointed frown. Or no. Not disappointed. Concentrated. She is trying to crack *my* code. It's an interesting faceoff. I am almost nervous to see how it will turn—

"Carrington?"

I jump so hard, I drop my pencil on the ground, and the woman who hates sour pickles looks at me funny. When I retrieve my pencil, I notice a man standing two feet from my table. Except he is not just any man. He's Abel's friend, the guy I met last week when I ran into them outside Ruth's Bakery. Hunter, I remember suddenly.

One corner of his mouth slides up, his green eyes twinkling and amused. "Why are you staring at yourself in the mirror?"

Dammit, Hunter! I was onto something!

I figured I could give self-watching a try this afternoon. If it's as successful as people-watching, then I could have really scored there. But apparently, public self-watching in a random restaurant mirror is a no-go.

"I had something in my teeth" is the random excuse I choose.

Hunter's laugh is more like an exhale, but his eyes hold zero judgment. They're nice eyes actually. Dark green like a Christmas tree and outlined in kindness. "Well, I think you're good now."

I smile and nod because that's what I always do when I feel like an idiot. This man just caught me staring into my own soul. Now I know what Meatball Sub Guy feels like...or *would* have felt like if he had noticed me.

"So, what'd you order?" Hunter asks, squinting at the menu with his arms crossed over his chest.

Not a bad body. A little taller and less muscular than Abel's, but not a bad body.

"Cold-cut with American cheese, tomatoes, and peppers."

"Gross. I hate tomatoes." His eyes cut to mine and he smiles again. That's when he notices my journal. "Whoa, sorry. Am I interrupting your genius?"

For some reason, that line makes me laugh. "No, you're fine. I have a good idea, but I can't fully grasp it yet."

"I know the feeling. I've been trying to think of a thesis for my paper for three days now. What's your idea?"

My chest tightens at the thought of revealing such an underdeveloped concept with him. "Oh, uh...self-discovery. I think."

"How far are you willing to go?"

"What do you mean?"

His eyes scroll over the menu once more before he takes the seat across from me. "When I was growing up, my dad used to say that self-discovery is like trying to swim to the bottom of the ocean with nothing but snorkel gear. It's a journey worth attempting but is ultimately impossible because...well, metaphorically speaking, you'd run out of oxygen pretty quickly. But realistically, you're always going to change, you know? You'll never know exactly who you are down to the bone. But that's the beauty of life. The question is—how far are you willing to swim?"

I should expect nothing less from a UMBC psychology student. But my mouth is frozen open in shock. That was...poetic. His green eyes bore into mine. There is a flicker in his voice that hints at a deep well of passion. I manage to close my mouth and sift through his words.

"Well, considering I don't do much self-discovery, I don't know if I can answer that question." My voice, compared to his, is hollow.

He sits back in the chair, no less engaged. "How much do you love poetry?"

"A lot." *Duh.*

"No, Carrington. How much do you love poetry? How much are you willing to give to your readers?"

"Everything." The answer is instinctual. "I want to help people and show them they aren't alone."

He leans forward again and folds his hands under his chin. There is a smile tugging his lips now. "So are you willing to drown for them? Give them every piece of your heart?"

His logic is a plug, and it just found the outlet in my brain. "You…" I shake my finger at him. "You're good."

"Eh." He waves my comment away. Okay, good and humble apparently.

"Why do you care so much?" The question cannonballs off my tongue.

For the first time since he walked into this sandwich shop, Hunter frowns. "Why wouldn't I care?"

It is not the response I was expecting, and yet it is the best response I have ever received.

"All right," I bite. "If I am preparing to…drown in self-discovery, where do I start?"

My phone chimes before he can answer, and my eyes automatically flick to the screen. It is a text from Abel. Ever since he started texting me this past Monday, we've been at it nonstop—except for when he's in class, and I'm baking with Ruth or staring at a blank piece of paper.

> You're gonna be so proud of me!

It's a terribly angled selfie of Abel with a plate of misshapen, slightly burnt chocolate chip cookies. He's never been a huge fan of the kitchen, but he *is* a huge fan of making someone feel special on their birthday. Today, his friend Leo turns twenty-five, as he excitedly texted me the other night. And what do you know? Abel sets his discomfort aside and bakes some damn cookies.

I must have heart-eyes the size of Jupiter because Hunter's eyebrow arches the moment I look back at him. It's a playful look. A *who ya textin'* kind of look.

"It's just a friend," I mutter.

He blinks at me. "The fact that you have to clarify it's 'just a friend' confirms it's not." His laugh is deep, flowing out from his belly, and very contagious.

"Okay, fine. I really like this guy. I've liked him for a long time."

"That's it!" He touches his finger to his nose and uses the other hand to point at me. I have literally never seen anyone gesture like that in real life in the twenty-four years I have been alive. "That's your way in."

"Into what?"

"The ocean. The way a person falls for someone and the way they go about it speaks volumes about their character. You want to do some self-discovery? Watch yourself around this guy." Hunter nods. "You'll be writing poems for hours."

Again, I should expect nothing less. "You're a genius."

"I'm really not," Mr. Humble says, standing up and gently pushing in his chair. "But I know that you're about to write the most amazing collection of poetry that's ever existed."

No one has ever said that to me. Not even my agent who sends me fruit baskets and Starbucks gift cards as a way to say she adores me, though it's really a tactic to bribe me to keep writing.

"Thanks," I say, and I truly mean it.

"No problem! Oh, and Carrington?" Hunter says before going up to order. "Make the first move."

My blood drops five degrees. "You mean..."

"Tell him how you feel." He nods. "I don't know what girls think, but if I were that guy, my respect for you would shoot through the roof." With that, he smiles that kind smile and turns around to order.

Okay, Cari. This is not rocket science. You are not climbing Mount Everest. You are not performing on World of Dance. You are not scarfing down hot dogs in a ridiculous carnival contest. It is just a text message.

> Hey Abel. Do you wanna go to dinner with me next weekend?

You have to start somewhere, and I can do this. If I could just... press send.

My heart, of course, is demanding I press send. My brain is asking me if I understand how stupid I am. But another perk of growing up with a clinical psychologist mother—albeit, a disappointed one—is learning how to quiet the section of the brain that is a bully. So, after breathing in for four counts, holding, and exhaling for six, I press send.

I pitch my phone across my bed. It bounces off the end and lands on the rug. (I really should buy a more protective case with all these crazy text messages). But I can't just sit here and wait for his reply. Not if I want to check into a psychiatric hospital. Instead, I switch on my TV and play an episode of my go-to comfort show: *Parks and Recreation*. I can almost lose myself in Leslie's peppiness and in Ron's hilarious glare, but my brain is pumping more and more cortisol by the minute.

Abel and I hung out a lot back in college. Once I realized he lived in Providence, we were at each other's houses all the time for movie marathons, New Year's Eve parties, and his annual luau every June. Granted, Noah and Kelsey were with us for those things too, but Abel and I are comfortable around each other. This will not be weird or awkward at all. Until I tell him how I feel.

If I develop the guts to by then.

I've only ever told one guy that I liked him, and that was my dumbass jock boyfriend back in high school. The difference was that I knew he liked me, too, and was desperate to get inside my pants, so I said to hell with it. *Let's have a closely-monitored, gossip-fueled high school relationship!* We lasted three months. My next serious relationship after him was with Kai, but Kai asked me out himself.

The point is, Justin What's-His-Face and Freakin' Kai don't hold a *candle* to Abel Harpen. Abel makes me speechless. Abel cures every worry I've ever had just by existing. Abel is everything I have ever wanted in a man. Bipolar disorder or not.

I can't take it anymore.

I speed-crawl to the end of my bed and reach down to get my phone, hyper-aware that my heart is literally screaming at the top of its lungs. A new text from Abel pops up.

> I'd love to go to dinner with you! :) Where would you like to go?!

I don't know.

I just fall back onto my pillows and squeal like a fucking sixteen-year-old.

8

We settle on Rozenbury, a restaurant in Catonsville
that is both cozy (with wooden decor and olive-toned walls) and club-
like (with glowing signs and an attractive bar). If it wasn't October, I
would have asked for a table outside. But it wouldn't matter anyway.
When we sit down, I am not focused on the buzzing energy of the
surrounding tables or the tall glass of sparkling merlot sitting in front
of me.

All I see is Abel.

"These chairs are so funky," he says in his usual cheery tone.

It snaps me out of my trance. I'd been staring at his wavy gold
hair that looks even better than it did the night of Meg's party, though
how, I don't know. It doesn't appear gelled or anything, but not one
hair is out of place. His eyes are as blue as ever, maybe even bluer.
They make me want to rip my heart right out of my chest and hand it
over to him. This thought almost makes me laugh at myself.

"What do you mean?" I somehow say. "They're just chairs." My
voice is already an octave higher. God, I'm ridiculous.

Abel doesn't seem to notice. "Look at the armrests." He leans back in his chair, arms raised slightly higher than his slouched posi-tion. He appears slumped and uncomfortable, but I know he's exag-gerating. He is trying to make me laugh. Mission accomplished. He straightens, and the smile on his face is happy, satisfied. Proud.

I have never wanted to kiss someone's smile so badly.

"So, okay," he says, "Let's see. What's new in my life?" This is how we started conversations back in college: by jumping right in. "Well, I spent four hours in the gym last night, so that was fun! But other than that, nothing is new. Literally nothing." He laughs. It's an entire five-star orchestra to my ears.

"Nothing?" I challenge with a grin.

"Nope. Not unless you count hours of homework and conducting correlational research on how social media worsens mental health." I want to ask how that's going, but he continues. "What can I say? I'm living the life."

"But you're one step closer to your dream," I remind him.

His smile broadens. "Clinical psychologist, here I come!" He takes a sip of his water. "That's only *part* of the dream though. I want to live in a big house."

"How big?"

"Massive!" He gestures with his arms as if he's capturing his future home in the palms of his hands. I'm laughing because he's laughing. "With stone, you know? I don't like brick or stucco. It's gotta be stone."

"Well, of course."

"And I want to have kids."

This isn't a surprise. We've had this conversation, or one like it, more than once, but we never stop each other once we get going on it. Because when you want something *this* much, it's hard to turn it off and swallow it down.

His blue eyes twinkle. "Four kids."

I know why four: because his parents had wanted that many, but after their third, his mom got sick again and said she couldn't handle having another. He wants to complete their legacy; and besides, he always said, he loves kids, and four is a cool even number. He takes another sip of water. "What about you, Cari Carrington? What's your future look like?"

He can probably guess my response, but there's interest and curiosity written on every square inch of his face.

"I'll be living somewhere quiet," I say, "and gorgeous so that I can write to my heart's content. I want a big kitchen so I can bake everything under the sun and set it all out on the island."

"How big?" His smile is twice as large now.

"*Massive*," I reply, leaning forward and piercing him with the same grin.

We giggle until the couple at our neighboring table glances at us over the rims of their wine glasses.

"Kids?" Abel asks like he doesn't already know.

This is the part that always sends my stomach into somersaults. Because it's *him* asking, and I can't even fathom sitting across from him let alone entertaining the idea of *us* having kids together. I figure it's unhealthy to think these conversations are foreshadowing anything, but honestly, who gives a damn?

"I'm scared to give birth," I remind him. *Terrified* actually. One time in high school, I googled the most painful things that a human can experience out of sheer, morbid curiosity. Blame it on the writer in me. Surprisingly, childbirth was number two, right behind burning to death. I am not doing that. Out loud, I say, "I don't want to know how much it hurts."

Abel nods. "Okay, but that's only one small part of the glorious experience of raising children. It's like taking your driver's test. It's scary in the moment, but it doesn't compare to the feeling you get when you pass or the years afterward."

I stare at him. "Did you just compare childbirth to a driver's test?"

"Mhm." He's fully smiling now, perfect teeth and all. My

defenses crumble like a three-year-old's sandcastle. He has a point though.

"Have you ever seen *Silver Linings Playbook*?" he asks.

I chew on my straw. "Sure, with Jennifer Lawrence and—"

"Bradley Cooper," Abel says. "Best movie ever. Hands down."

I've seen the movie three times, partly because I'm obsessed with feel-good movies involving mental health and partly because I know it mirrors Abel's situation and watching it somehow makes me feel closer to him and his mom.

"Excelsior," Abel murmurs. "Everything has a silver lining. Like, for example...the silver lining of childbirth is getting to raise that child into the awesome human being you know they're going to be."

I roll my eyes, and his laugh envelops me.

"I really thought you were going to be poetic there," I say.

"What are you talking about? That was incredibly poetic."

"You could've used a better metaphor."

"There is no better metaphor." The corner of his lip hooks up, and I shake my head again.

Our food arrives. Abel ordered the cauliflower taco because he says he's feeling brave tonight, and he can only try new things when he's brave. Apparently, a cauliflower taco sounds like the most eccentric meal a restaurant could ever sell. Turns out, Abel loves it. In the meantime, I try the salmon BLT wrap. I'm brave, but not cauliflower taco brave.

"Top three favorite memories from college!" Abel exclaims. "Go!"

"Okay, uh...." My salmon BLT stares up at me from the plate as I consider how most of my favorite memories from college somehow involve Abel. "Oh! Third place: the frisbee incident sophomore year."

Abel slams his hands down on the table. "*What?* No! How can that be in your top three? That's in, like, my top *worst* three."

It happened when we were playing frisbee on one of the enormous lawns on campus with Noah and Kelsey. It was September, but Mother Nature was still in her hot girl mood, so the weather was gorgeous. Abel called my name, whipped the frisbee across our rectangle of people, and somehow managed to smack me right in the head with it.

He screeched and sprinted to my side. "Go get her an ice pack," Kelsey told him through her high-pitched laugh.

Sure, it was painful, but I successfully avoided a concussion and got to sit with Abel for the next hour while he guiltily held the ice pack to my forehead. Now every September, I reminisce about the massive red mark that stayed on my forehead for three days.

"I just thought it was funny," I tell Abel now. *I thought sitting next to you was the best feeling in the world. It still is.*

"You thought it was funny because you weren't thinking straight after that."

"Tomato, tom*ah*to."

He shakes his head, but there is a gleam in his eye. "What's your second-place favorite?"

"My release party." That's a no-brainer.

"Oh yeah! I still have that picture of us holding up your book!"

"Me too!" Like I would ever delete it. Me in a maroon cocktail dress dwarfed in his arms, and *him* in all black but still managing to look brighter than the sun. *Please.* "Before I say my first-place one, I have an honorable mention."

"I'm all ears."

I really smile at this one. "That time I passed my psych midterm and you passed your calc midterm."

"The dance party we had in the middle of campus, of course." He chuckles.

We danced like monkeys to no music for five minutes straight in the middle of a public area with lots of questioning eyes. But we didn't care at all.

"That's a beautiful honorable mention."

"Why, thank you," I say.

"Okay, I'm dying here. What's your all-time favorite memory?"

I test the weight of what I'm about to say on my tongue because I don't know if it will feed the vibe or destroy it. But I can't fight the magnetic pull of his eyes.

"Honestly, Halloween night, freshman year."

For a second, his expression loses focus, and I know he's thinking back. Then it clicks.

"Right. The night we spilled the beans to each other." He leans back in his seat. His expression is still friendly, still warm and curious, but there's a small shadow in his eyes now. I know what he's doing. He's putting on his trusted, protective armor.

"Well, yeah," I say. "I feel like that night really marked the beginning of our friendship."

Halloween fell on a Friday that year, so Remy Ausberg threw one of his legendary parties. Kelsey had been hounding me all week about going, but I had the misfortune of a psych exam the following Monday, and I knew that if I was going to get into graduate school, my grades had to be *gorgeous*. So, Kelsey called me a loser out of love and took Noah with her instead.

Meanwhile, I'd relocated to the library and was studying for two hours until Abel walked in and took a desk across the room. He was bent over his notes, glancing at his textbook and scribbling onto his paper.

He skips parties and Friday night shenanigans to keep his *grades gorgeous, too,* I'd realized.

Just like that, he had unknowingly checked off another box on my list of Impossible to Reach Standards. Because *he*, a muscular, otherworldly handsome man with perfectly wavy hair, looked so out of place among these shelves of books and papers and calculators on a *Friday* night. He belonged in a crowd. He belonged at Remy's party with girls practically throwing themselves at him.

Instead, he was in the library. With his own books and papers and calculator.

I couldn't help myself. I got up and mustered the courage to say his name as I approached him. He looked up, and his face brightened so much it almost blinded me. We talked for all of five minutes before he said, "You know what? I've done enough work for today. Do you want to get some candy and watch a scary movie in my dorm? My roommate won't mind. He's at some party tonight."

He might as well have asked if I wanted to make out with him right there in the library.

Is fire hot?

Forty-five minutes later, after a quick run to the store, we were sitting on his bed with a bowl of candy between us, and he was flicking through the horror section on Netflix. The movie, however, was delayed because something about eating REECE's Peanut Butter Cups and sucking on Jolly Ranchers made us braver. We got to talking about the past.

I explained how I'd been a straight-A student in high school. Involved in honors programs. Captain of the softball team. Vice president of student council. I'd been involved in all of it because back then, I figured those would be the best years of my life. (In hindsight, high school means very little in the grand scheme of things.)

"Wow," Abel said. I remember how his eyes shimmered. "You should be proud of yourself. *I'm* proud of you."

I unwrapped a Snickers bar and tried hard to conceal my smile. "Thank you. So, what's your story?"

He shifted on the bed. His Adam's apple bobbed. His eyes betrayed the smallest shred of worry. But by some miraculous force, he decided to open up to me.

He told me about how he'd had his small circle of friends in high school, but that all changed when he turned seventeen and had his first full-blown manic episode. He stopped sleeping. He talked too much and too fast. He couldn't focus; his grades went down the drain. He snapped at his friends, spent five hundred dollars on shoes and gifts for his sisters they didn't need and other meaningless things. He had a major fight with his dad, even tried to punch him once. Abel had finally ended up in the hospital and was diagnosed with bipolar disorder.

Severe mania with touches of depression.

He started taking lithium, continued therapy—mostly out of guilt.

"I'll never forget the look in my mom's eyes," he told me that night, while we were sitting on his bed. "Complete and utter sadness."

He went on to tell me how he hadn't liked the medication, how it had made him feel funny and shaky and sick to his stomach. He didn't like having to go to the doctor to have his blood checked. He didn't like weekly therapy sessions. He rebelled often, pretended to be fine, stopped taking the lithium until he ended up right back in the seat opposite his therapist's, coming down off another manic episode. Forced back onto the meds.

Ultimately, he said, it was the look in his mom's eyes that stayed with him. He told me it seemed like she felt she failed as a mother, and he refused to let her go on thinking like that. So, he stayed on his meds and worked his ass off to get his grades back on track.

"Routines are good for me," Abel explained that night in his dorm. It was the last thing he said before he turned on a random scary movie and we pretended to watch it.

"You're right," he says now, as we sit opposite each other in Rozenbury, with our empty plates in front of us. "I'm glad I can talk to you about that stuff."

We're quiet for a moment. The sounds of laughter and discussion filter between us, but we're staring at each other. And it's the *way* he's staring at me, like he's seeing me for the very first time. Dammit, it's now or never.

"Abel?"

"Mhm?" He takes a sip of his water.

It's not rocket science, Cari. You're not presenting your dissertation. You're not giving birth—

"I just want to say that...I seriously adore you." The words come out misty like I've been crying. "You mean the absolute world to me, and you have since I tried to steal your food freshman year."

He laughs, remembering that day. I push myself to keep going "You're like this...angel. I swear. To be honest, life was boring before I met you."

Is it a full confession? No. But it's close enough for now.

His cheeks are glowing bright red. His smile is uncontainable. "Wow, Cari. Thank you. That is one of the kindest things anyone has ever said to me."

"It's true," I insist, unable to hide my own smile.

He looks at me again. "I'd say the same about you, too. I'm so lucky to know you."

Okay, now I give my heart full permission to inflate and explode.

We pay—separately because, as of now, against my wishes, we are still just friends—and Abel talks about his classes as we exit the restaurant. Then he does something completely unexpected.

He hugs me.

It's not an awkward one-arm squeeze like he used to give me in college. Both his arms wrap around my body and hold me to his chest. Not tightly. Just right. I'm pretty sure I pass away.

"Bye, Cari." His eyes aren't joking anymore. They are brimming with compassion and something else I can't name.

"Goodbye, Abel."

By the time I get back to my apartment, my body is reduced to watery legs, tingling skin, and a Grinch-after-the-revelation-sized grin. I'm basically moonwalking on air.

I brush my teeth and don't taste the mint toothpaste. I remove my makeup and don't feel the splash of water on my face. I change and don't register the different clothes on my body. All I can think of is that hug. That look he gave me. It has me feeling cauliflower taco brave.

I text him.

> I had so much fun tonight Abel! We have to hang out again soon!

I fall asleep, but only because I listen to a guided sleep meditation to force myself to calm down. When I wake up the next morning, I am more elated than I've felt since I dyed my hair rose gold pink. My hand shoots out to pick up my phone, and my brain floods with dopamine at just the *thought* of what he responded to me.

Except I'm slapped in the face with an unexpected surprise. He never texted me back.

9
____

"Carrington, sweetheart, that's frosting, not your high
school bully."

I immediately ease up on my stirring and turn to look at Ruth.
The apron she's wearing today is a darker purple than anything else
in this whole bakery. Even her eyes are underlined with purple shadows, but I don't think those are intentional.

She writes something on a notepad, but her cursive is so slanted, I
have to tilt my head to make it out: Three-tiered vanilla cake—
wedding on October 20. Tomorrow.

Ruth grabs a bowl from the cabinet. "You want to tell me why
you're trying to abuse my frosting?" There's no real irritation in her
voice. More like curiosity. I love my grandma boss.

"I'm sorry." I move to the sink to wash the sticky purple gunk off
my fingers. "I went out with a friend last night and may have screwed
up our friendship."

"What'd you do?"

"Kinda sorta told him that I like him."

Ruth tosses a cracked eggshell into the sink and glances at me.
"Good for you, Cari."

"No, *not* good for me. He never texted me back last night."

"Maybe he was on the toilet."

"For nine hours?"

Ruth measures out some milk and adds it to her bowl. "Maybe it was something he ate."

Not the cauliflower taco! I almost laugh until reality karate chops my stomach again. "I'm so stupid! I shouldn't have told him anything. Now he's going to hate me and never talk to me again."

"First of all, you are *not* stupid, so watch your mouth. Hand me the vanilla, will you please?"

I pass it over.

"Second of all—" She measures that out and pours it into her sweet-smelling concoction. "—is this guy worth it?"

I was expecting her to say, *If he doesn't respond, he's not worth your time!* Or, *A guy who doesn't recognize your amazingness* has *no amazingness!* Instead, my heart rate doubles.

"Yes. Absolutely."

She looks at me like she's waiting for me to do something. And when I don't budge—because I don't know what she wants me to do— she says, "Aren't you going to turn him into a poem then?"

I slap the counter and laugh. "You say that like I'm a fairy godmother just *dying* to get my hands on a pumpkin."

"No, you already found one." She turns to me, her rain-gray eyes wide for emphasis. "It's him."

"Turn him into a poem. I like that, Ruth. I'm going to have to give you credit when I publish this next collection."

"You better."

Despite the fact that Abel's nonexistent text is folding my heart into thirds, I like talking with Ruth. My grandma on my mom's side passed away two years ago—heart attack—and my dad's mom isn't in the picture. Apparently, there was another man with polished suits and a Corvette that made Grandma tell Grandpa *Adiós, sucker!* We don't talk about it.

The point is, Ruth is filling both of my grandmas' shoes *perfectly.*

Like a new pair of sparkling pumps. Or in my case right now, a pair of flour-dusted, stained tennis shoes, which are just as perfect. But those purple shadows under Ruth's eyes are really getting to me.

I purse my lips. "Hey, can I ask you something?"

"Sure thing."

"Is everything okay like, personally?"

"Of course. Why?"

We stare at each other for a second, and then I place my hand over my heart. "Ruth, I mean this in the nicest way possible. Never become an actress because that performance stunk."

"What do you mean?" She looks offended.

"I mean you're obviously *not* fine. We could call it a day and order some pizza. Drink fruit punch and talk about our problems."

"Nice try." She taps the note, reminding me about the wedding cake.

I move to the sink and wash some dishes while she continues to stir. "How is that fair? I open up to you about my monumental mistake, and I get the silent treatment in return?"

"Carrington, you did not make a mistake. And my issue isn't important right now."

"Aha! So there *is* an issue!"

She glances at me, but instead of an irked expression, it's one of gratitude. "We'll talk someday soon, but right now, I need you to help me with this cake."

I sigh heavily, only to be dramatic. "Aye, aye, Capitan."

Ruth laughs.

WHEN I WAS in fifth grade, one of my then-friends was boy-crazy. The lilac walls in her bedroom were covered with posters: Big Time Rush, One Direction, Gale Hawthorne from *The Hunger Games*—you name him, she had him. For a long time, I thought *I* was the crazy one because I didn't feel the same. I was not addicted to WattPad or

The Vampire Diaries like she was. But when we reached middle school, and the boys in our grade finally had their growth spurts, I realized my indifference was my superpower. It made them chase me. I could toss my hair without a care in the world, dead certain that I would *never* chase a man so long as I lived.

Until the universe said, *Cari, meet Abel.*

I am sitting on the carpet in my bedroom, head bent and shoulders hunched, legs splayed out in front of me. I'm writing a poem. I don't know why Abel hasn't texted me back yet. All I can do is give in to intrusive thoughts, assume he does not reciprocate my feelings and has found another girl. The anxiety is infiltrating my throbbing heart. That's why my writer's block has been temporarily obliterated.

> Well, he walked into my life:
> an angel dressed in light jeans.
> He gave a smile to me,
> and then my soul was clean.
> So now he stays in my lips
> to keep my conscience redeemed,
> and I would die
> a hundred times
> to meet him back in my dreams.

> An instant reliever.
> I hope that he leaves her
> so I can play lover
> in a game with no cheaters.
> My heart is dramatic,
> but Cupid's sporadic.
> It feels just like static.
> I'm so damn emphatic.

> He's like an artist
> 'cause my life was a canvas,

his presence was color.

He came in to paint tiny stars
down the groove
of my spine
and across
all my scars.

And so
I keep wishing
that he'll start thinking
we could become
more than what we are.

I need my artist.

He stands so close,
but his heart
stays far.

I will never be able to fully explain what it feels like to finish writing a poem. It is triumph on steroids mixed with cocaine. It is having both feet on the ground again after skydiving. It's even better than sex. This feeling right here—this breathless, fluttery accomplishment—is why I originally became a poet. Sure, I can bake a mean chocolate cake and mumble my way through the lobes of the brain, but true power comes from speaking in metaphors. If you do it right, the reader will never know it's about them. Having your thoughts on paper is pure, sweet relief.

I like this poem that I've just spit out. I am proud of this poem.

I eventually decide to title it "Brief Relief." Abel is my brief relief from writer's block. From my mother's disappointment. From cooking frozen chicken on lonely weeknights. He's not my *sole* source of happiness; I'm a best-selling poet and baker on the side, for Pete's sake. That right there is basically paradise. But Abel is at least 85% of that paradise.

Brief relief, lasting impact.

A memory surfaces in my mind.

It was August. Abel and I were a week away from being big fish seniors at the University of Rhode Island. Abel had recently reappeared after a manic episode but was still mourning his breakup with Camila. I had just gotten an acceptance to publish *Left or Right*, and fresh off that high, I couldn't stand seeing Abel so down in the dumps. A ray of sunshine does not belong in a depressing shade of blue.

I did the only thing I could think of: I invited Abel over to swim and pig out on the cheeseburgers my dad had grilled. Abel seemed to perk up as we played volleyball in my pool and compared our tans under the baking sunlight.

My memory strays to one conversation in particular. Our Bullshit List.

"You want to know what's bullshit?" I said, splashing my legs in the pool.

Abel looked at me. "What?"

"Combing your hair out when it's wet. This is going to suck to detangle." I pointed to my ratted brunette hair.

"Yeah, I don't have that problem." His hair was still beautiful, just damp and dark from swimming.

We were silent for a second, taking a moment to move our legs in the water and listen to the birds sing their own karaoke in the trees.

"I'll tell you what else is bullshit," Abel murmured.

"Let me hear it."

"Driving behind slowpokes in the left lane. I had to do that on the way over here, and let me tell you, Cari. Gosh, I was so irritated."

If Abel Harpen is mad—if *ever*—the worst he will say about someone is "What a jerk!" It is simply another reason why I adore him. His innocence is one in a billion.

"That is bullshit," I agreed. "But not as bad as having to stop for gas in the middle of January when it's below freezing."

"Oh, my gosh. You're right. That makes me wanna hurl!" He hugged his torso and made a face that had me laughing so hard, I almost fell into the pool. "What about folding laundry?"

"Yes, super annoying," I confirmed. "The stomach flu?"

"Wisdom teeth surgery?"

"Math exams?"

"Breakups?"

Our wide eyes had glued together. I caught the flicker in his eye at the mention of a breakup and slowly lowered my gaze to the pool.

"I think we found our bullshit winner," I said.

"Guess so." His voice was a little strained. I didn't like it.

"Abel, what do you look for in a girl? And don't say Camila Saunders," I tacked on quickly.

I figured maybe if he could get to the bottom of what he wanted and deserved, the breakup wouldn't be a problem anymore. I was trying to help him get back to himself.

"Well, Camila taught me a lot. I'll give her that." He leaned back and pressed his palms into the warm concrete of the pool deck. "I want a girl who's passionate and motivated, you know? Someone who goes after her dreams. Someone who is down to earth and funny and smart. And understanding," he added, with a happy helping of fervor in his voice. "Understanding of me and my situation and of my family. I know that if I find that, I'll have struck gold."

I knew I shouldn't have, but I'd started comparing. I'm *passionate and motivated!* I'm *down to earth and funny and smart!* I'm *understanding! He's talking about* me!

"I mean, Camila was all of those things," Abel muttered. "Until she wasn't."

"Camila is the jerkiest of jerks," I said, and he laughed. "She didn't realize she was the luckiest girl in the whole world. Imagine dumping Abel Harpen!" I shook my head because the idea was (is) literally insane to me. Maybe even clinically insane.

"Thanks, Cari." Abel's cheeks went pink. His smile was soft and grateful.

I should have kissed him right then—in my backyard, under a red and gold sunset, with our feet dangling in the water. Maybe if I had kissed him that day, everything would be different now.

But in hindsight, it is probably better that I didn't. His breakup was still too fresh. He probably would have thought I was trying to take advantage of him.

To this day, though, I remember the way he looked at me as we talked about his required girlfriend material. I'm not an expert on body language, but one thing had been blatantly obvious: his voice was nonchalant, but his eyes were on me, and they were pleading.

10

———

I CAN HARDLY SEE THROUGH THE SWEAT POURING INTO MY EYES.

My YouTube kickboxing instructor is a little on the self-absorbed side, but her abs and calf muscles could cut diamonds, so by default, that makes her cool. She has me wheezing through thirty seconds of boxer crunches with a weighted punch, and I think I might black out. That clock is an asshole for not ticking faster. When the buzzer sounds, I go limp on my stained yoga mat and pant like on overheated Siberian husky. Thirty seconds of rest has never felt so blissful.

Until my phone rings. *Oh, come on!*

I pause the TV, wipe my sweat on the sleeve of my sweatshirt, and click to answer the FaceTime call.

"Hey, Cari! What's going—" Noah squints at the screen. "Did you just go swimming?"

"I'm doing a kickboxing workout."

"At eight o'clock at night?"

I nod. "Helps the creative juices flow, you know?"

Noah gives me a look that translates to, *I don't buy it. What's wrong?*

In college, if stress was eating me alive, I would power through an intense workout as a means to cope. Noah knows this better than anyone. We took some tough classes together, and on the nights before exams, he usually caught me doing jumping jacks at nine o'clock in some common area with my notes open on a nearby table.

"I told Abel."

Noah looks confused for a second. Then it clicks.

"Finally! Praise God, finally. Tell me how it all went down."

I explain everything—down to the hug and the blush in Abel's cheeks. Noah cocks his head.

"Wait, so you didn't tell him you love him?'"

"Well, no, because—"

"Then it wasn't a *real* confession."

"I told him adore him, which is progress, okay?" Crazy Abs Kickboxing Instructor is frozen mid-sentence on the TV screen like she's getting impatient. "It doesn't matter anyway. He's ghosting me now."

Noah shakes his head. "That doesn't make any sense. Abel can be flakey, but he's not a dry texter. He's probably just busy with schoolwork or something. I can tell you right now that there's no way he had a bad time with you. There's just no way. It's mathematically impossible." He flashes me this professorial look.

"Show me the data then," I say.

"I digress. The point is, he's currently just being a clueless idiot. All men are."

"Coming from a man himself."

"At least I'm honest."

I register the passing landscape behind him and realize his phone must be in the car ProClip. "Where are you going?"

"Home." He glances down at the screen. "I was only supposed to be in Baltimore for the week."

"Home sweet Atlantic City," I say.

Noah is from Cape May, New Jersey. He chose the University of Rhode Island for two reasons: its business program and because he has family there. The second he graduated, though, he swung right back down to his home state. He lives in Atlantic City now because of his job.

"You have to come back," I tell him. "We'll go to a bar. We'll go out to dinner. We'll go streaking."

"Whoa!" Noah holds a hand up. "Save that for your time with Abel."

"Too far."

"Not far enough." He smirks.

Noah and I should have been siblings. Our brains work the same. Our banter is equally witty. We even look the same—or *did*, before I dyed my hair. We call our brother-sister energy the Force. That's why whenever one of us forgets to text back, the other demands, "May the Force be with you." While I was in New York, the Force disappeared to hibernate, but our friendship is a paused TV show. When we reconnect, it's like no time has passed at all.

"Hey, what happened to that girl you were seeing?" I ask, wiping another sheen of sweat off my forehead.

"Who? Nadia? Ugh!" Noah sticks out his tongue. "She smoked so much weed, *I* started smelling like it! That's not great for business in case you were wondering."

"Told her to hit the highway, huh?"

"I may have told her some other things, too, but mainly that. Yes. Besides, it's just me and Rudy now."

Rudy, his adorably overweight dachshund that I have only seen in pictures but have been plotting to steal since freshman year of college.

"Rudy's all you need," I agree.

"He is all I've ever needed—"

My phone chimes, and my heart skids to a stop.

"Wait! Wait!" I shout at Noah.

It is—at long last—a text from Abel.

I had even more fun Cari Carrington :) And
YES! What are you doing tomorrow?!

Cue the headrush.

Noah's grin is on fire. "No need to explain. Just leave some room for Jesus, all right?"

"Copy that." I feel breathless and bubbly. "Safe travels, Noah. Come back soon."

11

———————

Aside from my weekly yoga exercise, Sundays are typically reserved for cleaning. Reorganizing my journals that become cluttered throughout the week. Sweeping and scrubbing the crumb-covered floors. Tackling the small mountain of laundry in my hamper. It is my sweatpants, messy bun, and no makeup day. But when Abel Harpen offers to pick me up to go mini golfing in Towson, all of those productive activities get pushed to Sunday *morning*.

I am Dash from *The Incredibles*.

The journals get organized by color on my shelves; the floors are spotless; the laundry pile disappears. I am in my bathroom by 11:30 a.m., curling my hair and smearing on mascara. I am not trying hard. I am in love. By the time I double-knot my Converse, Abel texts me that he's here.

Halloween—our favorite holiday—is eight days away, so we're going to a Halloween-themed mini golf course today called, characteristically, Monster Mini Golf. I skip outside and spot his dark blue Toyota Corolla. When I climb into the passenger seat, "Sweet Dreams (Are Made of This)" by Eurythmics belts from his speakers. Not surprising. Abel's dad played lots of music from the '70s, '80s, and '90s while Abel was growing up. It is all Abel listens to, even now in a universe ruled by Drake and Billie Eilish. The rest of Abel's car is spotless, except for a spare sweatshirt tossed across the backseat.

"Good afternoon, ma'am." Abel smiles at me.

Joke's on me because we are only separated by the small center console, and the proximity to him is giving me heart palpitations. He looks unbearably handsome in a simple black T-shirt and those damn gray sweatpants. One time, Kelsey and I had a twenty-minute conversation on why the sexiest thing a guy could wear is gray sweatpants, but we never came to a final conclusion. As I'm sitting beside Abel now, I decide that there doesn't have to be an answer other than *mini golf can wait.* But he presses the gas, and we move away from the curb.

"Are you ready," he asks over Annie Lennox's sultry voice, "to be publicly embarrassed in mini golfing?"

I scoff. "It appears you have forgotten, sir, that I was the 2018 winner at the Mini Golf World Championship."

"Cute, but you're talking to the 2019 winner of the Mini Golf Galaxies Championship."

"Twenty-twenty-one," I shoot back. "I won Universe."

"Congrats. But does God invite you to drink lemonade and play mini golf with him on Sundays?"

I crack first and start dying laughing. We both suck at mini golf, but we adore some healthy trash talk.

We spend the majority of the car ride half-dancing to '80s music, but as soon as the classic beat of "Billie Jean" begins, we both go nuts. I go from screaming the lyrics to muttering them because Abel steals all of my attention before the second verse even starts.

I fully confess that I did not know true beauty until this moment. Until I watch Abel keep beat on the steering wheel and sing his heart out. His eyes cut to mine as Michael Jackson sings, his famous lines. I think I'm smiling, but it is way more likely that my jaw is on the ground. I know that Billie Jean isn't *Abel's* lover, but the way he sings her name over Michael's voice makes me want to be her.

As the song fades away, Abel leans back in his seat, one hand lazily draped around the wheel. "I think that's my favorite Michael Jackson song ever. What's yours?"

"I'm gonna have to agree with you," I say.

It is seriously not fair how much my heart burns for him—not fair to any other guy and *certainly* not fair to me. My heart is not even mine.

The second we see the golf course, we transform into squealing 6-year-olds. Each hole is divided by orange strips and fake grass where animatronic yet eerily realistic monsters are waiting to greet you. A wrought-iron fence runs the perimeter of the course with the words **BEWARE** hanging above the entrance. Abel swings into a parking space, and we can't shut up as we go to stand in the long line, doused in gold from the sunshine.

"This is so cool!" I shout.

"Look at the skeletons!" Abel tugs on my arm.

"No way! They have the Headless Horseman on top of that little cliff!"

"Cari, are you seeing that giant clown head at the end of the course?"

A little girl in front of us peeks over her shoulder, grilling us with a weird look. Her mother calls her forward in line, and as soon as she looks away, Abel and I lean into each other, howling with laughter. We decide then that if anyone asks, we are Professional Halloween Enthusiasts—just doing our job.

"Prepare to eat my dust," Abel warns once we get to the first hole. He rolls his shoulders and cracks his neck. Stretches his arms, twists his torso. Touches his pointer fingers to his thumbs and does a breathing mantra.

He will do anything and everything under the sun to make me laugh, and he won't quit until I have at least cracked a smile. But I don't have to fake it with him.

"Okay," he says once I've snorted. "Here we go." He brings the club down against the ball and sends it careening around a curve, smacking into one of the dividers. Nowhere near the hole. "Good luck beating that!"

We play our way through the course and brag about all our terrible shots. At one hole, it takes me ten strokes until I curse and just kick the ball in with my heel.

"Whoa! I didn't know we were allowed to play soccer here," Abel says.

"Actually, we are. I've just been holding out on you."

I am too busy flirting to notice the animatronic skeleton draped in a black hood directly behind me. Its robot hand reaches out, grazes my back with a skinny finger, and says something in a gravelly voice. I don't hear its words though because I'm screaming and swatting it away until my back presses against Abel. He secures a hand around my waist to steady me. The touch sears my skin even through a thick jacket and shirt.

"You're okay, Cari Carrington." He stabilizes me, smiles, pulls his hand away.

For a second, I consider pulling it back, pulling his lips to mine. Dropping our clubs, forgetting the Halloween golf course, forgetting the universe. This is ridiculous. I want to lose myself in him.

I am tired of waiting.

"Last hole's the jackpot!" Abel guides me to the gigantic, ceramic clown head with its mouth open and tongue acting as the ramp. "Ladies first."

Naturally, I miss, but I don't think my head is in the game anymore. Abel sets his neon blue ball down and looks at me.

"If I make this, ice cream's on me."

"Wouldn't I pay? I lost fair and square."

"Nope." He refocuses his attention on the ball.

My thoughts become a cyclone.

I am completely and utterly in love with the man in front of me. It's not just his looks—though if I were an artist, I would choose him as my permanent muse. It's how he points the club toward the clown's mouth and says, "Give me a lucky shot, come on!" It's in the crook of his lips as his eyes flicker back down to the ball. It's the groan that erupts from him when he misses. It's the grin he gives me as he shrugs.

"Let's get some ice cream anyway."

As I walk beside him to the ice cream stand at the opposite end of the course, I am a philosopher of love. If love is a poison, then it is delicious. If it's a drug, then I will willingly be high for life. Is this beautiful? Is this healthy?

"You never branch out," I tell Abel when he orders plain mint chocolate chip on a waffle cone.

"Says you with your three scoops of cookies and cream. Same order since junior year of college."

We grin at each other. Two peas in a pod. A perfect match. Why aren't we doing anything about it? Why aren't we racing for the car to drive back to my apartment?

Eating ice cream in thirty-degree weather proves to be an absurd idea. We finish in a rush and scamper back to Abel's car with shaking limbs and blue lips. He cranks the heat as soon as we're inside.

"What are you up to for the rest of the day?" I ask.

"Homework," he deadpans. "I'll probably be up all night honestly."

"You need to sleep," I remind him.

"Noted." The smile doesn't quite reach his eyes. "What about you?"

"I'm going to write." I cross my arms to keep warm.

"Could I read some of your new masterpieces?"

Since the day we met, Abel has always supported my poetry. I let him read a lot of it back in college, and for a while, he even had my contact saved in his phone as Poet Goddess. He did it to make me laugh, but I didn't have the guts to tell him that it made my whole body feel euphoric. I *would* let him read these new ones, too...if they weren't about him.

"Uh, not yet," I say as he turns onto the main road.

His lower lip juts out into a pout, but he quickly pulls it back. "I get it. Gotta polish them up first."

"Exactly." Sure. Let's go with that.

Abel is about to say something else but is cut off by the first guitar strum of The Cure's "Love Song." His favorite song of all time.

"You still have this song," I say. My heart melts like microwaved butter. I feel weightless and nostalgic all at once.

"I could *never* delete it."

Neither of us sings this time; we just let the lyrics and the swell of music fill the small space between us. Our eyes are trained on the road, but it's obvious the song is sinking its hooks in us.

Abel once explained that his father and mother danced to this song at their wedding—proven via old videos. It reminds Abel of love. *Real* love. The kind that lasts—even in the face of mental health concerns or whatever life throws at you.

I am acutely aware of Abel's arm resting on the console. I want to take his hand. I fight the urge to look over at him. Suddenly, the heat pumping from the vents is too hot. Abel turns it down before I say anything.

My eyes flicker to his hand again as the main melody crescendos. We are completely still, but I have a feeling his heart is beating just as wildly as mine is.

I want you. I'm tired of waiting.

Robert Smith reminds us that he will always love us, and then the song ends. It is replaced by "Summer Breeze" by Seals & Crofts—a song that is a little easier to breathe around. Abel clears his throat and grabs the wheel with the hand that was just draped over the console. He wasn't even touching me, but I feel empty without it there.

Traffic is light as we cruise down the road, and the sun has dipped behind some clouds. A little while later, Abel stops at the curb outside my apartment. Instead of saying goodbye and letting me out, he throws the car in park and climbs out too. As soon as I'm standing, he pulls me to his chest. His arms are so warm. I love that they protect me from the chill of the wind. I could stay here for centuries. Hell, entire eons.

"Have a good rest of your day, Cari Carrington," he murmurs. "I'll text you."

When I pull away, his face is *right* there. All it would take is to stand on my tippy-toes and our lips would touch. His blue eyes are magnets. We only stay like that for a second. He steps back and smiles, turning the rest of my body to liquid.

"See ya."

"Bye." My voice echoes in my ears.

This time when I get into my apartment, I go straight for my journal. I yank it off the shelf I just organized this morning, flip to an open page, and write for *hours*. The poems I churn out are not glitzy and cliché. They are packed with punchlines, sprinkled with wit, and brimming with tension of every kind. Each poem is another slice of my consciousness, another sliver of that cyclone of thoughts. At long last, I have found the cure to writer's block: fall deeply and madly in love. If love is poison, then poetry is the cup.

That night, Abel texts me, just like he promised.

12

Good morning Christie!

Good news: I am writing some immaculate poetry! I'm drafting the rest of the collection and plan to be done writing sometime around early December. Plenty of time to edit. Hope all is well in Manhattan.

Happy day,
Carrington

AFTER I SEND THE EMAIL, I TURN ON MY HYPER-ENTHUSIASTIC playlist—named for that special mood only writing and Abel Harpen can put me in. There is a lot of Tove Lo, a touch of Ariana Grande, and tons of Dua Lipa.

Abel and I stayed up talking until midnight about nothing in particular, and yet somehow, that was everything. After we would hang out in college, I'd get a splattering of text messages over the span of many hours. This is different. Something is finally happening. And if not, then this is a cruel, sick joke from the universe.

Kelsey has been texting me ecstatic messages for hours now, and it is only eight in the morning. Things like

> AHHHHH!

and

> PLEASE TELL ME YOU'RE GETTING MARRIED!!

and

> USE PROTECTION!

She is essentially the best friend who continuously waters your hope like a blossoming flower. Reason number 400 why I love her.

I twist my hair into a low ponytail and pair a faded T-shirt with jeans. I have work today and am leaving my house early to stop at the café down the street to purchase Ruth a caramel coffee. She didn't specifically mention that it's her favorite, but her exact words were, "I would buy a whole refrigerator to keep a lifetime supply." So, I'm lucky guessing. No way are those purple shadows of stress under her eyes getting any worse—not on my watch!

Just before I leave, my laptop pings with an email from Christie. She is nothing if not a speedy responder.

Such great news, Carrington! I look forward to reading!
Best,
Christie

Oh, yes. Things are looking up.

I AWARD myself a blueberry muffin because the ones on display in the café are testing my salivary glands and because I forgot to eat breakfast. The baristas scurry around to assemble Ruth's drink. The moment they add the creamer, I hear my name.

"Carrington, hey." Hunter walks toward me, dressed to impress in a dark blue blazer. His backpack is strung over his shoulder.

"Evidently, we have a talent for running into each other," I say. He's also got dress pants on and spotless C. & J. Clark shoes. He cleans up nice. "What's the occasion?"

"I have a presentation today." I respect how calm he is. If I had a presentation at UMBC, a repressed fear of public speaking would take me out. "That's why I'm here," he says.

"To drown your nerves in caffeine?"

He smiles. "To get a shot of extra energy. I hardly slept over the weekend 'cause I was prepping." He gestures to his backpack. There are at least twenty notecards in that front pocket, all ready to go.

"Well, you're going to be amazing."

His smile broadens. "Abel actually has a presentation today, too."

You mean, Abel is wearing a blazer and dress pants and fancy shoes, too? Damn. That's my first thought before I realize that he didn't mention any presentation—neither at mini golf nor on the phone.

"He's been in the gym every day for two hours. It must be his way of preparing."

"Yesterday, he was out with me," I counter.

Hunter's eyebrows furrow the tiniest bit. "Huh. At least you gave him a break. I don't know how the dude does it."

"He's Superman, didn't you know?"

"Right. It must have slipped my mind."

They call my order, and I snatch the caramel coffee off the counter. "I'm off to work."

"Oh, hey, real quick," he says. "What are you doing on Halloween?"

"Probably getting fat on candy," I answer honestly.

He laughs. "Well, a few of my friends are having a party. You should come. Abel will be there."

"Impossible," I say. "Abel hates parties."

"It's not a *party* party," Hunter clarifies. "I'm not a partier either. It's just some friends getting together to watch *The Conjuring* and drink some beer."

"Beer is gross."

He chews on that for a second and then nods. "Fair enough. I can get whatever drinks you like."

"You so boldly assume I'm going." I place a hand on my hip.

"Well, I already talked to Abel, and he said watching a scary movie sounds like fun."

"All right, fine. I'll think about it. Here." I shove my phone at him. "Put your number in."

He does. "How's the poetry coming along?" he asks, passing the phone back.

I am honestly surprised he remembers. That conversation feels like a lifetime ago. "Beautifully."

"That's what I love to hear. See you at the party, Carrington." He turns away before I can respond, but I am pretty sure he is chuckling under his breath. He has a nice chuckle.

Once I'm parked outside Ruth's Bakery, I text Abel.

> Hunter's Halloween party–lame or not lame?

We used to ask each other questions like this all the time to see if the other was supportive of a choice.

The freshman picnic—lame or not lame?

Pysch research fair—lame or not lame?

Moving to Manhattan—lame or not lame?

He responds instantly.

Not lame! I've never seen The Conjuring!

You won't sleep!

I warn with a crying laughing emoji.

I never sleep, lol!

It's supposed to make me laugh, but that text makes me frown.

13

Ruth is pleasantly surprised when I set her caramel coffee on the counter.

"For my favorite boss," I tell her.

"Oh, Cari. You didn't."

I wear her smile like a gold badge on my chest. "Yep. Now you can call me your favorite employee."

She snorts, then takes a sip. "Thank you. I needed this today." She sips the drink and her face transforms into a serene mask. "We have a lot to do, honey. Cupcakes for a sweet sixteen, red velvet whoopie pies for a couple's anniversary, and a birthday cake. *All* chocolate," she adds emphatically. "The woman I spoke to on the phone sounded like she'd murder me if the cake wasn't *all* chocolate."

We work the whole morning and half the afternoon while Country's Hottest Hits serenades us. I am not a die-hard country fan but seeing Ruth lip sync every once in a while makes my heart happy.

By the time I finish lathering the bases of the whoopie pies in cream, it is already four o'clock. Ruth is busy frosting the birthday cake. We finished the cupcakes around before noon, and they've already been picked up.

"Seal 'em up," Ruth instructs, gesturing to the whoopie pies. Her apron is dusted in flour and frosting. Mine could use a wash, too.

We work for another hour—her adding finishing touches to the cake, me wrapping whoopie pies and washing the tower of dishes that has appeared in the sink. When five o'clock rolls around, I'm officially spent.

"Finish those last two dishes and then you're good to go for the day," Ruth says.

I am about to hold a thumbs up when I notice the look in her eyes. It does not have a name, but I would place it in the unhappy category.

"Ruth." My voice leaves no room for excuses. "What is wrong?"

She gives the usual response: sniffs and looks away, like I'm asking a preposterous question. A woman like her should be carefree, not plagued by whatever it is that is so clearly plaguing her. She's too kind, too good at what she does. I can be patient, but right now, the empathetic softy in me takes over. I need to help her. Now.

"Please tell me."

"Carrington, I am *fine*."

I pull myself up onto the counter and cross my ankles and my arms. "I'm not leaving until you tell me."

Her rain-gray eyes widen. "Do not sit on my counter where the *food* is made."

Okay, yes, that was incredibly stupid of me. "Sorry!" I hop down. "Don't worry, I'll clean the counter again, but if it's any consolation, my ass is clean, too. *Butt!* Sorry!" I clap my hand over my mouth.

Ruth laughs and her whole face brightens. "I'm happy your rear end is clean, Cari."

I grab some disinfectant wipes from the back. When I return, that distant look is back in Ruth's eyes. "You really want to know?" she says.

The question makes me stop scrubbing. "Yes."

She sighs. Whatever this is, it is *hard* for her.

"When my daughter Amber was a little girl, she loved to bake with me. She couldn't reach the counter, so she'd pull a chair up to stand on, and then she would help me mix or add ingredients. Whatever needed to be done." Ruth pauses to laugh, but it sounds more like an exhale. "All my life, I had been a stay-at-home mom for her. My husband was a dentist—still is, actually. The job he has now is the reason we originally moved to Maryland. Harry will be retiring within the next year though. He's getting too old to be filling cavities." I laugh because she laughs. "The point is, we were always comfortable with our money." Ruth looks up from the cake and meets my eyes.

"I always had this dream to run a bakery, though. When Amber started first grade, Harry had his work, but I didn't really...have anything of my own, you know? Aside from being with my daughter, baking was everything to me. Harry realized that, too. He's always been very supportive of my dreams." A rosy color touches Ruth's cheeks. "Anyway, back then, we went out window-shopping one day —I *love* window-shopping—and we stumbled across this place." She gestures to the purple walls and purple countertops. Purple everything. "And it was for sale. I knew it was meant to be mine. Instantly.

"I'll tell ya right now, Cari. It was God's hand that brought me here. I got so lucky. Business was booming by the first hour I opened. I hired a couple of bakers to help me, and we were off and running, orders popping in every single day."

The way this memory lights up Ruth's eyes—it is making me emotional, too. I can see, taste, hear, *feel* her success as much as she can.

"Amber would come in every weekend and help us bake. When she got to high school, I officially hired her for part-time, and boy, was she dedicated. She took almost every home-ec class her school had to offer. And you know what she said to me, Carrington?"

I shake my head.

"She said, 'Mom, one day, I'm going to take over the business.'" There is a choke in Ruth's tone, a quiver.

She drops her gaze back down to the cake. "Two years. That's how long she worked here, before..."

Tread carefully, Cari, my subconscious warns me. *Channel your inner psychologist.* "Before?"

Ruth blows out all the air from her lungs. "Before Hayden."

I don't push. I just wait. There's an explanation balancing on the tip of her tongue; I can practically see it tipping forward.

"Apparently, they'd known each other for years, but she started dating him at the start of their junior year. That was when everything started to break. They were...too close, you know?" Ruth locks her fingers together. "Her grades started slipping. They started going out to parties, missing curfew. And then...we got the news that December."

"What news was that?"

"She was pregnant."

I swallow loudly without meaning to. "What happened?"

"A pregnant seventeen-year-old?" Ruth scoffs. "You can *imagine* what happened! We had these massive fights about keeping the baby or putting her up for adoption. I told Amber she wasn't allowed to see Hayden anymore, and she screamed that he was the love of her life. Except, he drank way too much and was hardly around for any of it." Ruth's nostrils are flared. She is intimidating when she's fuming.

"All of a sudden, my daughter was uncontrollable. She dropped out of school, made plans to move in with Hayden and his family. Harry and I tried to talk about helping raise the baby, we tried to compromise, we consulted a family therapist—we did everything and then some to try to get our daughter back. But she was just gone." As she says this, Ruth caves in on herself and suddenly looks very small and fragile.

"The baby was born the following September. It was a girl, Mia." Ruth's voice is painfully distant now. "Hayden wasn't even there. He claimed to be 'working—'" Ruth air quotes that, "—but God knows where he *actually* was.

"I thought once Mia was born that things with Amber would cool down and we'd be a family again. But the day Amber turned 18, she left. She'd been working night and day as a waitress at one restaurant and as a hostess at another. Harry and I took care of Mia when we could, but we had to call a sitter most days. I didn't even know Amber had been looking up apartments in the meantime. She never *talked* to me anymore. Except for..." Ruth blinks. I see a single tear glimmer on her cheek. "Except for the very last thing she ever said to me."

Don't push. Just wait.

"She announced she was leaving for an apartment in Connecticut and strapped Mia into her car seat. Then Amber turned back to me and guess what she said."

"What?"

Ruth slides her tongue over her bottom lip. I can see, taste, hear, *feel* her pain. It's agonizing. "She said, 'You were never going to be proud of me anyway. Sorry I couldn't be your perfect baker, but honestly...I don't want to be.'"

The oxygen around me dissipates, and my throat tightens around any words I could possibly offer.

"Then she got in her car and just...left." The look in Ruth's eyes is worse than haunting. "That was thirteen years ago."

"Did you ever try to call her or text—"

"I tried every day for at least a decade." That shuts me up. "She wants nothing to do with me, and I don't know why. I wasn't happy with the choices she'd made, but I tried to help her! I went with her to all the doctor appointments. I was *there* when Mia was born, for God's sake! I took care of her! I just...to this day, I do not know where we went wrong."

Every cell in my body down to its nucleus is dying to help this woman. Dying to take her pain away. Dying to bring her daughter back to her so that maybe, just maybe, they can make up. I feel powerless.

"The worst part is that she thinks I'm not proud of her. I'll admit, we fought a lot, but when it came down to it, Amber worked two jobs and then came home every night to nurse her baby and get maybe four hours of sleep. And having the guts to move to Connecticut of all places, even though she'd never been there! I was proud of her! *Am* proud of her. I texted that to her many times but got no response." Ruth wipes her face with the heel of her hand. "I guess she isn't ready to accept me back into her life yet.

"So, I'm sorry if I seem a little upset every once in a while. Amber turned thirty a week and a half ago. And my granddaughter, Mia, is thirteen now." More tears spill despite Ruth's efforts to stop them. "I wish things were different."

This is the part they didn't teach me in my undergraduate years. I don't have any idea what to say. A few responses work their way to my teeth—I understand because of my own mother; Amber is wrong for thinking you're not proud of her; it'll get better—but don't pass through. I feel *terrible*. Powerless and terrible.

"If I had it my way," Ruth says through a sniffle, "Amber would own this bakery by now, and she'd paint the walls whatever color she wanted. But kids have to find their own way. I just wish she understood that, despite everything, I am proud of her."

14

THERE ARE TOO MANY THOUGHTS FLUTTERING IN MY MIND. ANY psychologist or biologist who believes in the link between the brain and the gut is correct. My stomach has been twisting for the last half hour.

I can't get Ruth's story out of my head. It feels too painfully famil-iar, like I am looking into one of those twisted mirrors in a fun house. Ruth wants her daughter to know she's proud of her, and I'm wishing my own mother was proud of me.

I'm in my apartment, on my favorite squishy cushion of the couch, staring out at the sheeting rain. It began to torrential down-pour on my way home from work, so I had to change into some dry clothes. I should be enjoying the peace and quiet, but my thoughts are biting me. Eventually, I sigh and reach for my laptop.

Left or Right has been out for three years now, and people are still gobbling it up. That has always left me overflowing with gratitude, but right now, I'm on Amazon for the exact reason I should not be.

Reading reviews as a published author or poet is a major no-no. Strangers love to play Big Critic and judge every part of a book, down to the publisher's chosen font. It is a wormhole to hell.

I remember the first bad review I ever got. Ironically, it came from one of my mother's clients. Mom kept their identity a secret, but they *allowed* my mother to disclose their opinion on my collection. According to them, metaphors are not the way to shed light on such a serious subject. I, of course, could not agree because none of the metaphors I used were wisecracks. Their comment just stung a little bit, that's all. The *real* problem is when those stings start to add up and you begin internalizing critiques. Rule of thumb: DO NOT READ YOUR OWN REVIEWS.

Yet here I am.

I scroll with one eye open; the rest of my face is stuck in a grimace. *Expect the worst.*

Left or Right deserves every award. It murders your heart and then glues it back together. That's called poetry!
Jimmy Korligon

Waited to read this collection because of the hype around it. There's nothing worse than a gigantic letdown. Except NOTHING about *Left or Right* is a letdown!! READ THIS COLLECTION ASAP!!!
BookFetishGirl069

Metaphors are exhausted. Imagery is basic. This collection of poetry is the definition of overhyped. Don't recommend.
Chris T.

A wonderful voice for people who don't have one. Best poetry collection I've read in a *longgg* time!
MJ Offganger

My eyes flick back to Chris T.'s comment. It is a thorn in a garden of marigolds, and I continuously decide to prick my finger on that thorn. If I was going for my PhD, I would do my dissertation research on why the brain loves to linger on a negative point. If that topic is even good enough for a dissertation. Heck, if I know.

There are a few more thorns down through the list, but only a *few*. AubreyStarton__ThePoet thinks I have poor taste in style and rhyme scheme, while Jaxson H. does not believe in my presentation. *Was she even suicidal??* he comments.

The answer to that question is no. I did not write *Left or Right* on account of my own experiences, and whether that justifies my ability to write about the topic, well...that is up to Jaxson H.

I got the idea for the collection in December of my junior year in college.

I had a creative writing class in the afternoons that semester. One evening after class, I found my dad in his recliner with a can of Pepsi cracked open. The TV was on full blast, clearly annoying the hell out of my brother Tucker, who was seated at the kitchen bar with his textbook and notes open in front of him. He'd been a freshman at Roger Williams University at that point. Mom was nowhere to be found.

"She had to stay at work," Dad answered when I asked. "Apparently, one of her patients went berserk and wants to kill himself." He'd shrugged, sipped his soda.

I do love my father. He means well—truly. But he is also gifted with an illness-free mind, meaning he doesn't understand the magnitude of a situation when someone admits to being suicidal. He's one of those *Just-put-on-a-happy-face!* people. *It's all in your head! Just stop being sad!* He also fully believes my mother is a superhero who only knows success. *If you're feeling suicidal, stop in to see Joan Daughtler and all your problems will magically melt away!* Again, Dad is well-intentioned but misguided.

In the meantime, I fell into full-blown panic mode. My homework was forgotten; I skipped dinner without realizing I skipped dinner. Empathy is its own damn poison because all I could picture was that client's face.

Were they pale? Sweating? Shaking? Glaring? Crying? What did they feel like *inside?* What were they saying? How were they saying it?

"Do you think that client is okay?" I eventually asked Tucker, for the fifth time.

He had relocated to his bedroom desk, and I standing in his doorway, twisting my hands together. He looked up at me.

"Cari, I'm sure they're fine. Mom is good at her job. Relax and breathe."

To Tucker's credit, he never once snapped at me. He's my younger brother, but sometimes I feel like he should have been born first. He has that calming nature that an older sibling should have.

When Mom did get home, at 7:43 p.m., my mouth abandoned its off button. I fired question after question at her until she swallowed an Advil and turned to face me.

"Everything is under control, Carrington." Her voice was stern yet tired. "They are getting the help they need."

"How did you know they were suicidal?" I pressed. "Did they tell you directly or—"

"I can't share that information. You know that."

HIPPA laws aside, Mom is exceptionally loyal to her clients. Her lips are sealed tighter than a triple knot—with an extra layer of glue for good luck. She will take her patients' stories to the grave. Count on it.

Her curt responses only left me crumbs though.

I wanted more, but she wouldn't give me anything. I climbed the stairs two at a time, heart still pounding, cortisol still flowing. In my bedroom, I stood in the middle of the floor and scrutinized my surroundings, wondering what it would feel like to be suicidal. Not because I wanted to end my life, but because I could feel that person's pain in my bones. The metaphors were already growing in my brain like beanstalks, but I was ruminating on one thought in particular: that person has a choice. A massive choice. To live or not to live. What would I do with that choice if I were in their shoes?

That was when I sat down at my desk and opened my poetry

journal. One poem led to another, oranges upon oranges squashing those clichés and creating something entirely new. Something intricate and raw. My college writing professor would be so proud of me. (And he is.)

I wrote *Left or Right* based on someone I didn't even know.

It was tricky juggling schoolwork with my writing. Little by little, my love for poetry started to overshadow my fascination with psychology. Mom knew I was up to something. When she thought I wasn't looking, she would glance at my journal and try to use X-ray vision to figure out what I was spending so much time on. Unfortunately for her, I was extremely protective of my work, and I'd recently begun people-watching.

For three months, my life consisted of studying, note-taking, and writing. I talked with Kelsey and Noah briefly between classes. I hardly saw Abel; his mind was wrapped around Camila's waist and thighs. The only thing keeping me pieced together—ironically—was my collection about choosing life over suicide.

I wrote and rewrote several poems several times before typing them all up in a Word document. And in the meantime, I was researching big-name publishing companies.

My target companies were the ones with people wearing crisp suits or dresses with red bottoms—the type of people who lick salt from their margaritas and slither their way through negotiations because they can. The ones who peruse manuscripts while crunching on celery smeared with peanut butter. The Big Guys.

But that was only a dream. I wasn't like the Big Guys. I write with my hair up in a horribly assembled bun. I write wearing a stained, ratty T-shirt. I write with my retainer in. And I don't even like margaritas or celery.

I continued to write anyway. As soon as I was sure *Left or Right* was readable and somewhat enjoyable—as far as the topic allowed—I began churning out query letters.

Camila dumped Abel in early May, two weeks after I caught them making out at Remy Ausberg's party. Their breakup threw me for a loop. I was convinced that Abel and I would finally get together and run off to graduate school, hand-in-hand. (To our dream school, of course: UMBC.) But my poetry had become everything.

What a realization that had been.

It was scary—like, tiptoeing across a frozen lake scary. For a long time, the thought of giving up psychology made me sick to my stomach. I could not leave Abel, and, arguably more important, I could not upset my mother. She was so *set* on me becoming a clinical psychologist like her.

And yet there I was, sending out query letters via email once a week to every publishing company I researched. The only person who knew exactly what I was up to was Tucker. And he fed me all the support I needed.

By the end of June, I had twelve rejections. I thought that was kind of rude of them. Refusing to publish a collection on suicide prevention was like adding more sugar to the delightfully poisonous pie called Mental Health Stigma. But whatever, I guess.

Abel and I spent the summer before senior year rekindling the parts of our friendship that had been extinguished because of Camila. And it was on July 4th, as fireworks exploded over our heads, that I told him I submitted a collection to be published.

"*Shut. Up!*" he had exclaimed. "Wow, Cari! I'm so proud of you!" He'd yanked me into his arms. It was the happiest I'd seen him in a long time, and it was the happiest *I'd* felt in a long time.

A week later, I got an acceptance. Candace Lively from Polly&Pippy Publishing, reached out to me, claiming she fell in love with my work and wanted to publish *Left or Right*. Immediately. Polly&Pippy is one of the biggest publishing companies in New York.

The *exhilaration* I felt. The *possibilities* that opened up. I was on cloud twelve.

Tucker and I squealed like six-year-olds. When I saw Abel, he hugged me so tightly, I almost popped a blood vessel. Kelsey and Noah cracked open three White Claws and toasted to me. Nobody asked about what the future held because nobody seemed to care at that moment.

Until I told Mom.

I made sure to catch her on a day she was reading by the pool. Whenever she did that, it meant she had light stress. Little reason to freak out.

"You did *what?*" she asked, yanking off her sunglasses to stare at me directly.

"Polly&Pippy want to sign me!" I repeated happily. My journal was clenched in my hands for moral support.

"So...how much is this going to cost??"

"Well..." I had trailed off because it hit me right then that we were comfortable but not necessarily dripping in diamonds.

"Why didn't you say something, Cari?" Her tone was only *slightly* critical.

I can pinpoint that exact moment as the time a match struck in my body. It was the first time I accepted that my mother might not be on my team. Defense mechanisms activated. "Do you even want to know what it's about?"

She blinked at me. "I—"

"It's about suicide," I cut in. "Choosing life *over* suicide."

Alarm popped across her face. "Carrington, are you—"

"*I'm* not suicidal!" I'd interrupted, thwapping my journal down on one of our Adirondack chairs. "But if you bothered to check up on *me* every once in a while, instead of being so absorbed in your *clients'* lives, you'd know that I love to write! It makes me happy! I wrote this collection because I care about people!" My voice was rising. "I want to keep writing!"

She closed her eyes for an instant, and I literally watched her transform into Trustworthy, Cure-All Therapist. "It is amazing that you like to write, Carrington," she'd insisted in a calmer tone that made my left eye twitch. "That will come in handy when you work with clients—"

"I don't want to be a psychologist!" First gunshot. "I want to be a writer!" Fatal gunshot.

She stared at me, mouth frozen in the shape of an O. Halfway between shocked and, *Wait, I'm sorry, I think I hallucinated your last statement.*

"I really do," I said, twisting my hands together. "Ever since I started writing this collection, I've felt so much like me."

"Clinical psychology was your dream."

"*Your* dream," I corrected her. "Continue the family legacy, sign my soul away to school, graduate when I'm thirty-one, and then what? More work!" Even as I said it, I realized that, yes, this was my dream at one point, but times had changed.

I assume Mom works with all kinds of clients. Funny how the thing to uproot her from her calm demeanor was her own daughter thinking for herself. In the face of my announcement, my mother struggled to find words, her pink lips opening and closing like floodgates trying to stop a tsunami.

Eventually, she settled on, "If that's what you want."

"Yes." My tone was clipped.

She nodded. Without another word, she got up and walked back into the house, book clasped under her arm. I didn't feel triumphant or heroic. I felt frozen.

As I moved forward with the publishing process, Mom only talked to me in brief sentences. She helped me pay those disgusting bills but from an emotional distance—far enough away that I couldn't even get a real smile out of her anymore. Except I couldn't take my confession back. I wanted to be a writer, and that was that.

Senior year floated by like a massive cumulonimbus cloud. All at once, I stopped fretting over my grades, finally realizing they were not life or death. I was a straight A student. I'd proven myself enough already. I ended up passing last semester with two As and three Bs. Good enough for me. When I realized that *Left or Right* was bound to be a great seller (Candace's words, not mine), I made the life-altering decision: I was going to move to Manhattan.

At the annual twilight barbeque in April—three days before graduation—Abel and I were sitting on a blanket, gazing up at the magenta and pink sky. Noah and Kelsey were little ways down from us, playing another game of frisbee.

That night, Abel had sat a little closer to me, our shoulders touching.

"Remember me in Manhattan," he'd said, glancing over at me with those drop-dead-gorgeous blue eyes.

I had found Christie a month earlier and chosen her to be my literary agent. I wanted to be in New York with the Big Guys; now I could be.

"Trust me," I told Abel. "I could *never* forget you."

We stared at each other, the laughter and conversations around us melting into a distant murmur. He had been so close. Our noses were inches apart. I remember his eyes flickering down to my lips and my heart performing a back handspring.

"Abel," I'd whispered. It was the only word I wanted to say for the rest of my life.

His eyes touched mine again, as gentle as a caress.

"Abel, I—"

"Dude, Abel!" We broke apart as Tristain Something (I don't remember his last name) ran up to us. He was in practically all of Abel's classes that semester; they were close. "Get in on this football game! We need you, man!"

"Sure!" Abel smiled and stood up from the blanket. "What were you saying, Cari?"

He wasn't even facing me anymore. He had picked up his ketchup-smeared paper plate and checked his phone. I can also pinpoint *that* moment as the time I realized Abel Harpen and I might not end up together at all. I had been about to tell him that I was in love with him.

"Nothing," I'd replied, feigning happiness—per usual. "Get out there with your boys!"

Now, in my room in Catonsville, I blink at the computer screen, forcing myself back to the present moment. All of that feels like four lifetimes ago.

Maybe a part of me wrote *Left or Right* in hopes that my mother would be proud of me, but it ended up putting an even bigger divide between us. I wonder if Mom secretly feels like Ruth. I wonder what would have happened if her patient had never gone into crisis. If that were the case, would Abel and I have gotten a second chance now?

15

On Halloween night, for Hunter's party, I am Cleopatra. The white dress I'm wearing has a swooping neckline and only stretches to my thighs. I make sure to do the thick, curvy eyeliner, too, with a dusting of blue over my eyelids. Yes, I am Cleopatra—if she had rose gold hair. I doubt anyone else is dressing up tonight, considering the party is basically movie night. But as a Professional Halloween Enthusiast, I take it upon myself to celebrate *correctly*.

Abel understands the memo.

When he knocks on my apartment door, he is Pete Maverick from *Top Gun*—down to the camo green flight suit and the Ray-Ban Aviator sunglasses. In other words, he puts Tom Cruise to shame.

He whips off his glasses, pins me with those striking blue eyes, and runs a hand through his glossy, perfectly wavy hair.

"I feel the need," he murmurs, and I start giggling uncontrollably. He deserves a PhD in Halloween Enthusiasm. "The need...." He takes a step toward me, blue eyes intensifying. "For speed."

We both break down instantly, doubling over with laughter.

When he catches his breath enough, he holds out his arm. "Your chariot awaits, Miss Cleopatra."

Cleopatra and Pete Maverick stumbling down a hallway, howling with laughter and not even drunk—what a sight. I feel like we could be the subject of a bad joke that some horny guy might tell that pretty lady in red at the bar.

It is nine o'clock, which means trick-or-treating has technically ended for the youngsters of the neighborhood. But some of the pre-teen zombies and undead brides and Anakin Skywalker impersonators decide to rebel and stay out longer, their pillowcases slapping the sides of their legs as they sprint down the sidewalks.

Naturally, the first song Abel plays after he starts the car is "Somebody's Watching Me" by Rockwell and Michael Jackson—the *classic* Halloween banger from 1984.

"I made a playlist *specifically* for tonight," Abel says with a ghoulish grin.

It's perfect. "Monster Mash" followed by "Thriller" followed by "Ghostbusters" followed by "(Don't Fear) The Reaper." We spend the fifteen-minute ride dancing in our seats and screaming lyrics like banshees.

Abel parallel parks his Toyota Corolla outside Hunter's apartment complex and helps me out of the passenger seat. I am wearing high-heeled gladiator sandals—gold, of course—and there is a 98.5 percent chance I will fall and splatter my brains tonight. *You're welcome, zombies!*

Hunter's building is planted in the middle of the town square. The building is five stories high with a mix of brick, stone, and stucco siding. Potted ferns guard the entrance. The lobby resembles a smaller, slightly dustier version of a Hilton lobby—one that's on a budget.

The only person in the lobby is a tall man with hair that looks more pepper than salt. He glances up from his book—*Pet Sematary* by Stephen King—and smiles at us as we pass.

"I have to be honest, Cari Carrington," Abel says when we step into the elevator. He presses the button for level three. "I am a little nervous to watch this movie. I've never seen any of *The Conjurings*."

"You'll be fine," I assure him. "Just be prepared for the jump scares."

"How do I prepare myself for a jump scare?"

"Like this." We step out into a hallway with dark green carpet and white doors on both sides. I cross my arms over my chest and open my mouth like I am stuck mid-scream. Abel stares at me. "See that? Preparation at its finest. Then when the demon pops out of nowhere, you'll be like, psh! Please, bitch! You really thought!"

"Please, bitch! You really thought!" Abel adopts my sassy, self-assured tone, even adding a pretend hair flip.

"Perfect!"

Hunter lives in apartment 202, which I respect simply because it is a very gorgeous, even number. I'm a poet. Stupid, little details like this are my metaphorical Red Bull.

Hunter answers the door seconds after I knock. He has on a black skeleton T-shirt. It fits him well, especially in the biceps. His dark hair is unruly, sticking up on all sides. I have to hand it to him. With the black sweatpants and bedhead, he really nails the Just Rolled Out of Bed costume.

"Are you...a Greek goddess?" he asks me, eyes scrolling down to my sandaled high heels.

"I'm Cleopatra," I correct him.

He shakes his head. "Mmm, this is more...Aphrodite has an affair with Ra. Isn't he the Egyptian god of the sun?"

"I don't remember everything I learned in third grade. I'm very sorry."

"I got it!" Hunter snaps his fingers, ignoring my comment. "It's the hair. The hair is giving off those vibes."

"Are you just going to stand there and hate on my costume?"

"Who said I hate it?" I can't help but notice he has a nice smile. He turns to Abel and immediately holds up a salute. "Lieutenant Pete Maverick. Pleasure to be in your presence, sir."

Abel returns the salute. "The pleasure's all mine."

Boys. Really, though, their friendship is kind of adorable. Hunter opens the door wider. "Come on in, guys! Alcohol's on the bar. Abel, there are water bottles in the fridge."

"Thanks!" Abel says.

The apartment has laminate wood flooring that is the color of sand after a wave brushes over it. A few art pieces hang from the walls—mostly shapeless clashes of color that claim to be subjective beauty. Hunter did not originally strike me as an artsy guy, but I do tend to misjudge. In the living room, there are seven, maybe eight people. I recognize no one. A sectional couch sits in the living room, and two guys are redesigning it. As expected, neither of them is in costume.

"Leo!" Abel exclaims.

The guy with teal and black locs looks up from the pile of cushions.

"Harpen!" They perform a complicated handshake. "I didn't think I'd see you here tonight, man!"

"I changed my mind." I want to take Abel's smile and glue it into my scrapbook.

Leo's eyes cut to mine. "And you're Cari, I'm guessing?" His teeth are as perfect and white as Abel's. "Cool costume!"

"Thank you. I'm the product of Aphrodite's affair with Ra."

His brow furrows for a second and then he steals my move: he smiles and nods. "Awesome." He pats Abel's shoulder. "This guy is the little brother I never had."

"And by little, he means fourteen months younger," Abel clarifies.

I can't help but notice that every person Abel meets automatically becomes an extension of him. But it is not a surprise. He's a walking beam of light, attracting anyone and everyone who passes by.

"Abel!"

"Hi, Raquel! Hey, Violet!"

Raquel and Violet lead to Anissa and Chris and Alex.

Mr. *Popular* Beam of Light, that is. The fact that six of the eight people in this room are now greeting Abel and vying for his attention somehow makes his light even brighter. Abel Harpen is literally the sun.

Hunter appears next to me, crossing his arms and watching the classmate reunion play out in front of him with a lazy grin.

"Did I ever tell you about the time Abel one-upped our professor?"

"Do tell." I sound like an eight-year-old, seeking an update on elementary-school gossip.

Hunter steps closer to me, and I get a whiff of Old Spice. It takes me a half a second to refocus. "We were all in the same class together," he says, "Abel, me, Raquel, Leo, Violet. Our professor started firing off questions. It's what he did at the beginning of every class as a review. When he got to Abel, he asked something about what age kids are when they start to perceive distance."

I think back to my undergraduate years and realize that even though I probably killed that test, I do not remember the answer at all.

"Abel came right back with the answer." Hunter grins, his eyes trained on the back of Abel's head. "Like *that*!" He snaps his fingers. "Abel knew his stuff. Our professor loved to challenge us, so he fired more questions at Abel, and the dude was like *boom, boom, boom*! He couldn't trick him!"

I smile and glance back at Abel. "It was *incredible*," Hunter goes on. "And after, like, a straight minute of interrogation, our professor walked up to Abel and just shook his hand. It was hilarious. Everyone was dying laughing. That guy right there—" Hunter nods toward Abel "—is *awesome*. One of a kind." His face softens. "He's my best friend."

"You sound like you're in love," I tease.

"Yeah, actually I sneak over to Abel's apartment every night and we spoon."

"You, too?"

We break into a fit of giggles. Hunter scrubs a hand down his jaw. "All kidding aside, I know that deep down, Abel really struggles. I know he goes through a lot that he doesn't let anyone else see. But he is always upbeat and positive. I can't explain the amount of respect I have for him."

"Is that a protective instinct I'm hearing?"

This time, Hunter doesn't laugh. Instead, he flashes me a gentle smile. "I know Abel has dark shit to deal with, but if I have anything to do with it, the world is not going to hurt him."

What I see in his eyes is true, unmistakable empathy. A small flame ignites and licks its way along my ribcage.

"That's kind of you."

He shrugs. A stray curl dangles over his forehead. "Kindness, Carrington. That's all this world needs." Our eyes linger for a second longer, and then he moves away from the wall.

"Okay, guys," he announces, "let's get the movie started!"

Everyone hurries to the newly assembled sectional couch, squeezing in next to each other and passing bowls of candy. Abel grabs my hand—pure energy jolting through my arm—and pulls me to the end cushion.

"This is Carrington, everyone!" he tells the group. "My best friend from URI!"

The group raises their drinks to me. They shout, "What ups?" and "Heys!" and I even catch a "Look how cool her shoes are!" from the girl with the long, dark hair, who I'm assuming is Raquel.

I flash them my best smile and sit down next to Abel. We're situated on this couch with our thighs touching, which basically coats my entire leg in lava. Our shoulders are pressed against each other. His face is so close, we could turn our heads and our noses would brush.

The movie is nearly two hours long. While everyone else spends those two hours screaming, I think about what it would feel like to swing my leg over Abel's hips and get properly acquainted with his body.

16

———

As I sit at the bar in Hunter's kitchen, Raquel kindly mixes me an orange crush. We survived the movie—though Violet is two seconds from a panic attack, poor thing—and the boys are lounging on the sectional, groaning about some recent sports dispute. Abel is still perched on the end cushion, listening intently but managing to look like a golden retriever.

"You look like you've made a few orange crushes before," I tell Raquel when she adds a few splashes of vodka to the red solo cup. She even has a dishrag draped over her shoulder, for goodness' sake.

"I'm a bartender." Her eyes are brown and sparkly, and her hair is like a river at midnight—black waves cascading down past her shoulders. She has a tattoo of a rose twisting up her arm, the petals full and blooming.

We met only three hours ago, but I can already tell Raquel is cool. There is no better adjective. From the lock necklaces to the red Adidas pants to the dimples in her tanned cheeks, this girl is Cool with a capital C.

"Are you a student at UMBC, too?"

"Mhm." She plops a straw into the cup and slides it toward me.

"I'm pursuing my PhD in applied developmental psychology. I want to be a child psychologist someday."

Annnddd cue the golden spotlight.

"Wow." It takes me a minute to form multi-syllable words again. That's how in awe I am. "Brave choice," I say eventually, "working with kids."

Even her laugh is cool.

"Where are you from?" I take a sip of the orange crush and nearly flip off the stool, it tastes so good. Raquel has a magic touch—or is just extremely gifted at drink-to-drink ratios.

"Argentina." A hint of a Spanish accent filters into her voice. She punctuates the answer with a compelling smirk. A *cool* smirk. "We moved here when my mom was pregnant with my *oldest* youngest brother, Antonio. I guess I get my work ethic from my parents. They worked their asses off to keep us afloat when we first got to the States. While they were working, I took care of my brothers, went to school, and studied. Now here I am."

Simple, straight to the point, yet lacking in so many areas where I would love details: what are her parents' names, where did they work, how old was she when all this took place?

Before I can politely press her, she says, "I'd be living under a rock if I didn't know who you are. *Left or Right* saved my brother's life. He's a bit of an aspiring poet himself."

"Is this Antonio?"

"Manuel." Raquel hops onto the stool next to me with her own red Solo cup. "My youngest brother. He's been bullied a lot in high school."

"Why," I wonder aloud, "is high school just a place for sharks to roam around in miniskirts and football jerseys?"

"Spoken like a true poet." Raquel raises her drink to me. "Manuel was bullied because apparently, vaping and drunk sex is cool, but reading and writing poetry makes you lame."

My empathy swells. All I can do is blink rapidly and choke on a hundred apologies.

Raquel reads my expression. "The good news is he's graduating in May. Let me tell you though, he carried *Left or Right* around with him like it was the freakin' Bible. And now, thanks to you, my little brother's going to college for creative writing."

"Wow." There must be red splotches all over my face. "That's amazing."

Raquel chews on her straw. "Anyway, you know Abel from college?"

I need to redirect my thoughts after finding out I've been a super-hero to someone's younger brother. "Yeah. We met in undergrad at the University of Rhode Island."

She nods and glances over at the boys. I can hear Alex still trying to convince Violet that a demon is *not* going to appear on top of her dresser tonight. Raquel's eyes tick back to mine. "Did you and Abel ever date?"

"No. Why do you ask?"

Her lips have a habit of curling at the corners. "Because that boy has not stopped looking at you since you left his side."

I'm sitting with my back to the couch, but suddenly it feels like my spine is on fire. *Abel can't stop looking at me?*

Raquel's grin is gleaming. "This is the fifth time I've looked over there and caught his eyes on you. And that makes you one hell of a chick because Abel doesn't waste his time, let alone stare at girls like that."

My windpipe might as well have a twisty tie on it; I can barely breathe.

"Which, as far as I'm concerned," Raquel continues, "is something to jump on. I'm a little bit of a love cynic myself, but you guys —" She arches an eyebrow, "would be a perfect match."

I swallow at least eight different emotions: surprise, excitement to name a few. "Why are you a love cynic?"

"My girlfriend of five years left me for some guy who drives a muddy pickup truck." A what-are-ya-gonna-do shrug. "Haven't had much luck with women since."

"There's a big sea out there," I offer.

"Yeah, with catfish everywhere."

"Spoken like a true poet."

We clink our cups. "Seriously though," she says after taking a long sip. "You and Prince Charming over there better get it on soon. Otherwise, the world is going to explode from all this pent-up tension."

17

"What's my favorite color?" I ask Abel.

He pulls his car to the curb outside my apartment. "Yellow."

"What *shade?*"

He snaps his fingers. "Banana."

"Ding, ding, ding!"

We call this game So You Think You Can Know Me. Guidelines: see how well we remember little tidbits about each other for no other reason except shits and giggles. Because nothing says *I'm flirting with you* like stating a random fact about someone they thought you forgot.

"What did I want to be for Halloween when I was seven?" Abel throws the car in park and narrows his eyes at me. "Be careful. Trick question."

"Please," I scoff. "Give me a hard one. You wanted to be a doctor, but you couldn't find a lab coat in your size, so you ended up being Ironman instead."

His grip slips off the steering wheel. "How do you *remember* that?"

"My hippocampus and frontal lobe are stronger than yours."

"Shoot, that's right. I forgot you are the world's greatest cognitive psychologist. What's the difference between episodic and semantic memory again?"

I stare at him, nostrils flared, lips pressed together. He knows he has me.

"Oh no!" Abel cries. "That was the buzzer. You unfortunately won't be winning that $50,000 prize, but did you have fun playing?" He holds his hand to me like it's a microphone.

"Are you done now?" I ask his hand.

"Mhm." He smiles, all happy and proud of himself, which makes me laugh.

The very last thing I want to do is say goodnight to Abel. I mean, I'd rather eat a Carolina Reaper—with ice handy, of course—than leave this car. Abel seems to sense that. I wonder what pepper *he'd* sooner incinerate his tongue with.

"Do you want to come in for a little bit?" Asking is my way of ripping off the Band-Aid.

Abel's eyes cruise all over his car—his way of considering. I chew on the inside of my cheek.

"Only if your apartment is demon-free."

I raise my hands. "I clean with sage twice a week."

"In that case." He kills the engine. "After you, Cari Carrington."

It is insane how your eyes can be so selective and ignore discarded cups or journals or unfolded blankets until someone else steps into your private space. Then, and only then, do your eyes do their job. I try to be subtle as I organize my journals into a pile on the coffee table and carry water glasses to the sink. In my defense, Sunday—Cleaning Day—is still forty-eight hours away.

Abel joins me in the kitchen, and his eyes immediately flick to my fridge.

I am something of an obsessed magnet collector. There are flower magnets, stick figure magnets, cars, stars, block letters, magnets of the Eiffel Tower (a place I have never been but would *love* to go), emojis, the Statue of Liberty, and sticky notes of every color. Those are for my grocery and to-do lists as well as positive affirmations that a YouTube therapist swears by.

"Wow." Abel drags out the word.

"Too much?"

"No. This is a work of art."

It occurs to me that this is the first time Abel has been inside my new apartment. It is also the first time we have been alone-alone since senior year of college. My dress burns my skin.

"This makes my fridge look lame," he says forlornly. "I just have a URI magnet and my sisters' school pictures."

"You should spice it up," I suggest. "I mean, what are girls going to think when they come over to hook up with you?"

"Right, because I have a new girl in my apartment every single night." He rolls his eyes.

I know Abel lost his virginity to Camila (the girl's mouth was practically a megaphone; I heard her tell her table of friends from across the dining hall). But what I don't know is if Abel has had sex *since* Camila. He isn't Noah. He doesn't go around reciting his sexual experiences to anyone who will listen.

"Have you?" I venture.

"Have I what?"

"Hooked up with anyone recently?"

Abel purses his lips. "Nope. I've been focused on my degree."

His innocence always shocks my system because dammit, he could have anyone he wants. All he would need to do is look at a girl, and she'll want to have his babies. But he *doesn't* look. He is perfectly content in his own bubble of sunshine, wearing a pair of goofy rose-colored glasses.

"*Why?*" I ask without meaning to.

"Well, my master's and PhD are the next steps to becoming a clinical psych—"

"I don't mean why focus on your degree." I laugh breathlessly. "I mean, why haven't you hooked up?"

I guess I sound a little nosy. Abel's throat bobs. A flash of pink settles in his cheeks. "I have to be in love to have sex."

Oh.

The words *love* and *sex* did not twinkle until just now, when Abel says them. A ball of heat wrings its hands in my stomach.

"I don't like messing around," he adds. "The way I see it, my body is only meant to be with one girl."

"I get it." My voice is rich, a side effect of the heat that is now sinking below my hips. "Kai, the last guy I had sex with, clearly never learned the phrase *give and take.*"

"He definitely wasn't your type then."

"And what is my type, Mr. Expert on Women?"

"You told me once, remember?" He leans against the counter and crosses his arms. "Neuroanatomy was canceled, so we went to the common area."

The memory slowly rises in my brain like a warm fog. That's right. Senior year, first semester. Or was it the second?

"We started talking about our romantic types," Abel continues. "You said you had a list of requirements that your dream guy *has* to fit. But the big ones were generosity and caring about others."

How does he remember this tiny, insignificant conversation that took place three years ago? *Okay, Abel, you win this round of So You Think You Can Know Me.* I stare at him, mystified, amazed, and utterly speechless.

He gives me a soft smile. "What?"

"That's..." I have to try to remember how to talk. "Yeah, you're right. I didn't think you remembered that."

"Well, it was important to you, so it was important to me."

Kiss me right now, you handsome, clueless angel baby. Read the room!

When he doesn't, I clear my throat and pour myself a glass of water—mostly because it is a thousand degrees in here. I offer him some water, but he declines.

"So," I say, "I take it you're not concerned about keeping an up-to-date Tinder profile then?"

"I don't even have Tinder." He says it like he's apologizing, but I give him a giant smile and lead him into the living room. Sometimes, it is still mind-boggling to know a guy like Abel even exists—and is in my life for that matter.

"You wouldn't like Tinder anyway," I tell him. "It's just for people to perfect the art of sliding into someone's pants."

He couldn't care less. I am ecstatic that he couldn't. We sit facing each other on the couch, our knees bumping briefly as I ease my throbbing feet out of the gladiator heels.

"What else do you remember about my type?" I ask.

He tilts his head. "Let's see. Well, I know you're a sucker for blue eyes." He doesn't look at me when he says this, which is funny because I'm a sucker for *his* blue eyes. "Athletes—"

"Or—"

"Gym addicts," he answers, tacking on a grin.

"Correct."

"He has to be funny and a good listener."

"Man, you are on *fire!*"

"At least five-five but preferably taller." Abel twists his lips thoughtfully. "And isn't there something with legs?"

"Yeah," I say, feeling my cheeks flush from pink to scarlet. "I don't know why, but if a guy has strong legs...." I trail off.

Abel laughs, but it's not really a joke. Not since he showed up to work out with me one time in college wearing black drawstring shorts. In fact, he's the one who prompted me to add STRONG LEGS to my list of standards.

"Kai must have really strong legs then if he got your attention," Abel says.

"I only saw what I wanted to," I admit. "That was before I realized those legs are attached to a pompous asshole."

"What do the legs of a pompous asshole look like, I wonder?"

"Like chicken wings."

In the short seconds of silence after, heat floods my body again. Abel is the only person I have ever physically *ached* for. The fact that his hands are not on my waist right now is bruising my soul. Even during the months before I met Kai in Manhattan, memories of Abel would set my skin blazing. And we have never even kissed! You know you're screwed when the simple *thought* of someone turns you on.

Abel stares at me with those eyes that make me want to believe in Heaven because nothing is that blue or that perfect.

"Kai's chicken legs aren't the problem," I hear myself say. "I'm pretty sure it's me."

"Cari." All traces of humor are instantly erased from Abel's face.

"I'm flighty," I blurt. "Flighty and impulsive and obsessive. I don't know the difference between infatuation and love!"

What the hell am I doing?

"I have this weird anxiety that's always hovering around me but just out of reach. It's extremely annoying and makes me feel very insecure."

Why can't I stop talking?

"I'm not close with my mom, but I fucking wish I was. At this point, I don't even know how to build an olive branch, let alone how to offer it."

My eyes are glued to the clamshell gray wall. My throat feels like it just absorbed a fireball. I'm not one to spit out insecurities like that face-to-face; In poetry, it's easy. Here, with Abel, it has me feeling embarrassed.

He is silent for a second. Then he says, "Did I ever tell you that I sometimes wear mismatched socks to the gym?"

I shake my head, wondering how this relates to everything I just spilled.

"I do," he continues. "My therapist told me to try it because I love order so much that *any* change—big or small—makes me nauseous. But life is *full* of change. So, I have to take small steps. Try to accept the fact that I'm not perfect and that life is not a straight line. It annoys the hell out of me." He releases a long breath. "Two different-colored socks. What an atrocity!"

The small outburst is clearly meant to make me laugh. It works.

"But I'm insecure because of how much I wish I was perfect. Bipolar disorder kicks my butt a *lot*."

His confession rings in my ears like he shouted it through a tunnel. It wavers in my mind, disrupts my equilibrium.

Abel *is* perfect. Down to the way his left eyebrow arches slightly higher than the right one. Down to his smooth yet emphatic cadence. His knuckles and his slender fingers. The tiny birthmark at the base of his neck. The muscles in his biceps and shoulders. The glowing halo over his gold-tinted hair. His massive, overflowing, passionate heart. His gorgeous brain. That disorder that *makes* his brain gorgeous.

How can he not see any of that?

"I think it's cool of you to wear mismatched socks."

"And I think it's cool that you're spontaneous enough to move here from freaking New York City just to cure writer's block." He stares at me, drilling the point home.

Oh.

When he sees it click in my brain, he explains, "We are our own worst critics, Cari Carrington. To the outside world, we might not be so bad."

I can't help it. I start laughing.

"What?" Abel asks.

I snort, which makes me laugh harder. "It's just that..." More uncontrollable giggles. "Nothing!" I say, trying to calm myself down. "I just know you're going to be the most amazing psychologist."

He starts chuckling then, too. "Future Dr. Harpen, am I right?"

"Future Dr. Harpen," I confirm. "The best in the business."

Somehow, we move closer to each other as we laugh, the magnets in our hearts doing their jobs. My head ends up on his shoulder. His cheek ends up against my hair. Our chests rapidly rising and falling as we come down off our giggle high. He smells like sweet cologne, possibilities, and home.

We don't move and we don't say anything.

I have done book signings in Manhattan, where people have shown up in custom-made T-shirts with my poetry printed on them. I've been bar hopping with Kelsey on New Year's Eve. I have camped out at music festivals just to be close to the stage when some underrated artist performed. But *nothing* is as exhilarating as the tingle zipping through my body right now.

This is how it should feel every time, I decide. Like every nerve ending in your body is writing this person's name and highlighting it. I have never felt like this before—not with Kai, what-his-name from high school, or any forgotten lover in between.

Is *this* what it means to love someone? To feel tongue-tied and stomach-tied and brain-tied to the point where you can't remember how to speak, let alone put your feelings into words? To feel weightless and numb except for that one spot where your head meets their shoulder because heat is blossoming there like a giant sunflower?

"I should probably...head home," Abel says eventually. His voice is lower, huskier.

Or you could stay, I almost say. Instead, what comes out is, "Okay," and instantly feel cold the moment I sit up.

He smiles very softly, very attractively, and gets to his feet. All the heat retreats as I walk him to the door.

"If a demon pulls me out of bed or tries to kill me in my sleep, I'll call you." He grins.

"Ditto."

"Goodnight, Cari."

"'Night."

He turns down the hall, and I wonder how many more times we have to part like this before the barrier breaks and we give in.

18

Ah, November. The month where stomping on crunchy, amber-colored leaves becomes annoying and everyone's forced smile screams, *Can the holidays just arrive already?*

In my humble opinion, November has many good things to offer, but two things stand out above all others.

One is Tucker's apple pie that he serves after Thanksgiving dinner. Perk of growing up as Mom's Kitchen Chatterbox: he learned to bake, too. And I don't know if he laces those perfectly cinnamon-sweet slices with crack, but every year I swear I get more and more addicted to them. For as much as I adore baking, Tucker's apple pie is perfection on a plate that I simply cannot mimic.

The other good thing November has to offer is Katerine. Today is her birthday; hence, we have been on FaceTime for the last two hours —me with a glass of champagne and her with a glass of Perrier, per her decision to ditch alcohol.

"You know what, Cari? I am *feeling* twenty-four! It's my year," she shouts.

"I know! Your brain's almost fully developed! How exciting!"

Her expression goes blank. "Thank you for that, Dr. Random Facts."

"You're welcome."

"Anyway," she says, "maybe this is the year I'll finally get the guts to quit my job and move to Toronto."

"You took *one* vacation there, and that was two years ago."

"And it's been calling my name ever since!" she argues, swirling the Perrier in her cup. "I'll just have to convince Ben."

Her boyfriend of four years is a New York City guy through and through. He's a real estate agent who doesn't mind a bougie getaway every now and then, but who would quite literally cut his heart out and bury it in the soil of Central Park just to prove his loyalty to the city.

"Good luck with that one," I mumble.

"I just think Toronto will suit me. It's time for a change."

I can't say anything against that, considering I packed my bags and traded gutter smoke for the vague scent of water and fish. Manhattan is an opulent jewel, but it's not the only diamond in the jewelry box.

"Would moving make you happy?" I ask.

Katerine purses her lips. "I think so. When I was younger, you know, traveling used to make me anxious. But as I've gotten older, I've realized that there's actually some beauty in that." She sips her Perrier. "It's healthy to change your surroundings. Plus, you never know what opportunities will come your way until you try."

I am thoroughly proud to hear her say that.

She used to share a lot of those travel-anxiety stories with me. In one, she was a preteen and suffered an embarrassing choke-up panic attack in the middle of a cramped pizza shop on the boardwalk. In another, she was seventeen and barfed up a cherry slushie on some girl's foot in the middle of a Drake concert. At twenty-one, she "lost her shit" on the deck of her vacation cottage because it was the farthest she'd been from home sweet home. The only time she felt even remotely safe was when Ben took her to Toronto for her twenty-second birthday. We don't know why, but I choose to credit the cocktails and Ben's supposedly cozy arms.

"Exactly," I reply, raising my glass to my phone screen. "Toronto for the win!"

Katerine's smile creeps higher. "I know what makes *you* happy. Poetry!" She sings the word—terribly off-key. "Tell me about this new collection that you're writing."

My pulse quickens. It feels like I swallowed a swarm of butterflies. The feeling is not unwelcome. In the last few days, my journal has gained a healthy portion of witty, sarcastic poems that are a mirror into my lovesick brain.

"It's going fantastic."

"I need details!" I love that she cares, even if she doesn't read.

"Ever since Kai and I broke up, love has been a joke to me."

"I'm aware." Katerine rolls her eyes. "Ben and I couldn't even hold hands without you making some smart-ass comment."

I laugh. "Well, good news for you, I'm now putting my smart-ass comments into my poetry."

"I'm not following. Aren't you in love with Supermodel Dude?"

"Very."

"How can you be in love and still make fun of it?"

"Because," I say, "the collection is about my *reaction* to everything I'm feeling. Joking is how I make sense of the world."

"Don't tell me you make fun of his dick," she deadpans.

"Trust me, making fun of his dick is not on my to-do list."

She nods vigorously. "Get it, girl."

"Point is, my poetry has been revived. Writer's block can go suck a brick."

"How appetizing."

"Precisely."

When I write a poem I'm not sure about (which happens more often than I'd like), I text Hunter. Turns out he has an excellent knack for moral support. He usually responds with a list of reasons why I should A) relax, and B) consider the fact that there is most likely someone out there in the world who needs to read that poem as much as I needed to write it. He also concludes his arguments with *You can always rewrite later, Carrington,* which gets me every time.

Hunter has accidentally become my voice of reason. In fact, he has texted me twice throughout the span of this FaceTime call, responding to the four lengthy paragraphs I texted him earlier. I wrote a poem called "Smoking Dopamine," which is a metaphor for being high off your own neurotransmitters in the presence of someone you like. I wrote it, overthought about it, and splurged my anxiety to Hunter. His response:

> You can always rewrite later, Carrington.

"Well, I'll come visit on the book tour," Katerine says.

"That's kind of you."

"Well, you know me. The queen of kindness. I'm so kind I'll even lend you a sharpie to sign people's copies."

"Wow. Now you're really breaking records."

"What can I say?" She raises her cup. "Twenty-four is already transforming me."

We drink to that.

19

In the most astonishing news of the year, Ruth is wearing yellow today.

"Oh *crap*," I say. "Should I call 911? Are you feeling sick? How many fingers am I holding up?"

Ruth leans against the counter and crosses her arms. "Two and chill your roll, kid. I'm fine."

"All right." I press a hand to my heart. "I was really scared there for a second. I thought you were going to double over and start foaming at the mouth."

"Believe it or not, I do own and wear other colors when I'm not in the bakery."

"Nope. I never would've guessed." I lather my hands with soap and scrub them clean in the sink. "I am curious though."

"I'm scared to ask why."

My lips curl into a smile. I *love* my grandma boss. "Why purple? You could've chosen a more superior color. Like turquoise, for example."

"Watch yourself." Ruth pins the day's To-Bake list up on the bulletin board. "Purple is the color of the Baltimore Ravens."

"No." I gesture through the double doors. "*That* shade of purple screams cute cupcake shop romance."

"Something you're familiar with?"

I scoff. "Hardly."

Ruth grabs a few mixing bowls from the pantry. After a second of silence she says, "Purple was the color I was wearing when I met my husband Harry. We met at a bar."

This is a frame story taking its first breath. I want to feed it some oxygen. I want to watch it play out in black and white on a movie screen. I want to grab my journal and turn her story into a poem. Instead, I gesture for her to continue.

"I was nineteen. My friend Patty and I had spent the day sunbathing on the beach. We decided to go out that night on a whim because originally, we were just going to order room service and watch movies. But we got all dressed up and went out to a dive bar."

"A dive bar," I echo ridiculously. "You met Harry in a *dive bar?*"

"Absolutely. Spotted him the second I walked in. I was wearing this long purple dress." She shakes her head wistfully. "I had my hair all teased up. You better believe he couldn't take his eyes off me."

I can't help jumping up and down like a five-year-old. "What happened? Did you go up to him?"

"Heck no." She hands me her special recipe for sugar cookies. "I was out with my girlfriend. I made him come up to *me.*"

"Right on."

"Patty had caught the eye of another young man, so she started talking with him. Harry saw his chance and swooped in. I let him buy me a drink."

"Was it love at first sight?" I clasp my hands together and attempt puppy dog eyes.

"It was *attraction* at first sight," Ruth corrects. Her outer shell dissolves as she blushes. Ruth. Blushing. I should have a camera on me. "We talked 'til one in the morning about...life and love. Harry is an intelligent man, I'll tell ya that. He's very philosophical when he wants to be."

"And in the meantime, he fills cavities."

"In the meantime, he fills cavities," Ruth confirms. "That night he told me that purple is my color because it brings out the passion in my eyes."

"Stop!" I cry, pressing two hands to my face. "My hopeless romantic heart can't take it!"

"We've been married forty-one years. Bought the bakery when Amber was six." Her eyes darken at the mention of her daughter, but it's a quick flicker—less than a second. "Originally, the walls in here were a cream color, but Harry said it was missing *me*."

"So he was the one to suggest purple?"

"Exactly. Not only is it my favorite color—and the color of my football team," she hurries to add like it *can't* be left out. "Purple means ambition, which is what I needed to create this bakery."

I beam. "Everything has a story. It's a proven fact now."

"Precisely."

I turn on some country music—Chris Stapleton naturally because who else?—and we work in silence. By the time I finish mixing the dough, smears of egg yolk and flour decorate my apron. It is only after I pop the cookies into the oven that I ask my next question.

"How did you know you loved Harry?"

Ruth just got off the phone with an order for raspberry cheese-cake (some office work party for employees who have *specific* sweet cravings). She copies this down on a purple sticky note and turns to face me.

"I knew I loved him because I thought about him while I brushed my teeth."

I wait for the punchline, but her face is as straight as an arrow.

"Well, I think about my literary agent when I brush my teeth, but that's because I wonder if she thinks I'm wasting her time, not because I'm in love with her."

Ruth cracks a smile. "I *mean* that when you're in love with someone, you can't stop thinking about them. All you feel for them is compassion. You want to get to know them in every single way possible, even the weird stuff. *Especially* the weird stuff."

I think about Abel when I make peanut butter sandwiches. I think about him when I do yoga on Sundays and during every workout every day after. He owns my thoughts when I watch *Parks and Recreation.* He is every male protagonist in every Emily Henry book. Every streak of color in a sunset. And, come to think of it, I *do* think about him when I brush my teeth.

I don't think of anything in particular. Just him. His physical presence. The fact that he exists in the same time period and same environment that I exist in. The disbelief that anyone could ever *not* adore him. I think about preference and how Abel Harpen is my definition of top-tier perfection, but, say, Kelsey's definition of a semi-funny-semi-annoying Friend. Nothing more, nothing less. I think about telling Abel how I feel, and the sheer stupidity of that. I think of a wrecked friendship, and that is typically where the thoughts stop.

"Did you tell Harry you loved him first?" I ask Ruth.

"He beat me to it," she replies, pulling a cup of melted butter out of the microwave. "It just slipped out one night while we were at dinner."

"How'd it make you feel?"

She considers this for a second. "It felt amazing, but there wasn't a firework show if that's what you're getting at. I'd already known he loved me way before he said it because of the way he looked at me. Like I'm the only woman on earth."

Like she's the only woman on earth....

Is *that* what love is? A single look that spills all of your heart's desires? I have a nasty-lovely habit of showing every emotion on my face. My eyes are massive windows to my soul. How could Abel *not* know?

"What's with the burning curiosity today, Carrington?" Ruth asks. "Am I going to be featured in your next collection?"

I press my lips together. "Not quite. See, I...." *Open the floodgates, why don't you?* "I met this guy in college, and I've been in love with him for almost six-and-a-half years, but he was dating someone else, and then I moved to Manhattan and dated this *arrogant* jerk of an aspiring heart surgeon, who, by the way, was *weirdly* close with his sister. But then we broke up, and I moved here because my agent was like 'Where's your next collection, Cari? It's been two years.'" I slap the countertop. "And I panicked—moved here because I was supposed to go to UMBC after college, and what do you know? Abel is a student there now getting his master's. And I'm *so* in love with him I don't know what to do, but it is eating away at me, and I don't know how much longer I can take it."

I take a breath and then several more. Ruth just stares at me. Five very long seconds later, she comes back to life and adjusts her glasses on her nose.

"Abel is...the guy from college?"

"Yes."

"That is...that's quite the pickle," she murmurs.

"A stupid, sour pickle." I sound like a three-year-old, so I stop pouting and stand up straighter. "We've been friends for years. I can't risk it."

"Can't or won't?"

"Both, I guess." My voice loses its fervor.

Chris Stapleton sings through the silence.

"Carrington," Ruth says after a long exhale. "If it is meant to be, then it will be."

"Right, because fate is so perfect every single time."

"I didn't realize you were such an existentialist."

"I actually teach college courses on it every Thursday evening."

"Look," she says, ignoring my joke. "If you truly love him, tell him how you feel. You are the only one who's stopping you," she adds as I cringe and recoil. "What *is* stopping you? The risk of losing the friendship?"

"The risk of losing him for good." I can't even say it without my stomach dropping to my feet.

"You could lose him if you *don't* tell him."

Reverse psychology, or as I like to call it, My Personal Kick in the Ass.

"Okay." I harumph. "Point made."

"Just breathe and let things happen as they will. Go with the flow. I'm going to enroll you in my class on fatalism."

"Oh, goody. Can't wait."

The oven dings. I pull a toothpick from the container and test to see if the cookies are still gooey in the middle. Satisfied, I pull them from the oven and set them on the cooling rack, all the while thinking, I *need to regain control of this situation.*

How to make Cari Daughtler uncomfortable: throw the truth in her face. I realize I need to go with the flow. But going with the flow is boring.

"Tell me, Ruth," I say as I re-wash my hands in the sink. "How much do you know about bipolar disorder?"

20
____

"Risk"

Never date a writer,
especially in winter.

Cozy love letters
bring frigid spring blisters.

A writer's words
are the softest of splinters.
Cinnamon,
ginger
turning so bitter,

leaving you thinner.

You know all that glitters
isn't gold.

THE CAFÉ BUSTLES AROUND US AS HUNTER'S GREEN EYES FLICK up to mine with a look that is infuriatingly indecipherable.

"It's a first draft," I argue, tossing a fistful of rose gold hair over my shoulder. "I can always rewrite later."

He doesn't react when I throw his own words at him. Instead, he lays my poetry journal down on the table, leans forward, and steeples his fingers in front of his mouth.

"You make it sound like it's a bad thing to date a writer."

I had been prepared to whip out my gilded sword and defend my right as a poet to have mediocre first drafts. His comment throws me off guard; I wasn't ready to defend the *message*.

"Well, I don't know." I bite my lip. "I consider myself a lesser version of Taylor Swift in a way. If you wrong me, I'm going to write a poem about you, and those 718 followers you have on Instagram will all unite and commit the biggest crime known to man: *unfollow*."

Hunter cracks a smile. "Good thing I have 818 followers."

"That's my point though," I say. "Dating a writer is a risky business. Hence..." I point at the poem's title.

"I personally have to disagree."

I go back to unsheathing my gilded sword—ready for battle. "And why is that?"

He leans forward with his elbows on the table. "Because writers think differently than most people. They pick up on things that the average person, like myself, wouldn't think twice about. In fact, dating a writer would probably change my whole perspective of the world. She'd teach me to love monotony or something just by turning it into a cool metaphor." My shoulders lose their tension. He has a point. "And honestly," he goes on, "*if* we broke up, I'm sure her revenge poem would be absolute gold, which would make it hard to hate her."

"You poor baby bunny. Don't take the bait."

"Are you kidding? I would literally *win* Valentine's Day if I dated a writer. I'd get a five-page essay about how much my girlfriend loves me."

"Don't be so sure," I warn. "With that expectation, you'd be lucky to get a note card that says simply: 'I like you. You're pretty cool.'"

"Don't be ridiculous. It would say, 'I *love* you. You're pretty *awesome.*'"

We try to suppress our laughter because the café is miraculously empty today except for a thin woman with an amber-colored bob cut typing away on her computer in the opposite corner. We bite back our giggles out of courtesy.

Hunter suggested we meet here today after his class because I experienced a mini panic attack over this poem. He is kind enough to still be friends with me instead of thinking I'm nuts.

"Let me ask you a question," he says.

"Shoot."

He hesitates for a moment, considering his words. "What are you so worried about?"

"I'm worried a spider is going to crawl into my mouth while I'm sleeping and lay its eggs in my intestines."

A beat of heavy silence clambers by.

"Okay, let me rephrase." Hunter says, trying and failing to keep a straight face. "What are you worried about in relation to the *poem?*"

"Oh, um..." It takes me a second to shift my thoughts back after that horrid mental picture. "I—I don't...really know." Maybe it's that I'm scared of the possible truth of these poems in relation to Abel. Maybe it's that I think I wouldn't be a good girlfriend to him at all for reasons I can't figure out but that my anxiety is spewing at me.

"You texted me like twenty times, Carrington. Plus, you've been picking at your cuticles for the last twenty minutes. Clearly, there is something weighing on your mind."

"Call me Cari." It's the only response I can muster.

"Did you know there's beauty in imperfection? Just look at human evolution. Throughout our history, genetic mutations have popped up. Mental disorders have become prevalent. Genetic and environmental factors completely out of our control make us the beautifully *imperfect* creatures we are. Our entire existence is based around trial and error. It's okay to not have the poem perfect on the first try."

I roll my eyes. "Did *you* know you should've pursued philosophy? You're in the wrong field."

"Actually, most things in psychology are subjective and require deeper thinking." He grins at me.

"All right, I think we're done here."

Hunter barks a laugh. "Come on, Carrington—*Cari,*" he corrects when I shoot him a look, "stop being so hard on yourself. This is a *good* poem. It can be enhanced, sure, but it's great for a starter." Hunter may not be a poet himself, but he is probably one of the smartest people I've ever met, so I trust his judgment entirely.

I suck a piece of ice through the opening of my cold brew and chew it instead of answering because I simply can't. I can't bring myself to acknowledge the deeper meaning behind these poems for what it is: if I love Abel, I could lose him, too. I steer the conversation in a new direction instead.

"Tell me your story."

"Come again?"

"Your story." I tick the questions off my fingers. "What were you like as a kid? Did you do drugs in high school? Are you secretly a member of the CIA? Don't worry, I'll keep that last one a secret."

"Those are very specific questions."

"How else am I going to get to know you?"

He narrows his eyes at me. "Are you trying to pick me up or something?"

"No!" I pause to laugh. Really laugh. What an absurd idea. "You know, for a student pursuing his master's and PhD, you should know how people become friends."

"Had to be sure." Hunter holds his hands up. "But I love a good game of Twenty Questions. Ask away."

"What state were you born in?"

"Massachusetts."

He's smiling at me, and it's a nice smile. It's symmetrical. More than that, it's genuine. If smiles were colors, his would be golden.

"Where in Massachusetts?"

"Worcester. I grew up there, and then I went to college in Nashville."

"Belmont?" I guess.

"Vanderbilt."

I slap my hand down on the table because *duh*. He's a genius. "That checks out."

If laughs were colors, his would be green like a summer leaf. Easy, warm, inviting. "Next question."

"Do you have any siblings?"

"Only child."

"Okay," I say, hoping to stump him. "If your personality could be represented by an animal, what would it be?"

"An elephant," he answers instantly. "They're loyal, and they have great a memory."

"Favorite fast-food joint."

"Chick-Fil-A."

"Dream job."

"Neuroscientist."

"Favorite season."

"Fall."

"Worst attribute."

"Bad anxiety."

"*Best* attribute."

"Empathy."

I lean forward and grill him with my fiercest gaze. "What's 8,456 divided by 379?"

He tilts his head and squints up at the ceiling. His eyes dart back and forth for several seconds like he's writing the problem on a whiteboard. Approximately forty-five seconds later, he looks back at me.

"Twenty-two point three."

I frown and whip out my phone. A quick calculation tells me that he is, of course, correct.

I clear my throat. "So anyway, I wrote a poetry collection, and it's a bestseller."

"Speaking of...." He snags a napkin from the holder and a pen from his backpack. "Can I have your autograph?"

"Are you going to sell it?"

"Actually, I'm going to frame it and brag about it to my parents and friends when they come visit."

My lips split into a grin. I take the napkin and pen from him and sign my signature in swooping cursive.

"Artsy," he comments.

"You should see it when I have to sign a hundred copies. It gets less pretty every time."

Hunter's summer green laugh matches the green in his eyes. His dark hair hangs down over his forehead in tiny rivulets. Sometimes, it's curly. Other times, it has beach waves. It is hair that has a mind of its own, yet never mars Hunter's appearance.

"What got you into neuroscience?" My voice sounds airy and far away. Full curiosity mode.

"Short answer: My grandma passed away from Alzheimer's."

"Long answer?"

He sighs and glances at the lady in the corner like she's a safety net.

"Gran was my dad's mom. When she got sick, my dad really fell apart. I remember the night we went to the hospital, and she didn't recognize him. The look on my dad's face." Hunter tries to hide his shudder. "I'd never seen my dad cry. I didn't know dads *could* cry actually, but then he went out into the hallway with my mom and bawled his eyes out in her arms. It was the first time I realized the true depth of human emotion."

"How old were you?"

"Eight." He looks down at his hands. "Gran never knew how sick she was. After she passed, Dad got depressed. There was a point where Mom was worried he'd lose his job because he refused to get out of bed. It was hard 'cause...well..." He clears his throat. Brilliant UMBC Student, Hunter Gatelin, chokes up right in front of me. "I lost my grandma, but it was like I lost my dad, too." He heaves a sigh. "He's better now, but for a while it was...it was tough."

"I'm sorry," I murmur.

He nods and finally looks at me again. "I knew I wanted to do something with the brain then, and the older I got, the more I found out about neuroscience. If I can do research on the brain and the nervous system, I might be able to find answers."

"Answers?"

"For diseases like Alzheimer's and other mental diseases."

"You want to save people."

"Yes." He nods in determination. The empathy in his eyes is a glimmering pool.

This man is a story if I've ever met one. He is a young child growing up too quickly. He is a heart of gold. He is a mirror.

"Wow." I shake my head and grab another napkin. "Would you mind signing this? I need to get your signature before you become famous for discovering the cure for Alzheimer's."

He looks amused. "Are you going to sell it?"

"Don't be ridiculous. I'm going to frame it and make it the background for all my Christmas cards."

"In that case...." Hunter signs the napkin with a barely legible signature.

I squint at it. "Why thank you, Dr. Gatelin."

"You're very welcome."

I grin at him. "Guess we're even now."

"How so?"

"You know a shit ton about me, now I know a shit ton about you."

He waves a hand, brushing the whole conversation away. "You don't know me. You'll *never* know me."

"Because if you told me, you'd have to kill me?"

"Because I'm secretly a member of the CIA and am literally forbidden to give you any more details."

"I knew it!"

The smile we share is as effortless as breathing.

Every once in a blue moon, the planets align. By no means am I an astronomer, but that's got to count for something. Some intense mathematical equation or a dazzling high-tech photo opp. Regardless, perfect things must happen in that moment, which leads me to believe that the planets are aligning right now in broad daylight on a random Wednesday in November. Because Hunter might just be my friend soulmate.

Not at all in a romantic way, but in a way that gleefully exclaims, *Our energies are connecting, and it feels more natural than leaves twirling in the wind!* I can tell because of the way we laugh from the gut together. The way we can be weird and silly together. The way we started fist-bumping without realizing it. And the way I know he feels it, too.

This man is a mirror.

"I should probably get going." Hunter sighs. "I've got another presentation to prepare for."

"More research?"

"Always research."

"I'd love to hear it sometime."

He swings his backpack over his shoulder and cocks an eyebrow. "You'd love to hear about the effects of neural implants on nerve stimulation?"

"Sure." I stand up too. "That's my shit."

"Right on."

He fist-bumps me, and again, it feels as natural as sunlight slanting on the sidewalk.

"In the meantime, get some writing done," Hunter says. "You're really slacking off."

"Har, har."

He sticks his tongue out at me, and I thank the aligned planets for this incredible friend soulmate.

21

Kelsey's text message arrives at 1:23 a.m.:

> Friendsgiving on 11/21!! No bs excuses. We have to get better at keeping in touch. Meg said we can come to her place.

Noah replies instantly:

> Do I have to bring my own food?

Abel jumps in with three question marks.
Kelsey texts,

> What does Friendsgiving mean genius?

I jump in.

> You know some of us like to sleep?

My comment is completely ignored.

The text chimes are what woke me up. I'd been having a dream about picking flowers in a garden, and while it was entirely random, it was still peaceful. An exploding group chat was *not* supposed to interrupt that.

The glowing phone screen fries my sleepy eyes.

Noah asks,

> Ok what if I just buy a pie from the grocery store?

Kelsey retorts,

> Is that your idea of authentic?

> Well, I will have paid for it with my own money so YUP.

He sends that GIF of Shaquille O'Neal smirking and wiggling his shoulders.

My eyelids weigh eight pounds, so I let them drop. The blissful peace lasts approximately twelve seconds before my phone chimes again, and a zip shoots up through my arm. Abel's name appears across the screen.

> Friendsgiving, lame or not lame?

It takes me a moment to realize he's not texting in the group chat. This is a direct question to me. The only reason I bother responding is because it's Abel. I type,

> Not lame. It'll be nice to have everyone together again.

He replies seconds later,

> You're right.

The speech bubble floats across the bottom of the screen. It sets my heart on a low burn to know he's typing, but the sensation is clouded by pure exhaustion.

> Did you know that out of all the whales, belugas are the most vocal??

A small part of my brain oozes dopamine at the thought of Abel wanting to text me at all. But a larger, more tired and increasingly impatient side of my brain is asking why the hell that piece of information is important right now.

Even though I am past the point of tired, my thumbs still type a response.

> I did not know that. That's cool. I'm sorry Abel, but I'm exhausted and about to pass out. Can we finish this conversation tomorrow?

I add a smiling emoji for good measure.

> Absolutely!!! Sleep well Cari Carrington. Have the most amazing dreams ever!

He might as well have just driven to my apartment, tucked me in, and kissed me on the forehead. What an angel.

Kelsey and Noah do not appear to understand that one-on-one texting is a thing, so I put the group chat on *do not disturb* and snuggle up under my blankets.

～

SPOON-FEED ME SOME MOTIVATION, sit me in front of a laptop, and I could be a professional researcher. Well, as long as I have a full night's sleep.

Sunlight creeps onto the kitchen table, splashing bits of gold on my computer as I type furiously into the Google search bar.

Signs of mania.

I press enter and instantly feel guilty. Four years' worth of psychology classes plus a senior year internship *and* that introductory course I took in high school, and it's like all the information has fluttered out the window. This is the problem with psych classes though. I was never going to be a good psychologist by memorizing keywords from a textbook and regurgitating them on a test. I needed to *talk* to people and see the symptoms for myself. I couldn't have done that with Abel in college if I'd wished upon a star or downed Popeye's spinach. Abel is a master at hiding his emotions. But over time, I could have recognized more and more manic behaviors in him. That's the point. Book smarts plus experience equals good psychologist.

The reason for my research is because Abel's good-natured energy last night made me realize I don't really remember the symptoms of mania all that well. I want to know the signs.

A list appears on Google, splurging the basics: high elation in mood, little to no sleep, talking quickly.

I just want to make sure Abel is okay.

The summer after freshman year, he invited me on his family trip to Disney World. It had been a one-time thing (with *lots* of convincing for my parents), and I was forced to sleep on a cot next to his younger sisters' California King in the hotel suite. It was during that trip that Abel first explained to me what it feels like to be manic for him.

"It is the best feeling in the world," he said.

We were in line for the Haunted Mansion, and his mother was distracted when Abel's sister Charlotte asked her if the ride was really that scary. Abel would never talk about mania if his mother was listening. If words were cactuses, *manic* would draw blood—for him *and* his mom. But in the weeks leading up to the trip, Abel had been recovering and coming down off another episode. He was more vocal about the experience since he'd been back to therapy and had at least fourteen days of lithium medication in his system.

"It starts with a spark," he said under his breath, while we gazed up at the gruesome behemoth of a mansion.

"A spark?"

"Yeah. Like the need to *be* something or *do* something. And you feel like you can—that's the best part. It feels like someone injects Red Bull into your veins and then leaves you there to conquer the world."

"What types of things spark it?"

His cotton-candy blue eyes had touched my face for a brief second and then moved away. He'd started twisting his hands together in a way that was meant to look casual but was really an unconscious sense of safety.

"The holidays are a bad trigger for my mom. Once, she bought presents for the entire neighborhood and for people in the next neighborhood, too. That's why Dad handles Christmas shopping now."

I stared at Mrs. Harpen for a moment when Abel said this. Stared at her dirty-blonde hair and her tanned apple-like cheeks that grew plump when she smiled. I remember thinking she was beautiful and then wondering if that was the universe's way of disguising her struggles. I didn't know if that was kind or cruel.

"What about you?" I asked him.

More hand-twisting. More *intense* hand-twisting.

"Exams are a trigger." I had to give him credit for how even his voice sounded. "When I'm motivated to do well on something, it makes me over-prepare, and I feel so energized that I forget to sleep. I also get super goal-oriented out of nowhere. Ace this test, ace that one, take full charge of this group project." He shrugged.

"So, you're a high achiever." I grinned at him.

Thankfully, he grinned back.

"You could say that. Here, let me paint it out for you." He unlocked his hands and sketched a picture frame in the air. "My brain's like a shattered mirror. Each shard of glass is a different thought, but they're all glinting in the sun at the same time, trying to catch my attention. When I'm manic, I can see them all simultaneously. It's like I have a thousand eyes. It makes me feel like my brain and my body are more powerful than they actually are. I don't need sleep; I'm a god. I can do *every single thing* I put my mind to. I can address every piece of glass at once.

"But it's a double-edged sword. If someone gets in my way, they're a villain. The pieces of glass make me say things that aren't like me, and I later regret those things. It's constant guilt."

It's constant guilt.

After that, the Haunted Mansion line had shifted forward, and we left the conversation behind us.

This world is fucked up, I think now, sitting in my apartment, scrolling through mania symptoms on my laptop. Seriously fucked up.

How is it fair that Abel Pure Sunshine Harpen has to be stuck in emotional cycles like this? But then, how is any of it fair? How is depression fair, or OCD or anxiety or schizophrenia? *No one* deserves constant mental torment.

I exchange my laptop for my journal and write a poem, or—I try to. But the angry words boomeranging in my brain never quite resonate. I erase for a fifth time. Words are like people. You can't force them into anything; they have to come at their own will. Eventually, they do.

If I could,
I would trap all your scary thoughts in a jar.
Shake them up
and watch them shimmer.

I stare at the words until finally, the message hits.

No, mental disorders are not fair. They are scary and exhausting and overwhelming, but they are also a core component of what makes us human. Another chink in our already flawed existence. If everyone lived perfect lives, it would be boring as hell. We need gray mixed into the black and white. We need the ups and the downs. How else would people be so uniquely beautiful?

I set my journal aside and glance at my laptop. Google stares back at me, twiddling its thumbs, waiting for me to get back to its results of how mania manifests. So, I exit the tab and shut my computer instead because truthfully, it doesn't matter. When Abel experiences another manic episode, I will still adore him just as much as the day I met him.

That's it, I realize with a start. *That* is what love is. Understanding.

Code cracked.

22

———

"Porn is overrated."

I realize I said that out loud when a woman with swooping blonde hair and chunky glasses looks over at me with eyes as wide as dinner plates. What's worse: we're inches away from the banana stand. I have half a mind to apologize, but I just smile crookedly because what do you even say to defend yourself after that?

"On the contrary," the woman says.

My ears prick. "Come again?"

"Porn is *underrated*, dear." She switches her bag of produce to her other hand and touches my shoulder as she passes. It is a gesture that says, *I'm sorry you aren't a fan of watching people bump uglies.*

I am physically disgusted as Katerine starts howling with laughter. She's on FaceTime and has just played witness to that catastrophe of a moment.

"That woman is my new favorite person on earth!" she gasps.

I back away from the banana stand, suddenly craving literally anything else. I guess it's not *my* fault Katerine chose this moment to call and tell me Ben is a sex god. It's not my fault they're a porn-positive couple. I'm just the listener...who apparently needs to steer clear of middle-aged women in the grocery store.

"Cari, I'm telling you," Katerine says, "reverse cowgirl, *blindfolded*, in the *shower*. It will change your life."

I turn the volume down on my phone. "How does that even work in the shower?"

She explains graphic detail after graphic detail.

"Wow." I choose a head of cauliflower and place it in my cart. "You should quit your accounting job and go work for one of those magazines that does scientific research on orgasms." I intentionally keep my voice low this time.

"No thanks. I'll leave the writing to you."

Movement in my peripheral steals my attention. I do a double take.

Raquel—the bartending chick from Hunter's Halloween movie night—is browsing the fruit section. She looks like she belongs in LA. Beige cashmere sweater, dark brown cargo pants, layers of gold necklaces and matching gold hoops. Even her lips are plump and glossy. Always picture-ready.

"Hey, Kat, can I call you back?"

"Always."

I end the call and jog toward Raquel. She's intensely scrutinizing a pack of raspberries.

"Raquel!"

"Cari, hey." She spares me a quick glance and goes back to examining the raspberries. Coolest chick in the world—you have to compete against *fruit* to keep her attention. "What's up?"

"Nothing much." I pop my left hip, copying her stance. (I'm cool, too.) "A woman thinks I'm lame for not watching porn, but whatever."

"*Huh?*"

I clear my throat. "Don't worry about it. So, what are you doing for Thanksgiving?" It's the first topic that pops into my head after porn. Is that weird?

"Nothing," she replies matter-of-factly and tosses the raspberries into her cart.

My feet jerk me into motion as she starts pushing her cart. Follow the leader, I guess. Follow the independent queen of a leader.

"Nothing?" I press.

"Nah." She stops to pet some peaches. Yes, pet. She doesn't even pick some up; she just stands there, running her fingers over the fuzz. I would judge her because A) she makes peach-petting look dope, and B) I would probably do the exact same thing. I *have* done the exact same thing.

"No plans with your family?"

"Well, yeah. Antonio is coming home from Boston, and my grandparents are coming from Argentina, so my mom's cooking up a whole feast. But that's just on Thursday. Other than that, I am free as a...well, I was gonna say turkey, but that's a bad example."

She sounds genuinely excited to see her family. I wish I had a supersonic vacuum so I could suck a shred of that excitement out of her, turn it into a capsule, and swallow it down.

Thanksgiving in the Daughtler household is always a sight to behold—*especially* since I moved to Manhattan. Our Thursday is a conglomeration of awkward hugs from my teenager cousins (whose phones are "like, the coolest thing in the world"), heated subtext about some marital issues between my Aunt Lorraine and Uncle Benny, Dad's war-cries at the TV when the Patriots don't score, and the mutilated cherry on the grotesque cake: mom's forced attention.

How's New York, honeyyy? Always asked like she had sand under her tongue. *Still using the pepper spray we gave you? How's the apartment holding up?* All to which I always wanted to reply, *I'm your daughter. Stop acting like I'm some friend you lost touch with after high school.*

If there's one person that can revive my holiday cheer, it's Tucker. After we choke down Mom's overcooked turkey and clumpy mashed potatoes, we let the family congregate in the living room while we lock ourselves in the den, play Connect Four, and catch up on life.

It's been a brother-sister tradition since we were young. Of course, the catching up part started after I left for the Big Apple.

I haven't seen my brother since he graduated in May, but from his Snapchats, he clearly hasn't ditched the jagged haircut and Avengers T-shirts. What a massive nerd. A massive nerd that I love.

The point is, my family doesn't exactly follow the prototypical American example. We're more like the Addams Family...you know, minus the wealth and macabre appearances.

"Sounds like a blast," I tell Raquel.

"Cari, have you ever had tres leches cake?"

"I have not."

"Hmm, I see you've never lived." She continues down the aisle and snags a pack of strawberries.

I'm not quite sure what triggers the idea—whether it's the sight of the strawberries, the thought of not living, or the mention of my weakness: cake.

"What are you doing on the twenty-first?"

Raquel turns to me, her brown eyes narrowing a fraction of an inch. "The Monday before Thanksgiving?"

"That would be the one."

"Most likely reading research articles, why?"

"Hear me out—"

"I'm hearing—"

"I know research articles are like your chips and dip—"

"My what—"

"But what if you came to a Friendsgiving instead?"

She cocks her head. "Who's coming to this Friendsgiving?"

"Abel." I lead with him because I know they're friends *and* because it's Abel. Who would pass up an opportunity to be in the presence of such amazingness? Raquel's eyebrows quirk. "And our friends Kelsey and Noah."

A beat of consideration. "If I'm gonna be crashin' your guys's party, then I might pass."

"Good thing I'm formally inviting you." I smile so big, I feel my eyes scrunch. "*Plus*, how else am I going to try tre leche cake for the first time?"

"*Tres leches*," she corrects with a grin.

"That, too."

"You drive a hard bargain, Miss Carrington."

"Well, I was going to be a salesperson at one point in my life."

"Really?"

"No, not at all."

She stares at me for a minute before bursting into laughter. It's one of those wheeze laughs that comes straight from the gut and gets caught in the throat. The best kind of laugh.

She wipes her eyes. "You're silly."

The coolest girl in the world thinks I'm silly. It must be true then.

"Is that a 'yes' I'm sensing?"

"Yeah, I'll be there."

"Yay!" I start my happy dance without even realizing it: a dumbed-down version of the moonwalk with some semi-hazardous jazz hands.

Raquel doubles over. I tell myself to simmer down before I knock over an entire row of fruit, and that's when I notice the three teenagers looking at me like I have maggots crawling out of my nostrils and eye sockets. I smile and wave. They scurry away.

Once Raquel stops wheezing, she says, "You're pretty cool, Cari."

I will wear that compliment like my mother wears her cross necklace—everywhere.

The second I get back to my apartment, I text the group chat.

> I'm bringing a +1 to Friendsgiving, hope that's ok. Her name's Raquel.

Abel wants to know:

> RAQUEL TORRES??

> Yup.

Kelsey asks,

Who's she?

Abel answers.

Only the coolest person on the planet.

He took the words right out of my mouth. He proceeds to ask,

Can I bring my friend Hunter??

I immediately second his request. Having Hunter there would be a blast.

Kelsey texts,

The more the merrier dude

Raquel might bake some tres leches cake!

The group chat proceeds to explode.

23

There are certain things I hypothesize that I will never do: sit on a guardrail in the middle of the highway, see the earth from outer space, go swimming with Great Whites, try pistachio ice cream. Top of the list: go to an indoor pool with Abel Harpen. At night. But never say never.

Turns out, Abel is full of surprises, and swimming at this privately owned gym is one of them. Did I think recreational swimming in this joint was reserved for retired old-timers and jacked gym rats? Yes, until 7:43 p.m. tonight when Abel texted me to put on my swimsuit. I didn't even ask; I just sent a thumbs up. I might be a tad pathetic, but who gives a shit?

"Are we going to be arrested for breaking and entering?" I ask as Abel leads me onto the pool deck.

"Nope. I just text Darla when I want to come swim and she leaves the door open."

"Is that legal?"

"I'm not sure," Abel says, unperturbed.

"Wait, who's Darla?"

"The gym's owner. Oh, she is the *sweetest* woman ever. She

always asks how I'm doing and how my family is doing. One time, I even ran through one of my research presentations for her. It was about the effect of age on mental illness. She loved it, can you believe it?"

Can I believe she loved it because on top of solid research, Abel is a modern-day Adonis and hopelessly hypnotizing whenever he opens his mouth? "Yes, yes I can."

Abel chuckles and tosses his drawstring bag onto the cream-colored tiles, next to a bench. Then—*oh my God.* The fabric of his shirt slides up over his head as he tugs it off. His back is to me, so I'm greeted by the lines of muscles there. My mouth actually falls open. The pool lights wash his skin in a dancing turquoise haze. Like, *hello,* this man's bare back makes me want to contribute my genes to the continuation of the human race. When Abel turns, I whip my head in the other direction.

"Last one in is a sore loser," he exclaims.

"I'm already a—" *Holy abs,* "—sore loser."

"I'd have to disagree, but we'll see. Race ya!" He lunges forward, hugs his knees to his chest, and executes a perfect cannonball. When he emerges, his wavy hair is darker and drooping and utterly adorable. Would it be weird if I took a picture of him and made it my lock screen?

"Come on in, Cari Carrington."

"You don't have to tell me twice." I yank off my cover-up. I chose to wear my famed solid-red bikini tonight. It's striking and historically proven to give guys a hard-on. Not that I'm trying to seduce Abel or anything...but if he happens to catch feelings tonight, I guess it's out of my hands.

When I was little, I was scared of getting gallons of water up my nostrils, so I never learned to do a good cannonball (don't judge me). Instead, I do a mediocre star jump, crashing in inches away from Abel. The water isn't icy like I expected, but it's not quite bathwater either. It is golden ratio perfect—probably because Abel is here.

"I'd rate that jump approximately four-point-five out of five," he says when my head breaks the surface.

Thank Aphrodite for waterproof mascara; otherwise, I'd look like Pennywise's lesser-known younger sister. "Why the half-point off?"

"Your arms were at least four degrees lower than they should have been, thus making the shape a little deformed."

"I'm sorry, I didn't realize you were a shape critic."

"It's one of my hidden professions."

"In addition to...."

"Let's see." He manages to tread water and count off on his fingers. "Jolly rancher taste-tester, five-star pumpkin carver, professional diver...*Oh*, and head astronaut for NASA, but that one's just my weekend job."

I send a wave of water at him, which he successfully dodges by ducking under.

"Peace!" he cries when I try to splash-attack him again. "It's not my fault NASA called *me*."

"Right, I'm sure floating around next to your own feces is a real honor."

He presses his hand to his chest—to his bare, muscular, utterly flawless chest. "It is the *greatest* honor."

When I go to splash him again, he catches my arm and pulls me under. I screw my eyes shut and feel my cheeks puff out full chipmunk style. Okay, fine. I was never the best swimmer. I'm not a professional mermaid, for fuck's sake; I never learned to look pretty underwater. Let's hope my solid-red bikini is still working its magic.

Seconds later, we come up again. I wipe the water from my eyes and realize Abel is climbing over the pool's edge.

"Where're you going?" Please tell me I didn't scare him off with my breath-holding-chipmunk-face.

"You can't open your eyes underwater," he says gently, turning back to smile at me. "So you didn't witness the beauty."

"The...beauty?"

"Hold on."

Abel (dripping wet, burly Abel) pads across the pool deck, his swim trunks *very attractively* hugging his waist. Not that I'm staring. He digs around in his bag until he retrieves a pair of bright-orange goggles.

"Oh, hell no."

He gives me a delightfully endearing look. "What do you mean?"

"I'll look like a clownfish in those."

"Good thing clownfish are cool!" He dives, perfectly.

How can I look sexy wearing goggles that are so bright, they shame the sun?

Abel emerges from the water and swims over to me. It only takes one and a half strokes because he is as tall as I am short. He doesn't hand the goggles to me at first. Instead, he slips them on over his own head, and when he looks at me, I laugh so loud it echoes.

"I know, right? I could totally model for swimwear." He poses and puckers his lips.

I laugh harder because he's right. He *could* model for swimwear, even in tiny, otherwise ugly goggles. He just makes them work. Modeling companies, start calling!

"Your turn." He removes the goggles and holds them out to me. "It'll be worth it, trust me."

I sigh. "Trust? You? How brave of me."

His laugh is silver bells. I want to implant them into the cochlea in both my ears. I tighten the goggles and put them on. Then, I cross my arms and wait for Abel's reaction. The lenses are only slightly tinted, so I don't miss it when he presses his lips together.

"Clownfish?" I say.

"The most beautiful clownfish ever."

I think he just performed open-heart surgery on me, but he doesn't give me a chance to check. He takes my wrist and gently pulls me back under.

Oh. Beauty. Yes, now I understand. The pool lights alternate colors, giving the illusion that we're suspended in the atmosphere of a new planet—somewhere far outside the Milky Way. It is quiet and colorful and mesmerizing, but nowhere near as stunning as Abel. He floats next to me, blue eyes pried open and glittering with awe. When he looks over at me, he does so seemingly in slow motion. I don't know if it's the lack of oxygen to my brain or the out-of-body sensation, but I swear we lean toward each other. Yes, because now I'm looking *up* at him instead of *over* at him. Now his body is right there; now his mouth is *right* there...But then I remember that I probably look like an orange blobfish, and my nostrils react by expelling every ounce of air saved in my lungs. I shoot up toward the surface. I tear the goggles off my face and splutter through an embarrassingly loud cough.

"Are you okay?" Abel swims gracefully at my side while I desperately doggy-paddle to the shallow end.

"Yeah, I—" More hacking. "I'm great. I'm actually—a professional water-inhaler."

"You, too?"

I wish Abel didn't stand up out of the water because when he puts his hands on his hips and stares down at me with those blue eyes, I feel pitifully small. I also feel pitifully flushed. His body is on some marble-carved, Greek god shit.

"Are you okay?" He's staring into my soul in a way that still feels gentle and respectful of my privacy.

"Most of the water has made its exit, yes."

Did I really just screw up an almost-kiss with Abel Harpen? The odds of us ever getting that close again are slim to none. Maybe a *little* higher considering we're friends, but then what? Friends don't kiss friends! A common misconception is that the devil on your shoulder has the louder mouth, but in reality, the angel is equally annoying. Would I really let myself kiss this unnervingly handsome cinnamon bun of a man just to finally have the experience of tasting his lips if it all meant losing him in the end? And how do I know I wasn't just hallucinating? He was probably closing the distance between us to tuck away the goggle's rubber strand that sticks out. Yeah, that's definitely it. There is no way—*no chance*—that he feels what I feel. Zero. Zilch. Nada.

My brain might just disintegrate.

"Well, perfect," Abel exclaims, smiling with those flashy white teeth and that singular dimple in his pink cheeks, and *dammit, why is he taking my hand!* The amount of energy I feel at the touch of his skin has to be unhealthy for my nervous and cardiovascular systems. "Tag, you're it!"

I blink through the dopamine fog in my brain. "I'm sorry, what?"

"We're playing tag!"

"Since...when?"

"Since now, silly!" And down he goes, into the colorful world of water where my lungs are still sinking to the bottom.

But lungs are overrated.

I dive after him, goggles back on my face and chase him around the deep end like we're two toddlers on a summer afternoon. It feels *good.* It feels euphoric. It feels like I've left the pressure of a poetry collection, and judgmental mothers, and graduate school, and mental health concerns far behind, back on the pool deck. We are *us* in this moment. Untouchable. Free.

I catch Abel's calf just before he can kick away. The triumph lasts for three-point-five seconds though before I realize, shit. Now *he's* it. He tags me back before I can even make an attempt to escape.

"It's not so fun when your opponent is six five and faster than you!" I whine when we come up for air.

"Actually, I'm six-foot even."

"*Oh.* Gosh, I'm sorry. Would you like a gold star?"

"No, thank you. I have plenty."

I'm not exactly Michael Phelps, so my energy depletes faster than a whoopie cushion. I give up trying to tag Abel again and instead float on my back. After a moment, he joins me. We stay like that for some time, deep breathing with our limbs spread out like two starfish until Abel murmurs, "This reminds me of my sisters."

"Floating?"

"Yeah. When they were younger, we used to have contests to see who could float the longest. Dad was always the mediator."

"Who was the reigning champion?"

"Charlotte. By a long shot. Melanie and I would get bored, but Charlotte...that girl could float for hours."

Melanie and Charlotte Harpen. One blonde, the other brunette, and *equally* beautiful. Sweeter than peaches and cream. Precious beyond words. I love them. I miss them.

Melanie is the artsy sister. I remember walking into Abel's kitchen for a glass of water and seeing the collection of Melanie's artwork housed on the fridge. Back in the day, it was a collage of unicorns, rainbows, and glitter. But as she grew, the drawings got more defined, more three-dimensional. They turned into realistic dogs, objects, and even people. When Melanie turned ten, she drew a portrait of Abel. It was his lock screen for at least two months.

Charlotte, on the other hand, is the sports addict. *She's like our dad,* Abel always used to say, walking around the house wearing football jerseys, out kicking soccer balls in the mud, shooting hoops with the neighborhood boys. December of our sophomore year, Abel invited me over to decorate Christmas cookies, and I distinctly remember Charlotte's being in the shape of a football. She's a tough girl with a heart of gold.

I bring my feet down and start treading water again so I can look at Abel directly. "You haven't talked about your sisters recently. How are they?"

Abel continues to float. "Charlotte's in eighth grade. She runs cross-country and plays basketball. In the spring, she runs track. One hundred and four-by-four. I text her before every race, tell her I'm proud of her and that I love her. And that she's a beast." Abel pauses to laugh. "She's always been a beast."

My heart sighs dreamily.

"Melanie is in seventh grade. She won the school art contest last year with her painting of a garden. It's *fantastic*, Cari. I don't know where she gets her talent. I FaceTimed her after she won, and we talked for like, two hours about how much she loves drawing."

His blue eyes lose focus for a moment, but they fill with sparkling adoration. "I can't tell you how much my sisters mean to me. I love them more than life. I would do anything for them in a *heartbeat*. God knows they've been there for me." His lips part to say something else, but no sound leaves his mouth.

"What do you mean?" I ask gently.

He sighs and stops floating, turns to face me. "Do you remember that really bad episode I had during junior year? The one that made Camila dump me?"

It stings to hear him ask it—stings on so many levels. I nod.

"Well..." He averts his eyes from me. "Mel and Char came with our parents to pick me up when the hospital discharged me. They'd seen me at my worst before, but I don't think they understood it until that moment. I don't know if Mom or Dad explained it to them, but... they were there. And they hugged me. Didn't say one word, didn't ask if I was crazy, or insane, or wacked-out bananas. They just hugged me."

I did not think it was possible to love those girls more, yet here I am, doing it.

"Do you ever...get worried?" I ask.

"About what?"

"That they might...develop..." My eyes fill in the rest of the question.

Understanding shows on Abel's face, and his lips turn down at the corners. "Sometimes. I worry about Charlotte a little more, only because she's a bit more hyper and reactive. But they've been getting psych evals for years—Mom insists on it—and so far, they've both come back without a diagnosis. For that, I thank the stars twice as hard."

Let this be a lesson to everyone: family perfection is a myth. You know that annoyingly beautiful family on top of the hill in their castle of a house that's covered in swaths of ivy or surrounded by wildflowers or fill in the blank? They cry, too. They grieve, too. They accidentally burn food, and crack vases, and overspend, and pass gas. They argue. They love too intensely. They struggle with their mental health. They're human, too.

"I'm hungry," Abel says all of a sudden. "Are you hungry?"

"I could eat."

"How about a couple of sundaes from Clive's?"

I blink at him. "What's Clive's?"

"An all-night diner not too far from here."

Though I'm upset to leave the pool and this moment of intimacy, my stomach has been growling for the last half hour. "I would love a sundae from Clive's."

24

We devoured our sundaes in a few bites and thanked the waitress with the Barbie-pink lipstick smudged on her teeth for serving us so late. She said it was no problem, that her husband was with the baby tonight and that they had been fighting recently.

After hearing that story, Abel suggested we leave, and on the way to his car, says, "How did you manage to get ice cream on your *elbow*? It was in a cup!"

"What do you mean?" I climb into the passenger seat. "You don't make a mess when eating ice cream? You're kind of weird for that."

"You're right," Abel says, turning the keys in the ignition. "Perfection is boring."

I look over at him. "Say that again."

He was clearly joking, but when he sees my narrowed eyes, he swallows noticeably.

"I want to hear you say that again, Mr. Harpen. Come on now."

He sighs and runs a hand through his mostly dry hair. "Sure thing, Dr. Daughtler. Perfection is boring."

"No, no, no." I set my cup in the holder. "You have to look me in the eyes and say it."

"Now you really do sound like my therapist."

"Is she that demanding?"

"She calls me out a lot." He shrugs. "Guess I need it."

I level my gaze at him. "Say it again."

His eyes soften, as does the rest of his face. "Perfection is boring. It's still there, you know."

"What is?"

"Your psychologist self."

I hate when I can *feel* the blush creeping into my cheeks. "I hardly remember anything from school."

"You're telling me that if I pointed to a section of my head, you wouldn't be able to tell me the lobe of the brain?"

"Probably not."

He quirks an eyebrow and points above his left ear. What do you know; I couldn't keep my lips sealed if I tried. "Temporal," I blurt.

"Aha! Let's take a step deeper. What region of the language center?"

"Broca's," I mutter.

He gives me this sad-parent look. "The lack of faith you have in yourself is disconcerting."

"All right, well, that stuff is like riding a bike," I reason. "It's burned into my brain for good. There's no way I could recite all the diagnostic criteria for schizophrenia or something like that."

"That's why we have the *Diagnostic and Statistical Manual of Mental Disorders*, or—"

"*DSM*, I remember."

He chuckles and veers onto the main road.

"I don't think I would've been cut out for a PhD program anyway." I stare out his windshield as the dark silhouettes of trees swoosh by. "Like, sure, I got As in my psych classes, but I averaged a B-plus on most exams. I was never going to pass the GREs like that."

"Screw the GREs," Abel says. "They're dumb."

"Mhm, what was your score?"

"That's not important." I shift uncomfortably in my seat. This conversation is strangling me. Abel notices. "Look, Cari. It's one thing to go into a separate career because you love writing. But please tell me you didn't give up on psychology because you were scared."

His voice is anything but judgmental. It's soft, almost pleading.

"No. I..."

What am I trying to say? That I love writing? (I do). That I hated psychology? (I don't). That I cracked under the pressure of wanting to be like my mom and be perfect—

"Oh." That's all I say. One syllable, one realization.

"What?" Abel asks.

"I'm just like you, but the opposite."

"Huh?"

I glance at him. "Perfection is boring."

His eyebrows furrow. "I'm...sorry. I don't—"

"I felt like psychology would trap me into wanting to be perfect. There's so much competition out there, so much room for error and career-ending mistakes. I didn't want that for myself."

He presses his lips into a line, somewhere between offended and amused. "Did you just poop all over my field?"

"No!" I push at his arm and laugh. "We need strong people like you to be clinical psychologists so that struggling clients can get the help they deserve! I just wasn't cut out for that. Writing is my home. *Poetry* is my home."

He's smiling again. "I love that. I have so much respect for you, Cari Carrington. You are a massive inspiration. But then...I've always thought that."

"What do you mean?"

"Was it not obvious?" He flashes those blue eyes at me. "When we met, I thought you were the coolest person in the universe."

I've learned to take compliments throughout my life, but this is Abel Harpen speaking, so all I ask is, "*Why?*"

"What do you mean *why?* You almost stole my food, and then you told us you were obsessed with the brain, and *then* we found out you were a writer!" I shrug, so he nearly yells, "I don't know *anyone* who just casually writes poetry collections!"

"Well, I..." My blush is probably putting a tomato to shame. "I don't know. I was just...me."

He sighs. "Can I be real with you for a second, Cari?"

I've been dreaming of those words. "Sure."

"You are one of my top-ten favorite people I have ever met."

This is definitely a sugar-induced coma dream. "For real?"

"Yes! One hundred percent."

"But all I do is sit around with a journal."

"No, you're more than that. You're funny and passionate and dedicated. And *way* smarter than you give yourself credit for."

I'm pretty sure the space shuttle is picking up on the vibration of my heart right now.

"Well, you're one of my favorite people on earth, too," I tell him. "I've never met a kinder, more selfless person in my life."

"You're lying."

"Nope. You're my favorite matrix glitch."

He turns slightly toward me as his eyes stay glued to the road. "I'm your what?"

"My favorite matrix glitch," I repeat. "How many guys are attractive *and* nice? Nope, doesn't compute. You're one of a kind."

He blinks, passing headlights reflecting in his eyes. He looks genuinely at a loss for words. Did I just make Abel Harpen speechless? Please don't wake me up from this dream. In the meantime, "Take on Me" kicks through his Bluetooth, and I feel utterly alive.

"Wow, Cari. That was...wow. Thank you." He shakes his head once, and the smile that blossoms on his lips leaves *me* speechless.

"It's the truth," I insist when I recover.

His smile grows.

When we get back to my apartment, Abel kills the engine and accompanies me upstairs like the chivalrous gentleman he's always been. "Here's another reason why you're one of my favorite people," he says when I pull my keys out of my purse.

"Enlighten me."

"You make everyone around you feel special." He's leaning against the wall, grinning down at me. "You're genuine, Cari. That is so rare."

I can't speak for a second because he's caught me in a fishing net, dangling me above the ocean of his eyes. He's so handsome, I think I might combust. "Thank you." I'm not sure if I say it out loud or in my head.

He nods—out loud, then—and straightens away from the wall. "Goodnight."

"Goodnight," I echo, a bit breathlessly.

He turns and walks away. It is *painful* to watch. I feel it in the pit of my stomach, in the bones of my toes, in my eye sockets, and everywhere in between. I want that man. I want him so badly, I entertain the idea of saying fuck it and running down the hall after him. But somehow my feet, damn them, tug me into my apartment. When I close the door, I feel a clamp close around my heart.

How does one deal with being hot and bothered by the mere presence of someone? In my case, lots of charged poetry. I make a cup of chai tea and settle on my favorite cushion with a fluffy blanket and a fresh mechanical pencil. I only write one word before there's a knock at the door.

I groan and leave the comfort of my warm blanket cocoon. I swear to God if my neighbor Dianne's cat got stuck under the bed again—

I freeze when I come face to face with Abel. His expression is rugged, cheeks flushed.

"Abel? What's—"

I don't get to finish my question because suddenly his lips are on mine. Fully and passionately. His large hand is snaking around the back of my neck, and my body is propelled into what I think might be heaven. He moves me out of the doorway and against the wall, pressing his body against mine in a way that is so sinfully delicious, I could pass out from pleasure.

I can feel him—*every* part of him. Is this real? Is he real? Am I real? Is anything real? His lips leave mine only to press against my neck. My moan is embarrassingly loud. Abel takes it as a challenge, tipping my neck back further and dragging his tongue along my carotid artery. My throbbing pulse must egg him on. He kisses a trail down to my collar bone, and my hands burrow under his shirt. His skin is softer than silk; my fingertips graze the defined muscles in his back.

I am going to be so pissed when I wake up from this dream.

Abel's lips find mine again, hot and feverish. Greedy. Desperate. I need them—need *him* closer. We are chest to chest, and it is not enough. I can't think. Can't form full words, let alone coherent thoughts. There's just...

Him.

His burning lips.

His quick, roaming hands.

His broad chest pressing into my lungs.

His shifting hips.

His—

It's gone in an instant. All of him. My eyes flutter open, disoriented, confused, high out of my mind. He comes into stunning focus: a beautiful man with wine-stained cheeks and wide blue eyes. Pinker lips than usual. Neither of us speaks. Because what do you say? Where do you go from here?

"I..." His jaw clenches hard. "I'm sorry."

"Sorry?" My voice is three octaves too high. "For what?"

I smile at him. He turns away.

"I...I shouldn't have done that."

My heart folds in half. It's a new kind of pain.

"I'm sorry, Cari," he insists, turning back to face me. There is fear overflowing in his eyes that makes my chest tighten. "We can't be..."

Together.

He doesn't say it, but the word ricochets in my skull. For the first time in my life, I don't want to look at him anymore. I don't want to look at anything. I want to wake up.

When I don't say anything, he sighs. It's a deep sigh. A regretful sigh. He shifts between his feet for several seconds before deciding to leave, and just like that, he's gone.

I don't move for at least a minute. Or two. Or ten. I can't breathe. He's gone. The open doorway is the chasm swallowing my heart right out of my chest. He's gone.

He's gone.

I slam the door, and when the tears come, I know it's not a dream.

25

———————

Calling all psychologists! Here's a question for you: how is it possible that losing someone can *physically* make the world darker? I'm offering my brain to you. Study my perception; get to it. Find me an answer. Find me a cure.

Here's why I believe my man Murphy was right when he said everything that can go wrong, will. I lose my closest friend (and the man I'm hopelessly in love with), and a few hours later, I have to get up and go to work. An eight-hour shift, which, okay, may not be that bad, except there's a line stretching out Ruth's door. She warned me November is a busy month, but I thought "busy" would just be a few more phone call orders than normal. My first mistake.

As I race around helping Ruth take orders and count change, smoke starts curling from the oven door. Burned cookies. Charred black. Naturally. Ruth is out front, handing a sealed apple pie to a couple in matching flannels. I try to keep my cool, but I think my cool dissipated last night around 11:15 when I was sobbing in the shower. I discard the cookies, retrieve some fresh dough. And, as fate would have it, a costumer decides to be a dick.

Thank you so much, Murphy.

I hear the guy before I see him.

"Twenty-five dollars for a small pack of mint chocolate chip brownies? That's practically robbery!"

I drop the ball of dough on the tray and peek out front. The guy is only five feet tall with straw-like yellow hair and heated brown eyes. Ruth tells him to quiet down.

"You're out of your mind if you think these prices are worth it!" he shouts.

No one steps forward to argue. In fact, the crowd is dead quiet—the power of social influence, am I right? Normally I'd look the other way, too, but I lost Abel Harpen, so the world has become dark. So has my mood. So has my patience.

I march over to the register. Every pair of eyes moves to my face, including Mr. Whiny Pants. Ruth gives me a warning look, but I ignore it.

"Excuse me, sir," I say. "I can't concentrate on baking in the back because your inconsiderate bitching is loud enough to wake a cemetery. Here's a suggestion. If you don't like the food here, don't come here. The place would be so much nicer without your attitude anyway. Now, move along, you're holding up the line."

Not even a cricket would dare to chirp in this silence. The guy slams the box of mint brownies on the counter and strides out.

"How can I help you?" I ask the shell-shocked woman behind him.

Dull murmuring resumes in the crowd, and I can feel Ruth burning bullet holes into my skin with her eyes. That's when I realize, *shit. I am so fired.*

Thanks again, Murphy.

When the last customer leaves, I make a show of washing the mountain of dishes, as if that can make up for my snide comments. Ruth comes to stand next to the sink and crosses her arms. She looks like one of the four horsemen, here to drag me to hell.

"Just let me finish these last couple dishes, and then I will hand in my apron and get out of your hair."

She doesn't answer, which sucks because now I'm forced to look up at her. I can't decipher her expression. I can't even make an assumption.

"Why would you do that?" she says.

I blink. "Um...because I talked back to a customer?"

"Talked back?" She shakes her head. "You *obliterated* a customer —in front of *other* customers."

Cue the self-loathing dread. "I know, but...I can't apologize, Ruth. He was being a complete jerkwad to you—"

"A what—?"

"And I wasn't going to stand there and let him open his mouth like that."

She doesn't tell me to get out of the store or look for a new job. She asks me something I'm not at all prepared for.

"What's going on with you?"

I stop scrubbing butter out of a bowl. "Nothing I'm fine."

"Bull."

We lock eyes. Ruth never so much as hints at a curse word. This is deeper than I thought. There's no escaping my grandma-boss now.

Memories roll back through my brain for the millionth time today. Abel's lips, his body. How *good* he felt pressed into me like that. The searing moment he realized, too, that we can't be more than friends because it would simply end in heartbreak. I gnaw on my lower lip.

"Abel kissed me."

Ruth uncrosses her arms. "The guy from college?"

I nod. "He dropped me off at my apartment last night only to come back, knock on my door, and kiss me. It was *amazing*."

"But?"

My stomach flip-flops. "He stopped and apologized like he made some big mistake. Then, he said, 'we can't.'"

"Can't what?"

"Be together." My throat constricts.

"Then what?"

"He left."

I bite my lip harder, and pain seeps into my skin. It stings, but not as badly as the memories of last night. What a joy physical pain is. It subsides and heals. I would rather get my nipple pierced. I would rather skinny dip in the Arctic Ocean. I would rather a tarantula bite me. Because all of that would be a cakewalk compared to losing someone I love. This is a worst-case scenario. Code red situation. My biggest fear playing out in real time.

"I'm sorry, Cari."

I don't say anything, just continue chewing on my lip.

This is ridiculous. The last time I cried over a boy was in kindergarten, and that was because the prick stole my crayon. I didn't even cry when Kai left! I just scribbled his face out of all our pictures with a red marker while Halsey's "Nightmare" blasted in the background. This is different. *Abel* is different.

"Have you tried texting him?"

"Yes." Twice last night and once this morning. "No answer."

Ruth sighs. "I'm sure if you guys are as close as you say, then he'll come back."

"Doubtful." I dry the bowl and place it in the cupboard—a little too forcefully, but nothing breaks.

"Well, it's not like it's your fault. *He* kissed *you*."

"Which makes it worse, actually," I retort. "Because I know he felt the same way I do but realized that it wouldn't work out."

"If he's right for you, he'll be back."

I roll my eyes, so *not* in the mood for another lesson in fatalism. "Can you just tell me I'm fired already?"

"Why would I lie to you like that?"

I glance over at her, severely confused.

Ruth takes the last dish from my hands and dries it. "I can't exactly fire my favorite employee when all she did was come to my defense. That takes some real courage. Unfortunately, you did mouth off to a costumer though, so as punishment, you're cleaning the floors and bathroom for two weeks."

My lips curl into a smile. "Aye aye, Captain." I untie my apron and hang it on the hook where it belongs. Where it will stay.

"Not again, though, Cari, do you hear me? You're on thin ice." The smile she gives me is 30 percent boss, 70 percent grandma.

"Things I'd Like to Tell You Now"
(By Carrington Daughtler, age 19)

I think about that day often.
The two of us,
separated
by polished wood
and glasses of ice water.
The day you
gave me a tour of your heart
right there
in the middle of the restaurant
and I was
tongue-tied
and cross-eyed,
even brain-tied
because the vulnerability
in your eyes was
more beautiful than
the Northern Lights
at Christmas time.
But it was April when you told me.
I think about that day often.
The two of us,
separated
by one confession.
THE confession
that's been rattling
my amygdala

for eight months:

I'm

in love

with you.

There. I said it.

To a page.

Three hours later.

Next time I say it,

it'll be against

your lips

where the confession belongs.

I was a freshman in college when I wrote this poem. It's in one of my old composition journals that I used to carry around in my backpack just in case inspiration struck. And on that day (the day Abel and I met in the dining hall to study for our psych final but ended up talking about life for an hour and a half), inspiration had been *strong*.

Now the poem just pokes holes through my lungs.

I set the journal aside.

When I was younger, I was obsessed with Kat Stratford from *Ten Things I Hate About You*. I wasn't allowed to see the movie until I was in middle school, but that girl managed to change my whole perspective on life the moment she told Patrick to not think for *one minute* that he had any effect whatsoever on her panties. Classic line. Classic bad bitch. Whenever I was feeling down back in the day, I would just channel my inner Kat Stratford, and life would fix itself.

That's what I need to do now. I have been down in the dumps for too long, and if I spend one more minute here, I might puke. I need to dress up and go out. Not give a fuck. Because with or without Abel Harpen, I am still me. And no man can change that.

26
____

Raquel and I uber to Mount Royal Tavern, a bar with low lighting and a ceiling that replicates the Sistine Chapel's. (Nothing like getting wasted under the eyes of God.) I texted Raquel because I realized that she is my only female friend who actually lives here in Baltimore, and I needed a good old-fashioned Girls Night Out. She'd responded two seconds later with an enthusiastic *Hell yes.*

When the Uber drops us off, my adrenaline spikes to its peak. I feel like a high school mean girl, making my entrance in slow motion with the wind wisping through my hair. Raquel and I walk in, linked arm in arm, dressed like we just left Bergdorf Goodman in New York City. And *man*, do the eyes look our way.

Let me be clear. Girls' Night Out is not about getting drunk or looking for a hot stranger to sleep with. It is about looking good, feeling good, and having fun. Let's normalize *this* definition so that the bad bitches who want to do just that *can* without the fear of being labeled heinous names.

Sheesh, this society, I swear.

It's Friday night, so the bar is crammed wall to wall. Raquel and I have to elbow our way to the counter just to order two shots, and when they arrive, we clink our glasses together and sip the liquor down. I feel bold. I feel beautiful. The fun part about being a light weight? It doesn't take long for the buzz to kick in. I get a lot more social when I've had a few, so thoughts of Abel start to scurry away as Raquel and I mingle.

We meet Leslie, the modern-day equivalent of Princess Aurora with long tendrils of golden hair and a pink thigh-length dress. She's even wearing a tiara.

"It's my twenty-first!" she exclaims, hoisting her shot glass to the Sistine Chapel above.

The place erupts for her.

We meet Keith and Riley, perhaps the most adorable gay couple I have ever had the pleasure of knowing. They tell us they met at the Inner Harbor, Keith pausing to take a photo of the sunset and Riley stopping his jog to gawk at that sunset. Then they looked into each other's eyes for the first time, and...cue the audience *awws*.

We meet Parker, a fully pierced, fully tattooed mountain of a man who owns a pet groomer shop up the street. He shows us pictures of all the cute puppies and kittens he's groomed over the years. We become fast friends.

I also meet Griffin while Raquel is busy flirting it up with Princess Leslie. Griffin has crystal-green eyes and a jawline chiseled by the hand of Zeus. I talk with him (and swoon for him) for all of five minutes before I catch another pair of eyes across the bar. Not just any eyes. Eyes greener and more familiar than Griffin's, with an equally familiar smile underneath.

Griffin notices. "Oh, God. I'm sorry. I didn't realize you had a boyfriend. I would never move in on another man's girl." He turns to face Hunter. "You're lucky, man!"

"No, wait! He's not—" I start, but Handsome Jaw Guy has already disappeared through the crowd.

"Thanks a lot," I tell Hunter when he comes to stand beside me.

I have my back pressed to the bar, so he copies my stance.

"I swear I did not intend to scare away your new man."

"I think I might get a restraining order on you. No one bumps into someone this much. Are you stalking me?"

"Why would I waste my time stalking *you*?"

We grin at each other and sip our drinks.

"Good, because stalking is extremely unsexy and not something to be romanticized."

"Well, then, it's a good thing I'm neither stalking nor romantically interested."

Ah, my friend soulmate. "Speaking of romantic interest," I say, "where's the girl you're taking home tonight?"

"Nice try, but I'm out with the boys."

He gestures to a cluster of men across the bar, and for a split second, my heart sprouts legs, ready to run if need be. *Is Abel here?* Wait, no. That was stupid. Abel doesn't drink. No way he'd be in a bar on Friday night. But then...if he's not here, what *is* he doing? Does it involve putting his head between a girl's legs? *Cari!* I nearly hiss at myself. *Stop with the intrusive thoughts!* Abel doesn't sleep around!

"I've been doing research and writing a paper all week, so I figure I've earned this." Hunter holds up his beer.

Normally I would dry heave at the sight of beer (gross), but the buzz in my brain is pretty good at keeping me chill. "How'd your presentation go on neural implants, Dr. Gatelin?"

He takes a long swallow and licks his lips. "Amazing."

Raquel returns then with a gleaming smile.

"Hey," I say. "Did you get a kiss from the princess?"

"Nah, but I got her number."

She turns to Hunter. "Hate to kick you out, but we're in the middle of a girls' night," she says, pressing her hand to her hip. Queen.

"Were you not just simping over a Disney character?" he asks.

"The girl can do what she wants," I refute.

"And her *name* is Leslie," Raquel adds.

Hunter holds up his hands. "Whatever. You guys are really cramping my style anyway. I should get back to my friends."

"Yeah, to the loser club!" I shout and hold my hand up to high-five Raquel.

She eyes me sadly over the rim of her glass. I clear my throat and high-five myself. Hunter chuckles. "I'll see you guys later."

We leave the bar around midnight, not quite drunk out of our minds but thankfully not sober either. The Uber drops us off at my apartment complex, and after we climb the stairs and I get my door open, Raquel belly flops onto the couch.

"I'm crashing *right* hereee!" she sings.

"Sounds goooood."

The moment I sit down next to her, intrusive thoughts return. What is it about sitting still in a quiet room that allows the dam in my brain to crack and burst? Being buzzed is only fun when you're happy. Now I'm just drunk and sad—a very depressing combo.

"Hey, you good?" Raquel nudges me with her boot.

"Just thinking about...bipolar disorder."

She sits up. "*Why?*"

"'Cause I wish it didn't exist."

"Oh my gosh." She covers her mouth with her hand. "Cari, I had no idea."

"What?"

"How long have you been struggling?"

"No." I laugh, and it sounds squeaky. "I don't have the disorder."

"Oh." She plops back down again. "Then why are you fussin'?"

"I'm talking about *other* people. People who do struggle. Like, imagine having to go through that medication dance, trying to figure out which pills will work and then having to take them. Of having to fear that the next manic or depressive episode could end you up in the hospital!"

Raquel's eyes are so narrowed, I think they're closed for half a second. "Have you been watching *Sixty Minutes* or something?"

"No, I just...worry."

Why am I worrying right now? That's the better question. I should be dancing on the coffee table to some old Katy Perry song, flinging my bra around for the heck of it. Now *that's* what I call a moment of freedom. Freedom from...the fact that I do miss Abel. I can't help it. My Kat Stratford energy only lasts so long. I'm worried if Abel's okay.

Ever since I met him that day in the dining hall what feels like a century ago, I've had this protective instinct for him. Stronger than a Karen looking out for her bubble-wrapped child going to summer camp, but not that controlling. More like, if anyone tries him, I'll kick their ass with a crowbar and blowtorch. Because Abel Harpen is a baby golden retriever frolicking through a meadow doused in sunshine. Consider me the Bubble Wrap.

I don't want to trigger an episode for him.

That is my biggest fear: if the Bubble Wrap starts to suffocate him.

By now, my nails have dug lines in the couch. I need some more tequila—STAT. Raquel doesn't notice my anxiety; she's too busy reaching for the ceiling for no apparent reason.

"I don't know, Cari."

"What do you mean?"

"I've never met someone who gets drunk and worries about people with mental health disorders. You should've been a psychologist."

27

———

"Fun fact about the Megalodon. Its bite can crush a car," Hunter says.

We stare at the outline of its jaw, towering over both of our heads.

"Where'd you learn that?" I ask, not breaking eye contact with the massive teeth that could slice through my skull.

"Google," Hunter answers just as distantly.

"Well, what are we waiting for?" I ask. "Snap a picture of me with my prehistoric killer!"

Hunter steps back and takes a photo of me standing in the Megalodon jaws as I pose with a thumbs-up and a cheesy smile.

A week has passed since Abel and I made out against the wall of my apartment, and I still haven't heard from him. So, when Hunter texted me asking if I was up to spend a Saturday at Baltimore's National Aquarium, I all but thanked him for bringing me back to life.

Hunter shivers. "That's terrifying. I have awful thalassophobia."

"Gesundheit."

"It's the fear of open water, Cari."

"Then why the hecking heck are we at an aquarium, genius?" I snatch the phone from him and laugh at the picture.

"Exposure therapy?"

"You want exposure therapy, let me take you out on a boat to the middle of the Pacific Ocean—"

"No!" I glance over at him. He nervously shovels a hand through his dark hair. "I'm good right here on dry land, thank you."

I shrug. "Can't blame a friend for trying. Just know that I'm inviting you on my next beach trip."

"I would rather have a boil lanced."

I crack up. "That's foul."

We move along so that the little boy behind us can start crying when he sees the jaws and reach for his mother.

"What other weird fears do you have?" I ask.

"Thalassophobia isn't weird. It's common."

"Okay, well, I don't think sasquatch hunting is weird, but I've been judged for that on so many levels."

He peeks at me from the corner of his eye. "You're definitely someone who watches *Finding Bigfoot*."

"All twelve seasons," I confirm. "But you didn't answer my question."

"Okay." He stops to stare at a stingray as it floats on the bottom of a tank. "I'm scared of being buried alive."

"I have a simple solution. Get cremated."

"What, and have my soul watch my earthly body burn? No thank you."

"You're right. How about you just overcome every fatal incident and live forever."

"You want to know what I *hate*?" Hunter asks, ignoring my comment. "TikTok."

I gawk at him, clutching my chest. "Are you even human?"

"I'm more human than the rest of you because I'm not married to my phone."

This is a whole new side of Hunter that is coming to the surface.

He's no longer the reserved, doctorate student that's been my fill-in therapist for all my poetry anxiety attacks. He is lively and opinionated. Emphatic. I *love* it. I feel like an archeologist brushing away dust and soil to uncover the fossil underneath.

"What else do you hate?" I ask.

He presses his lips into a line before saying, "Black Friday. Samsung. January. The color brown."

"Whoa! All this time, I've been hanging out with a secret pessimist!"

"I love a lot more than I hate," he defends.

"Can I get that in writing?"

"Okay, fine. What is something *you* love?" he asks as we cross paths with a particularly massive sea turtle.

"Cheap pickup lines," I answer instantly. "They're hilarious."

"Cheap pick-up lines," he repeats. "All right, what's the cheapest pickup line someone's ever used on you?"

A memory swims into focus in my brain, a memory that stains my cheeks pink and pushes a laugh up my throat. "I took a philosophy class as a gen ed my freshman year of college, and this one time, I sneezed really loud during the lecture. The guy seated on my right leaned over and whispered, I kid you not, 'I would say God bless you for that sneeze, but it looks like he already did.'"

Hunter's eyebrows furrow the tiniest bit before he starts howling.

"He'd never spoken to me before that moment," I get out between my own guffaws.

"What'd you say?"

"I said, 'Thanks, I know.'"

Hunter laughs harder. "I think I can top that."

"You're a cheap pickup line enthusiast, too?" I squeal.

"No, but I've got some game."

"By all means." I gesture for him to proceed.

He shakes his hands out, settling into character, and then he looks down at me—bright-green eyes lined by dark lashes, and...all right. He's not bad-looking from this angle, I have to hand it to him.

"Hey, do you know how much a polar bear weighs?"

I shake my head.

"I don't know either, but it's enough to break the ice. Wanna get a drink?"

I laugh so loud I draw more attention than the freaking fish. Hunter's smiling at me with this proud look on his face, and it's making my sides burn, making tears prick my eyes. It feels so good to laugh from my gut.

"You know, in this hypothetical situation, I might've said yes to that drink, not going to lie."

"What did I tell you? I'm not just some graduate student at UMBC."

"I like this you, Hunter."

"This me?"

"Yeah, this version of you. It's fun. We'll call him...Real Hunter."

"Actually, that's not a proper title because I am the real me in every situation, even when my personality changes based on context. It's called the Working Self-Concept in social psychology, and—"

"Oh, goodie, Dr. Gatelin, thank you for the lesson. I was so intrigued."

He rolls his eyes, but he's still clearly amused. We pause to ooh and ahh at the massive skeleton of the Omega finback whale hanging from the ceiling.

"What's something you love?" I ask after snapping a picture.

"Sunsets."

"Ah, the sentimental type."

"You could say that."

"I promise I'll take you to watch the sunset sometime."

"Only if we can get drinks, too. Platonically, of course," he hurries to add.

"Drinking at sunset sounds lovely," I say.

"Then we'll make it happen."

28

A part of me is expecting the message, and a part of me is not. My phone lies face up on the kitchen table, displaying the four-word text that has my heart both throbbing and sobbing.

Cari, can we talk?

From Abel. 2:38 a.m. I didn't see it until this morning because at 2:38 a.m., I was passed out in bed, dreaming about spotting a Megalodon in the ocean.

I don't know what to do. The obvious answer is to say yes so that I can finally know what he's been thinking this whole past week, but I'm nervous. It will most likely be an apology. A *sorry-but* type of deal that I'm supposed to smile through even though it's going to be the death of all my hopes that we could ever work out. *I'm sorry, but I'd still like to be friends.* Meaning, the make out session was a mistake, and we will never go there again. Am I ready to hear that? Am I ready to accept that? I don't know! What does someone do when they have been in love with a person for six years straight, and the answer turns out to be no?

I feel sick. Do I play bad bitch and send him the *Sorry, I'm Busy* excuse? The problem with that is, deep down, I'm not a bad bitch like that. I couldn't be. Plus, I'm not busy. It's Sunday, and I already cleaned my apartment. Do I send the clueless response with fake cheeriness? *Sure, we can talk! Is everything okay?* The problem with *that* is, everything is far from okay, and we both know that. Plus, this is Abel Harpen we are talking about. I couldn't fool him if I tried.

Ok.

I send it and bite down on my thumbnail. One second becomes a century. Two seconds, and I gain about forty gray hairs. My stomach feels like it is defying gravity and crawling up my esophagus *Exorcist*-style. My jaw is in danger of snapping.

Ding!

My heart triple beats, but I make myself wait and grab a glass of water instead of lunging for my phone. Doing this restores a tiny shred of dignity in my soul, and it almost tricks me into believing I don't care as much as I do. I swallow half the water before allowing myself to look.

Great! Do you wanna meet at Lucky's?

My eyebrows scrunch.

What's that?

A restaurant near the Inner Harbor.

I sigh. Getting friend-zoned under a lavender sky while the turquoise water ripples softly through a sparkling window does not exactly sound like my dream romantic scene. It sounds more like a water painting where the colors *should* be pretty, but really, they are all just smudged and smeared, and the overall picture is actually a quease-fest.

I respond,

I'll see you there.

Then, for no apparent reason other than the fact that I must be having a mild anxiety attack, I clean the apartment again. Undo and remake my bed, organize my closet, which was already color-coded but is now color-coded alphabetically. I even steam my favorite turtleneck for the hell of it, all the while refusing to acknowledge that I am only trying to make myself busy so that I don't think about what my conversation with Abel will entail. But it is playing in my head the whole time like an endless mudslide. *Sorry, Cari, but...*over and over and over again. I consider taking a dose of NyQuil just to knock myself out, but that seems too pathetic, even for me.

Five o'clock arrives too early. I put the address in my GPS and follow it toward the Inner Harbor until I parallel park and walk the rest of the way. Turns out Lucky's is along the stretch of the water where the giant ship floats—the one that looks like it belongs to Jack Sparrow if he ever decided to dock in Baltimore. The sky is not lavender, but rather a deep, dark purple, leaning toward the shade of black licorice. People are everywhere, walking hand-in-hand, talking and laughing, the streetlights and glowing restaurants reflecting in their eyes. I find Lucky's pretty fast because a group of teenagers comes barreling out the door, slapping each other on the back and howling. The sound of sports broadcasters hits me like a tidal wave until my eyes adjust to the low lighting. I blink and see the red velvet booths encased in dark wood, the flat screens floating above the bar, the white and black checkered flooring, Abel sitting near the hostess's podium.

He stands up when he sees me, and I hate myself for how much I want to kiss him. He is wearing a black crewneck—the gold UMBC letters screaming against the dark background—and khakis. On anyone else, it would look blander than unbuttered mash potatoes. But he is a model. Even the light is attracted to him; it glints off his gold hair, making it appear amber. A few small curls dangle over his forehead. The swell of pink in his cheeks is hard to miss considering it contrasts with the sea blue of his eyes. They jump from uncertain to pleading to friendly in half a second. New record.

"Hey, Cari."

"Hi." I am surprised by how chipper my voice sounds because my body feels like a crumbling sandcastle.

Abel tells the hostess two, and I don't miss the way her eyes give me a swift once-over and fly back to Abel—where they stay. She guides us to a booth in the back corner. When I sit down, I immediately feel stuffy and claustrophobic, so I peel out of my jacket. It is just the circumstances. Any other night, this place would have me talking his ear off in a good way.

We spend five minutes perusing the menus in silence because apparently, you can't just come right out and say, *I have zero feelings for you, but we should still be friends.*

My appetite dies with the thought.

"You have to try the onion rings here. They're amazing," Abel says.

I nod, forcing a smile. My fake cheeriness is dissipating fast, and I know he can sense it. His eyes linger on my face for a beat too long.

Our waitress has a flopping brunette ponytail and a voice that is eerily close to Snow White's. "HI THERE! MY NAME'S MINDY. HOW CAN I HELP YOU TWO TONIGHT?" Apparently, Mindy is a shouter, too.

I order a Sprite; Abel goes for water and an order of onion rings.

"SURE THING, CUTIE! BE RIGHT BACK!"

I would have been offended if Mindy was not clearly forty and if her wedding ring hadn't caught the light and nearly blinded me.

When my eyes catch Abel's, I push my menu to the side. It is now or never.

"Abel, I—"

"I want to say—"

We both stop and smile a little. I feel the heat spread from the back of my neck down my arms.

"You go first," I say. There was no concrete thought in my head anyway, other than *let's just get this over with.*

He nods and toys with the paper of his straw, twirls it around his finger as his eyes drop to the dark wood table. After a shallow breath, he says, "I'm sorry I've been MIA." I feel the statement in my intestine. "I just needed some time to figure things out and understand why I...why we..." He gestures vaguely between us. "It was not right of me to disappear on you like that and not respond to any of your messages. I was just...confused."

"Why?" It comes out like an accusation instead of a question.

His lips part and close three times, and his gaze stays glued to the table. He twists the paper straw through his fingers. "I...I've always liked you, Cari."

A submarine crashes into my torso.

"Well...not always romantically," he amends. "We've just been such good friends, and I used to think of you like that. As *just* a friend. But ever since I saw you in the park last month, I realized how much I missed you when you left for New York." He smiles a little. "It was kind of a shock to my system to see you sitting there—first time in two years. And then we started reconnecting, and..." He shakes his head, but his face is all soft and velvet. Happy. "I wanted to kiss you on Halloween, but I didn't know if you felt the same way, and I didn't want to make a fool of myself. I was planning to tell you eventually, but that night in the pool just felt so right, and...Are you okay?"

"I think I'm going to pass out." I press my palms to the cool table, trying to think through the dizzying rush in my brain.

"Here. Drink some water." He slides his glass toward me, and I take a sip to appease his concern.

I really do feel like I am going to black out. There is no way Abel Harpen just confessed that he has feelings for me. I am definitely back in my apartment, drunk on NyQuil and hallucinating. I take another sip of the water to be sure that's not the case.

"You okay?" Abel asks.

"Yup." After a few deep breaths, I will be.

He eyes me cautiously, clearly unconvinced.

"I'm okay," I insist. "Go on."

He stares at me for another minute before nodding. "I should have told you how I felt before forcing that kiss on you. I feel awful for that, and—"

"Don't," I nearly cry. Realizing I'm leaning forward with my hand outstretched to him, I draw back. "I liked it."

My face has never been redder. I can feel it. His eyes widen the slightest bit, but the force of the blue is almost too much to handle. I swallow and glance away. This is not how I expected the conversation to go. If I'm not careful, I might have an excitement stroke and end up in the ER.

His face brightens five notches. "Oh. Well, that's good then." The corner of his lip hitches up. "I still should have said something first. Next time I will."

My body heats. "Next time?"

"If that's okay with you." The look in his eyes makes my stomach heat up until he shifts and leans forward in the booth more conversationally. "I haven't been with someone in three years, not since Camila. I get nervous that I'm not...good enough for certain people. That I can't have a relationship without breaking it in some way. Like, I don't want to snap on anyone."

"How would you snap?" I want so badly to hold his hand, to comfort his sore, scared heart.

"Become manic. Say something or do something bad." His eyes are trained on the straw paper again, but this time, a worry line grooves his forehead. This is something he has really thought about. Something he is actually terrified of. He tries to go on but swallows.

"Abel." I ease the paper out of his hands so that he looks at me. "I've had a crush on you since I freaking met you." He looks startled, so I hurry on. "I was too scared to tell you because I didn't want to lose you. But I care about you too much to ever let you feel like you can't be loved or not allow yourself to love again." He blinks a few times. "I'm not saying we're going to lose each other, but we can't say what the future holds. That's the beauty of it, though."

"How is that beautiful?"

"Because the pain is worth it if it means we can have something that is important to us—for however long it lasts."

His incredulous expression melts into understanding. "What a writer thing to say."

"You got me there."

We grin at each other, and I want to pull him into my arms right now and never, ever let go. It feels like someone just plugged me into an outlet. I'm glowing. I'm floating. It is a wonder we spent eighteen years crawling through our youth before meeting each other. If I thought the world was bright before I met Abel Harpen, I must have been severely blind.

"I really like you, Abel." Six years of weight leaves my shoulders as I say it.

I want him more than a place on the bestsellers list. I want him more than a penthouse overlooking Central Park. I want him more than thousands of Instagram followers. Because even though I am grateful for my place in this world, I have never felt truly happy unless I am with Abel. He has to see that in my eyes.

He does. And as he does, a smile spreads across his face that drowns out the sound of basketball games on the TVs and laughter rushing over from the bar and forks clinking on plates. It drowns out the entire restaurant until there is nothing else but me and him.

As it should be.

I am not a believer in fate...but this kind of makes me want to believe in God.

29

———————

I follow Abel back to his apartment. We stumble through the door, laughing so hard our heads could pop off. On the way upstairs, he showed me a low-quality meme of an overweight raccoon wearing a silver chain with the words *That wasn't very trash money of you* typed below. For some reason, that picture knocked me out. It isn't until I wipe the tears from under my eyes and take a long breath that I acknowledge my surroundings.

Abel's apartment screams Abel. The cream walls are lined with bookshelves (all filled) and the occasional Marvel poster because his little-boy self still aspires to be Iron Man someday. The foyer leads directly into a fairly spacious living room with a black futon couch that sits across from a small flat screen. An Xbox and controller sit on the stand as well, and one shelf down is his collection of games. My eyes move to the wooden coffee table with the model of the brain sitting in the center, and my heart gives a fond squeeze. *Of course* he has a model of the brain there as if to say *this is the most interesting thing in the entire universe.* Behind a makeshift wall of more book-cases, I find his bed. A queen-size with a navy-blue comforter and matching pillows. Made up without a single wrinkle. My body floods with heat, which definitely surfaces in my cheeks. I don't linger here long but just enough to notice the family picture hanging above his bed.

It is a professional black-and-white shot of him sandwiched between his sisters with their parents standing behind them. They are all facing each other and laughing at something I instantly wish I was there to hear. They look so happy. So untroubled.

"Being away from my family is hard," Abel murmurs beside me. "I miss them a lot, so Mom had this printed last Christmas."

My eyes stay on the photo a second longer before I look at him. "Growing up is difficult."

"Not just that," he says softly. "The city is a pretty lonely place."

"I feel like that's an oxymoron."

He laughs. "I just mean that I can be surrounded by people and still feel alone."

My empathy spreads its wings.

I loved Manhattan, and not just because I got to do book signings where the lines stretched out the door. I loved it because everyone was chasing something different together. We were all nobodies trying to be somebodies, trying to form connections so that, just maybe, we could get a small taste of happiness. Of fullness—the kind that lies under your soul like a foundation and keeps you going. Even when I was just a face in an ocean of faces stampeding through the city, I never felt alone because I knew that the people around me had just as much determination firing through their blood. We were all going places. New York has a way of making *everyone* feel important.

But as I stand here looking at Abel's shadowed eyes and slight grimace, I can almost understand what he means.

"You're not alone," I say. It comes out forcefully, like I'm begging him to take the words to heart.

"I know." With a change of tone, he waves the matter away. "Sometimes I just feel down is all."

There is more to that sentence than he is letting on, but I let him drop it and guide me into the kitchen instead.

The dark laminate flooring matches his cabinets. The L-shaped countertops are spotless and stocked in the corner with boxes of 100 percent whole-grain Cheerios and packs of rice cakes, trail mix, kale chips, and what appears to be crispy chickpeas because Abel Harpen goes for healthy. He fixes two glasses of water from his plain old fridge with the magnet from the University of Rhode Island and his sisters' school pictures.

"So, this is what the world of Abel looks like," I say, gesturing vaguely to the apartment and accepting the cup of water.

"Please don't critique it too badly."

I narrow my eyes at him. "There is not a speck of dust anywhere. Come on, fess up. Where are you keeping your maid held hostage?"

He nods to the door on my right. "Closet."

"She better get gourmet meals for doing this good a job."

I expect him to quip back, but he just smiles faintly and guides me into the living room. I understand that it might be a touchy topic. He explained once that when he feels mania coming on, he starts cleaning. Something about wanting to maintain perfection, or at least reach for it in the midst of losing himself.

"When my surroundings are clean, it makes me feel better about the chaos in my mind." He'd told me that over FaceTime on one of my first nights in Manhattan the fall after college graduation. And after that conversation, we drifted apart—him with his master's program and me exploring my new element of being a successfully published poet. I can see his words manifesting now. This apartment really is stunning. It makes me self-conscious about my own apartment.

I flop down onto the futon-couch. "Pretend to be Freud! Psychoanalyze me!"

"Hmmm. He'd probably say that the reason you pursued writing instead of psychology is because you struggled with unconscious sexual attraction to your father but couldn't compare to your mother."

I sit up. "Oh my God. You're right! I *don't* compare to my mother!"

He laughs and swats my feet off the other end of the couch so he can sit. "Freud would also probably find a way to sexualize this coffee table though."

"Do you think he was on drugs?"

"I'm pretty sure he was abusing cocaine, but don't quote me on that."

"What a man."

Sitting here with Abel reminds me of all the nights I spent in his dorm room watching *SpongeBob* and laughing so hard the popcorn spilled out of the bowl, forcing Abel to retrieve a vacuum to clean our mess up before his roommate returned. On those nights (typically Fridays if we didn't have an exam the next week), we would forgo the school talk and the family talk and just enjoy each other's company. Cry-laughing like two outrageous twenty-year-olds high on life and without a care in the world.

That's when I see it.

"Oh my God," I blurt, springing off the futon and lunging for the scrapbook lying on the bottom shelf of his TV stand. "I forgot about this!"

Abel scratches the back of his neck, his blossoming smile bashful.

I sit back down with the scrapbook clutched in my hands. *To Our Lovebug, Abel,* it reads in white, sticky foam letters across the front, and underneath, a picture of his senior college photo—pristine tux, perfectly wavy hair, a thousand-dollar smile.

His mom made this for him as a graduation present. She had just started seeing a new therapist and was on new medication, which seemed to be helping tremendously until a week before the ceremony, when she figured she was better and decided to quit the meds. That next week, she was in the hospital, missing Abel's graduation. Luckily, she'd finished the scrapbook before then, but I remember trying to lift Abel's spirits as we posed for pictures in our caps and gowns. It is a sad thing, but this scrapbook proves how much she really does love her son. And he keeps it close because he loves her, too.

I had looked through the book with him at his party that night after graduation, but I haven't seen it since.

"Let's take a walk down memory lane, shall we?"

"Start with page fifteen. That's thirteen-year-old me in my underwear with suspenders and a top hat."

"Don't worry, we'll get there," I promise.

Behind the cover is a picture of Abel as a baby, staring wide-eyed up at the camera with blinding blue irises and a smile that could melt a pat of butter. He is captured clapping his tiny, precious hands together. A letter accompanies the photo:

Abel,

Your momma and dadda are so very proud of you. We have watched you grow from an adorable infant into a kind, selfless, smart, loving man who is not afraid to chase after his dreams. You are a blessing to this world and a light for everyone around you. Never change, son.

With buckets of love, Momma Bear and Daddy

I glance at Abel.

"I used to call my mom Momma Bear because it made her laugh." He reminds me, failing to hide a smile.

"That is the most wholesome thing I have ever heard in my entire life."

His cheeks pinken. "Thank you."

The book is a time capsule for his entire life up until this point. The early pages are a collection of his elementary school days when he was briefly obsessed with *Star Wars* and Heelys—the sneakers with the rollers on the heels. There he is, pictured mid-motion as he rockets down the driveway in those shoes, toes pointed up toward the sky, hand raised in a half-hearted wave. There is a picture of him on Christmas morning, cradling a green lightsaber to his chest. As I flip through the pages, those lightsabers turn into Iron Man action figures and photos of Abel posing with his baby sisters—first Charlotte, then, a couple pages later, Melanie. After that, the pages pay homage to the *three* of them: Abel on the living room floor with his little sisters climbing over him like he's a jungle gym. Abel hugging his sisters beside their freshly-decorated, ginormous Christmas tree. The three of them with pink, green, and white blobs of ice cream in waffle cones outside a sixties-looking ice cream shop.

In every one of those pictures, Abel's eyes are sparkling. He looks happier than I have ever seen him. He was probably ten or twelve then.

"I love this one," he says, pointing to the photo on the next page: a family picture of the Harpens in front of *The Pirates of the Caribbean* ride in Disney World. "Mom dared Dad to wear an eyepatch and pirate hat." Indeed, Mr. Harpen is all decked out in pirate attire, could even pass for a Disney actor if he had ditched the khaki shorts and *First Time in Disney* T-shirt.

"Ah, here it is," I squeal, flipping the page. "You should wear suspenders and a top hat to defend your master's thesis."

"And go in my underwear, too?"

"They'd remember you, guaranteed."

He chuckles. "I'll keep it in mind."

The next picture is his freshman year school picture: pressed blue and white button-down, hair a mountain of waves on top of his head, angular cheeks. Even with braces, he looks like a young movie star.

I whistle. "All the girls must have had a crush on you."

"Most did. It was kind of annoying actually. I couldn't really have any female friends because a lot of them started rumors that I liked them back. Well, except for one."

"Is this a little-boy crush I'm hearing about?"

His face warms again. "When I was fifteen, I had a massive crush on a girl named Whitney. She was in my biology and algebra classes, and we always sat together."

My dopamine levels jump at the thought of Abel having a crush. It's like reading a good book where the author finally spoon-feeds you more information about a character's past, sheds more light on what makes them *them*.

"Please tell me you asked her to homecoming."

"Derek Longleman beat me to it. They actually dated for the rest of high school, and I think they're even still together now."

"I'm sorry."

"Don't be." He laughs. "It was nine years ago. Plus, she didn't talk to me after..."

He trails off, which is okay. I know what "after" means. *After* his first manic episode—the one that landed him in the hospital and in hot water on the high school popularity food chain.

"Nobody really talked to me after that," he murmurs.

"Their loss."

This brings a smile back to his face.

We continue down memory lane together, even though his first episode is getting closer and closer. There's a photo of him with three other boys.

"Mason, Rine, and Nick," Abel explains, pointing them out from left to right. "My best friends." My arched eyebrow asks the question my mouth doesn't. "Mason was the only one who stayed. It's why *he* is my best friend to this day."

The next picture is of seventeen-year-old Abel lounging on the couch in red Christmas tree sweatpants. He's smiling, but the smile appears to be painted on. Otherwise, he looks absolutely drained. Beside me, Abel's head drops for a moment before he looks away.

This must be it.

"First episode?" I ask gently.

"A month after, but...yeah." He's not even upset for himself. He is upset because of how his mother reacted to the knowledge that her son had developed bipolar disorder, too. Hurting her was the last thing he ever wanted to do.

It is a risky question, but I have to know. "What do you think triggered it?"

He laughs without humor. "Genetics." He raises his eyes to mine. "But...Rine had also gotten in with a bad crowd. Did a full personality one-eighty. I think he was jealous of me or something because he started spreading rumors that I went behind his back and had sex with his girlfriend, which I would *never* do."

"I know you wouldn't, Abel."

He takes a deep breath. "So, I lost a lot of friends because it was high school, and everybody has to believe everything they hear. Guys called me names. Girls only wanted to have sex. Nobody really cared about me, and I guess...that's what triggered my mania. Losing my friendships and my reputation."

My jaw could split in half for how tightly I'm clenching it. I am not a violent person, but this story makes me want to shove all the people who hurt him into a frozen meat locker and swallow the key. How could *anyone* bully Abel Harpen? It defies all logic.

"I'm sorry," I whisper.

"The bullying got worse once the mania started because I couldn't shut up, and I got myself into a lot of trouble saying things I shouldn't have. I was sent home one day after I shoved Rine up against a locker. Dad and I started arguing back at the house, and I threw a punch, and... that's when Mom started crying." He pauses to take a shaky, grounding breath. "Next thing I knew, I was in the hospital. Mom had called 911."

I blink back thick, heavy tears. "You don't deserve any of that pain."

He is frozen for a full minute before heaving another large breath and trying for a smile. That's Abel, though. Smiling through the negativity. His eyes meet mine.

"It turned out okay in the end."

He gestures for me to continue flipping through the scrapbook, and a few pages after his high school graduation, I see myself. We are standing in front of the Fahrenheit rollercoaster at Hersheypark, its infamous drop looming over us. He's giving a thumbs-up, and I'm grimacing cheek to cheek. Luckily, we'd both survived the ride.

The next couple pages are of us at Abel's house for the holidays or riding our bikes in the cul-de-sac in front of his house during the blazing summers. There's the time we took Charlotte and Melanie to the Roger Williams Park Zoo. There's the selfie Abel took with me, Kelsey, and Noah in the theater when we went to see *Us*—the doppelgänger horror by Jordan Peele that had me avoiding mirrors for at least a week. There's a picture of Abel gazing into Camila's eyes, the two of them looking so in love, I'm getting a secondhand high. Pictures of Abel with his brain model, and a picture of him in his black cap and gown, golden tassel moved proudly to the right. A photo of him with his sisters and father at the ceremony. Of Kelsey and Noah hugging his waist and fake crying. Of me crying real tears in his arms. It is the last picture in the scrapbook. Another note accompanies it:

Little Lovebug,

Your parents are so proud of you. You have wonderful friends and a wonderful future ahead of you. Never lose sight of who you are, son. Go out there and show the world the love it is desperately missing. Your family will always have your back.

Love you endlessly,

Momma Bear and Daddy

"Are you crying?"

"How are you *not*?" I demand, wiping my runny nose with the back of my hand.

Abel reaches for a tissue and hands it to me. He doesn't even lean away when I obnoxiously blow my nose like a horn. I remember crying the first time I looked through this scrapbook, too. It is the most precious mother-father-son gift in the world.

Abel sighs and leans back on the futon, folding his hands in his lap.

"You know, Cari Carrington, you are the only person besides my family who has seen this scrapbook."

I look at him, astonished. "Really?"

He nods. "You're one of my best friends."

"Best friends," I confirm, flopping down into his lap like a giddy child.

We have always been physically affectionate like this. There were times in college when I would hang on his arm because I was bored or worried about a psych exam or presentation. Abel even let me hang on him and sniffle all over him when I was sick. Never complained once.

This physical contact feels stronger than that friendly sibling love though. He has just removed the last of his armor for me, and now I can see him piece by shimmering piece. I stare up into his beautiful eyes and lose myself there. Lose my breath. Lose every thought I've ever had. His smile slowly fades as his eyes grow...what? Hungry? Desperate? Who cares—it doesn't need a label. His lips part slowly, and I vaguely register that his face is moving closer to mine. As mine leans closer to his.

He stops just before our lips touch, and I taste his breath instead. Somehow, it is minty, and I wonder if he chewed some spearmint gum on the way back here. He blinks, taking my breath away until his eyes are open again.

"Cari," he whispers. Every fiber of my being hangs onto his voice. "Can I kiss you?"

For an answer, I close the distance between us because I need to. That tiny shred of space was killing me.

He takes my bottom lip in his for a brief moment, flicks his tongue across it, pouring kerosene onto my heart and lighting a match. More distance as we break apart. His minty breath washes across my face once more. It was a whisper of a kiss. I need more.

So does he. When our lips meet again, it is fierce and rushed, fire on fire, feeding the flames in our bellies. I sit up and straddle him, which makes me feel like I'm not even in my body at all. The sensation leaves pinpricks in my fingers.

"Is this okay?" Abel breathes.

I inhale through my nose. I can't even open my eyes to look at him. I'm afraid if I do, I might have a heart attack or a seizure. *It's just the nerves*, my brain whispers. *You're okay, deep breaths.* I will the feeling back into my fingers. I don't want to lose this moment to the anxiety of losing Abel or the fear he won't like me if he sees me. I want to be here: skin, nerve endings, heart, and all. I want two feet on the ground with my fingers in his hair. I want to burn this moment into my mind, brand it there. Leave it there. Where it belongs.

Slowly, I open my eyes. The intensity of his concerned gaze hits me like a taxi cruising down a street in New York City.

"Cari?"

"I'm okay," I murmur. "I just...I want you."

He understands immediately. His forehead touches mine and he nods.

"Good. Because I have never wanted anything so much in my life."

He stands, holding me in his arms like I weigh nothing, and carries me to the bed behind the bookshelves.

30

———

"I'm clean, just so you know," he tells the hollow in my neck, but I forget his words as soon as he kisses me there.

His tongue trails a line all the way up to my ear, and when he catches my lobe in his teeth, I moan so loud it is a wonder the neighbors don't start pounding on his door to say, "I have kids! Keep it down!" His fingers dig into my thighs, welcoming a rush of heat between them. Our shirts disappeared the moment he sat me down on the bed, and now I'm working at his belt like if I don't remove it in the next thirty seconds, both of us will disintegrate.

"Cari, let me get a—"

"I'm on the pill." I slink his belt through the loops of his jeans and throw it on the ground.

I yank his jeans off and grunt in frustration when they get caught lopsided on his hips. He chuckles and kisses my forehead, easing the jeans off the rest of the way himself. Meanwhile, I've shimmied out of my own jeans. He climbs on top of me, and I taste those sweet lips again. Our tongues dance together; our fingers intertwine. He's hard between my legs, and I'm tired of waiting. That's the moment I lose my panties, and I all but tear his boxers off him.

When he touches me (*finally*), my back instantly arches. It's my heart, no doubt, pounding its fists against my ribcage and forcing my chest up to the ceiling. I don't think I've ever moaned louder. This could be a poem. I feel myself slipping into verse—free verse because the way he's touching me is too poetic to be crammed into a strict sonnet or haiku.

"Cari," Abel pleads. "I need you."
And
that's
when
I
feel
him.

Sour first
like squeezing lemon juice
onto my unsuspecting taste buds:
stings
but fucking breathtaking,
and we're drunk
(happily)
on a carousel,
colors
twisting and melting
under the hot November
moonlight.
Up and down.
Up
and
down.
Swallowing swear words
has never tasted so good.
Sweet now
like cherries

in a shared Shirley Temple:
good
and fucking breath-taking.
A mouth full of
tongue and teeth
and dirty whispers
sits on the record player
in the corner of
the carousel,
spinning
on full volume.
I turn it up louder.
The ground shakes.
Or is that just my legs?
I turn my face
up to the clouds,
and it starts
to downpour:
warm
and fucking breath-taking.
I smell his skin
like mint,
like coffee—
distinct
and savory.
It bleeds
into my skin,
leaving a mark
on my neck.
I'm tripping
down the carousel steps
into a lap
of open legs
and open arms of

desperate hands.

They reach inside me

all the way

to my combusting heart.

Squeeze once.

Twice.

Third time's a charm.

It breaks free,

enclosed in his dripping fingers,

and escapes my chest

in one quick thrust.

It belongs to

him

now.

But did it ever

really belong

to anyone else?

The downpour continues.

When Abel pulls out of me, my body instantly feels too empty. My hands feel too shallow. My tongue feels too cold for my mouth. He lies beside me, digging his fingers through his disheveled hair.

"That was...."

"Amazing?" I supply.

He exhales. "No, better than amazing."

I feel myself smile.

Six years of wishing, of deciding whether or not to let him go, and here we are: legs intertwined under his navy-blue comforter.

"We should go again," he says. "I like making you feel good."

"Really?" I must sound astonished because he looks over at me. "I'm not used to hearing that."

The first time I had sex was in high school. It was with the captain of the boys' lacrosse team: Justin Outlynder. But I didn't care about lacrosse. I liked him because he was tall, brunette, and knew how to finger me something fierce. We did it for the first time in his bedroom while his mom was downstairs cooking us a homemade pizza. The sex was sloppy and, to be completely honest, a disappointment. He wasn't as big as the girls' locker room gossip said he was. Every time we had sex after that, it was because we were bored.

Kai was a different story. Dating him was like secretly learning how to be a porn star. We did it in the shower, on the pool table in his den—pretty much every flat surface in his apartment and mine. But he was all take, no give. In the year that we dated, he only made me finish *once*, and that was because he wanted something to brag about to his country club buddies.

So, hearing Abel say that he *likes* giving me pleasure is a whole new ballpark entirely.

"The fact that you aren't used to hearing that makes me die a little on the inside," he says. "You are amazing, and you deserve everything."

I stare at him, stunned speechless. He gives me that charming smile that's tinged with innocence because despite the blush-inducing things he just did to my body, Abel is still an angel who can't pass up an opportunity to be kind. It has me pushing him back down onto the pillows and straddling him—a new angle that I am immediately obsessed with.

I lean down and kiss him slowly, trying to commit the taste to memory. I'm a detective, uncovering what makes his chest rise faster, what makes his breath shorter, what makes him whisper my name. I familiarize myself with his neck and his fingertips and his hips, feeling my heart accelerate each time he groans. It's never loud though, always brief and cut off as if he loses himself for an instant but quickly reels it back in. I don't like that. I want him to let go.

At first when I take him in my mouth, his eyes pop open.

"Cari?"

I look up at him from under my eyelashes. "Yes?"

"You don't have to do that."

"Do you not like it?"

"No, I—" Pink floods his face. "I do, but I don't want you to do something if you're not comfortable just because I like it."

Oh, Abel. The kindest of the kind. "Who said I don't want to do it?"

Before he can respond, I go down on him again.

I learned what makes a good blowjob over Cobb salads with Katerine last May. She'd been experimenting at the time with Ben, and her description was *very* detailed, per usual. I figured she was just exaggerating until I tried the tricks on Kai, and what do you know. It was a slam dunk.

Abel seems to agree.

I can practically see the restraints breaking loose in him. He digs his fingers into my hair, silently begging, and I comply until a groan tears out of him so intensely, for a moment, I think I hurt him. But then I see the glaze in his eyes and watch his jaw go slack.

I don't let him finish in my mouth. I climb on top of him instead, grinding until I'm just a chorus of cuss words with his accompaniment of groans. His hands lock on my hips, and he holds me down against him. I'm screaming his name. I've never screamed a man's name during sex. This isn't poetry anymore; it's erotica.

When he reaches down to touch me, it catapults me over the edge, and I'm gone. The feeling is so powerful, I nearly black out. All I know is that we're both moaning into each other's ears—loudly unfiltered the way we should be. No restraints, no armor, just skin on skin and the most intense pleasure I have ever felt.

When it's over, I don't bother moving. I like him inside of me; it makes me feel whole. He doesn't move either. He just wraps his arms around my waist, rests his head on my chest, and takes the moment to breathe.

Yes, sex with Abel is (as I've just learned) *absolutely incredible*, but *this* is the cherry on the cake. Holding him, resting my cheek on his hair, and running my fingers through it. Cradling him to me, where I can protect him from all of life's demons.

31

"Something's up with you," Ruth says. She's standing in the threshold of the bathroom, watching me twirl around with a mop. "Nobody's this excited when they're cleaning a public bathroom."

"What do you mean? I love inhaling sewage and stale urine. It's my favorite thing in the world." Correction: it is a *tolerable* thing now that I know what Abel's bed feels like in the morning.

The man even made breakfast: waffles with whipped cream and sliced strawberries for me, a dippy egg and smeared avocado on toast for him. "Waffles and eggs," he'd said, "are two of the only things I can reliably make." I swear, sometimes it is just not fair that Abel Harpen exists. He is the universe's proudest creation.

"This isn't a proper punishment then," Ruth says, crossing her arms over her purple apron.

"You can't break me," I swath suds across the gray tile. "Might as well just cancel the punishment altogether."

"And what would that teach you about mouthing off to customers?"

"You mean defending and standing up for what I believe in?"

"Now you're just splitting hairs."

I dip the mop back into the bucket of soapy water, but in my head, I still feel Abel's arm draped over my body. The sunlight leaking through the blinds. The chill racing up my naked body when he kissed me awake. That's called waking up in heaven.

"Trust me, Ruth. I'm walking on air."

She eyes me up and down, but her graying gold curls and *There's so Much to be Thankful for!* sweatshirt do not make the look intimidating at all.

"Make sure he's using a condom," she says as she turns to leave.

I choke on my spearmint gum. "W—how did you know? He is by the way. *Did,*" I correct myself.

Ruth stops in the doorway and laughs. "Child, I was young once *and* I have a daughter. Just do me a favor and promise you're being safe."

"We are."

I love my grandma boss—*adore* her—but sex is not something I discuss with people over the age of forty. Not since Mom sat me down when I was ten and explained how a Mommy has an outlet and a Daddy has a plug. *Shivers! Cringe! Enough!*

"How is your daughter?" I blurt out, desperate for a subject change. "I mean...have you heard from her?"

Ruth's smile ebbs like an ocean wave. "Nope. As far as I know, Amber's still living in a townhouse in Connecticut with my granddaughter Mia. I don't know if she moved or if she...met someone. I always get this sliver of hope around the holidays that maybe she'll call. Maybe she'll finally give me a second chance, you know?" Ruth studies her purple nail polish.

"Why don't you call?" I suggest lightly.

"So she can ignore me? Absolutely not. That would tear me to shreds. It has been bad enough for the past thirteen years."

I sigh and lean my mop up against the wall. "I know it's scary. My mom and I hardly talk. Right now, she's probably still wishing I'd gone to graduate school to get my master's and PhD, and it crushes me. I was never going to be a great psychologist. But...I also still have this nagging want for a mom. I want to be closer with her, but I don't know how to be."

Something in Ruth's eyes changes. She watches me resume mopping, the swish of the water and mop the only sound between us.

"I'll make you a deal," she says eventually.

"I don't make deals anymore. Not since New Orleans."

"I'm not even going to ask what that means. Look, Cari. I think you're right. We can't keep running from what we want most. If I call Amber, you have to call your mom."

The mop comes down a little harder than necessary on the floor. It's my crash from cloud nine. "No way."

"Why not?"

"She annoys the hell out of me. If I called her, she'd just find a way to turn the conversation into a guilt trip or a hundred questions about if I've been looking for graduate programs anywhere else besides UMBC."

"Carrington, I'm sure a PhD program is not all your mother cares about."

"You haven't met her."

Ruth takes a step forward. "What's her favorite song?"

"Excuse me?"

"What's her favorite song? Favorite color? Favorite season?"

My eyebrows pull together. "'Like a Virgin' by Madonna, green, and spring, but how does that have anything to do—"

"So she's *not* a one-dimensional cartoon character who's only obsessed with psychology. Imagine that."

I narrow my eyes at her. "Very clever."

Ruth shrugs with that little triumphant crook in her smirk. "The offer is still there. I want to call my daughter, and I know you want to call your mom."

She knows she has a point.

I chew on my lip, dipping the mop back into the bucket. "I'll think about it."

Ruth sighs. "Good. Don't forget to wash your hands at least five times when you're finished in here."

32

"So, I'll be in Baltimore on the eighteenth to stay with Meg. We should go out and get a drink! You, me, Meg, and Abel."

"You know Abel doesn't drink," I tell Kelsey, switching the phone to my other ear.

"He can order a club soda for fuck's sake. I miss you guys."

"We miss you, too."

I have not mentioned to Kelsey yet that Abel and I slept together because I'm worried she'll get so excited that her skull will burst open and colorful confetti will rain down where blood should be.

"Don't forget Friendsgiving is that next Monday. Noah texted and said he'll be there on Sunday night." Kelsey is using her mother-boss tone now.

"Yes, ma'am. And don't forget that I'm bringing my friend Raquel."

"Right!" Muffled conversations sound from the other end of the phone. "Okay, I've gotta run. Some customers just walked into the store, and they look like they came from old money. Love you!"

She doesn't give me a chance to respond.

"Who was that?" Hunter asks after a brief stretch of silence.

"That," I say, taking a sip of my Frappuccino and setting it back down on the table, "was our hostess for Friendsgiving. Abel invited you, right?"

"Yep." Hunter turns to look at the stranger who has just entered Starbucks and brought a rush of cold wind in from outside.

"Enough chit chat," I say. "What did you think?"

"Stomach Pain" is a poem I wrote yesterday evening after I got off work. I had been thinking about what Ruth said: how she is sure my mother isn't a flat stencil drawing of a person, and that lead to me obsessing over what it means to be liked. No one is one-dimensional.

Hunter's green eyes flick to mine. He leans forward, placing his elbows on the table. "This was the best poem you've ever written."

I transform into a four-year-old in the Barbie section at Toys R Us: I squeal at the top of my lungs. Hunter laughs and awkwardly catches the eyes of the coffee-goers around us.

"I knew it!" I slap my palms down on the table. "I had a good feeling about this one!"

"It can still be better, so don't let your ego get too inflated. But," he smiles, "this one was amazing."

I take my journal from him and reread my own work.

"Stomach Pain"

To be liked
is to have a
cherry-pink heart
and strawberry soul.
Red roses for dimples,
mind easily controlled.
A Picasso of a body
and Jesus-like manners.
A rainbow of a brain
that's humble in the glamour.
Sweetheart goddess

with the minuscule mouth
who doesn't shout
when his hand goes south.
Who's just the right amount
of shyness
and honesty.
Though honestly,
that could never be me.

I grin at Hunter. "How much should I start paying you for taking time out of your day to read my poems and offer beautiful criticism?"

"Zero dollars and zero cents."

"Oh, come on," I argue as he takes a sip of his drink (just a normal coffee with some cream and sugar—he's so lame). "You deserve *something*. You have your own life with your own goals of becoming a neuroscientist, and yet you're here. That deserves at least twenty an hour."

"I'm here because I like to read your poetry, Carrington. And for the self-esteem boost of saying I'm friends with a published poet."

"Ah, there it is."

"Seriously. You don't owe me a thing."

"But—"

"I have a question for *you*," he interrupts.

"Okay."

"How's the self-exploration going?"

Huh. With all the writing and the baking and the ruminating over sex with Abel and the silly text chains we've had since I have not taken a moment to reflect. It is a skill I am pretty good at though. When I was a young girl, Mom taught me how to analyze my emotions.

Step one: acknowledge with labels. Right now, I'm feeling pretty upbeat. I wrote a great poem, the sun is gleaming, and Abel likes me. All is good.

Step two: list physical feelings. My chest feels light and airy. I have the childlike urge to jump in a colorful bouncy house. My cheeks hurt from smiling.

Step three: thank the emotion and move on ("This," Mom used to say, "will keep you from dwelling on it.") *Thank you, happiness! It's been a pleasure, as always!*

"I feel like I'm coming into myself," I tell Hunter. "I know what makes me tick and what makes me laugh. I feel very grounded in my body."

"Meaning...."

"Meaning I've been present these last couple weeks. I'm fully aware of how I feel. It's nice."

"That's amazing." His smile is almost as big as mine. "It's incredible that writing gives you so much insight."

"I mean, it's no research on neural implants."

"You're right. It's way more interesting."

I swat at his arm. He chuckles.

"Speaking of, I have to get going. I'm meeting with my advisor."

"Ooh, about new research? What's the topic this time? Neurogenesis? Impact of addiction?"

"Blood flow and neural activity."

"Sounds like you're in the big leagues now, kid."

"Yes, and sometimes the workload makes me want to die, but it'll be worth it in the end."

"When you save a life."

"When I save a life," he confirms.

With that, he swallows the rest of his coffee, tosses the cup in the recycling, and tells me to have a great rest of my day. He's off to go conduct research and strengthen the mental health field. I love him for that.

33

IF THERE WAS A CATEGORY ON *JEOPARDY!* CALLED *THINGS ABEL Likes that No One Would Ever Have Guessed*, $500 would be What are Hallmark Christmas movies? Because yes. The man adores a good romantic holiday cliché. Well, all right. It's more about the Christmas decorations and sense of family and adorable, friendly puppies, but I like to poke fun. Here we are on my couch (on my favorite squishy cushion), bundled up in a fuzzy blanket, watching Hallmark's newest reinvention of the same old tropes.

Girl goes home for the holidays—back to Small Town Nowhere where everyone knows everyone, and this is the first time she's been back in years. Since her dad passed away that one Christmas. Now she has to meet the new man her mom has allowed herself to fall for and reconnect with that old crush she had as a young girl even though "the love of her life" is waiting for her back in the city. Turns out, Childhood Crush has actually grown into quite a hunk and is still living in Small Town Nowhere, taking care of the restaurant that his parents used to own. Our protagonist gets snowed in with Old Crush, a flame is rekindled, and next thing you know, she chooses him, and they get married however many years later around Christmas time, which she has now come to love and appreciate again.

If you couldn't tell, I have never been a fan of Hallmark Christmas movies. Abel, on the other hand, has the warmest smile on his face.

"They're a big, happy family again." He doesn't break eye contact with the screen.

"It was inevitable," I reply, patting his knee.

The credits roll, and in five seconds, another movie begins. Same concept, different faces and places. This story opens at an outdoor ice rink, complete with snow-topped pines, gloves and stocking hats, and a hot chocolate stand. I'd rather watch *The Grinch* (the Jim Carrey version because what other version?), but I can't pass up an opportunity to see Abel glow like this.

"My parents used to take us ice-skating all the time," he says. "It's my mom's favorite holiday activity."

"My mom's favorite holiday pastime is caroling, believe it or not. She's this stoic woman with all her patients but put her in a Santa hat in front of some strangers, and she'll sing a mean 'Jingle Bells.'"

Abel laughs. "My mom took us caroling once. Melanie was still a baby, and she started crying at the first house. It was hilarious. None of us can sing at all. My dad was so off-key that this one couple gave us extra cookies and told us to take a break and eat. Priceless! My mom though, let me tell ya. She never got tired of seeing the people smile." His face lights up. "And Dad never complained once either, even though it was only, like, twenty degrees out. I have that most amazing parents in the world."

My heart smiles. "I'm happy to hear you say that."

"Well, you know. My mom is my mom. She's incredible but... complicated. Did I ever tell you she had me when she was sixteen?"

My jaw drops. "No, you didn't."

Abel nods. "She and my dad went to high school together, and apparently, she was having a manic episode when she got pregnant with me. Yeah, she was sixteen and Dad was seventeen. They could've given me up for adoption, but they kept me.

"The first couple years of my life were great, and I honestly think that's because Mom worked so hard to stay on her pills and go to therapy. She didn't want me to see her during an episode. But...that changed when I turned four. Mom was a college dropout, but she'd gotten a job as a waitress at a diner near our old house—my grandparents' house—and Nanna and Pop were always super supportive. One night, though, she came home *screaming* about this table she waited on. They didn't give her a tip, and she was going on and on like, 'I fake a smile for these effing idiots all day, and they're ungrateful! I take on more hours, but it's useless! Everything's useless!'" An echo of Abel's fear shows in his eyes. "She wouldn't stop talking. My grandparents couldn't calm her down. My dad lived a few minutes away but was out working that night. It's like Mom was...a whole different person. I'd never seen her act like that."

I have to admit it is hard to picture Abel's mother acting out and screaming. It's something I have never witnessed. Every time I've been around, Mrs. Harpen's just had a book in her hands. Of course, it's not surprising that I can't picture it either. The people who struggle the most tend to hide it the best.

"My grandma found out that Mom had stopped taking her pills. She practically dragged my mom into the kitchen and stood there until she took a dose. It was the first time I realized that my mom was sick, and each time after that...her mood swings made a lot more sense.

"It's not necessarily rapid cycling," Abel explains. I remember suddenly that rapid cycling is the experience of mania multiple times in a single year. "But sometimes Mom would come home with this *crazy* energy. She'd get in at like one or two a.m., and I'd hear her arguing with my grandparents in the living room. To my grandparents' credit, they never threw her out. They were supportive and patient through all her hospital visits, all her episodes. I think they're the reason Mom tried so hard to be a good model for *me*.

"She always tried to tuck me in at night, always asked me how school was. Never took any of her anger out on me. When I was a teenager, she told me I'm the thing that always brings her back. That always makes her want to get better again."

I fidget with the fuzzy blanket as he speaks. Mrs. Harpen was not perfect, but she tried her hardest to be there for her son, and that speaks volumes about her character.

"She and my dad got married when they were twenty-four. They've been married *sixteen* years. Isn't that incredible?"

It really is. I run my tongue over my teeth, thinking through all that he's told me. "So, your dad stayed in the picture the whole time."

"Never left my mom's side." Abel resituates on the couch to face me fully. "He took on three jobs after Mom had me. Quit the wrestling team and everything just to support us. I won't lie and say watching someone else have an episode is a cakewalk. Mom got on my nerves a lot, and I did so much to distract Charlotte and Melanie while Mom went to the hospital, but my dad has been through more of her cycles than I can count. He stays calm during her mania, checks her into hospitals, worries himself sick that she'll be okay. I don't know how he does it."

My fingers twist around the blanket as he continues—Hallmark drones on in the background.

"It's hard...choosing to love someone who is struggling with a mental health disorder. It's not a physical wound that you can just put Neosporin on and watch heal. It's an everyday battle that gets better and worse constantly. But...it's not *impossible* either—loving someone who's struggling. Education is the most important thing in my opinion, along with patience and understanding. Understanding that it's not *them*, it's the intrusive thoughts or the paranoia or the desire to feel something other than medical-induced numbness." He gestures emphatically with his hands. "Trust is a big thing, too. Being someone the person can trust and talk to. I guess the biggest thing, though, is knowing when to take a break to protect your own mental health."

I nod, remembering when Mom had to go to work trainings on the importance of self-care.

"A lot of times after Mom gets back from treatment, my dad goes to stay at his parents' for a few days to decompress and recollect himself. But he always comes back. He says he can't imagine life without my mom. She...shows him the beauty in life and family. And the way he sees it, mental illness is just a way to make us stronger and kinder. Honestly, I wish more people would be like my dad. That way, people who *are* struggling might not feel so alone."

I wish I could take his words and surgically implant them into every single person's brain. Mental illness does *not* make someone weak. Even if a relationship doesn't work out, that is not an automatic green ticket for Person A to call Person B an insane maniac. Mental illness may exist to make us grow wiser and love harder. *Why* is that so hard for people to accept?

34

———

Good morning Carrington!

I want to check in on my favorite client's upcoming poetry collection! And remind you that Polly&Pippy are looking to have that manuscript by late next month or early January. I know you are writing some absolute gold! Keep it up, girl!

Best,

Christie

I READ THE EMAIL AND MAKE A MENTAL NOTE TO RESPOND TO my wonderful agent when my legs aren't liquefying beneath me. This stair-stepper machine must be laughing its ass off at how much I'm huffing and puffing, but I feel great. I joined this gym the moment I arrived in Baltimore, and when I'm not attempting yoga at my apartment, I am here.

Emerald Gym is small but crammed nearly wall to wall with equipment. It's not by any means a gym specific for old-timers, except the air is constantly tinged with clove and cinnamon, and most of the people here have gold or graying hair. The walls are forest green. The people are easy-going, no meatheads in wife-beater tank tops. Other than the chorus of clanking weights or breathless conversations, the music pouring out of the speakers is 2010 pop. I swear this gym is a grandma's basement in disguise.

That is why I love it so much.

Well, I don't love the burning in my thighs. My forearms are propped on the bars, and my head is hanging down so that I can focus on each step as it passes. This damn machine is going to have me hearing green and tasting "Telephone" by Lady Gaga in about two seconds. Thankfully, my ten minutes are up.

I suck down my sour strawberry energy drink until my taste buds are screaming, and then I retreat to the pocketed area at the far end of the gym with the mats so I can work my core.

Thirty crunches into the set, I have an epiphany: I am meeting myself all over again.

I have met myself two times before. The first time was during my third year of high school when I took my first writing class. Originally it was a dumb elective squeezed into my schedule for more credits, but it quickly worked its way into the spotlight in my heart. Mrs. Wu said I had a special talent hidden in my back pocket. That semester, I met Writer Carrington.

The second time was the summer before freshman year of college when Mom's passion rubbed off on me and I became obsessed with the brain. Lobes, functions, nervous system, impacts on behavior—I was a junkie, hence why I listed it as my major. Enter, Psychology Carrington.

And now, here on this gym mat that smells like disinfectant spray, while my core is being shredded like grated cheese, I meet Cari Carrington. She is twenty-four, unafraid to dye her hair rose gold on account of some writer's block. She is seriously addicted to satirical poetry and refrigerator magnets. She is a Professional Halloween

Enthusiast. She is all sharp edges and growing muscle. A sucker for dark humor. A slut for sarcasm. A full, undeniable lover who doesn't know what love is but is quite obsessed with the feeling. Desperate for connection. Sick of silence. An adult-child who is still trying to find her way in this big, bad wolf of a world. But she's okay with not having all the answers. She is okay with imperfection. Cari Carrington: the antihero of her own story, dressed in sweatpants and crew necks, attached to her journals like they're her Bibles. What a sight to behold.

I finish my fifty crunches and collapse on the mat. My core is in flames. My smile is ice. I feel redrawn—this time in red ink instead of blue or black. Cari Carrington isn't a stick figure or a rough sketch. She is a brightly colored oil painting that gives the *Mona Lisa* a run for its money. Three-dimensional. Complete yet imperfect.

To anyone else, this level of self-reflection may seem excessive. But I'm a poet. Details are everything. And Cari Carrington is the best me I have ever been.

After I finish my core exercises (a four-pack on its way to a six), I wash my hands in the locker room and hurry out to my car. While the engine's warming up, I respond to Christie.

Thank you so much. I have a feeling this will be my best collection yet. As always, thank you for the support!

Sending buckets of love,

Carrington

THE FIRST CHRISTMAS song of the year plays on Ruth's radio at 12:34 p.m. this afternoon. It is only November eleventh, but hey. I'm no Grinch. It turns out, Ruth might be.

"Turn that off!" she demands, waving frantically at the speakers. "Have some respect for Thanksgiving."

"What?" I call over Mariah Carey. I am being dramatic. It's not even that loud.

"I swear, these people are Christmas crazy! They never slow down to acknowledge what's right in front of them."

She has a point. Thanksgiving is shamefully underrated. I wonder if that's because it is a holiday built solely on gratitude and not materialistic gift-giving. Regardless, I won't lie and say I'm not hopping on the bandwagon with the rest of the Christmas nuts. I *love* the holidays because I get to go shopping for all my favorite people. It is one of the best feelings, watching someone you love open a present, knowing it will make them happier than happy.

"Just so you know," I say, setting a tray of freshly baked pumpkin pie (on a purple plate, of course) in the display case. "I am grateful, Ruth."

"I know you are, sweetheart." She dries her hands on a purple dish rag.

Mariah Carey continues to sing.

"I'm grateful for the shining sun," I say, "and this amazing bakery and the incredible woman who runs it."

That earns me a giant grin. "Thank you," Ruth says. "I'm grateful for you, too. I wasn't saying *you* specifically are unthankful, but it just makes me sad when people rush forward so much. They don't take the time to..."

"Smell the roses? Drink some coffee? Chew their food mindfully?"

"All the above, I guess." She leans against the counter with a pensive look etched into her face. "Young people don't understand how fast life goes. They're always in a rush. When you get to be my age, you'll realize how time flies."

I close the display case and turn to face her fully. "Yeah, no kidding. Sometimes it feels like just yesterday I was in elementary school, playing kickball at recess and not caring about anything else."

"And now you're here, working for an old woman."

"Oh, *trust* me," I say, holding up my hands for emphasis. "I wouldn't trade *this* for *anything!*"

Ruth laughs. I love her laugh. It is so deep and full, overflowing from the depth of her soul.

"I'm glad to hear that. As far as Christmas is concerned, patience, honey, patience. That time will be here before you know it."

35

Did I think I would be eating lunch in an '80s-themed steak grill with Abel and his cousins today? No. But stranger things have happened.

It has been a week since Abel and I slept together for the first time. Thanksgiving is officially six days away, which is why his cousin Peter is showing me his new toy dinosaur while we nibble on some olive-oil-drenched bread. Since Abel was young, his uncle Ethan (Mrs. Harpen's brother) and aunt Quinn have traveled all the way from Frederick County, Virginia, to Abel's parents' house in Providence for the week leading up to Thanksgiving. Now that Abel has started graduate school in Catonsville, they decided to stop here on the way up to have lunch with him. I have only met them once: spring break during our sophomore year in college when they came for an impromptu visit. Back then, Peter and Luka were still babies.

Now they are five and six and talking my ear off.

"His name is Dino," Peter explains, slamming his figurine down on the table and imitating a fake roar.

"I have a blue one, but I left him in the car," Luka assures me. He seems to be having the time of his life coloring an '80s Ford Mustang neon green on the child's placemat.

I smile and nod. "I'm sure it is just as cool."

"Even cooler," Luka promises.

He has a head full of blonde curls framing his plump, rosy cheeks. Peter's hair is straight as pine needles—the color of a penny—more resembling Quinn's hair than Ethan's. Both boys have Abel's shockwave blue eyes: cobalt blue with a splattering of indigo. Good genes run in the family, I see.

"Oh, Carrington, honey. It is *so* good to see you again. I feel like it's been twenty years—what a crime!" Quinn gushes. She is a strawberry cream pastry of a person: sweeter than holy hell and always smells like a vanilla bean (her favorite perfume). She takes a sip of her red wine and gestures emphatically with her pink manicured hand. "Tell us, tell us! How's the writing business?"

"Busy. But also amazing."

"Ah! I knew it!" She shakes her wrists, and the Pandora charms jingle on her bracelet. "When is this new collection coming out?"

"Well, publishing takes a while. If I can get my manuscript in by late next month, hopefully the book will be out in..." I count in my head. "August or September of next year."

"Phooey!" she pouts. "That's so long from now!"

"I know. But with the cover design, the advance reviews, and the whole printing process, it takes a chunk of time."

"Well, rest assured, when it comes out, the girls in my book club and I are going to read it *cover* to *cover*." She winks at me like it's a pinky promise.

Quinn Marsh: the bougie aunt I have always wanted.

As far as Ethan goes, picture Abel but add fifteen years and put a surfer dude spin on it. The man's a jeweler, but he looks like he just washed right up out of the ocean. Thor-like hair matched with a doughy torso and broad shoulders. The same piercing eyes in the same blue shade. Ethan and Quinn are a hot couple.

"Wait, Carrington, when did you say the collection's coming out? I've been looking for some new coasters at the house."

Quinn smacks her husband's arm, but I start giggling.

"I'm only kidding," Ethan clarifies. There is a massive gold cross dangling from a chain around his neck. It is dotted with minuscule rubies. He made it himself. I learned very quickly not to say the words "metal" or "stones" in his presence because he will transform into a professor and give you a three-hour lecture on polishing wheels and chemical baths.

"Abel, dear, this place is amazing," Quinn exclaims. "Thank you for recommending it."

It *is* a cool place, The Aftershock in Arbutus. There is not an inch of wall space available around the countless photos capturing precious moments in '80s pop culture: perms and mullets, leg warmers and neon colors. Pictures of Rubik's Cubes and Cabbage Patch Kids. Professional shots of Bon Jovi, Guns N' Roses, Blondie, Michael Jackson. There are even newspaper clippings of the *Challenger* explosion, the Chernobyl disaster and the AIDS epidemic. In the far corner, there are old-fashioned arcade games—*Pac-Man, Frogger, Donkey Kong*. All the waiters and waitresses have their hair all teased up. And what other song should be playing over the speakers except "I Wanna Dance with Somebody" by Whitney Houston?

No doubt Abel is in heaven.

"I feel like I got in a time machine," Ethan says, bobbing his head to the beat.

"My dad was always obsessed with the '80s," Abel explains. "I grew up with this music."

"That's right! Man, back in the day when Carson was dating your mom, he had this really cool BMW M3 in bright red. It was awesome."

"He still has it. He drives it on occasion." I can see Abel's eyes twinkle whenever he talks about his dad—his perfect role model.

"Get the heck out!" Ethan shouts. "How come I've never seen it?"

"He prefers not to drive it in colder weather."

"Huh. Maybe I can convince him to get it out this weekend. I tell ya, that man never left the '80s. It's how I knew he was perfect for my sister. Babe, did I ever tell you that Alana met Carson when she was fourteen? Had Abel at sixteen!"

I smile and glance over at Abel. His face has never looked brighter. He peeks at me from the corner of his eye, and a blush creeps into his cheeks as he takes my hand beneath the table. Gives it a warm, soft squeeze. A silent "thank you for coming" that I return when I squeeze his hand back.

"Abel," Peter whispers as he walks his dinosaur up Abel's other arm.

"What's up, buddy?"

Peter's blue eyes jump to my face and quickly jerk away. He leans closer to his cousin, cupping his hand around his mouth. "Do you like her?" he whispers loudly.

Abel laughs and then leans into whisper, "Yeah. I do."

Peter presses his lips together with a mischievous smile like Abel has just spilled the beans on some grand secret it is now his job to keep...though he probably won't. Kids, am I right?

"Abel!" Luka slams his crayon on the table. "Look at the car I colored!"

"Oh, my *gosh*. No way! A *green* car?" Abel gasps. "I want one! Do you think you could buy me one with all the pennies in your piggybank?"

"I have to ask Mommy and Daddy first." Luka hands Abel a pink crayon. "Color with me! Here. I'll give you this car." He passes Abel an outline of an '80s Chevrolet.

Abel flashes me a quick, lovely smile, and I have to resist the urge to say, "Go ahead, bud. Go color your beautiful, childlike heart out."

"Oh, what the hell. *Heck*! I mean, *heck*," Ethan corrects himself quickly. His sons giggle uncontrollably. "Luka, pass me a crayon, too!"

This day marks the beginning of a week of activities, some I am excited for and some I am dreading. For example, Kelsey is coming to town early tomorrow to stay with her sister Meg before our Friendsgiving on Monday (pro); I have to pack my suitcase and prepare to drive seven hours north to my home and have my mother ask about all the graduate programs I have not applied for (con). So, for the rest of this festive lunch, I would like to be fully present.

"Hopefully I'll get to see you again soon," I tell Quinn.

She leans forward and pats my arm. "Sweetheart, I just *love* seeing you. Do me a favor and stay in Abel's life, all right? Keep my nephew out of trouble."

"I will do my best," I promise.

Our waitress Becky arrives then (a life-sized Barbie doll in neon blue and yellow). "Hey, everyone! I got some gnarly food here for ya!"

Our table cheers. Abel's hand finds mine again.

36

I CAN IMAGINE HOW A MUSICIAN MIGHT FEEL. AFTER WRITING for weeks and weeks, a ten-track body of work shapes itself into existence. The project the world is *hopelessly* thirsting for. The excitement, the triumph, and above all, the nerves. You get stuck on that stupid What-If Cycle. Wait...hold on...what if this is trash? What if this is laughable? What if the critics take a giant shit on it? What then? They say you have to focus on you—write what *you* want to write. But what if the world doesn't care like you want them to? What if they miss the underlying messages?

I have been writing and rewriting my poetry, flipping back and forth through my journal, fixing this and tweaking that. I have some great poems here that I know are worth something, but the collection as a whole still feels empty. The project currently resembles an unfurnished house: no L-shaped couch with a squishy cushion, no blender or toaster in the kitchen, no toiletries in the bathroom or queen-sized bed with a teal comforter. Just a skeleton of a home. That is what has me on the What-If Cycle. What if I have been going about this collection all wrong?

As of right now, the working title is *Two Feet on the Ground.*

Fifty-six poems (give or take) about exploring this new version of myself while experiencing new love. Two feet on the ground means being fully immersed in what life gives you. I don't think I love the title. It feels basic and oddly impersonal. It could be the title of any poetry collection, and that's the problem. My work needs to be individual and unique to who I am. Something that really screams Cari Carrington.

Kelsey's text message interrupts my brainstorm (what's new?).

I just crossed the Maryland line!

Stop texting while you're driving!

Tomorrow is going to be a lot of fun.

I ARRIVE at Meg's apartment on Monday night at precisely 5:50 p.m. I have two passengers: Raquel, dressed in a dark-turquoise blouse and white jeans (cooler than cool), and a fresh pumpkin pie, which I whipped up at the bakery this morning in addition to dozens of other orders.

"I am starving," Raquel says as we climb out of the car into the crisp November air.

"Perfect." I grab the pie and complimentary bottle of champagne and shut the door with my hip. "Kelsey always makes sure there's more food than we can eat."

"How do you know her again?"

"We met in undergrad. She's a little type A and unfiltered, but she's one of my best friends."

We hardly make it up the porch steps before the door swings open and Kelsey pokes her head out. Her hair is in Dutch braids tonight, revealing the massive gold hoops in her ears, which match both the gold chain around her neck and of course, her slick eyeliner.

She freezes when she spots Raquel. Before I can open my mouth to introduce them, Kelsey steps forward.

"Hey, I'm Kelsey."

"Raquel." Said with a smooth, crooked smirk and twinkling eyes. This girl knows how to charm everyone, I swear.

"Please, please! Come in where it's warm. Cari, put the pie on the island."

"Roger that."

We step into the blissful warmth, immediately enveloped by a chorus of "Heys!" and "There they are!"

Noah shoots off the couch. "My favorite poet."

"Don't strain yourself with that lie," I say, setting down the pie and champagne and pulling him into my arms.

Abel consumes all the light in the room just by sitting on the couch, bent over with his forearms on his knees, a glowing smile on his lips. I catch his eye—those blue, blue eyes—and feel my organs liquefy in the best way possible.

On Abel's right is Leo, whom I remember from Hunter's Halloween party. Tonight, his teal-and-black locs are secured back by a band, and he looks like the kind of guy I could grab a drink with and step outside to talk about life. I make a mental note to become best friends with him.

Hunter sits on Abel's left, and something lightens in my chest the moment I see his smile. It is a smile only a true friend soulmate could give: playful yet tinged with genuine affection. I can't help but smile back.

"Cari, I don't believe you've met Warren," Meg says, entering the living room in a to-die-for dress the color of a starburst singed by sunlight.

Behind her is a guy who has a jawline cut from steel. Evergreen eyes, olive-toned skin, summer-kissed hair. *Not bad, Meg.*

"This is my boyfriend Warren."

Warren steps forward to shake my hand. "Meg told me you're a writer. I don't like to read, but it's pretty cool to know you, considering how accomplished you are."

"Thanks, I get that a lot."

People either love reading or hate it. It comes with the job, and you learn to grin, bear it, and shake hands anyway.

Abel appears behind me. "Oh, she's not just accomplished, she's *incredible*. She has the most creative brain out of anyone I've ever met."

And, in rare circumstances, you have Abel Harpen to take some of the grinning and bearing away. Somebody pinch me.

"I can second that," Noah chimes in. "In college, she used to keep us from doing homework so she could read us her poems. And they were *exquisite*." He drapes an arm around my shoulder.

"Guess I'll have to read your collection then," Warren says, probably to be kind.

"Guess so," Noah says.

I nudge him off my shoulder and tell him to cool it. In exchange, I get the *what did I do?* look.

"Food's ready!" Kelsey sings.

We gather into Meg's dining room, which is all mahogany wood, scented candles, and oil paintings. Her *uncle's* oil paintings, that is. Roderick Witchett is like Clark Kent in his insurance job. But underneath those thick-framed glasses and striped tie is a rugged artist with his own colorful, beautifully disarrayed studio. He excels in realism, which is why there are paintings of bowls of fruit hanging on the walls around the table. My favorite piece is the sliced watermelon on a cutting board. The gleam of the knife as it waits on the counter, the polka dots of black seeds, the pink-red juice as it dribbles down the cutting board—chef's *kiss*.

"So!" Kelsey announces, yanking me out of my admiration. "We have buttered mashed potatoes, roasted vegetables, sweet corn, sugared apple fritters, and, of course, steaming turkey!"

Leo clears his throat. "And for the lone vegetarian in the room—" Everyone giggles. "Green bean casserole!"

We cheer. We bang our silverware on the table like a bunch of salivating hooligans. We pass dishes to each other, complimenting someone's earrings or another's shirt, laughing over sarcastic side comments. With that collective first bite, we go dead silent, and then the groaning begins. Praise spills from our mouths, muffled by corn or turkey or Leo's green bean casserole. Kelsey and Meg have always been amazing cooks. Add that to the long list of perfections that make the Witchetts who they are.

"Man, this takes me back," Kelsey murmurs, staring at the mountain of corn on her plate.

"To the time you blew up that turkey in the oven after the Patriots lost?" I suggest.

Leo hears that. "Wait, *what?*"

"Good one," Kelsey says. "But no. It takes me back to all those times the Core Four had lunch together before Thanksgiving break."

"The Core Four?" Raquel asks.

Noah chimes in, "Prince Charming, Wild Child, Miss Writer, and myself."

"Why do *you* get the normal description?" I demand.

"Prince Charming?" Abel cocks his head at that one. He's seated right here beside me.

"We ate together every day of the week," Kelsey says wistfully. "And I prefer Wild *Woman*, excuse you."

"That feels like just yesterday." If I squint at my plate, it almost looks like one of those thick paper plates they handed out in the dining hall, with grease pooling under my mozzarella sticks.

"Six years later, and we're still a family," Kelsey says.

"Six years later, and Abel is still hotter than holy hell," Noah sighs.

We burst out laughing. Water squirts from Leo's mouth.

The evening carries on. We go for seconds and thirds...and fourths on the apple fritters (don't judge me; it's a holiday). By the time we settle into the living room, we are all happy and warm and drunk, except for Abel, who is content with his glass of water.

Hunter has been talking my ear off for the last half hour about why *Star Wars* actually *isn't* the greatest franchise of all time. The alcohol on his breath smells so sweet, I don't even care to tell him he's an idiot for arguing such a thing.

"We need some music up in here!" Raquel calls. She's been talking with Kelsey all evening, the two of them glowing like goddesses on the leather couch.

"Queuing it up right now," Leo says. "Abel, this one's for you, bro."

Abel looks up from Noah's phone. The two of them have been howling over TikToks for almost an hour now. When "Let's Groove" by Earth, Wind & Fire comes on through Kelsey's BlueTooth speaker, Abel's face lights up. Him and his '80s music. Raquel is the first one to stand and swing her hips to the beat, reigning in a chorus of whistles and hollers. The energy pulls Kelsey to her feet, and the two start twirling each other around. The beat is too compelling to stay seated, so I stand at the same time Meg pulls Warren to his feet. Noah is in the middle of the room, drunkenly waving his arms over his head, and my sides hurt from laughing.

When Abel stands, the beat gets five times more hypnotic, the lighting five times lower. The whistling five times louder. He struts to the center of our gyrating circle and executes the cutest, hottest Disco Point the world has ever seen. We shout and scream for him, and when he does the Moonwalk, I actually fall to my knees. I can't help it. He is smiling cheek to cheek, beaming in the low lighting and having the time of his life. It is so precious, my body threatens to explode. And then, by some miraculous force of the universe, he dances his way over to me and pulls me off the ground.

"Let's dance!" I think he says. It's hard to hear over the blood pounding in my ears.

He guides me back into the center of the dancing bodies. We boogie together, swaying and head-bobbing and laughing until every worry I have ever had disintegrates into the synthetic beat.

My soul elevates somewhere outside my body. My skin blazes.

My eyes are wide, and the alcohol zings through my bloodstream. Consider me high on life. This is what it feels like to be utterly, beautifully alive: surrounded by the people I love, with Earth, Wind & Fire blazing up the speakers.

~

I AM STILL HAPPILY humming "Let's Groove" when Meg offers me the spare bedroom. Kelsey and Raquel are already sound asleep on the couch, and Hunter, Leo, and Noah are packed onto the blow-up mattress like sardines, snoring away. Abel leans against the wall, yawning into his hand.

"In fact, you can both take the spare if you want," Meg says. Her arm wraps tightly around a swaying Warren. "Just don't be giving head. I washed those sheets like two days ago."

I laugh hysterically. Abel's face warms three shades, and he offers a small smile.

Meg tugs Warren down the hallway to their bedroom. "Goodnight!"

"I am honestly surprised you have not crashed yet." Abel takes my hand and guides me down the opposite hallway.

"Didn't I ever tell you I'm a night owl?"

"Oh, I know you are." Right. We went to college together.

I collapse on the queen-sized bed and run my hands along the silky gray comforter because it feels like a cloud. Able laughs softly. He is standing in the corner, pretending to fumble with the light switch.

"What are you doing over there?" I demand. "Come take my clothes off."

He clears his throat. "Cari, I can't."

"Of course you can. It's easy. You just undo the buttons—like this."

He strides across the room and catches my hand as it frees a button on my blouse.

"I know how to." He smiles. "What I mean is I *shouldn't*. Not tonight. You're drunk. It wouldn't be right."

"That's lame."

"Not really." He adjusts the pillows behind my head. "I could never take advantage of a woman like that. I was raised too well."

"We could just make out. I'll even keep the moaning down."

He gives me this look, like, *You're the cutest thing in the world, but come on now.*

"Fine," I say. "But you're not sleeping on the ground to keep up some chivalrous act. It's not worth the back pain."

"If you want me here, then here is where I'll be." He brushes his nose against mine.

An alarm chimes on his phone, and he twists around to stop it. I watch him cross the room to his backpack and retrieve a tiny plastic case. It rattles slightly. He swallows two pills with his glass of water and wipes his lips on the back of his hand.

I know he has to take those pills. I know they stabilize his mood. I know that a lot of people—*too many people*—have judged him over those pills. Rejected him and kicked him to the curb because of those pills. But to me, those pills are tiny blessings. They keep the person I love safe and healthy. They keep him here, dancing the disco and smiling crookedly at me.

He helps me slip under the covers and brushes a strand of hair off my face. *Goodbye, happy alcohol rush.* I am officially hitting the drowsy button.

"Goodnight, Cari." Abel leaves a ghost of a kiss on my cheek.

When he wraps an arm around me, the warmth and silence lull me into a peaceful sleep.

37

THE FIRST THING I SEE WHEN I WALK INTO MEG'S DINING ROOM in the morning is Noah chugging a glass of orange juice. When he spots me, he sets the cup down on the table a little too harshly.

"Care for some pancakes?"

I take one from the plate and tear off a piece with my teeth. "Are you hungover?"

"My brain feels like a slushie right now."

"Ah."

I sit down in the chair beside him, taking in the rest of the crew as they wolf down the heavenly breakfast Chef Meg has prepared. We're one short. I noticed this as soon as my eyes snapped open this morning.

"Where's Abel?" I ask.

There is a collective clenching of jaws.

"Balcony." Leo says eventually, gesturing to the French doors. "Been out there for about half an hour now."

"Talking to his dad on the phone," Hunter fills in. "Apparently his mom's mental health took a turn for the worst."

I crush the pancake in my hand. "What does that mean?"

Nervous glances ping-pong around the table.

"She was in out-patient for a long time," Hunter says. "But just recently, she had another depressive episode...tried to kill herself."

My lungs scorch my ribcage.

"He got the call about an hour ago. His dad said she was rushed to the hospital late last night." Raquel has abandoned her food. She looks at it instead of me. "You missed all the panic this morning."

I squeeze my poor pancake into a gushy deformed lump. "She's alive though, right?"

"Yeah. Abel's going to drive home today to be with his sisters while their dad goes and visits their mom in the hospital," Hunter says. "His dad called back a little while ago with another update." He motions toward the balcony. "I'm sure Melanie and Charlotte are scared sick."

Oh my God. My brain isn't fast enough to process the emotions slicing through my body. So far, I have only registered my sandpaper tongue and shaking hands.

Don't put Abel through this.

I don't know who I'm pleading with. All I can think is that he does not deserve that pain. And his mom does not deserve to feel that low. No one does.

One of the French doors swings open. Abel steps into the dining room, tugging his UMBC sweatshirt up around his neck and blowing on his hands. His beautiful eyes are tinged red.

"What's going on, man?" Hunter breaks the silence.

Abel draws a breath. "She's being transferred to a psychiatric hospital for more intensive care."

"Well, that's a good thing, right?" Leo asks.

"It *should* be." Abel pours himself a glass of orange juice but only downs a third of it. "Assuming they do their job properly and rule out all possible explanations."

"Like?" Raquel ventures.

"The medication," Abel says. "Certain meds heighten dysphoria. I mean, yeah, she has BPD, but the medication dance can be a monster of its own." A beat of silence strangles us until he adds, "I'm going to get my stuff together."

It only takes five seconds after he leaves the room for me to jump out of my seat.

"Anyone want more pancakes?" Meg asks, stealing attention so I can escape the table.

I zip down the hallway and pause with my hand on the doorknob. This is the bedroom we slept together in not four hours ago, where he held me so gently, and I felt warm and whole against his chest. Now the air in the room feels thick with dread. I could be disturbing the dead.

"Abel?"

I find him brushing his teeth in the bathroom, spitting spirals of blue paste into the sink. He rinses his mouth and glances over at me.

"It's all right, Cari." Typical Mr. Sunshine, masking his fear.

"I can go with you...if you want." I hadn't considered it but seeing him frown is like a shark's tooth in my spleen.

"It's okay." He brushes past me and heads for his bag on the bed.

I watch him dump his toothbrush in along with the case of pills and yesterday's shirt, which he yanks off his body in one quick motion. The sunlight peeking through the windows covers his bare back in a sheet of gold, underlining the dips between his muscles in purple shadows. My feet carry me toward him before I even realize I'm moving.

"Hey." I touch his cheek to turn his face toward mine.

His honey-colored hair is a mess of curlicues. I thread my fingers through some of them softly and draw his lips to mine. Any other occasion, kissing Abel is like sipping a margarita on the white sands of Aruba. But this is like kissing a slat of splintered wood. I pull back.

"I'm sorry." He turns away and retrieves an army-green T-shirt from his bag. Breaking away from my arms, he slips it on over his head. "I just can't stop thinking about my mom. She must be so scared and lonely."

"Has she ever...." The question stales on the tip of my tongue.

"No. Never. This is the first time."

His voice is so thick. I can hear the tears welling up the back of his throat. I have never seen Abel cry. I've seen him get *close*, like when his mom had to miss his college graduation and when Camila dumped him and told him he was "fucking insane." But he never shed a tear—at least not around me. I'm sure the walls of his house would tell me something different. *This* isn't like those times. He has triple-knotted his sneakers, and I swear it is an excuse to keep his head down because God forbid a man lets someone see him cry.

I'm not Camila, for fuck's sake.

"Abel."

I grab his hands to draw him to his feet, but he resists before clasping around my waist. His forehead touches my shoulder, and for the first time that I have ever seen, Abel weeps. Heaving, long sobs. His shoulders shake. I can feel the tears seep through my shirt. I hold onto him for dear life, afraid that if I move a muscle, he'll disintegrate.

I recognize the fear he's experiencing. It is exactly what I felt that night Mom's patient went into crisis and I began writing *Left or Right*. But the way Abel's crying...it feels much heavier. Like the weight of the universe is about to snap his shoulders like popsicle sticks.

"What. Am I. Gonna. Do, Cari?" His voice breaks between the cries.

"What do you mean?" I hold him tight to my chest.

"If my mom can't handle it...how am I supposed...."

The thought dawns on me, bringing a hefty dose of fear with it. I try to swallow the hole that forms in my throat.

"You're not your mom," I whisper.

He shakes his head. I can't tell if he's disagreeing with me or if the weight of the statement is just too much to comprehend right now.

"You're not." I insist, holding him tighter. "You have your own support system with your own amazing resources. Suicide, it's...a long-term solution for a short-term problem." He cries harder, and I bite the crap out of my bottom lip. "What I mean to say is...your mom is *okay*, Abel. She will get the proper treatment she needs, and she will be *just fine.* And as long as I have a say in it, I will never let you get that low. You mean too much to me to ever let that happen."

"I just..." He fights for breath. "I don't want to...be my disorder."

Something in me snaps. Something desperate and emotional and raw.

"Look at me." I take his face in my hands and lift his head from my shoulder. His eyes are liquid aquamarine jewels, refulgent and brimming with sorrow. I struggle to keep my voice even. "You are Abel Harpen, aspiring clinical psychologist. You're kick-ass at math. You love Hallmark Christmas movies and pictures of baby golden retrievers. You can cook some mean waffles. You love your family more than life. You're every girl's gym crush. You love milk and chocolate protein shakes. Your least favorite month of the year is January, and your favorite is May." I grip his face to look directly into his eyes. "You want to have kids someday and live in a big house. You never talk politics with your friends because you hate when everyone is at each other's necks. You are a *mental health advocate*, fighting to erase the stigma *every single day* of your life. Abel Harpen, you are not your disorder. You are a human being who struggles in your own unique way. That does not make you less of a person." I press my forehead to his, begging him to hear my words. "Don't let the stigma take you."

I don't even get to open my eyes before his lips, still wet from the tears, press against mine. He kisses me fiercely, almost harshly for a whole minute before slowly pulling away.

"Thank you, Cari. What did I do to deserve you?"

"Don't start," I mutter against his lips, craving just one more—

"I have to go." He kisses my cheek and turns away, scooping his bag off the bed. He swipes under his eyes before heading toward the door.

I follow him down the hallway. "Text me, Abel."

"Absolutely."

Our friends are waiting by the door—a rugged, hungover, beautiful little family. Hunter steps forward and pulls Abel into a hug.

"We're here for you, man."

Have I mentioned recently how much I adore Hunter?

"Thank you," Abel says.

The rest of the bunch steps forward to offer hugs and words of encouragement. I go back to biting my lip and trying my hardest not to cry. I need to be strong for Abel right now.

"Goodbye, Cari."

I follow him onto the porch, the November wind whipping my hair into a cyclone around my face.

"Bye, Abel!"

He only waves, no smile.

Hours later, after the slight hangover left my head and I was able to drive back to my own apartment, I get a phone call while I'm in the shower. It disrupts "Escapism" by RAYE, which had been serenading me through the Bluetooth speaker. I grab a towel and hop out, reaching for my phone. **Little Homie** flashes on the screen above a picture of Tucker with candy corn for teeth.

"Hey, Tuck."

"Hey. What time are you going to be here?"

Here? Where the hell is here? I rack my brain and come up empty-handed.

"Uh..."

"Cari." Tucker's voice takes on that little sibling edge of annoyance. "Mom said she wanted us home on Wednesday."

"It's Tuesday."

"I was able to get a sub for my class a day early, so Lauren and I decided to come home today."

Lauren, my little brother's new girlfriend, is the school nurse at the same school he teaches at. He went to get some Advil *once* and never left her office after that.

"The reason I'm asking is because Dad is trying to get us to play *What Do You Meme?* for the third time in a row. I mean, yeah, it's funny to see him crack up at all the dumb pictures, but I don't know how much more Evil Kermit the Frog I can take."

"It's your fault for going early," I say, combing through my knotted hair.

"When will you be here?"

"Tomorrow afternoon." *Kill me.*

"I brought extra apple pie."

"Tomorrow *morning*," I amend.

"I'm excited to see you, Sis." I can hear him smiling.

"Me, too."

Tucker is not just my little homie. He is my little everything.

"Oh, I gotta go. Mom is about to show Lauren my baby pictures, and if she shows her the one of me in the tub—Mom! Not that one!" I hear distant laughter through the speaker. "See ya, Cari."

"Bye," I say to the dial tone.

I set my phone down and take a long look in the mirror. My hair frames my face in a velvet, rosy outline and reaches just past my shoulders. A part of me is praying Mom will cool it and let me be her daughter this time. This time, this time, this time. It is always the same hope, and it always leads to the same letdown.

Ah, yes. Nothing like spending Thanksgiving with family.

38

My childhood home in Newport looks like it was built by an artist specializing in surrealism. Cinnamon-colored vinyl, dotted by rectangular and semi-circle windows, stretches from the navy-blue door to the peaked roof. The porch and the protruding living room windows are outlined in forest-green wood, contrasting against the banana-yellow siding of the east side. I can't make this shit up. I grew up in an architect's drunk experiment.

Mom's speckled rubber pumpkins stand guard beside the door, complimenting the obnoxious *Happy Thanksgiving!* homemade wreath that hangs on the door. Miss Debra, the elderly woman who lives next door and who *swears* she is *not* a control freak, made it for Mom and Dad two years ago.

I swallow my animosity (for Tucker's sake) and ring the doorbell. To my delight, Dad answers.

"Tiny Carrot!" he exclaims, pulling me into his arms.

Tiny Carrot has been my dad's nickname for me since birth. Apparently, I was such a happy baby that he swears my skin glowed orange. Whatever that means. The truth is, I love the nickname. It reminds me that no matter how old I get, I will always be my father's little girl.

I register that he seems to have lost some weight. "Hey, Dad. Have you been hitting the gym?" Normally, he resides in his chair with a cracked Coke Zero.

"Oh, you know it." He steps back and throws a few punches at the air. "Your old man's a lean, green, fightin' machine now!"

I raise an eyebrow. "Really?"

"Okay, fine. I saw the new Chris Hemsworth movie and got inspired."

It is a known fact in our family that if Dad was gay, he would do everything in his power to be with Chris Hemsworth, even if it meant sacrificing his life to Hollywood fame.

"Now *that* sounds more plausible." I pat his arm.

The front door opens directly into the living room. I see Aunt Lorraine charging toward me.

"Tessa! Tasha! Get in here and hug your cousin!" she shouts. When she faces me, her sour look turns sickly sweet. "Cari, baby, how are you? Benny, get up and greet your niece."

My uncle tries to disguise his groan as a cough. Ah, yes. Nothing like family time.

My teenage cousins Tessa and Tasha saunter in from the kitchen, faces glued to their phone screens. They could be twins: braided brown hair, dimples, and glasses. We exchange one-arm hugs. I try to ask them about school and get one-word responses. *Okay, that's enough of that.*

Thankfully, Tucker and Lauren round the corner next. I de-age about six years, lunge for my brother and secure him in a headlock. I shake my hands through his hair, raging about how grown-up he is and how this beautiful girl hiding a smile behind her hand is so lucky to be with him.

"Is that my daughter?"

Mom appears, her white-blonde hair twisted back in a clip. She's dressed in that same orange-brown Crewneck she wears every year: the one that says *Thankful for Family*. Right.

"Carrington." Her voice is teary, though why, I'm not sure. It's not like I've been off the grid, faking my death for the last year. She hugs me, and I swear I'm hugging a tree trunk, it's so stiff.

Tucker clears his throat, and I remember I'm supposed to play nice this year. "Hi, Mom."

She is fifty-five, but I swear she drinks an anti-aging potion because she looks thirty-five. Creamy smooth skin on an oval face, green-blue eyes like a kaleidoscope of sea glass. I should look just like her, theoretically. I did *once*—when I was eleven, but then puberty shook my hand, and my face lost its baby fat. My body stretched like a beanstalk but filled out in all the right places. And, of course, my latest encounter with writer's block made me prefer rose-gold hair over being brunette.

"I'm so glad we could all be together." She steps back from me and addresses the whole room.

"Me, too." Dad drapes an arm around her and kisses her cheek.

Joan and Douglas Daughtler—an image of marriage perfection. Barf.

"Why don't you ever kiss me like that, Benny?" Aunt Lorraine elbows her husband in the gut and giggles like it's just a silly little joke between them. My father's sister is something else. A TikTok video blasts full volume from Tasha's phone. She doesn't apologize, just turns the volume down a smidge.

I turn to hug Lauren, who smells like one of the vanilla cream pastries in Ruth's display case. A nice distraction from my extended family.

"Hey, Miss Model, how are you?" My voice is muffled by her caramel-golden hair.

I call her that because she *could* be a model. She's got the whole damn look: full, glossy lips, hourglass body, sharp chin and jawline, sparkling brown eyes. I mean, she could star in Rihanna's Savage X

Fenty Show with magenta light illuminating the catwalk. I'm sure Tucker would cough up a diamond ring then—no hesitation.

"Hi, Cari." A voice of honey, too, are you kidding? "I'm good."

"Still saving little kids' lives?"

"If you mean taking temperatures and providing Tylenol with parent permission, then *yes*." She curls her hand into a fist and jabs the air, which I love. She has a lot of those little mannerisms, and if Tucker wasn't dead set on this girl, I'd date her myself.

"Yeah, my students are doing really well. Thanks for asking," Tucker interjects, shoveling a hand through his hair.

I smile at him, all those late-night *Mario Kart* wars and water gun battles and cherry seed spitting contests of our youth flashing through my mind. This Marvel-obsessed, gym-aholic, boring civics teacher is one of my favorite people in the world. My brother, my little homie, my rock.

Okay, I guess coming home is not all that bad.

"Tonight we are watching *A Charlie Brown Thanksgiving!*" Mom announces. Her tone suggests this is an order, not a suggestion.

Lauren, the cutie patootie of the group, presses her hands to her heart while Tucker and I choke back our groans.

"Isn't there a game on tonight?" Uncle Benny asks, scratching his bald head.

"Don't be ridiculous," Aunt Lorraine says. Her peach-pink lipstick is smudged across her teeth, but none of us have the balls to tell her. "Whatever Joan wants to watch is perfect."

Dad tries to fish-hook us all into (another) game of *What Do You Meme?*, and I sneak a quick peek at my phone. It has been twenty-four hours since Abel drove home to Providence to be with his sisters. I texted him multiple times.

11:45 p.m. (yesterday):

> Hey, did you make it there safely?

9:00 a.m. (this morning):

How are the girls? You guys holding up okay?

12:00 p.m. (this afternoon):

Any news on your mom?

1:00 p.m. (one hour ago):

Abel.

No answer. I know he is probably busy trying to keep his sisters occupied, busy worrying about his mom. They only live just under an hour away; I could drive there if I felt so inclined to. I try to push the anxiety to the lowest pit of my small intestine so the enzymes can disintegrate it. Sadly though, even that doesn't work. I still feel it in my chest cavity...the fear. Blame the repressed therapist in me, but I feel sick when I can't help someone. This is completely out of my control. When I was younger and life threw me one of these curveballs, Mom would identify them as "gray moments." It was a metaphor: life is not black and white; it is a collection of gray moments in different hues, some darker and some lighter. Therefore, there is no sense in having a black-and-white mindset or trying to find an immediate solution. Sometimes waiting is the best thing to do. Looking back, I think that was the best advice my mother ever gave me. Waiting is not easy. But I trust Abel will reach out when he is ready. I just have to learn to sit in the gray.

It amazes me how I can eat three slices of extra-cheesy pizza from Domino's, wash them down with a cold Sprite, and not even have a touch of heartburn. Dad is not so lucky. He pops his heartburn pill as he pops in the Charlie Brown VHS tape. Yes, my parents are the only people alive who still own a VHS tape. Apple TVs are a tech headache and all that.

I am tucked into the corner of the couch between a fur-lined pillow and Tucker's shoulder. Lauren is on his other side, curling around his arm. This space was my only option. It was either here or sandwiched between my silently bickering aunt and uncle on the other couch or my screen-addicted cousins on the blow-up mattress. Dad settles into the loveseat beside Mom, and they immediately link hands.

"God, I'm pretty sure I can quote this whole movie," I whisper to Tucker, the Linus and Lucy theme covering my voice.

"In Japanese," he whispers back.

We giggle into our hands.

"How are you?" he whispers five minutes later.

"Kinda craving some spearmint gum."

"No. I mean, how *are* you?"

"Oh."

"Yeah."

"Successfully published. Working on my next project. Head over heels in love. Life is good."

"So, you haven't fucked it up yet?"

I glance at him, ignoring Mom's side-eye.

"Wait, how do you know about Abel?"

He breaks eye contact with the TV and shoots me a look. "You drunk-dialed me and told me that you guys reconnected. And then you vented about his hair for twenty minutes."

"When was that?" I whisper-hiss back.

"October, I think."

Not surprising. "He's in Providence right now, visiting his family."

"How are they?"

"Long story."

"Not good then, I'm guessing."

"Been better."

Tucker knows all about Abel's mental health struggles from the times I came home during college and spilled my infatuated guts to him.

"Well, I'll pray for them."

Tucker, like our parents, is a fully devoted Christian. Got baptized in a glittering pool of water in a church and everything. To each their own.

"Thanks, Tuck."

"Mom seems chill," he whispers after another five minutes have passed.

"I haven't had time to poke the bear yet."

"Don't." He takes a handful of popcorn from the bowl Lauren offers. She passes it to me, but I decline. "We don't need a repeat of last year."

"It's not my fault she didn't like the new look." I touch a tendril of my hair. "I'm just being me."

"You and I both know it was a moment of complete impulsivity and boredom."

I snicker and bump his shoulder.

"I don't know," I murmur half a beat later. "I want to make things right, but she makes it so hard."

The antics on screen are reflected in Tucker's speckled, hazel eyes. "Maybe you perceive it that way 'cause you're scared."

"Of *what*?"

"I don't know. *You're* the ex-psychologist."

I don't hold back when I shove his shoulder this time, and he topples into Lauren. The movement catches our parents' eyes again. Mom sighs.

"Come on, kids. You're missing the good part!"

Snoopy appears in a chef's hat, tossing plates around the table like they're flying saucers.

39

I spend Thanksgiving morning on the quilted couch as a mug of coffee burns my palms. It is a Daughtler Thanksgiving tradition that each year, our family gathers in front of the TV and watches old home videos.

This is Lauren's first time seeing baby Tucker splashing around in the bathtub. Toddler Tucker steering his Big Wheel down the driveway, his little feet pedaling so fast his sneakers are a swirl of blue. Tween Tucker murdering a saxophone solo at his sixth grade band concert. Teen Tucker chucking up a peace sign beside his brand-new Marvel Avengers poster and holding tickets to see *Captain America: Civil War*. I'm pretty he still has that poster framed in his apartment now.

"Lauren, do you know you're dating a Marvel freak?" I ask.

"Considering he made me watch every single movie from start to finish and explain how they all connect in the end?" She bites her lip and nods once. "I'm aware."

"Don't pretend you didn't love it," Tucker coos.

"No comment."

The footage of me is equally cringe-worthy. I was a bit of a movie-star-wannabe child. For my sixth birthday, Dad got me these purple star glasses that I wore every moment of every day, even during school, because they made everything (even *math*) an event. A lot of kids asked me where I got them or if I was ever going to take them off. I fired back with these concocted stories that zipped through my brain on a moment's notice: I won the glasses in a handstand contest. I fought a big-kid third grader for them (she ran scared).

Honestly, I should have known right then and there with my classmates gaping at me that I was going to be a writer. The stories came so naturally. Of course, Tucker calls me a pathological liar. Tomato, *tomahto*.

Another segment flashes on screen: me at approximately seven or eight years old, standing on a chair to reach the kitchen counter, lazily mixing a bowl of ingredients as Mom flips through a cookbook. If she looks thirty-five now, she looks twenty-five in this video, white-blonde hair spilling out from her messy bun, a soft smile pinching a corner of her mouth. She was stunning—*is* stunning. So unbothered by the disarray of bowls and splattered dishes in the sink. I remember that day perfectly: the day she let me help bake brownies for a Christmas party. It is almost nice to see, like this video proves a time *did* exist when my mom and I were close. No such thing as psychotherapy or complex poetry or grad school programs yet. It was just us and that bowl of lumpy brownie mix. The good old days.

Tucker coughs intentionally in my direction, and I roll my eyes.

"Sit on an ice pack," I mouth at him. In other words, *chill out*.

"Get off your ice pack," he mouths back. In other words, *extend the olive branch to our dearest Mother*.

I take a sip of my hundred-degree coffee, which I instantly regret.

DAD'S SNORING could wake the dead in Europe. He is passed out in his recliner, mouth dangling open, arm draped over his torso. Uncle Benny doesn't seem to mind. He has *American Ninja*

Warrior on full volume, digging around the Dorito bag, and sucking orange paste off his fat fingers. Everyone else has their escape routes from Dad's snoring: Tucker and Lauren disappear into the kitchen, Mom and Aunt Lorraine busy themselves with a game of cards in the basement, the girls disappear to the den to watch YouTube. I move into the sunroom—my favorite place in our house, by far.

Cream-white walls and windowsills housing sparkling windows that drink in the autumn sunlight. The peaked wooden roof, the dangling silver chandelier, the deep-blue wicker furniture. The best part? It's heated.

I tuck my legs beneath me and stare past the covered pool and Mom's dead vegetable garden. The field behind the house is ringed with towering, ancient evergreens that have been guarding the space since I was a little girl. Out here, Dad's snoring is only slightly muted. In the past, that used to annoy me, but being here in my favorite childhood space is softening my heart with some good old nostalgia.

My eyes drop to the books neatly stacked on the glass coffee table: The *DSM-5-TR. Fighting Trauma: A Guide to DBT Techniques. America, the Overmedicated. CBT Benefits, According to Research,* so on and so forth. Mom's unofficial library.

I can't help myself. I reach for the *DSM—Diagnostic and Statistical Manual for Mental Disorders*—and open to its table of contents. Neurodevelopmental Disorders, Feeding and Eating Disorders, Mood Disorders, everything in between. Something tugs one of the many strings in my heart. A string that has long since retired. Had I continued on the path of psychology, I would have had a copy of this on my own coffee table. I flip to a random section, Schizophreniform, and work my way down through the criteria, pretending I'm in front of a client. *Have you ever experienced at least one of the following: delusions, hallucinations, disorganized speech...for at least a month but no longer than six months?*

"Doing some light reading?"

I jump as Mom steps into the sunroom and shuts the door gently behind her. I blow a strand of hair out of my face. Tucker's voice pinballs through my brain: *Be nice.*

"Yeah," I say. "Where's Aunt Lorraine?"

Mom sits in the chair opposite me, faint crow's feet crinkling at her eyes as she smiles. "Between you and me, I needed a little break from her and all the gossip."

I feel like I swallowed an ice cube—that uncomfortable, out-of-place sensation settling in the pit of my stomach. When was the last time I sat with Mom like this? *Red alert*, my sympathetic nervous system screeches.

"When you were a sophomore in college, you used to diagnose the characters on the Netflix shows you watched." Her cadence drops as she finishes the sentence, like syrup spilling out of the bottle and pooling on a pancake. I hate syrup.

"And you yelled at me for that," I remind her.

"I didn't yell," she says. "It's just not nice to assume someone has a disorder without an official diagnosis." I am about to tell her the characters were fictitious when she adds, "You were good at it though."

"Fake diagnosing?"

"Thinking critically. You never made a decision based on your first guess, you always went deeper, picking apart the character's mannerisms and attitudes."

I did this for shits and giggles. Just because a tormented psyche used to fascinate me.

"My little psychologist."

That phrase hits me like I just sucked all the juice from a lemon. I feel my face contort, but before I can push out any sour words, my phone rings.

Abel.

"Hello?" I half-shout.

"Hey."

That's it. Just *hey.*

"Are you okay?" I urge. "How's your mom?"

"She's coming home." His voice sounds like it has been forced through a cheese grater.

"That's great," I say, unintentionally glancing at my mother. There is a line between her eyebrows.

"Yeah."

Muffled voices sound in the background, and I can just barely recognize one as Melanie's.

"Your sisters okay?"

"Charlotte's been in the shower for a century, and Melanie just went to take a nap in the den."

My heart twists. Normally, Charlotte is outside with a basketball or playing *Madden* on their Xbox, trying to pull Melanie away from her pastel crayons and sketchbook just to have another player. Or Melanie is coercing Charlotte away from the treadmill in their at-home gym just to have a model for her to sketch. Or, the two of them are joined at the hip, howling like hyenas over some ridiculous inside joke. The point is, they never spend more than five minutes apart, except for when school forces them to. It is alarming that they are choosing to be apart, doing passive activities instead of things they normally love.

"Okay." I try to sound chipper. "How are *you* holding up?"

A brief, heavy silence. "I'm...waiting for the water to boil so I can make spaghetti."

His sisters' favorite.

I don't even have to be in the room with him. I know exactly what his face looks like right now. The right corner of his lip is pinched; his eyebrows are drawn upward, leaving indents in the golden skin of his forehead. His blue eyes are tinged violet—a commonality for every time he chokes back tears, which is evident in his gravelly tone. I have known him long enough to know when he is really hurting.

"It's going to be okay—"

"Hold on. My dad's calling," he says and ends the call before I get to say goodbye.

I sit there and stare at my phone.

"Everything all right?" Mom ventures, trying for kind and concerned.

It takes me a moment to gather my thoughts. "No," I say after a moment. "Abel's mom tried to kill herself."

"Abel *Harpen*?"

"Yes."

"I haven't heard you talk about him since senior year of college."

Wow, it has *been a minute since I've sat with Mom like this.*

"I'm in love with him," I blurt. No reason to withhold the information now—not after such a close tragedy.

Mom doesn't say anything at first. She just crosses her legs and rolls her tongue across her front teeth.

"All right," she says. No bite in her tone, just acceptance. *For once.* "So, is Alana okay?"

"She's fine, I just...don't know if Abel will be."

"What makes you say that?"

I gesture to my phone. "He's not himself."

She sighs. "Well, that's understandable, Carrington. He almost lost his mother. That's scary."

"Yeah, but..."

I know Abel. I know he is going to do everything in his power to make sure his mom is okay...*and* his siblings *and* his dad. He will put himself last. I know this like the back of my hand, from all those times in college when he sacrificed club meetings or study groups just to sit with a friend and help cheer them up when they were down. He did it for me, after I didn't get the grade I wanted or when I missed that internship deadline junior year. He sat with me and talked about the most random things until I was laughing so hard my belly ached. I didn't realize the toll it took on *him* until I ran into him during one of my bathroom breaks from a night class. He was exiting the men's restroom, vomit stained on his upper lip. He had worried himself sick over a test he hadn't studied for, all because he was taking care of his (at the time) newly medicated mother. He ended up acing the exam, of course, but that look on his face when we spotted each other in the desolate hallway...*I'm busted!* on a whole new level. The desperate *I'm okay, I swear!* expression that tore my heart to shreds.

Abel's selflessness is his fatal flaw.

"But?" Mom prompts.

"He has Bipolar I. I'm worried about him."

I unconsciously flip through the *DSM* until I find the bolded letters typed against an orange background: **Manic Episode**, the criteria below making my stomach roil.

Mom says, "I remember you telling me Abel is consistent with his therapy and medications."

"He is."

"Well, then, just let him know you're here for him during this difficult time. Something as simple as that can make all the difference in the world."

I close the *DSM* and plop it back onto the coffee table.

"You need to focus on yourself, Carrington," Mom says. "This is not your fight."

"Not my fight," I echo; it turns into a scoff. "What happened to being there for him?"

"You can be there for someone and still set boundaries. For example, you can tell Abel you are there if he needs someone to talk to. But you can't *force* him to talk to you. Understanding what you can and cannot control is a healthy step."

"Yeah, like how you tried to take control of my decision to go to New York."

It stings the atmosphere once it's out, but I can't take it back.

Mom blinks at me, her jaw hardening like refrigerated chocolate. "That was different, Carrington."

"Right." I stand, stretch on my tiptoes, and head for the door. "It's always different when it's you."

40

———

I hardly taste the lemon in my tea this morning, and the words in my poetry journal hardly touch my soul.

Abel has been silent since our brief phone call this past Friday. I thought that in the forty-eight hours since, he would have reached out. Nothing.

I chew on my pencil eraser and glare up at the glowing menu of the café. My gaze must be intense because a woman in a pantsuit takes one horrified look at me and hurries past. I can't help it. My brain is locked in another writer's block chokehold. Basically, this is Gandalf vs. the Balrog: *Creativity...You shall not pass!* My leg bounces twenty-five miles an hour.

When the bells over the door chime, I know it's Hunter before I even look up. We are friend soulmates. I can sense him—in a way that is not sexual or creepy. He is simply my other half, baked into a taller, muscular frame with bright-green eyes.

"How was Thanksgiving with the family?" he asks, placing a sheet of paper in front of me.

I pull the paper into my lap. "Not a picnic."

I used to sleep in on the Saturday after Thanksgiving, but this time I dragged my massive blue suitcase down the stairs at eight o'clock a.m., roused only by the smell of Tucker's sizzling bacon and my strong desire to say *adiós*!

"You're leaving already?" my brother asked, turning to face me, spatula in hand.

"All good things must come to an end."

"That's stupid."

"You're stupid."

"You're childish."

"I love you."

Tucker cracked a smile. "I love you, too."

I did wait to have breakfast with my family before heading off down the road. And after Lauren squeezed my hand and Dad said, "Be safe, Tiny Carrot," Mom pulled me into her arms. It was the look on Tucker's face that made me hug her back. *Be nice.*

"If you need me, call me," Mom had said.

"All right." *Not going to happen.*

Of course, Uncle Benny and my cousins were forced to act like they gave a crap whether I left or stayed. Aunt Lorraine told me to consider getting Botox in my lips.

Now, in the café, Hunter sighs and falls into the chair across from me. "It's all there." Meaning the paper in my lap.

I glance down at it. "Jeez, Hunter, your handwriting's atrocious."

"I believe the words you're looking for are, 'Thank you, Hunter, for sacrificing some time away from research to read my poetry and offer more suggestions.'"

"Thank you, my sweet Hunter, for sacrificing some time away from research to read my poetry and offer more suggestions!"

"Was the British accent really necessary?"

"Come on. You know who you're talking to?"

He chuckles and rises to go order his usual: black coffee with cream and sugar, which I *still* do not understand how he can stomach.

His notes truly look like they were written by a five-year-old hyped up on Pixy Stix, but I'm able to make out a few sentences. Mostly grammar cleaning, correcting confusing pronouns, suggestions to add more meat on the bones of open-ended poems.

"Small stuff," Hunter says, returning with his steaming cup of mud.

"Thank you."

"You're pretty chill with criticism."

"This isn't criticism. This a friend helping a friend make their poetry better."

He takes a sip of his drink. "True."

My eyes flick over the nearly illegible handwriting, making out words like *Strengthen this* and *describe this more*. As the suggestions whirl through my prefrontal cortex, I can feel my brain squaring off with the writer's block. Creativity *shall* pass! I jot down a few ideas in my journal, then fold the piece of paper and stick into the notebook's spine.

"How are *you* with criticism?" I ask.

"Terrible," Hunter admits. "I know it's not an attack on me, but every time I get reviews back on research, it feels like they're out to kill me."

"Members of the IRB *are*."

"Funny. I've just always been super protective of my work."

"I'm sensing some self-deprecation here."

His green eyes, I've found, have a habit of reaching into my soul, even when we aren't talking about me. "I'm passionate, that's all. These are human beings I'm dealing with. I want to get it right."

I clear my throat and try to pitch my voice down an octave or two. "You're going to have some bumps in the road, Hunter. No one ever said saving the world was an easy job."

He considers my words for a moment, eyes flicking to the far wall then down at his cup. "Okay, okay, point taken. Have you heard from Abel?"

My heart shrinks. "For only five minutes last Friday."

"I haven't heard from him at all. He even lost our streak on Snapchat. I know he's dealing with something really tough right now, but I want to make sure I didn't do anything to piss him off or make it worse."

"You didn't." That, I can say for sure. "I think he...just needs to be there for his mom right now." *I just hope he doesn't lose himself.*

The sounds of the coffee shop swell around us: blenders, mixed chitchat, Katy Perry's "Never Really Over." The subject of Abel seems to have darkened the whole atmosphere of the café.

I sigh and take a crack at breaking the ice. "Have you noticed that we always have deep conversations in this place?"

"It must be the coffee bean smell," he says. "It goes to our heads."

"Like weed."

"Have you ever tried weed?"

"No, but I've heard things."

He laughs. I laugh. We go back to being carefree friend soulmates, but something heavy throbs in the pit of my stomach. I can't let go of the fear that Abel isn't safe.

"Take the rest of the afternoon off," Ruth says, sweeping the last specks of dust off her purple ceiling fans.

I'm standing below, steadying the ladder she's perched on. "No way. What about the—"

"Look around, Cari." She switches the Swiffer to her other hand. "It's a ghost town in here."

"A beautiful, purple ghost town."

"I told you business slows down for a few days after Thanksgiving. You should take the offer while it's on the table because trust me, once December first hits, we are going to be in crunch time."

"The holiday crunch."

She climbs back down the ladder, and my eyes track her every step. Once she's safely on the ground again, she turns to face me. "Seriously, Cari. Go home."

"You sure? 'Cause I don't mean to toot my own horn, but I'm a pretty talented dishwasher."

"I can take care of the dishes; you just go soak up some sunshine. You've been looking a little pale."

I think I am supposed to take offense at that, but I just grin. "When December first comes, you know who to call."

"Uh, you're still working on Wednesday!" she calls as I run to get my purse and sweatshirt.

"And when I arrive that morning, I will have Maryland's largest bag of peanut chocolate-covered pretzels for my favorite boss."

"Go on," she shakes the dust cloth at me "Get outta here."

I drive to the only place I think of that isn't my apartment: the park. It is a nice fifty degrees today, and the sky is a van Gogh-esque mix of cyan and azure: the type of blue that Mother Nature only reserves for *perfect* autumn afternoons. The kind where fallen red-gold leaves have flash mobs in the wind and you swear you can *taste* pumpkin spice in the air. Good thing I always keep spare journals in the pockets behind my passenger seat!

At this time of day, early afternoon, the park is full of dog-walkers and an abnormally large amount of Saint Bernards—three to be exact, which is more than I've *ever* seen in one place, what are the odds? Too many toddlers to count scramble around the jungle gym twenty feet away, and a group of pregnant women in neon-colored jackets speed-walk by, chatting about how *Lexi's new haircut is just hideous*...at least, that's what I catch.

I settle on a bench and open my journal. This notebook has nothing to do with my upcoming poetry collection. It is one I keep for convenience's sake if an idea ever strikes me while I'm out and about. There are little splatterings of ideas in this journal, abandoned or forgotten though never erased—just in case. Short, descriptive paragraphs of things I've seen throughout the years. This journal dates all the way back to senior year of high school. There are a lot of names in here, some crossed out, some with hearts; there's even a heart around Kai Bell's name. I gag audibly and flip the page.

A fresh, blank page. My best frenemy.

Sometimes it is good to get away from the poetry, to let my brain flow as it wants. I write about everything I see, from the whispers of white clouds to the giggling toddlers caught in a game of Red-Hot Lava on the playground. I am so entranced in the scene I'm writing that at first, I think I've only imagined someone calling my name.

I look up in time to see him jogging toward me. "Cari!"

"Abel!"

I jump to my feet. He lifts me up and twirls me around, and I don't even care that droplets of sweat flick off his skin onto mine. He's here. He sets me down and I wish he didn't have to.

"You're back," I say with my heart in my throat.

He looks perfectly normal, happy even. "Of course I'm back. I have a research meeting with my advisor this week."

The elephant could not be larger between us. "And your mom?"

"She's home. She goes to therapy twice a week and is on new medication, but I'll take it! Charlotte and Melanie are back at school. Dad's heading back to work tomorrow. Everything's great!"

His breath is heavy from the jog, but his smile is like a shot of heroin for my system. Perfect white teeth, rosy cheeks, sweat-slicked golden hair piled high on top of his head, a few rebellious, hopelessly handsome curls swooping this way or that. Those blue, *blue* eyes. This Abel is so different from the one I last saw on Meg's porch step. In fact, he's glowing.

"You sure you're okay?" I ask.

"I'm perfect, Cari Carrington. In fact, I want to take you to dinner tonight."

I stare at him a moment, struggling to believe he's back to feeling great. Scared to believe it, actually. But the thought of dinner with him sounds too great to pass up. "I'm glad you're okay, and I'm glad your family is healing."

"Dinner," he sings in my ear, shooting goosebumps down my

neck and shoulder. I let him kiss the tender spot below my jaw and then step away—for the kids' sake and gossiping mothers-to-be, now on their fifth lap up the path.

"Where are we going for dinner?" I ask, my breath short from that one kiss.

"You choose. Anywhere you want to go, I want to go."

41

———

When Abel picks me up two hours later, freshly showered and dressed in white jeans and a deep green polo, I immediately feel shabby in my simple black dress and heels.

"I should change," I say, eyeing his sculpted chest under the green shirt fabric.

"Why would you do that?" He pulls me against him. "You look *beautiful*."

He kisses me right there on the curb in front of my apartment building—kisses me in a way that stains my cheeks red and gets my heart pumping in turbo time. When he snakes his hands around my waist and slides them down toward my butt, my soul snares on my organs. He has never kissed me like this in public, for all the passing cars and bicyclists to see. It is not that I'm embarrassed. I just don't want to share this moment with total strangers. I want Abel all to myself. If I am going to touch him, then I am going to *touch* him...in a bedroom or the occasional bar bathroom where we can do so in private. But he's so physically passionate right now. That's unusual.

He finally steps back, the orange setting sun streaking off his

Aviators. Still tangling with my confusing feelings about this PDA, I gesture to his car. "Shall we?"

He opens the passenger door for me and then hops into the driver's side. His natural smell envelops me as I settle into the leather seat—sandalwood with a hint of eucalyptus—and I relax a bit. He puts "September" by Earth, Wind & Fire on full volume and pulls away from the curb. I have to laugh as he taps the steering wheel and belts the chorus from his lungs. Every so often he glances over at me and lip syncs pieces of the verses, and I have to sing along because this song was made with some type of drug in it. It is addicting from the very first note.

We cruise past shops and restaurants aglow with buzzing energy and the laughter of people who clearly want to lose themselves in the sweet autumn evening. It's perfect weather, fit for a football game or a bonfire. That is why Abel and I decided on Smokey Grill, a restaurant/bar outside the city with outdoor seating around a roaring firepit with live music and the best hot wings in the area, according to Yelp.

"Whoa," I say as Abel practically stomps on the gas. I lean over and check the speedometer. "You're pushing fifty-five in a thirty-five zone, buddy. Slow down a little bit."

He taps the brakes and laughs. Well, actually, he nearly doubles over laughing. I look at him as "Jump" by Van Halen begins over the speakers. Abel's smile is so wide, for a second I think it might split in half.

"Wow. Should I retire and become a comedian or something?" I ask.

"No." Another laugh explodes out of him. "It's just the way you said that! 'You're pushing fifty-five in a thirty-five, *buddy.*'" He cackles. "That was *hilarious!*"

My brow creases as I stare at him. I love his laugh, but his energy is suddenly over the top, which is uncharacteristic. I'm worried about him again.

"Are you okay?" I ask.

"I'm amazing, Carrington." His eyes widen for emphasis and he slaps the gearshift before pulling the car into the parking lot and killing the engine. He hops right out and loops around to open my door for me.

I push down the fear. Tonight is about reconnecting, and even though my stomach is twisting its hands, I will not turn tonight into a game of Twenty Questions with him. I want so badly to have fun. To have fun and let go.

I have never been to Smokey Grill; I only saw pictures of it advertised in catalogs or on social media. I can see why it is so popular though, architecturally for starters. Dark walnut panels intersect and jut outward, creating rectangles and one giant triangle above the main entrance, holding pieces of glass in place that are painted in zigzags of fiery reds, plum purples, and summer greens. Floating balls of light are visible through the main doors, and as we get closer, I still have no clue how they are hanging from the peaked wooden ceiling. I assume via clear strings, but I don't want to ruin the magic for myself. As we step inside, the smell of sautéed mushrooms and crackling firewood wraps around us. The hostess leads us across the velvet burgundy carpets and through the maze of cherrywood tables, packed with people sipping cocktails. We step onto the patio and head toward the sparkling fire that spits a shower of sparks into the darkening night sky. At the opposite end of the patio, a band serenades the crowd with Joan Jett and the Blackhearts' classic "I Love Rock 'n Roll." A few brave couples have even stepped onto the dance floor, shaking their bodies, drinks in hand.

I gawk up at the indigo sky. "This place is incredible."

"I've only been here twice. Once was with Hunter and a couple of other friends at the end of our first semester, and the other time was for my mom when my family was here visiting over Mother's Day weekend."

The mention of his mom sends a needle through my heart, but he doesn't seem fazed at all. He is smiling, weaving his straw wrapper in and around his fingers. Bickering aside, if *my* mother attempted to take her life, I don't think I would be ready to go out for a fancy dinner so soon. The shock and the grief of what-ifs would still haunt me. But either Abel is more resilient than I thought, or he downed two cans of Red Bull because his energy is *tangible*. It is like his mother does not even exist at the moment.

"I'm ordering a bucket of those wings! No, wait—they have a wing Ferris wheel! Cari, look at this." He shows me his menu. "All the types of wings on a *Ferris wheel*! I'm ordering that."

"It probably costs an arm and a kidney."

"Only thirty-five dollars." He waves the matter away.

"If you say so, but you're sharing the wings with me. And I'm ordering a side of wedge fries."

"Don't forget the honey mustard."

I shake my head in mock disappointment. "Just admit it already. You're from Mars. No one in their right state of mind eats french fries with honey mustard instead of ketchup."

"Actually, I'm from Mercury. It's why I tan so easily. Plus, you're the one who has no taste. Ketchup is so..." He gestures vaguely with his hand. "Expected."

"And delicious."

"No."

"Call ketchup the romance trope of the condiments," I say. "It is expected, but it works so well."

"That doesn't make any sense."

We laugh so hard we slap the table. I'm not really sure what is so funny, but when his laugh turns into another wheeze, I lose it all over again. He leans back in his chair and pushes a fist to his mouth, trying to stop. His face turns beet red, and my sides scream.

This is love, I think, trying to speak through uncontrollable laughter and at the same time not wanting to speak at all and risk missing even a sliver of a second in this alternate universe where there is nothing but us. Us, us, us. What a beautiful word.

Abel takes a sip of his water and a steadying breath. "You're such a silly goose."

A waiter sets a bowl of steaming sliced bread and tiny packets of butter on our table. When Abel orders the wing Ferris wheel, we giggle into our hands again, and the waiter's eyes flick back and forth between us. That look says, *Why did I get stuck with the goons?* He doesn't try to offer us a drink menu before skidding away with our order.

"Life is perfect." Abel reaches his palms toward the glittering fire that sits in the center of the patio. "I'm here with the most beautiful girl in the universe, and I get to hear '80s music performed live for free. I didn't even know this band was going to be here tonight, Cari!" He gestures to the lead singer, dressed in torn leather, ripped jeans, and combat boots.

He leans into the mic with that Mick Jagger swagger. They have since switched to a cover of "Eye of the Tiger," and honestly, they are murdering it. But my eyes stay trained on Abel, waiting expectantly.

"What?" he asks, smile pinned in place with invisible bobby pins.

"And your mom's alive." I feel bad bringing it up, but it seems like a crucial point to be thankful for tonight.

He laughs, carefree. "*Duh!*" He lifts his glass of water. "To life."

I raise my glass to his. In college, Abel was a kind, happy-go-lucky, young genius, acing all his exams, forming lasting friendships with all his professors, and making everyone around him feel valued and important. He was always a positive force, but tonight, it seems like the positivity is *pouring* out of him. It is a tsunami of optimism. I have never seen him like this—pointing at the floating balls of light, loudly exclaiming how *beautiful* they are. "Have you ever seen something so *gorgeous* in your entire *life?*"

A redhead at the table next to us and her bright-eyed brunette date break their dreamy eye contact to glance over at Abel. He doesn't seem to notice or care.

Our waiter appears with a miniature rotating Ferris wheel, complete with twinkling lights. Each cart is filled with crispy hot wings. Cups of barbecue, buffalo, garlic parmesan, and cilantro lemon sauce glisten on the platform below the wheel. A second waiter hands me a basket of steaming wedge fries.

"Are you kidding?" Abel gasps as they set the Ferris wheel on our table. "This is *amazing!*" He smiles at the waiter, and whatever hostility he was harboring toward us visibly dissolves. No one can resist Abel.

The two waiters disappear.

"I am trying every single one of these sauces," Abel promises.

"Are you feeling cauliflower taco brave?" I ask, plucking a wing from one of the carts.

He looks up at me, puzzled. When I realize he has no clue what I'm referencing, my heart sinks the tiniest bit.

"Cauliflower taco brave? When we went to Rozenbury last month and you tried the cauliflower taco?" His blank stare sets me back in my seat. "You don't remember that?"

"Vaguely," he answers a beat later. "But what does it matter? We're here *now!*" As if that is the only answer I need. He gathers a couple wings onto his plate, smears each type of sauce on each individual wing.

I try to ignore the sting zipping through my chest. I was under the impression that every moment spent together was burned into his memory like it is in mine. *Quit ruining the moment,* my conscience hisses. *He's a human being. He's allowed to forget.*

"Here's to here and now," I say and dip my wing into the cilantro lemon sauce.

The wings are *exceptional.* Yelp was right. We devour them one by one, the sauces smearing across our lips and plates. We probably seem drunk, laughing over the smallest things, but it really is just the autumn evening. The warmth of the fire, the lead singer's sultry voice.

As I finish my last wing, the crowd cheers. I turn around in time to see the band welcome a saxophone player onstage. He's got the whole look: dark shades, frizzy hair, million-dollar smile, glimmering instrument. The cheering lifts to a roar.

"For this next song," the lead singer says, "I want to see all the couples out on the dance floor."

More cheering. A few couples rise immediately and scurry to the space in front of the stage.

"We're slowin' it down now," the singer explains and cues the keyboardist.

The first few notes of George Michael's "Careless Whisper" echo into the night, and the crowd goes wild. Abel's jaw drops. I already know what he's thinking.

"Absolutely not," I say.

"Oh, come on. I'll buy you an ice cream."

"I don't dance like this."

"Now I *know* you're lying."

The challenge bounces between us. The introductory notes swell, casting a romantic spell on the audience. It becomes harder and harder to look away from Abel's eyes. They melt everything inside me. I sigh.

"One song."

"This is *the* song," he says and takes my hand.

We walk onto the floor among a crescendo of hoots and hollers. Even the lead singer smiles at us. My cheeks burn.

"Relax," Abel whispers.

His hands drape on my waist, sink to my hips. The closeness is already making my heartbeat funky. His cologne wraps around me, pulls me in, and for a moment, it is just me against his chest—*us*, swaying to these hypnotic notes until the familiar saxophone melody plays out, and everyone screams. The singer's voice is smooth and rich, paying true homage to George Michael. It almost seems like he's on stage himself.

Abel's lips graze my ear. "You are *so* beautiful."

My eyes flutter closed. The song is a blanket, settling over my shoulders, sinking into my bone marrow. Abel cradles me against his chest. Even the stars whistle as the chorus rings out and every mouth sings that they will never dance again. I chance a peek up at Abel, only to find his eyes trained on me. There is a hunger in them, an undeniable desire. It sinks its teeth in my heart. Heat trickles through my abdomen, sinking lower and lower.

Abel twirls me and pulls me in so that my back is flush against his chest. His breath glides down the side of my face, and I can feel *every* part of him, even his own heartbeat, knocking against my shoulder blade. There is nothing but him and this song.

The saxophone riff plays again, and his lips find my neck. It is a brief kiss—only a taste of what I want him to do. No, I don't like PDA, but I'm finding it hard to remember why at the moment. He spins me around again until we're nose to nose, and all of my concern floats away.

"I want to take you home," he murmurs, eyes glued to my lips.

"Do it, then."

We don't even wait for the song to end.

42

———

WE BURST INTO MY APARTMENT, ARMS TANGLED, LIPS MOVING feverishly together. I reach out blindly and slam the door shut. His hands, shockingly cold, slip under my dress and drift up until he grazes my bra, squeezes my breasts. A moan slips through my lips. We stumble through the foyer and accidentally knock over the vintage coat rack in the corner. We don't even break away to look at it; our mouths split into smiles and connect again.

He nudges me back against the wall and unzips my dress. It falls to my ankles in a puddle, and my bra lands somewhere across the room. Even parting to remove our clothing takes up too much time. I want him, and I want him *now*. Shirtless, our chests collide, hearts punching each other as my hands tackle his belt and zipper. I palm his erection and earn a groan. In fact, he kicks his pants off the rest of the way and lifts me up so my legs are wrapped around his waist. Our next kiss nearly hurts, it's so passionate. I can't get enough of him.

My hands need to clutch him closer; my nose needs to overdose on his smell. My heart needs to cut through muscle and bone to fuse with his. This isn't enough. Frantic making out is child's play. I want all of him in one shot, no half-doses.

I've only partly registered that my panties have disappeared because my hands are working tirelessly to remove his boxers. When we're finally free from our clothing, he lowers me back onto the ground. I sink down until my toes touch the linoleum, and he pulls back to look at me. We're panting, our breaths dancing together as we lose all sense of time in each other's eyes. His sweet, heavenly blue eyes....

That's when we snap.

He falls to his knees, clutches my thighs, and places his head between them. My head falls back against the wall.

"I don't...think you understand," Abel murmurs. My fingers lock in his hair.

"Understand what?"

His speed quickens, and I cry out.

He pauses, looks up at me. "How much I want you."

It happens so quickly: blinding, hot pleasure zigzags across my vision, pings through my body. His mouth brings me to the highest edge I've ever encountered, and just like a feather in the wind, I'm tipped over. I scream his name.

He kisses a trail up my thighs, leaving goosebumps in his wake, and I try to think if there was ever a time when my skin didn't bend to his will. His lips find my ear.

"I need more of you," he whispers.

"What are you waiting for?"

He swoops me up into his arms and beelines for the couch. "Come on," he urges breathlessly.

I climb onto him and gasp at the sheer relief. For a second, neither of us moves, frozen at the feeling of wholeness. Oneness. It never felt right with anyone else, but he is my metaphorical puzzle piece. A perfect fit.

And then, as if one more second without friction will kill us both, he pushes me down onto him, and that's it. We move spastically, desperately. The mere sight of his parted lips and sparking blue eyes nearly finishes me off. His hands alternate between my ass and thighs, squeezing at just the right moments, causing new sounds to escape my mouth. Sweat slicks my forehead, but we don't slow down. The pressure is building ferociously. He leans forward, causing my back to arch, and it only takes five seconds for the pleasure to zing through me again.

He pulls out, flops me onto my back, and reenters my body—all in one swift movement. My nails scrape across his back, but he doesn't wince. He just moves. In, out, in, out, his gasps pulsating against my cheek.

A lot of people say that good sex dulls your senses. That there is nothing else besides the person in your bed. But I disagree. In this moment, as Abel slides deep and deeper into me, my senses are *heightened*. I can taste color. I can hear emotions. I can feel sounds. It is *exhilarating*.

Abel burrows deeper and reaches down to touch me. It is all I need. He lets me have my moment, grinding his hips into mine, and then he stiffens as he reaches his own release.

That is when I realize he's not wearing a condom. Granted, I'm on the pill, so I know there is at least a 91 percent chance that I did not just get impregnated, but that's not the problem here. The problem is that this time, he didn't even stop to ask.

JUST TO BE SAFE, I swallow a Plan B the next morning after Abel leaves. I had to practically push him out the door.

He's working at his internship this morning, and after a *full night* of sex, binge-eating pretzels out of the bag, and more sex, I figured he would be *exhausted*. I am. My body feels like a piece of seaweed lapping over the waves—no intention of fighting the current anymore. Abel, on the other hand, was all jazzed about getting to campus so he could brighten his advisor's day by presenting newly cleaned data. He kissed me on the cheek and practically skipped out the door.

Thankfully, I'm not scheduled to work today, so I belly flop onto the couch. I can still smell Abel's rich cologne; it's ingrained in my throw pillows. Not that I mind.

Last night was the best sex I have ever had. Aside from the momentary sheer panic I felt at the possibility of getting pregnant, I have never come undone so frequently and so quickly as I did last night.

If I were in grad school, I would love to run some good old qualitative research on why the kindest men with the sweetest hearts become hot, dominant forces in bed far more often than their conceited male counterparts. Men like...well, Kai Bell, who don't know a dildo from a dil-*don't*.

This day was originally going to be dedicated to editing my poetry collection, but I would rather just lie here and pretend Abel's head is still between my legs. My latest poem "Funny Bone" flashes to mind—a piece that links falling in love to hitting your funny bone on a damn doorknob. The instant before the pain blossoms and a dizzying swarm of metaphorical hornets zips through your body, leaving you speechless. That's where I am right now, a realm between reality and la-la land where time sits on the back burner, and I feel happily numb.

My phone chimes with a text from Abel.

> Bowling tonight—lame or not lame?

I reply with a smirking emoji.

> Shouldn't you be at school?

> Theoretically.

> Well, I theoretically want to go bowling tonight.

> I'll take that as a yes!

He adds a grinning emoji.

Get to class, Ferris Bueller.

That reference made my heart melt.

I mean it. Don't make me hunt you down.

Now THAT'S something I would love.

I smile at my phone.

Not to be weird, but this man makes me want to squeeze my heart into a glass, mix it with some club soda and fruit syrup, and serve it to him on a silver platter. He makes me want to invest in some construction paper, glitter, and rainbow markers to draw stick figures of us holding hands.

Shush. I want a full research paper on all the assessments you conduct today by the time you pick me up at…let's say 5 p.m.

Page count?

Forty MINIMUM.

Piece o' cake. See you at 5!

I drop my phone on the cushion beside me and stare at it like it's a bouquet of lilies and peonies. Somebody get my heart a chill pill.

I reach for my poetry journal and for Hunter's list of suggestions. The list is crumpled and creased now from taking up residency in my tote bag for twenty-some hours. *God, his handwriting.* I squint, trying to make out the slashes and the slants and the scribbles. It takes fifteen minutes for me to read through the whole list. One point in particular catches my eye: *Consider this, is too much love dangerous?*

I stare at the question. Read it. Reread it. It snags on a region of my brain that is momentarily blank, and I struggle to come up with an answer. It's an interesting angle that I haven't yet considered.

Is too much love dangerous?

This is not a question someone typically asks in the sweetheart honeymoon phase of a relationship. Which makes it the perfect concept to explore in a poetry collection. I bounce my pencil between my fingers as I chew on an idea. Then I begin to write.

"Ocean Floor"

I put my trust
in a tank of oxygen
and allow the pressure
of your sea-rearing eyes
to shove me down,
secure a metal clamp on my chest.
The ocean
is bigger than I thought.
The sunlight
can only reach so far,
growing dimmer
as I sink deeper.
It is here—
at the train track
of your optic nerve—
that my oxygen runs out.
The current pulls me
toward the recesses
of your brain.
I have no choice.
My toes graze
your ocean floor,
and I wonder
if I will lose myself here.

I dot the period and pull my pencil away. Something about this piece feels oddly true but in a way I can't put my finger on. I love Abel with every organ and cell in my body. Yet, Hunter's question has planted a seed in my soul. Am I overlooking something in Abel because I choose not to see it?

43

I IGNORE MY GUT INTUITION, MOSTLY BECAUSE I WANT TO GO bowling. I am a sucker for some loud, ruthless competition.

The place Abel and I roll up to is about ten minutes from my apartment and looks shabby—splotched, cracked white brick, faded white-and-red-striped awning, and blinking *Welcome In!* sign. The inside is a spaceship to Saturn. A hazy purple light washes over our skin as we walk in, and we come face-to-face with rows of claw machines in various shades of tacky neon hues. The carpet is a whirl of planets and stars in a night sky. Ahead, bowlers whip the ball down the lane. I am in my element.

"You're on," I tell Abel, sashaying past him to the front desk.

He keeps my pace. "If I remember correctly, you averaged a mean ninety the last time we went bowling."

"That was in college, you naïve little goose. I've gotten better. Consider me your worst enemy."

"Says the girl who works in a bakery and writes poetry for a living."

"Precisely."

"Excuse me." Having gotten our attention, the teenage girl behind the counter toys with her nose ring. "Is it just you two?"

"Yup. Winner—" Abel points to himself, then to me, "—and loser."

"Right. How many games?"

"Three," I answer.

The girl leans on her hand and clicks lazily through the computer, taps on the keyboard with her three-inch-long ice-blue nails. "Cash or card?"

Abel whips out his credit card before I can and grins when I scold him. The girl blows a gum bubble while the purchase registers. Her eyeliner could slice my finger.

She hands Abel back his card. "Shoe size?"

Once we have thanked Miss Sunshine, chosen our balls, and entered our lane, the urge to trash talk overflows in my veins.

"You are going down like the bacon I accidentally overcooked for breakfast."

"Is that all you got? You're going down like a one-hit wonder," Abel replies.

"Well, *you* are going down like a man named Stan who lived in San Fran with a fake tan."

He narrows his eyes and walks up to me, towering a full foot above me. I don't back down.

"Poet addict," he says.

"Psychology freak," I spit back.

"Loudmouth."

"Airhead."

"Bench warmer!"

"Sink-clogger!"

"Cheek-biter!"

"Ass wiper!"

We glare into each other's souls and then burst into uncontrollable laughter. We can't catch our breaths for a total of five minutes before Abel gestures to the lane.

"Wild animals first."

"Why, thank you."

I pluck my turquoise ball from the stand and strut forward, sending the ball rocketing down the lane. Six pins topple over.

"Take that, oxygen thief," I call over my shoulder. My next attempt takes down three of the remaining pins.

"I don't mean to brag, but..." I shrug and take a seat next to him on the couch.

"That's nothing," he says. "I've seen better bowling from a drunk woman in a gold sweatshirt."

"Was that one of the many girls drooling over you?"

"No, it was my grandma on her seventy-fifth birthday." He rises before I can comment further.

Abel is admittedly a much better bowler than I am, but I would never say that to the sexy crook in his smile or to his hilariously adorable victory dance at receiving a strike.

"Beginner's luck," I mumble.

"Call it whatever you want. Loser buys soda and pizza."

It is a cutthroat game. His beginner's luck dissipates after that first stellar show-off, and we average seven or eight pins per turn. In the end, his hundred-one passes my ninety-eight, and I begrudgingly slap a twenty dollar bill down on the concession counter.

In between greasy pieces of pepperoni pizza and loud slurps of Sprite, we play another game. And then another. As his last attempt sends the pins clanging against each other, I sink to my knees in defeat.

"Winner, winner, chicken dinner," Abel sings.

"Oh, please. You probably rigged it!"

We're very touchy as we return the bowling balls and set our shoes back on the counter for Miss Happykins to reshelve. Touchy as in, that friendly shoving that secretly means *Rip my clothes off and pin me against the wall before I lose my shit*. He traps my hips in his hands as we approach his car, and it's not the wall, but somehow, it's hotter to have my backside pressed against the chill of his car.

Once again, we make out in plain sight—for the world and half the galaxy to observe over a bowl of buttered popcorn. This time, I don't care at all. *Let 'em look*, I decide. The way Abel's tongue slides across my lower lip might as well be its own genre of porn.

His body presses into mine, and—here comes the dizzying head-rush. The *Oh, God*. The burning in my belly. The curving of my spine so I can be fully flush against him, be fully in his space, fully become *him*. It never gets old.

"Car sex?" he suggests.

"In a sketchy parking lot at ten o'clock?" I pull him back to my lips so I can bite his.

"Yes."

"At least pull around back to the alley," I say.

It is one thing to make out in public, another to have full-on vaginal sex. I didn't think I was this crazy until we speed down and around the corner to an even sketchier parking lot between the bowling alley and another brick building that I swear I saw in an episode of *Ghost Adventures*. But whatever. All that matters is that it is dark. We dive clumsily into the backseat, giggling when we kick random objects—presumably a headrest and maybe even the gear shift at one point.

As Katerine once suggested during her experimental sex adventures with Ben, romantic lovemaking is good every once in a while, as long as it is balanced out by the occasional raunchy fuck in a bathroom bar, or, in our case, the backseat of a Toyota Corolla, which doesn't offer much space to begin with. So, we wriggle around, fighting to remove our pants and climb on top of each other.

"Condom," I hiss as he drags his tongue along my neck.

"I don't have any."

That's a mood killer. "Abel."

"What? You're on the pill."

"And I am still scared of getting pregnant."

His hands go slack on my waist. "You're not going to get pregnant." My brief silence is enough time for him to come back and kiss me, reigniting the fire between my legs.

Dammit.

"You better make me scream your name."

He does. Twice, to be exact. And then I let him finish in my mouth, which makes me want to hurl both my lungs and spleen out, but I don't say anything. It was my idea anyway.

On our way back to my apartment, it vaguely occurs to me that car sex isn't my style. Katerine has a point, but that doesn't mean I have to agree. My stomach still hurts, and an unexpected sense of shame rolls over me as Bon Jovi's "You Give Love a Bad Name" serenades us from the car speakers.

Abel eats me out on my couch an hour later, but I don't feel any better or any sexier. I feel just as ashamed for reasons I can't label. And forty-five minutes into a 2 a.m. showing of *Footloose,* I sprint to the bathroom, miss the toilet by two feet, and puke on the tile.

NOT PREGNANT, just embarrassed and sick from the taste of a man's ejaculation. (Seriously, why is that so praised?). Abel hadn't heard me get sick; he was too engrossed in watching Kevin Bacon's warehouse dance and finishing off a bag of saltine crackers from the depths of my snack cabinet. In his defense, I've always been a quiet vomiter. But I spent a good chunk of time on my knees in front of the toilet, occasionally dry heaving again.

I have only ever thrown up from anxiety one other time: senior year of high school before a two-hundred-point debate in AP history class with a teacher that acted more like a justice in the Supreme Court (pompous prick). This was a different anxiety. This was mortification—particularly at the realization that my desire for Abel's body made me do things I'm not very comfortable with in hindsight. Condomless car sex in a back alley and actually swallowing his semen...yeah, that's not me. It is not Abel's fault he is so infuriatingly good-looking, but maybe Hunter does have a valid point: maybe too much love *is* dangerous.

Do I know what love is?

All of this to say, it should not surprise me when Abel shows up outside my door on Wednesday evening with a small bouquet of roses and a tiny package wrapped in silver paper. And it doesn't surprise me that I let him in. I'm not angry at him. I'm angry at myself.

"What's all this?"

"I can't buy something beautiful for a beautiful girl?" he asks.

"You can." I lean in to accept his kiss (a quick peck; I keep it short).

We move further into my apartment, and I steer us to sit at the island because I'm afraid if we sit on the couch, I *might* end up pregnant. Besides, love is supposed to be more than sex, right?

"Open it." Abel is beaming. He looks so good, smells so good.

The package contains a small velvet box. Inside, I find a necklace with an aquamarine stone set in silver. My birthstone.

"Now, *this* is thoughtful," I say, even though it looks to be an expensive necklace. My heart squeezes.

"March sixteenth." He looks so pleased. Consider it an early present."

"Early by four months." My eyes flick to his as an uneasy feeling cuts through my gut. "How much was this?"

"Like I'd tell you." He lightly pokes my side.

I get lost in his eyes instantly, and my thoughts melt.

All of a sudden, he perks up. "Do you want to make chocolate chip cookies?"

"Right now?"

"Yeah!"

"Uh..." I scan my kitchen. "I don't know if I have any ingredients—"

"Let's go buy some!" He bounces on his toes.

I'm worried that he's spent too much money on me, but this I know for certain: I absolutely cannot say no to those refulgent eyes and that adorable dimple.

So, I splurge on chocolate chips and eggs at the nearest grocery store, and a half hour later, Abel and I are mixing the dough while Christmas music plays from my phone.

We scream-sing; we laugh; we reminisce about old clubs in college; we smear bits of dough on each other's hands; we watch the cookies rise in the oven like bright-eyed five-year-olds.

I retrieve a bottle of white wine and pour myself a glass. Just as I am about to ask Abel if he would like some water, he says, "Ooh, let me try some of that!"

My stomach drops. "You...want...some of my wine?"

"Yeah!"

"Rockin' Around the Christmas Tree" echoes off my cabinets.

"You don't drink," I remind him. As if he needs reminding.

"It's okay to indulge every *once* in a while, Cari Carrington." He laughs it off, carefree as ever.

"You just...you're not a drinker, Abel."

"Hey, stranger things have happened than me wanting to drink." He laughs. I can't quite join in.

My hand hesitates with another glass. This isn't right. Something is wrong. "How about we just—"

The timer dings (saved by the bell). His attention immediately shoots toward the oven, and I hand him an oven mitt to retrieve the hilariously misshapen cookies. They do smell wonderful and I'm excited to eat them. I put one between my teeth and hand another to Abel.

"Oh, no thanks," he says.

"What?"

"I'm hungry for something else now." He is at my side in an instant, lips brushing my temple.

This time, the normal physical reaction *doesn't* come. Anger flares up instead.

"Are you kidding? We made cookies because you wanted them, and now you don't?"

"Why do you sound so cranky?" he mumbles against my earlobe.

I push him off me. "Why are you here?"

He looks at me like I called him a long-nosed elf.

"Why are you here?" I ask again. I love being intimate with Abel, but it's all we do. I want to look at him, laugh with him, hear his voice when he speaks. A part of me is tired of giving in. "Is it just because you want to get in my pants? Is that what *all* of this is about?" I gesture around at the kitchen and the roses sitting in a fresh vase of water.

Shock crosses his face. "No!"

"I feel like all we do is have sex! You come over, we have sex. We go out, we have sex!"

"You don't like it?" he challenges, voice rising, eyes flared with anger.

That drains the fire from me. "I...Well, of *course* I like it, Abel, but I feel like that's all you want from me! You never used to be this way. What is going on with you?"

"I never used to be this way because we weren't together," he fires back.

"It's just not like you."

"Cari—" He says my name in a way I have never heard him say it. He takes a moment to breathe. "I came over here because I'm in love with you, all right? I've been in love with you for months." My heart rams into a brick wall. "I can't get enough of you. Every word, every gesture, it drives me *nuts!*" He puts his hands on my shoulders. "I just want to be near you, always. You make me feel more me. You make me want to freakin'...shout from the roof tops 'I'M IN LOVE!' I am *crazy* about you, Cari Carrington."

I'm not sure when I stopped breathing, but who cares? How long have I been hoping, *wishing* he'd say those words to me?

"I'm crazy about you, too, Abel. I've loved you since I met you."

His smile blossoms. The physical reaction returns. Hard.

"So, let me love you," he whispers in my ear.

I let him pull me to the bedroom. The cookies are forgotten on the counter.

44

I am reviewing the day's lengthy list of orders when Ruth drops the news.

"I called my daughter."

The atmosphere gasps. The bakery is empty for now, so I turn to Ruth to give her my full attention. "Daughter as in Amber?"

"Amber is my daughter, yes."

"Holy cannoli. This calls for a shop closure and glasses of wine."

"Eh-eh! Orders." I narrow my eyes at my grandma-boss, trying to gauge her expression. She looks amused and ready to burst.

"Well, tell me the story before I disintegrate in suspense."

"My sister flew in for Thanksgiving, brought her son and his wife, their kids—four boys, can you believe it? Anyway...it's always harder around the holidays, I don't know why, but seeing them all this year and not knowing where Amber was or what she was doing, it broke my heart." She taps the counter as she speaks. "It's been that way for thirteen years, but this year...I don't know. This year was different. Maybe it's that the boys are growing up."

Ruth pauses long enough that I ask gently, "So you decided to call Amber?"

"After everyone left on Sunday," she says, "the house felt emptier than ever. I just couldn't take the silence anymore. Harry said a call was past due, and this time, he put his foot down."

"Did she answer?"

"Not at first. I had to leave a message."

I wish I could have been a fly on the wall for that phone call. Healing in its most vulnerable phase—what a sight. Ruth doesn't tell me what she said in the message, and I don't let myself ask.

"A couple hours later," she goes on, "Harry had gone to bed, but I stayed up to watch this Ryan Reynolds movie."

"Ah, a fellow *Proposal* fan?"

"No, it was *Deadpool*." I realize she's not kidding. "My phone started ringing, and when I saw it was Amber, I thought my heart had literally stopped. What's that called when you stop breathing and think you're having a heart attack?"

"Panic attack?"

"That's the one. I had a panic attack. Hands shaking and everything."

"Tell me that you answered though."

"Well, of course I did. She said...'Mom.' That's it, just...'Mom.' I started crying, you know? 'Cause...well, I hadn't talked to her in..."

"What was the conversation like?" I ask gently.

"Awkward at first." She laughs. It sounds shaky. "I couldn't talk, I was an absolute mess, so she had to wait for me to get myself together. Finally, I asked her how she was, and she said she's good. She told me..." Ruth dabs at her eyes. "She told me she's working as a chef at a restaurant in Connecticut."

"A chef." The irony sinks into my bones.

Ruth nods. "That's right. The restaurant is called Malloby's."

"But...when she left here, she said she didn't want to be a baker." I hate to bring it up, but it seems a crucial question.

Ruth swallows and turns slightly toward the counter. "She's always been in the kitchen. Back then, when she was eighteen, she didn't want anything to do with her old mom anymore. She wanted to

go out and live her life how she wanted. I was so scared for her, but..."
Tears glisten down Ruth's cheeks. "She managed to carve her own
path, and she loves her new job so much."

I feel tears prick my eyes, too.

"We were on the phone for almost two hours. She said she's been
seeing a man named Grady. They've been together for three years."

"And Mia?"

Ruth swipes at a runaway tear. "A little marine biologist, apparently. She's in the biology club at her middle school. Amber bought
her a book on the zones of the ocean last Christmas, and she read it in
a week. Apparently, she wants to travel and study adaptations of
marine life in different parts of the ocean." Ruth smiles. "The kid's
going to be a genius."

"Wow." A marine biologist...Now *that's* someone I would love to
talk to. Imagine the poetry someone could spit out in a life that
consists of peeling out of wet suits, shaking the salt-water out of their
hair, and bearing witness to a tear-jerking sunset on the earth's hori-
zon, all while drinking prosecco on a shimmering boat...probably.
Either that or lots of research notes written in quick, near-illegible
handwriting. Okay, not my cup of tea (I prefer my wine and writing
on *solid ground*), but to each their own.

"Towards the end of the call," Ruth continues, "Amber told me
something else." Ruth presses her palms into the counter. "She said
she'd been homesick for a long time, but she didn't have the guts to
call me." She presses her palms harder into the counter, so much so
that her knuckles go white. "'Course, that broke my heart."

"Didn't have the guts?"

Ruth releases the counter and looks directly at me. "She thought
that I...hated her. That if she called home, it would just make things
worse." I clutch my T-shirt as I hear this. "I can't really blame her,"
Ruth goes on. "We used to get into some pretty nasty fights when she
was a teenager."

Sounds familiar, my conscience whispers.

"But I...*never* hated her." Ruth punctuates each word like each is its own sentence. "Never. You feel frustrated, you know, and you don't know what to do, and you say things you don't mean." Ruth clears her throat. "So I asked her, would she like to come home now, for a visit or anything. She's got a lot going on for the next few weeks, but she said she'll come home for Christmas."

"That is incredible, Ruth." Her teary eyes and watery smile make my heart feel like it's on a rollercoaster.

She hugs her arms around her torso. "I am...*so* happy. God gifted me my daughter back. It was all a misunderstanding." She laughs, disbelieving, relieved, close to tears again. "Here I was debating whether or not to call her for thirteen years, and she was too scared to reach out because she assumed I...." She can't even finish. She plants her face in her hands and shakes her head.

I wrap my arms around her and chew the heck out of my lip. This part hits a little too close to home. Could it be that...*my* mom feels the same? I mean, I've never even met Amber, but I relate to her more than I think I ever have to anyone.

Ruth pulls herself together. "Now, you have to live up to your end of the agreement."

"Agreement?"

"Don't tell me you forgot." When I don't answer, she says, "I called my daughter. Now you have to call your mom."

I scratch the back of my neck. With Thanksgiving in the rearview and how that ended, I'm not sure I can. "Did I agree to that?"

"Yes. No backsies now." She disappears through the swinging doors.

Calling my mother? That's an idea I prefer to think on while drunk and sitting on a pile of my own personal poetry, half of which is about her, which, okay, probably says that I *do* need to call her. But I'm stuck in the Stubborn Phase. Ruth is more of a woman than me, I suppose.

"Carrington?" she calls.

I tack the to-bake list on the bulletin board. "Yeah?"

"Someone's here for you."

Come again?

I push through the double doors and freeze.

"Cari!" Abel exclaims. "I'm so glad I'm at the right place. I could not, for the life of me, remember what this bakery was called. Ruby's? Randal's? Whatever. It doesn't matter now. I found you." He beams at Ruth. "Can I borrow Cari for a second?"

Ruth's eyebrows furrow, and she glances at me.

"Abel," I say. "It is 10:30 on a Thursday morning. Don't you have class right now?"

"Yeah, yeah, whatever. I want to show you something!"

My eyes flick to Ruth. She's still standing there, and yet I can read her eyes just fine: *What is going on here?* And then when reasoning kicks in: *This is the Abel?*

"I'm working right now—" I try to say.

"It'll take *ten* seconds of your time. Honest," he promises, turning to Ruth with his right hand raised like this is some kind of oath. "Come on, come on!"

"She's in a shift right now, sir," Ruth finally insists.

"And I *fully* understand that," Abel says. "But I just bought the most *amazing* thing, and I *have* to show Cari Carrington."

"Cari Carrington?" Ruth's eyes fly back to me.

I swallow. "One minute, I promise."

Abel is bouncing on his toes and leaning on the counter. I know he isn't going to leave—or get to class, where he *belongs*—until I see this grand purchase he is dying to show me at 10:30 in the morning, so I have to go with him.

Ruth's stare burns boils into my back as I follow Abel, quickly, outside. We stop on the curb, narrowly avoiding a jogger whose sweatband I can smell well after he passes.

"Ta-da!" Abel holds his arms out toward a blue-gray Kia Optima, shining in the spotlight of the sun.

He must be joking.

"An early birthday present for myself. What do you think?"

I think I am hallucinating. "Abel, your birthday is two weeks away, and...how much did this cost? Aren't Kia Optimas like, really expensive—"

"I had money saved up." He waves the matter away. "Plus, Mom and Dad helped chip in."

Okay, I may not be a graduate student with a kick-ass advisor and research opportunities blooming on the trees, but even *I* think that's a fishy claim. Mr. and Mrs. Harpen are the homemade gift-giver types. Not cheap—*thoughtful*, as Mr. Harpen once explained to me when Melanie unwrapped a friendship bracelet on her eleventh birthday. The silver beads read *Artist 4 Life* on an orange thread. You're telling me they bought Abel a Kia Optima? And so soon after Mrs. Harpen nearly took her life?

"Abel, I don't—"

"I have never been this happy, Carrington." He laces his arms around my waist and kisses me, and God help me. His smile is like hearing a baby laugh or watching a butterfly land on a kitten's nose. It *physically* makes the world a brighter place. For example, I swear the sun rays shining on his new car just twinkled.

"We should have shower sex tonight," he says.

The sun rays die down.

"Or," I say, "we could take a break from sex and watch a movie. We'll try the Hallmark channel. They have something new on there every three seconds."

"Or I could go down on you in the shower." He laughs. "What could be better?"

Something is very wrong; he has not been acting right in days. I want to ask a hundred questions. This energy and behavior are too much to process. It occurs to me that he may be having a manic episode, but I shut the thought down before it can grow. My heart wouldn't be able to take that.

"I don't want to have sex tonight."

"Fine." His arms drop from my waist. His jaw sets in a way I've never seen before, and he turns to leave.

My heart crumbles instantly. "You can still come over."

"Actually, I have other things to do." He's at the driver's side of the car now, pulling the door open.

"I'll call you." No answer. "I love you!" The door slams shut. The engine starts. He pulls away.

My heart plummets to the concrete. The door swings open behind me.

"Times up, Cari Carrington," Ruth says. "Come help me with these orders."

My nausea returns with a vengeance.

45

Today, Hunter has agreed to come to my apartment to talk about poetry. For one thing, it is downpouring, and I do not feel like taking an earthly shower just to walk to my car, let alone hearing my tires splash through gutter water as I cruise down the street. For another, I have never been so anxious in my life and am struggling to make it past my bedroom threshold without a plush blanket draped around my shoulders.

After yesterday's run-in with Abel, my stomach has been a mess of triple knots. His look streaks across my mind again: the clenched jaw, the hardened blue eyes, the odd quirk in his eyebrows. It's not right. None of it is right.

He wasn't just upset about the sex. Abel is one of the only men I know who prioritizes grades over gratification. I distinctly remember crossing paths with Camila while waiting in the same ridiculously long line at a vending machine between games at a volleyball tournament back in college. (It was unfit to attend college and not go to at least *one* sporting event. Plus, I'd had a few friends on the female team.) Camila, the loudmouth that she was, had complained to the girl beside her that she was not "getting any" from Abel at the moment, and when the friend asked why, Camila had responded with a drab "His degree, I guess?"

I won't lie, Camila is hot. She had the silky dark hair and the high cheekbones, always perfectly highlighted, and the full lips outlined in light maroon. Every guy wanted to rip her clothes off, yet sweet Abel had drawn the boundaries and stuck to them. He probably made her some tea, sat her down, and explained the matter face-to-face like the gentleman he is.

So he wasn't just angry with me because I didn't want sex. I tell myself that maybe his professor was an asshole the day before our interaction. Maybe he woke up on the wrong side of the bed with a throbbing headache (it happens). Maybe a research opportunity had fallen through. Maybe sex with me is just as amazing for him and has become his stress outlet (per my many fantasies). I tell myself I should not be this anxious over one bad interaction.

But my heart still won't calm down.

I glare at my reflection as I brush my teeth. By that, I mean push the brush around my mouth until toothpaste foams at the corners of my lips. My face looks fat. My hair is a grotesque pink lump on top of my head. There is a zit forming on my chin. I spit in the sink and try to smile. Bad idea. That new moisturizer I spent $45 on hasn't done its job; my skin is still as dry as a crumbling cinnamon cake left out in Los Angeles heat. But after another fifteen minutes of re-moisturizing, applying light concealer and mascara, and combing through my hair, I look like a try-hard who buys her makeup off eBay.

I hate your guts, Unreachable Beauty Standards. Go to hell.

Hunter arrives at 11 a.m. sharp, naturally, and I trudge to the door, still cocooned in my blanket.

"Should I come back later?" he asks.

"Nope. *Mi casa es tu casa*, or, whatever."

He obviously doesn't know what to make of any of this. "Okay?"

I lead him wordlessly to the kitchen table, which I purchased from IKEA last year and normally love but hate today because there is a dusting of crumbs where I sit. It makes me self-conscious.

"So," Hunter tries, "um, I read your most recent poems, and—"

I cut him off. "You want some water or something? Coffee? Actually, I'm out of K-Cups, so I can't give you that."

"Uh, no." He must feel as if he's looking at me through glass. I can't change that." I'm good. Thank you though."

He resumes his spiel about how he loved my poem "Ocean Floor," and another poem about giving in to temptation because sometimes you feel like you don't have a choice, but I can hardly listen. I bite my hangnails and stare out the window, seeing Abel's glare in my memory. That uncharacteristic, frightening glare.

"Cari."

I force myself to look back at Hunter. "Yeah."

"I said you should try reworking '1:04 a.m.' through a more stream-of-consciousness vibe. And..." I must be staring into space again. "Where are you right now?"

I can't answer. He tips his head, waiting for one. "You are a shell of a person right now."

"That seems a little rude." I can't summon up any real conviction. In fact, my voice sounds as hollow as he says.

"It's not rude," he counters lightly. "You just aren't you. Are you willing to talk about what's going on?"

"You mean, am I willing to have a therapy session with a technically unlicensed therapist?"

He smiles, but not with his eyes. "This isn't a therapy session. It's two friends talking. There's a difference."

I pull the blanket higher on my shoulders. Guy talk is usually reserved for my girlfriends, particularly Katerine, who always has a boatload of advice and/or thoughts on my situations. But since he asked...

"It's Abel," I say. "Yesterday, he was...I don't even know."

Hunter leans forward, immediately attentive. "You've seen him this week?"

"Of course." I look at him like, *hasn't everyone?* "We've been hanging out every day."

Hunter lets out a breath of relief. "So, he's okay. Good. He just hasn't been in classes, and—"

"What?" That can't be true. "Abel *has* been going to class. He left my apartment Tuesday morning to go to the university." I realize that I just revealed something about our relationship and bite my lip, which does nothing to erase what I spilled.

To his credit, Hunter doesn't comment on it. "Well, he wasn't in class, I can tell you that. I've texted him multiple times, Snapchatted him more, and no answer. I've just been worried because of his mom and everything." Hunter is visibly nervous.

My eyebrows draw together. There's another sinking sensation in my stomach. Abel skipping classes can only mean one thing.

Hunter's jaw sets. "What happened yesterday?"

I can't hold out anymore. I tell him everything from the surprise appearance at Ruth's Bakery to the new car and Abel's unexpected reaction to me not...wanting to have sex with him. That part I rush over. It still makes my skin crawl. I understand that my body is my own, and I have the right to reject sex, but hurting Abel kind of makes me hate myself. (But did I hurt him? Was he even himself in that moment? No...I won't think about that.)

Hunter would be a five-star therapist. He keeps a neutral expression and focuses on the core pieces.

"He...bought a Kia Optima?"

"Yes."

"And...got irritable when you...?

"Yes."

My gut is cycling like that Twister ride at a carnival. Hunter is putting the pieces together, and I know he's going to arrive at the same place I did, where neither of us wants to be...but somehow, it's still fascinating to watch him work it out.

"If you don't mind me asking," he ventures. "Has he been... pushing sex on you?"

"Not necessarily," I lie. "He just...wants to have it...all the time."

Then he asks the one question I don't want to hear.

"Has he been taking his meds?"

It's a kick to the stomach. My mouth opens, but no answer comes out.

He has to be, but I know better. I rack my brain for any moment that I saw him swallow those pills in the last week, like the night he did when we stayed at Meg's for Friendsgiving. I come up empty. My hands are sweating.

"You think he stopped taking them," I say, hoping Hunter will deny it.

Hunter's eyes darken. "Mania can lead to impulsiveness, like unnecessary, expensive purchases or unprotected sex or drinking—"

I start to hyperventilate. I never saw him take a pill, and I never made sure he did.

"Hey, hey, hey." Hunter is at my side instantly. "It is just a thought, Carrington. We can't say for sure unless we talk to him."

"Would he even tell us that?" It comes out as a shriek, and Hunter doesn't answer.

I'm not panicking because Abel may be experiencing mania. I am panicking because I could have done something to prevent it but didn't. I just didn't want it to be true.

"Cari, *breathe*," Hunter instructs. "The most important thing in these situations is to stay calm. We can keep an eye on him and—"

"No, I need to help him. I promised him, Hunter. I promised him in college that if he ever had a manic episode with me, I would not let him fall."

Surprise flashes across Hunter's face. "You really love him, don't you."

It is a statement, not a question.

"YES!" My chest rapidly rises and falls. I'm starting to lose feeling in my arms. "I can't watch him disappear!"

"Breathe," Hunter puts his hand on my shoulder. "We're not going to lose Abel. *You're* not going to lose him. Breathe."

I stare into his eyes, trying desperately to match his deep breaths. One. Another. Slowly, achingly, my airways start to open up.

"Don't let the stigma get to you," Hunter says. "Abel may struggle with his mental health, but that does not mean it will destroy him. He has a very strong support system. We all want the best for him, right?"

I manage to nod and take a shaky breath.

Hunter squeezes my shoulder. "Just do your best to stay calm."

I say okay and that I will try, but unfortunately, I have never been one to sit around and keep my chill.

I knock on Abel's door and, when he doesn't answer, ring the doorbell a few times. Suddenly there he is, looking like a million bucks in a blue T-shirt and gray sweatpants.

"Cari! What are you doing here? You kind of look like hell, no offense. Did somebody run over your cat? Wait, you don't have a cat, what am I talking about?"

I walk past him into his apartment, which is even cleaner than the last time I was here. I can clearly see my reflection in the floor. It even smells like fresh Lysol in here. He's been super-cleaning.

"Want to play a board game? I just bought five at a yard sale two days ago." He consults a shelf where the new games are piled up perfectly (largest to smallest and color-coded). "I have *Sorry!*, Monopoly, checkers—"

I blurt it out. I have to know. "Did you stop taking your meds?"

He turns to look at me and laughs. "What?"

"Your meds. Have you been taking them?" Nausea curls up my throat.

He laughs again, but this time it sounds more like a scoff. "The—I don't...need them, Cari. I am just fine without them. I've been doing so well! Why should I stay on meds if I don't need them?"

So it is true. I promised him in college that I would be there for him. I promised him I would know the signs and help him before he ever got to this point.

"Abel." My voice quivers. "You *do* need them."

"How do you know?"

"Because—"

"How do I know you don't just want me take them because you like me when I'm boring?"

"*What?*" Panic tears at my bones. "Medication does *not* make you boring, Abel—"

"I feel *amazing*, Carrington! Aren't you happy for me?"

"You're manic," I spit out. Now I'm angry, more at myself than him.

His face morphs into something of a cross between hurt and disbelief. "This is who I am, Carrington. I'm not manic—"

"Yes, you are—"

"This is who I *am*! You—you don't like me when I'm at my best? You don't think I'm worth your time now?"

"I never said that—" My anger transforms into frustration.

"So what if I stop taking the meds? I don't need them!" His face is bright red. "I don't fucking need them! They slow me down, Cari Carrington!"

"Abel, listen to me." I try to reach out for him as he paces. "You are manic and you need to get back on your meds right now."

He freezes mid-stride. The look in his eyes sends ice water down my spine. "You can't just walk into my apartment and lecture me about how to live my life! Especially when *you're* the one who moved to fucking New York City and dyed your hair pink! Yeah, like *that's* gonna solve your problems!" My mouth snaps shut; pain knifes through my chest. "The second *I* do something, it's all 'Abel, you're manic. Abel, you messed up!'" His mouth is twisted into a sneer. "How about looking at your *own* choices instead of shoving your nose into everyone else's business!"

I cannot speak. My lungs have stopped working. My heart is so sore. Somehow, I choke out, "Abel, I love you. I would never—"

"Bull-*shit*." This echoes off the walls. "You know what? I don't need this. Get out of my apartment."

"I'm not leaving you—"

"Get the fuck out, Carrington!"

It's a whip cracked against my back. I spin on my heel and barely make it to the door before the sobbing starts.

46

————

THE LAST TIME I CRIED THIS HARD WAS IN SIXTH GRADE, WHEN I accidentally brought the wrong flash drive to school and, instead of pulling up a presentation about ancient Egypt, revealed my dad's photo album from when he went to see Kiss live and had his face painted chalk-white with freaky black eye makeup and red lipstick. Mrs. Benning was *not* happy.

This is shame on a whole new level.

Shame for denying Abel's symptoms, for making him so upset that he tumbled past his limits and exploded like that, for not knowing what to do now.

I am a massive fraud. Ruth is right; I *should* call my mom, but only to give her a twenty-minute speech entitled, *This is Why I'm No Psychologist.* I talk big like I understand mental illness, like if I translate those struggles into beautiful metaphors in my poetry, I, too, will help people. At the end of the day, I want to leave a positive impact on this world just like my mom and Hunter and Abel and all the other students out there, fighting tooth and nail to get into the right branch of a clinic or psychiatric research facility so that they can cure fill in the blank. And yet...I couldn't even save Abel from himself.

I suppose I could quit poetry, quit the gag, and become a bank teller or a cook at some gas station off the highway. Not that there is anything wrong with bank tellers or cooks at gas stations off the highway. I would be completing my civic duty as an American: wake up, work, eat, sleep, repeat. No deceitful poetry involved to give people the wrong impression that I understand *anything* about a.) the human condition and b.) life itself.

Cars zoom past me, and I try to shield my mascara-smeared cheeks from each one. Crying in your car with the four-ways blinking at nine p.m. is not ideal, especially outside the apartment complex of the man you're in love with after he's just thrown you out. When a blue Jeep Wrangler speeds past with three blondes, scream-singing Doja Cat, I decide I've had enough. I turn off my four-ways and merge onto the road, only realizing I'm heading toward Hunter's apartment when I turn onto his street ten minutes later.

His door swings open before I even get to knock. A woman steps out—strawberry blonde, almond-shaped eyes the color of walnuts, *perfect* eyebrows. Her mouth drops open when she spots me. So does Hunter's. Fortunately, Hunter is great under pressure.

"Who the hell is—" the woman starts.

"Sasha, this is Cari. She is a friend of a friend, and I'm...not sure why she's here?"

Sasha crosses her arms, waiting for an answer. I choose to ignore the formal "friend of a friend" bullshit and cut to the chase.

"Abel's manic. He's off his meds. I made it worse."

Hunter's mouth snaps closed. "Sasha, thanks for coming. See you later."

"Who's Abel? Is that code for some freaky—"

"Tell Lucia I love her." Hunter executes a smooth exchange of pulling me into the apartment and tactfully pushing Sasha out.

Sasha scoffs. "Like I'm gonna tell my cat that lie."

"Have a nice night."

"If you have sex with her, we are done!"

"I'll call you."

"Hunter, you are a two-faced player."

"Don't forget to take the back road because there's construction up two blocks."

He gently shuts the door before she can say something else. She does, but it's muffled, and two seconds later, we hear her stomping down the hall.

Hunter's shirt is half-buttoned. He sees that I notice. "It's complicated," he says.

"No, I wasn't judging that," I say. "I'm judging the fact that you guys are done and it's only nine fifteen." If I hadn't just sobbed my eyes out, this would have me on the floor laughing.

Hunter exhales and leads me further into the apartment to the living room with the sectional couch. "I take it you didn't stay calm?" he says.

"I tried to."

"And by that you mean..."

"Went over to his apartment, told him to get back on his meds, and he told me to get the F out." More tears threaten my eyes. "How much of an idiot am I?"

"You're not an idiot." Hunter massages the bridge of his nose. "Did he physically hurt you?"

"No. He just has a lot of energy."

Hunter scratches his chin and then grabs his keys. "All right, come on."

My heart skips two beats. "Where are we going?"

"People struggling with mania often feel isolated. If he's alone in his apartment with all that energy, it could lead to something bad."

"Something dangerous?" My brain pictures a few horrible things, and I wring my hands.

Hunter shuts the door behind us and locks it. "Hard to say."

We speed-walk down the stairs and out to Hunter's car. It's starting to rain again, droplets sprinkling in the streetlight.

"Should I even go inside?" I ask. "What if that upsets him?"

"We'll play it by ear."

"No offense, but that doesn't sound like a solid plan."

He navigates onto the main road. "There is not a one-size-fits-all plan for someone who struggles with mental illness, Carrington, just the golden rule of trying to stay calm."

We swerve down a back road, avoiding the flashing orange lights of construction ahead. Hunter has the heat on, but I'm still shaking.

"I feel absolutely sick to my stomach," I murmur.

"It's okay to be overwhelmed."

"No, I feel so *stupid*. I was blinded by my feelings for him, Hunter. I didn't want to know what was going on with him. How is that healthy?"

"Sometimes love makes you crazy. That's it." His jaw clenches and releases. "It doesn't have to be some earth-shattering guilt trip that you inflict on yourself. It can just be what it is. Do you get what I'm saying?"

"Not really."

"You shouldn't punish yourself for feeling what you do. Abel has bipolar disorder, with symptoms both general and unique to him. That is *completely* out of your control. Don't let yourself think you are responsible for this. You're not."

The rest of the ride is quiet, other than the windshield wipers and the rain that is pouring harder now. Hunter's words sink in, and for the first time all day, so does a sense of calm. Not peace, necessarily, but a moment in the eye of the storm. I take a breath. Unfortunately, the moment doesn't last.

We arrive at Abel's building. Hunter asks, "Where's his car?"

I look up from my hands. He's right. Abel's car is missing from its usual space in the lot in front of the building.

"He was just here."

Hunter exhales again. This time, he can't hide a twinge of anxiety. My own anxiety jumps, a flame turned up on high.

"Should we call him?" I ask.

Hunter whips his phone out of the cup holder, and I hold my breath while it rings. Hunter curses. "No answer."

"Okay, um...check his Snap location," I suggest.

"Good idea."

We find that Abel's last Snapchat was four minutes ago at a bar in Baltimore City. That's it. My cortisol levels are fucked—anxiety through the roof.

We don't say one word to each other. Hunter just pulls the car around, and we speed off toward the distant city lights.

~

THE BAR, as it turns out, is actually a club: Greyhound. I can feel the music's bass in the roots of my teeth.

"Stay close," Hunter says as we approach the door. I understand what he means as soon as we step inside.

Smoky pink-and-blue lights flash in time with the music, and there are so many people in here, it's difficult to breathe. I have never thought I was claustrophobic, but as of ten seconds ago, I'm not so sure. At the front of the room is a small, elevated platform, home of a fist-pumping DJ, who's shouting something unintelligible into a microphone. People scream, dance harder. On the plush couches in the corners of the room, couples are packed like sardines, laughing, making out, sniffing substances off their hands. Everywhere I look, eyes that aren't Abel's.

Someone with shaved, rainbow-dyed hair stumbles past me, nearly splashing beer all over me. Hunter manages to pull me out of the way.

"How the hell are we going to find Abel in here?" I shout into Hunter's ear.

I can only see Hunter when the lights flash, washing his face in red, then purple, then blue. He scans the crowd, and I see his shoulders visibly hunch up toward his ears. He doesn't like it in here. Yet, he charges on, taking my hand and leading us through the thrashing, gyrating bodies. I come face-to-face with extravagant glittery eyeshadow, large, curly hair, sweat-slicked chests, exposed nipples through fishnet crop tops, flirtatious grins. We make it all the way to the opposite wall, clouds of weed smoke curling in the air. Still no Abel.

"Dammit!" Hunter shouts. "Where *is* he?"

"Make some motha'fuckin' noise!" the DJ screams, and my eardrums shatter.

The crowd shifts, and for one second, I see him. It is faster than a blinking eye, and only because the lights flash gold right across his face.

"There!" I start toward him, jostled by a couple very earnestly grinding to the fresh beat. I push through a group of women in skirts up to their hips.

But then I stop, and Hunter (I think, I hope) bumps into me. It *was* Abel I saw, only...

"Cari." I hear Hunter's voice in my ear. "Stay calm."

When will I listen to his advice?

I march forward to Abel and the girl he's dancing with, or, should I say, dancing *on*. She's bent at the hips, and...need I say more?

"ABEL!" I scream.

He looks over at me, but not before *she* does—all five-foot-three and massive cleavage, white-blonde hair down to her hardly-covered ass.

"How could you do this to me?" I ask Abel. At the moment, my grief that he's with another woman outweighs my fear for his well-being.

She looks me up and down. "What's your problem, bitch?"

"What are you two doing here?" Abel shouts. He doesn't sound or look happy.

Hunter approaches him gently and says something I can't hear. Abel shakes his head, rolls his eyes.

"Hey!" *she* shouts. "Do you need a hearing aid? I asked you what your problem is!" She's so close to me now that I can smell the liquor her breath.

Over her shoulder, Hunter continues trying to talk to Abel, but

Abel throws his hands around, blue eyes wide and angry, shouting back. Hunter places a hand on Abel's arm and leads him toward the exit, glancing back at me to follow. I brush past Little Miss Loud Mouth. She doesn't like that. When my head yanks backward (the bitch grabbed my hair), I turn around and slap her hand away. All my anger, all my self-loathing, my sadness, and guilt goes into that slap. So as to say, I *know* it hurts her.

I grill her with a glare that comes from one of my meanest inner demons. "Go take a cold shower." Acid drips from my voice. She tries to sneer, but I can tell she wasn't expecting this from the visibly sober, visibly heartbroken Nobody in the room. Tough shit.

I turn away and follow Hunter.

The icy air outside is refreshing for all five seconds before the wind chokes me. Hunter has Abel on the sidewalk, tenderly trying to calm him down...to no avail.

"You're *crazy!*" Abel screams. "You can't pull me out of there and tell me what I can and can't do!"

"Abel," Hunter says. They're both washed in the dim gold of the streetlight overhead.

"You don't get to talk! You don't know what it's like to have everyone look at you like you're insane! Like you're *batshit!* Well, guess what! I'm not the bad person! *You* are! *You're* the one who's batshit!" He looks between me and Hunter, teeth bared, eyes blazing. "I'm not the bad person!"

Knots of late-night city goers pass us. We're sidewalk drama. Some people glance at us, and I see some concern, hear a laugh or two.

"Abel, please," Hunter says. He's not as tall as Abel, and from what I can see from my place behind Hunter, it seems like they are about to square off.

"What?! Do I *embarrass* you?" He holds his arms out at his sides. "Do—are you *embarrassed* by me? Do I sound fucking *crazy* to you? Well, I'm *not! You* are! It's you! All *you!*"

"You are manic!" I shout, mostly because I can't stand this. More specifically, I can't believe what I'm seeing. My brain can't equate the person in front of me to sweet angel Abel I've known since college.

His eyes turn to me, nostrils flared and chest heaving.

"This isn't you!" Tears burn my eyes. "It's the disorder talking." Hunter tells me to stop, but I go right on, "You don't drink or party in nightclubs or dance with other women—"

"You don't know me!" he yells.

"Yes, I do!" Now the tears trickle down my cheeks. "I fell in love with you because of who you are! And you love me!"

In one step, he's directly in front of me, his breath hot on my face. "That was a *lie!*"

Something in my chest shatters. Hunter says, "That's it, Abel." He takes hold of Abel's elbow. "Stop this right now."

"Don't fucking touch me!"

Hunter attempts to pull him toward the car, but Abel shoves him away with a face like fury. Hunter trips over the curb and falls into the street.

"Don't touch him!" I shriek and lunge for Abel's other arm. Hunter is back on his feet, phone at his ear. In another moment, I hear sirens, distant at first but coming fast, and I realize Hunter is talking to the police.

Now everything seems to go silent. Abel is shouting at me, his lips forming obscene words, but I can't hear that, or what Hunter is saying into his phone, or what the people across the street are yelling. I can't hear the cars passing by or the screeching brakes of the cop car that stops in front of us. I can't hear what they say to Abel or what he bellows back at them.

When the officers close Abel in the back of the car, Hunter puts his arms around me, but I can't feel them. I can't feel anything but the sharp, sickening cracks that are puncturing my heart.

47

I LEAN FORWARD AND VOMIT A SECOND TIME INTO THE trashcan. Back at Hunter's apartment, the living room light is too bright. Hunter pats my back. As soon as I come up for air, he presses a glass of water into my hand. I sip it tentatively.

"It's going to be okay." It is the fourth time he has said this.

I gag at the acrid taste in my mouth. "How are you...so calm?"

"What do you mean?" His voice is only slightly hollow. If he is scared, he is *exceptional* at hiding it.

"Abel just got arrested."

"He wasn't arrested," Hunter says. "He was transported to the hospital. They can help him better than we can."

This is supposed to make me feel better, but it doesn't. In fact, I feel like I may get sick again. Here's another bullet point in the list of *Why I'm No Psychologist, Mom!* I witness a single manic episode and get so upset that I vomit.

Suddenly I think I know why Hunter is so calm. "Have you worked with manic patients before?"

"Not directly, but I've shadowed clinicians who do." He realizes I'm waiting for more. "You see a lot in this field, I can't lie. At one point, I was searching for evidence of brain structure abnormalities in patients who struggle with schizophrenia. I met a young patient one time who had gone off his meds and was desperately trying to tell me that his parents were Russian spies who wanted to poison and kill him." Hunter's eyes are distant. "I couldn't calm him down. He started shouting at me, saying I was probably part of it. I didn't know what to do. That was my very first time interacting with someone who struggled with schizophrenia." He presses his lips into a grim line. "Mental illness can be scary, but...that's only the stigma talking. Over time, you realize that these people are just people. They're not monsters or crazy criminals. They're *just people*, struggling and in need of support and love."

His fingers tenderly brush mine as he takes the cup back. Hunter Gatelin is like a precious lily pad floating in a roaring ocean. He is cautious and calm, thoughtful and patient, a combination I haven't encountered in many people before. *My friend soulmate*, I think, and then I start to cry.

"Cari?"

"Abel said it was a lie. He doesn't love me." I have to force the words out. Hunter places a hand over mine. "Why would he say he loves me if he doesn't mean it?"

"I'm not sure," Hunter says and sounds genuinely upset by it. "It certainly doesn't sound like Abel to lie about something like that."

I cry into my fists for a few minutes before something occurs to me. I feel my face go bone white. "Did he only say he loved me because of the mania?"

A crease forms between Hunter's eyebrows. "I don't know."

My brain could burst at any second from the confusion and the denial and the sick feeling that my question might be true. Come to think of it, I hope my brain *does* explode. It might leave a mess for Hunter, but at least I'll be out of this strange *Twilight Zone* episode where Abel Harpen hates my guts. New research question: do manic outbursts expose someone's true feelings? Like that saying, *drunk words are sober thoughts*. Does Abel really think I'm a "fucking waste of his time"? That insult surfaced in my memory while Hunter was driving us back to his place. Abel had screamed it right before the cops showed up. Even if he meant it, I don't hate him for that. And I hate that I don't hate him for that. Basically, I just hate me.

The feeling chokes me, like squeezing lemon juice onto my tongue or swallowing a mouthful of sand. You could place two anvils on my shoulders, and I wouldn't be able to tell the difference between their weight and the shame I'm sagging under. Under Abel's hurtful (honest?) words, under the mania, under his absence. The air is thinner here without him. Is he scared? Is he still screaming? Are the officers being careful with him?

"Cari." Hunter pries my fingers from my palm, and I realize I've pressed my nails too far into the skin. Indents remain.

"I..." Cannot verbally articulate the poisonous thoughts incinerating my brain right now. So, I ask a question instead. "Is it normal?"

"Is what normal?"

"To...hate yourself?"

Hunter leans back on the couch, clearly trying for clinical detachment even though he can't stop frowning. "I think at first. Especially if you are close with the person. Sometimes they can say some pretty hurtful things."

A fucking waste of time, Abel shrieked in my face. Hurtful...that's an understatement. I let the dam crack and cry for a good twenty minutes—I think. I'm not really counting. Time does not exist right now. Hunter eventually wraps an arm around me, and I collapse into him, a mess of snot, tears, and smeared mascara. He doesn't complain once. I cry. And cry and cry and cry. Harder than I cried after that stupid flash drive mix-up in the sixth grade. It is officially a new record.

My heart broke about an hour and a half ago. Now I'm just sobbing myself dehydrated. I can't take anything else. Abel is all alone in the hospital. His harsh words are a poltergeist in my mind. My self-worth has shattered. Because, okay, I believe him and his jarring words. I *am* a fucking waste of time. Would that confession make all therapists cringe and want to offer unsolicited advice? Probably. But it can't be uncommon. It is one thing to flip off the general haters, but when the person you love starts attacking you? It hurts because they sit on the stage in your heart.

What exactly qualifies someone to be a "fucking waste of time" anyway? Is it the numerous piles of journals cluttering my apartment? Is it boring to date a writer? I know it's dangerous (guard your reputation, and all that), but is it *boring*? Maybe it's the way I can't, for the life of me, say the word *anemone*. It's one of the most commonly mispronounced words in the English language, so I'm not special in my pronunciation skills. Is it the way I can only remember basic facts about the brain? Like intro-psych-level lobes and functions? No grad student wants to hang out with a naïve undergrad, surely, with their cooler research opportunities and all that. Maybe it's the way I never paint my nails. I can't stand the way they look when they start to chip, so I just skip the routine altogether. But what if the lack of color means I'm a fucking waste of time?

This spiral is going to suffocate me. At least I've quit crying and am only staring at the wall now. The blankness is somewhat soothing.

I say, "You know those thoughts that float around your head, and you don't want them there?"

"Intrusive thoughts?" Hunter supplies.

"Yeah." I don't take my eyes off the wall. "How do you make them stop?"

Hunter takes my face between his hands and gently turns my head so I'm looking at him. "Name something you can see."

I blink. "The zit on your cheek."

"Uh, right. Okay, name something you can touch."

"Couch." I drag my fingers along the leather.

"Something you can hear."

"Cars." There are occasional honks outside.

"Something you can smell."

I wrinkle my nose. "Old Spice?"

He blushes a little and then says, "Something you can taste."

"Vomit."

"Okay, let me get you some gum."

He disappears into the kitchen for a moment.

"Was that supposed to help?" I call after him.

"It's a mindfulness activity." He reappears with a piece of spearmint gum. I unwrap it quickly. "It's supposed to keep you in the present moment and stop the thought spiral."

I consider his words. "It only worked for four seconds."

"Yeah, I hear that a lot." He sits back down beside me. "But four seconds is better than nothing."

It occurs to me that if any other man told me to try a five senses check-in, I would mark them off as absurdly cringe. But not Hunter. That is such a Hunter thing to suggest. I reach for his hand and offer a weak smile.

"You're right. Thank you."

He smiles, black hair spilling over his forehead and down into his sharp green eyes. Tonight, those emerald irises remind me of weeping willows in the dead of summer. He is sad about Abel, too. He just won't say anything because he doesn't want to add to my distress. That both puts a band-aid on my heart and breaks it all over again.

"What are we supposed to do now?" I ask. I realize I'm still holding his hand, so I gently let go. "It's going to kill me to wait."

"Use this time to work on yourself," Hunter answers. "And trust that Abel will be okay."

I grind my teeth.

"It's all right, Carrington."

I hear the words, but I struggle to believe them.

That night, I fall asleep on Hunter's sectional couch. The couch Abel and I sat on last month with all his friends during *The Conjuring* (and me, secretly wanting to give Abel a lap dance). The couch feels ridiculously empty tonight, even as my eyes are shut and I'm forcing my brain to dream. I have a nightmare, actually: one where I break my hand on the glass door of Abel's hospital room. It's locked from the inside.

48

Good morning Christie.

Due to unforeseen circumstances, I am suffering a bad bit of writer's block again and will need to reschedule our Zoom meeting to a later date. The passion has currently left my bones. I understand the guidelines of my contract and will have the manuscript in to Polly&Pippy by the agreed date: December 31. Thanks for understanding.

Take care,

Carrington

I SEND THE EMAIL AND CLOSE MY LAPTOP BEFORE CONSULTING my Saturday to-do list entitled, *Things to Take Care of While the Love of My Life is in a Psychiatric Hospital.* It's soaked in tears—gray splotches that have smeared the ink so bad it is nearly illegible. But I manage.

1. Clean the kitchen.

2. Post on writer social media (it's been too long).
3. Read that self-help book Tucker got me two Christmases ago.
4. Contemplate therapy. (Google who will take my insurance.)
5. Catch up on *Stranger Things*.
6. Cry because that's healthy, according to some college website.
7. Meal prep if I feel like it.

I wrote this up to feel productive, to prove that I am *not* a fucking waste of time. That I am, actually, a driven human being who can continue to function in the face of difficulties, disregarding the fact that I spent the whole morning weeping on Hunter's couch during breakfast, under a blanket with blobs of blueberry yogurt dripping from my mouth. But I was able to drive back home to my apartment. That's productive. I was able to send Christie this email. *That's* productive. See? I'm not a fucking waste of time.

So why do I still feel like that kid who's picked last in gym class? It is a very miserable feeling, considering I *was* the kid who was always picked last in gym class (in elementary school at least). I try not to linger on the thought—another piece of advice from that wise college website—and move through my to-do list.

The kitchen counter requires extra elbow-grease scrubbing that I bail on after about fifteen minutes. I repost a quote from another writer: "Writing is like bacon: if it ain't sizzling, it ain't good" and turn off my comment section. The self-help book tries to convince me I'm a badass by simply getting out of bed and existing despite "all the bullshit you've been through, girl." It feels more cheap self-affirmation than valuable self-help, but what do I know? I contemplate therapy while lying upside down on the couch with my feet on the back cushion and my head dangling over the edge.

I have always supported therapy. I grew up in a household that force-fed it to me, hello? But do *I* need it? I refused to look at myself in the mirror this morning out of crumbling self-esteem for what Abel had said to me, but that's to be expected. I'm human. Of *course* I am going to have a reaction like this. Does it mean I need to go spill my guts to a therapist? Not necessarily. I understand when I should go: if symptoms start to negatively impact my daily life, and I'm not there yet. As far as I'm concerned, this is still normal grief. Normal denial and self-hatred.

Catching up on *Stranger Things* transitions to bingeing unnaturally upbeat talk shows where women lift up other women.

"You don't need him!" the host insists over a roar of agreement from the crowd.

The woman in question, a redhead from Kentucky whose husband left her for his boss's daughter, wipes under her eyes and nods with a quivering lip. I'm crying and nodding, too.

"You *don't* need him," I say out loud. "You're not a fucking waste of time either!"

Probably. She's got a great jawline and that beautiful flaming braid down her back. She'll be some other dude's self-proclaimed queen again in no time. I startle awake three episodes later in a puddle of my own drool and start to cry again. Mostly because I didn't want to wake up. Mostly because when I am conscious, Abel takes up 95 percent of my brain. Where is he now? Are psychiatrists evaluating his state? Is he scared? Are they treating him kindly? And then, I realize I've fallen back into the thought spiral and feel a fresh dose of Pathetic.

The to-do list only carries me to eight o'clock because I do not feel like meal prepping. I decide to FaceTime Katerine. When I get a text saying she's out to dinner with Ben's family, I FaceTime Noah instead and listen to him recount his most recent sexual encounter. I interrupt him ten minutes in and ask if it seems like we talk about significant others too much. He asks where Abel is. The conversation turns bleak and depressing. I hang up and cry again.

Good thing I don't have work today. Ruth probably wouldn't appreciate four teaspoons of tears and snot in the mix for her holiday pastries. But this means I have to clean myself up for Monday...the day Abel *should*, legally, get discharged from the hospital, assuming the hearing goes well and the psychiatrists determine he is no longer in need of in-patient treatment. The muscles in my neck are about ready to quit; I've been tensing them so much over this whole ordeal. I could try Hunter's five sense check-in again, but do I really want to be "in the moment" right now? This moment sucks. I could call Hunter, but a part of me doesn't want to bother him anymore.

I check my laptop and find an unread email:

Hi, Carrington.

It is nice to hear from you, though I am so sorry about your writer's block. It may be beneficial to take a few days away from the project. Refreshed minds always think better. Take care of yourself, sweetie! We will touch base in a few days.

Best,

Christie

I feel like I should send her a fruit basket with a card saying *Thank you for your undying patience!* But fruit baskets, while a sweet gesture, feel like a half-assed thank you. I'm a writer for cream's sake. Christie deserves a ten-page letter on why she is everything and more to me.

Too bad I'm not in the mood.

I used to write a lot of lengthy thank-you letters. Back in high school, it was what I was known for, especially around the holidays. By graduation, I'd churned out at least seventeen letters—mostly for the girls on my softball team and the group of girls I sat with most days at lunch. The Mixing Pot, as I called them behind their backs. There was a girl of every stereotype at that table: Chloe, the cheer captain-slash-student council president-slash-leader of damn near every club; Mae, the steminist who *really enjoyed* correcting our understandings of chemical compounds; Joselyn, the dumb blonde who was actually a brunette until junior year; Leslie, the quiet bookworm who thought we didn't notice she was reading *Harry Potter* under the table; and me, the athlete with pork chop thighs and cheesy jokes. We sat together all four years, even supported each other through breakups and emergency cram sessions. I thought that was what friendship was, so I wrote them all sentimental letters for graduation, commenting on the time we talked about this and when Joselyn made that joke. I never got a real thank-you in return. We didn't even sit together at graduation or take pictures afterward. In hindsight, I didn't really speak to them outside of our Mixing Pot table.

So, I don't write thank-you letters for people anymore. Who knows where they ended up. Crumpled on an ignored desktop? Shoved in an old folder? Accidentally burned in the transitional Post High School Bonfire? Forget that.

And that is why my current project feels silly. It is an entire collection that might as well be called *Abel, I Love You*. Never once do I say his name in the poetry, but it is as obvious as the grass is green. Even if I were to formally dedicate it to him, would he even appreciate it? Like the girls in the Mixing Pot failed to? Or would he call the collection a fucking waste of time, too? My work reflects *me*, my passions, my regrets, my life. What if after all that, it is still not enough?

And what does that say about me?

Why do I care so much?

I want to be a carefree bad bitch, but that façade would take too much of my energy.

I have chewed through all of my nails, so I look away from the window and head to the bathroom to...I don't know. Take a bath maybe? Apparently, that is what I want since my hands automatically move to the faucet and I start to undress.

Seated in the warm water, hair twisted into a bun on my head, I contemplate therapy again. Is this normal grief? What even *is* normal grief? How do I turn off my brain? The bathroom is too quiet, save for the *drip, drip* of the faucet and the whirring fan.

Sometime between taking a dreamless nap and seeing Christie's email, I googled self-care ideas. A bath was one. But I think the link mentioned bath *balm* or *bubble* bath, not *Sit in your own filth and wallow—double thumbs-up!* I get out of the tub.

The only other distractions I can come up with are sweeping the kitchen and making a cup of tea, another suggestion from the self-care website. But those activities only take me to 9:45, so I cut the chase and climb into bed, or, as I like to say, give in to my thoughts.

Guess I am a fucking waste of time.

Feel that pressure in your chest, Carrington? That's called anxiety.

Abel's probably eating gray slabs of uncooked meat...Is that legal? Is that the stigma talking?

I fall asleep after crying another gallon of tears.

The knocking on the door is part of my dream. I know because my subconscious dream-particle body moves to answer it—in my hospital room. The door swings open (No, they don't keep locks on the door, silly!), and I see Hunter, dressed in all white.

"Hunter, when did you become a nurse?" My voice sounds oddly high-pitched.

"Are you in there, Carrington?" His sharp green eyes search mine.

Am I—

I jerk upright in my bed. The knocking is *not* part of my dream.

"Carrington!" It's Hunter, calling me from outside the apartment.

I wrap myself in a fuzzy robe and move to the door, this time for real. Hunter's there, but not dressed in white. He's wearing jeans and a Twenty-One Pilots T-shirt.

"I'm glad you're still alive. You haven't been answering my texts." He walks inside before I can even get out of the way.

"Won't you come in?" I offer.

He pauses in the living room. Now I can take in how buzzed he looks, full of nervous energy. His eyes find mine. "How are you?"

"Like, seriously?"

"Seriously."

"Not well." It feels good to say out loud. I trudge to the couch and faceplant on it. "I'm making myself sick over him. Asked my agent to kindly leave me be and everything."

"Cari." The couch dips as he sits beside me. "You can't let yourself go like this."

"Isn't this *love?* Crying and worrying about someone?" I admit, my tone is nastily sarcastic.

"I...I don't think it's *healthy* love, Carrington."

I glance up at him through fresh tears.

"It's not my place," he forewarns, "but...do you know where he ends and you begin anymore?"

"Of course I..." Don't. Because I come up empty-handed with reasons. My eyes blur more. Hunter pulls me to his side, and I cry into his T-shirt. *My friend soulmate...what would I do without you?*

"Who the hell am I?" I sob.

Hunter's hands relax on my back. "You're Carrington Daughtler. Number-one best-selling poet of *Left or Right.* You love cafés but only go to one if you bring your journals to write. Scary movies don't scare you. People-watching is your research. You see the world through your emotions, and it's like you can't ever get enough of life, even if it sucks sometimes. You clearly want to move in with your boss." That one makes me laugh. It feels nice to be held by Hunter. "You refuse to let people walk all over you; I mean...you moved to New York City before coming here. You're hilarious and upbeat and *smart* as all get out. I read your poetry, and I *know* that you understand how humans work. There is this light inside of you that is so bright and welcoming. It's hard not to like you, Carrington. *That's* who you are. Kind and creepily observant." I laugh again. We both do. "Please don't lose yourself in Abel. He's a great person, too. But he's just Abel—his *own* person. He's not perfect. He's not all-knowing. He's not the end-all-be-all. Carrington, you are *you*, and I would prefer not to lose you."

I look up at him. My friend soulmate...with his unruly black hair, kale-green eyes, tender smile, and the now tear-soaked Twenty-One Pilots T-shirt. My heart fills with love for him. The kind of love that you can't even name because it just feels so natural and sifts through every crack and crevice between your bones. The kind that warms your nervous system with gratitude. For the first time in some twenty hours, the pressure eases off my shoulders.

Hunter isn't a blusher. He just grins and glances away—at the journals on the table. "Time to write some poetry."

"Oh, please no. Anything but that."

"Well, you're not going to sit here and wallow over something you can't control."

I turn my face against a cushion and groan. "Why not?"

"Come on, get up. We're going for a drive."

"What about—"

He grabs my face. His stare drills into me. "Abel *will be fine.* He is incredibly strong. You and I both know that he will fight until he wins himself back. He won the battle before, and he will win again."

Two deep breaths. I nod. "Your faith is very refreshing."

He shrugs. "How else are we supposed to get through life?"

Once I have brushed my teeth, tackled my knotted hair, and put on some presentable clothes (a massive sweatshirt and leggings), I allow Hunter to drive me to Who Knows Where. I don't ask. I just allow the cold November air to fill my nostrils and my pores and my soul. December is four days away, which means Abel's birthday is only thirteen days away. I nearly make myself sick over the possibility of him spending his twenty-fifth birthday in a psychiatric hospital (assuming he doesn't pass the evaluation for discharge), but I promised Hunter I would try to limit the what-ifs for a while, so I inhale the air and try to focus on the fact that it is *still* November air.

Hunter pulls into a parking lot at the park. I give him a questioning look.

"It's thirty degrees."

"We're not getting out," he explains nonchalantly, like I'm funny for thinking so.

"Then...."

He reaches into the back seat and retrieves my poetry journal. "You're going to talk through your writer's block."

"That's worse than being psychoanalyzed."

"I doubt it." He hands me the journal.

Sometimes working on a long-term creative project is like having to get back on a carousel that's already made you puke, stumble in your own vomit, and take three doses of Dramamine. Other times, that carousel is beautiful and twinkling and lovely. Right now, I'm experiencing the former.

"Can we please just bird-watch instead?"

Hunter turns the car off and pins me with a look. "Cari."

"*Fine.*" I groan like a toddler. "I don't feel like writing because the whole collection is about my feelings for Abel. The highs, the lows, the in-betweens. Uncertainties and fears."

Hunter nods, his lips pressed together. "I've gathered that."

"Excuse me if I don't feel like writing while he's in the hospital, or after he..."

"After he...?"

I sigh. "After he called me a 'fucking waste of time.'" I look out the window when I say this because it feels silly to admit that I'm not a bad bitch with golden armor around her heart, that these things don't just roll off my shoulders.

Silence, and then, "That must have hurt. A lot."

"Yeah, and the sky is also blue." *Like, is that even a question?!*

"There's no denying that," Hunter says gently. "Can I ask you something?"

"If it's that you want me to spit out a new poem right now, the answer is no."

"That's not it. What do you think it means to love someone who struggles with a mental health disorder?"

Now, I turn to look at him. I'm about to answer the usual—honesty, patience, communication, etc.—until I remember that Hunter's questions usually require more thought. Something Abel told me one time comes to mind. He explained that his father never left his mother, despite the cycling of her mania. Carson's love, patience, and kindness toward Alana, (and himself; let's not forget that) is the ultimate example of true compassion in our fucked-up, stigma-fueled world. The exception that should be the norm.

"It means...educating yourself," I realize. "Being a trusting, solid presence in their life. And setting boundaries to protect your own mental health." Abel's words echo in my head.

"Yes," Hunter says. "Now, that last part."

"What about it?"

"Do you think there is a difference between setting boundaries and identifying when you have been pushed past your limit?"

I cock my head at him. "Are you asking if it's okay to break up with someone because of their mental health?"

"Not necessarily. I'm asking if you think there is a stigma around protecting your *own* mental health. Doing what's right for you, even in this situation?"

"I..." My stomach clenches. "Probably. But how does that work? How do you know when it's time to...let it be and move on? I love Abel. I don't want to..."

Hunter's eyes fill with that empathy that makes me feel seen and understood. "What's going through your head?"

Annoyingly, tears sting my eyes *again*. "I don't ever want Abel to think he was...too much to handle, or...God forbid, get worse. Mental illness is not an excuse to break up with someone!"

"No, it is not," Hunter agrees instantly. "But...would you agree that lines need to be drawn if your partner's mental illness starts to negatively impact your own mental health?"

My mouth quivers. Tears stream down my cheeks. Snot trails down from my nostrils.

"Cari."

"Don't say it." I nearly choke on the emotions.

Have I ever been in this much pain? When did the harsh self-talk get so loud? The guilt, the shame, the...

I can't take this anymore.

My hands ball into fists, and I wail like a four-year-old, but who gives a shit? Could it be true...? Am I *not* the one for Abel? I may have tricked myself into thinking I have the strength to support him, but honestly, I haven't written a word in days. I've hardly looked at myself in the mirror. I can't stop crying. I can't even eat a full meal—the knots in my stomach are *way* too tight. I have shouldered Abel's pain and mania and everything in between. I can't take it anymore. Does that make me a bad person? Or is it possible that the answer to that question is...*No, Cari, you're just human.*

"I need to let go," I sob. "But I can't! Why?"

"Because you genuinely love him. Nobody said this was going to be easy."

I hear Hunter. I know the truth in my heart; I know what has to be done, but the thought sends a spear through me.

"So, he gets out of the hospital, and I break his heart?"

"He's going to check out of the hospital, and you're going to have a conversation," Hunter corrects tenderly.

I shake my head, hard. "I can't. He's going to hate me. I can't have that."

"Do you hear yourself?"

Man, screw Hunter and his intelligent responses.

"How will I get past it?" I moan.

Hunter doesn't answer. He just looks pointedly at my journal.

The lightbulb sparks to life in my brain, so bright, I get chills despite the tears. "You...you're too good."

He smiles, but it's a sad smile. He clearly hates having this conversation as much as I hate sitting through it. We both despise this turn of events, wish on our lives that it didn't have to be this way. But it just is what it is. Radical acceptance and all that.

I heave a sigh as the idea forms in my brain.

"Tell me what you're thinking," Hunter says.

"A new angle," I say. "For the collection."

Hunter's eyebrows raise in interest.

"A collection about how to love someone who struggles with a mental illness and knowing when to…let go." Just saying it, I feel a hundred knives plunge into my body.

I witness something I never thought I would see: tears forming in Hunter's eyes. He fakes a nose brush, wipes them away quickly. My own tears drip down to my chin.

"I still love him," I say.

"You always will. It doesn't have to be goodbye forever."

My hands are shaking, but I want to write. I pull my knees up to my chest in the passenger seat and rest my journal on my legs. Hunter starts the car so we can get some heat. The radio comes on and "The Chain" by Fleetwood Mac plays softly through the silence.

49

───────

I don't go into Sheppard Pratt Hospital. I wait in my car in *front* of it because I am a jittery, mascara-smeared, shaking *mess*.

After I emailed Christie my plans to alter the poetry collection (she, of course, was fully on board, as long as I meet my deadline), I called Carson Harpen. First time in four years: I haven't talked to him on the phone since Christmas of sophomore year of college, when I called him to ask where Abel should park at the Christmas lights showing (Abel had been driving and passed his phone to me in the passenger seat).

Yesterday, my conversation with Mr. Harpen went something like this:

Him: Carrington?
Me: Hi, Mr. Harpen.
Him: Good grief, it's been too long, kid.
Me: I know. I'm sorry about that.
Him: What can I do for ya?
Me: I know Abel's in the hospital. We've gotten really close

*these last couple months, and I want to be there to support him
when he checks out.*

Him: That won't be until the hearing is over.

Me: Right. Do you know when that will be?

*Him: Hard to say in today's world. (Pause) Tell ya what.
When the information is released, I'll reach out to you, and
you can come see him when we pick him up.*

Me: You're coming down to Maryland?

*Him: Of course. It's always been an important thing in our
family to be there for each other. Abel decided that when he
was a teen. After he's released, he comes home for a few days.*

Me: Oh, I don't want to intrude.

*Him: No, stop that, kid. You wouldn't be. Abel needs his
friends, too.*

Me: Thank you so much, Mr. Harpen.

*Him: Thank you for always supporting my son. I'll call you as
soon as we know.*

Turns out, Abel needed an extended stay after his initial admission to the hospital. *So he can get proper treatment,* Hunter reminded me a few days ago. *He will get through this.* Of course, Hunter was right. Here I am, pressing my frozen fingers to the heater in my car on December 1, waiting for Abel to walk through those doors.

Ten minutes after my arrival, he does.

Blue T-shirt. Gray sweatpants. No coat. An unreadable expression: neither happy nor at peace. A steady hand on his shoulder. Mr. Harpen.

I stumble over myself to jump out of my car, but not before a woman with gorgeous honey-blonde hair cuts across my path.

"Abel, baby!" Mrs. Harpen sprints to her son. Wraps him in her arms. He hugs her back, so tightly I think he might be suffocating her until she draws back, and I see the tears in her eyes. She kisses the side of his head a dozen times.

"Hi, Mom."

She gives him a motherly concerned look, and he must know exactly what she's asking because he nods reassuringly and pats her arm.

"There's someone else here to see you, too, son," Mr. Harpen says.

And then our eyes connect. The vibrant blue of his irises traps my heart in a stutter.

"Carrington." It's barely a whisper.

I step toward him, losing the fight to keep my tears at bay. When we're close enough to touch, he's the one to ask.

"Can I hug you?"

I fall into his arms. *His* arms, not the arms of a crazy person or a psychiatric patient. Those labels can all burn in hell. He is as warm and gentle as ever. Himself, again.

"You didn't have to come here," he says. I hear the tremor in his voice. "Not after...."

I shake my head. "I *wanted* to be here."

He lets me go to wipe under his eyes. Even though Mr. and Mrs. Harpen are off the side, chatting quietly, the silence between me and Abel is deafening.

"I guess we need to talk, huh?" he says. He knows. He can see it in every worry line on my face.

I try desperately to breathe around the sinking feeling in my stomach. "It doesn't have to be now. You should be with your family."

He sucks in a long breath. "I missed Melanie and Charlotte like crazy."

I smile because there he is. The caring man I fell in love with.

"We'll talk soon," he says and gives my hand a soft squeeze. For the last time?

"We'll talk soon."

I wonder if my heart will ever stop crumbling when he walks away from me. Mr. Harpen offers me a kind *thank you* of a smile and follows after his son.

It takes me a moment to realize Mrs. Harpen hasn't moved.

When I look over at her, she's staring at me with familiar blue eyes, only a shade lighter than Abel's. I look down and notice, for the first time, the book in her hands: a battered copy of Joyce Meyer's *Battlefield of the Mind*. Judging by the tense expression on her face, I expect I'm about to get a lecture for something until she starts to speak.

"You've always been there for Abel."

"I try to be," I say, feeling timid. Alana never showed much affection toward me.

She blinks, pushes a strand of Barbie-like blonde hair over her shoulder. "Thank you for that. It's rare to not have people give in to stigma."

"Trust me." I almost manage to laugh. "With a psychologist for a mom, I would never."

Her chin raises a notch. Something pulls at her lips that I can't quite call a smile. "Take care of yourself, Carrington. Life's too short as it is." With that, she turns and follows her husband and son to their car. The book swings in her tight grasp.

Her words ricochet in my brain until I register the cold wind seeping through my jacket. I head to my car and try to accept the fact that a piece of my heart will forever remain on that sidewalk.

50

I only leave my apartment to go to work. Otherwise, I'm piled under fluffy blankets on my couch, writing through countless hand cramps. You'd think I swallowed six Pixy Stix with the way I'm churning out poems. For that reason, the rewrite is not taking as long as I suspected, and after a gleeful Zoom meeting with Christie, I feel more than motivated again. In *this* area of my life at least. Other areas, not so much.

For example, I haven't bothered to decorate my apartment for Christmas. It's all barren bones in here: clamshell-gray flooring that looks duller now that the streets are dusted in snow. Good thing my neighbors are in the spirit because otherwise, I'd never get around to seeing lights blink in time with "Silver Bells" and every version of the song.

I have also neglected to keep to my cleaning routine, so not only is the apartment dreary, it's also a pigsty. Pots and pans clutter the sink (I'll get to them eventually); takeout boxes form a mountain in the trashcan (there's still some room left); toothpaste and makeup stains adorn the bathroom sink (nothing some water can't wash away). I just have other things on my mind at the moment.

Like, replaying the small interaction I had with Abel two days ago on his birthday.

I'd texted with some party-hat emojis:

> Happy 25. Eat some cake for me. And let me know if you finally get that Hot Wheels track you've been wanting since you were seven.

He responded an hour and twenty minutes later.

> Didn't get the Hot Wheels track. But I did eat some pretty good cake. Thank you for the kind words!

He went on to ask me how I was doing, which had my heart kicking in its usual Abel-fueled way. He didn't have to ask, but he did. I lied and told him I was great: writing a lot of poetry, cooking great meals, getting my fill of *Rudolph* and *Frosty the Snowman*. He texted back that he was thrilled I'm doing well and that he hopes I have a great Christmas and New Years. Which led me to believe I wouldn't be seeing him before then.

Probably for the best. In the week and a half since I saw him outside the hospital, some healthy (or overwhelming) self-reflection helped me realize that maybe...just maybe...Abel was a distraction for me. Love doesn't have to be categorized as a distraction, but when you sacrifice your whole sense of self to be with someone, it does. And I sacrificed my own happiness to keep him close.

Unfortunately, the shame hasn't packed its bags and left yet. I still feel like I have an ugly soul for 1) denying his symptoms, and 2) exacerbating the problem. Like, yes, in terms of extending olive branches, we are good now, but not really. We're not the *us* we were three weeks ago. Now, there's an awkwardness to our text chain—a formality that hasn't been there since the first few weeks of our freshman year in college, when we would occasionally text each other questions about class material. The new tone makes my bones ache.

I want things to go back to the way they were. But how can that be, after you've realized that someone might just not be good for you...as painful as that is to consider? Hunter, the humble saint he is, reminded me that sometimes, people are in our lives for *seasons* and specific *reasons*.

"So, if it's not to be my soulmate and get gray hair with me while we file our taxes, then what's the point?" I asked him last week, over glasses of warm tea, *not* coffee for once.

"Well." Hunter stared at the tiny dancing flame in my Vanilla Cookies candle. "What do you think?"

"Can't you just be the therapist that tells me all the answers?"

"Again, I'm not your therapist." This has become a joke between us. Well, I always think it's funny; Hunter just gives me a mix of a grin and a grimace. A grinmace. "We're two friends talking. There's a—"

"A difference, I knowwwww." I rolled my eyes and lightly punched his arm. "Fine. Maybe it's because...Abel is meant to go on and be a movie star, and I'm meant to be that writer that trends on social media as the I-Knew-Him-When attention hog."

Hunter pursed his lips.

"Or maybe," I said, "I'm meant to be one of his future patients. Get diagnosed with—"

"That would *not* happen."

"Why not?"

Hunter looked at me like I had asparagus for teeth. "Major conflict of interest."

"Whatever."

"Could it be that...you are meant to write this poetry collection to help someone else in the world who is dealing with similar struggles, and to be able to do it, you needed Abel?"

I nearly spat out my tea. "Stop grilling me with these dead-on explanations. They freak me out!"

We then proceeded to talk about cheap Christmas gift ideas.

Hunter's idea has made it into the collection, though. "Renting

My Home" is a poem about moving into someone's heart, but only for
a short while:

> I would splash Robin's Egg Blue
> on the walls,
> but the landlord
> prefers Royal Blue
> because it compliments
> his irises.
> I leave some opened boxes
> in the kitchen
> so I can spare myself
> the search
> for a spatula
> or duct tape later.
> And the coffee
> in my mug
> stays warm for 0.3 seconds—
> how long I have
> before the doorbell rings
> and the Grandfather Clock chimes:
> "Cari,
> time is up!
> On to the next adventure."
> I'll leave my sandal
> in the freezer
> and my heart
> in the bathtub.
> Thank you for your hospitality.

Writing during winter is lonely. Some writers will argue with
that, call winter *a wonderful time to write* with all the crystal-like
snow and holiday addicts who leave their Christmas lights up till
Valentine's Day, but that's only half the picture. Writing during the

winter *also* means barricading yourself indoors to have five minutes away from those sleigh bells jingling so that you can write a single sentence in peace. (The Pentatonix version *is* lovely though.) Plus, there's the reminder of the significant other you *don't* have and the box of cookies you *shouldn't* binge but do anyway because you can't write and *not* eat.

Winter feels a hundred times lonelier this year. I sit on my couch, scribbling away in the journal so that I can get the poems typed up and send the manuscript to Polly&Pippy by the thirty-first. It won't be difficult. It is just quiet in my apartment. Super quiet.

Past holiday seasons flash through my memory. When Tucker and I were really young, we would sneak back downstairs to hide under the kitchen table to wait for Santa. I wanted to see how he could eat twelve cookies so fast. But Dad always caught us and chased us back up to our beds, playfully threatening to install a security camera downstairs—if we were caught again, no presents. We never snuck back down.

In high school, I used to wake up early and make everyone cups of hot chocolate, secretly hoping the gesture would persuade my parents to let me skip family brunch and hang out with Xina, my best friend at the time. It only worked *once*, and I had to do all the dishes when I got home.

I typically spent Christmas Eves in college at Abel's house, along with Kelsey and Noah. The Core Four, at our absolute greatest, playing Cards Against Humanity until Mr. Harpen invited us into the living room to listen while Melanie or Charlotte read the Nativity Story. Abel and I had always sat together, always jokingly poked at each other, always laughed the hardest at each other's jokes. Except for junior year, when Camila attended the Harpen Christmas Eve. Ugh.

Abel....

My chest aches.

I miss everything about him—down to his wonderful smell and the way his golden hair sometimes curls over his forehead. I miss his laugh and those *perfect*, white teeth. I miss his warm arms and the glow of his smile and the feeling of his body entering mine and the way we were.

The way I was.

Confident? Maybe. Happy? Absolutely.

My most recent poem, the one I wrote twenty minutes ago while listening to a group of carolers serenade the traffic jam outside, is entitled "Red Wine, My Bitch." Because now I can't talk to Abel like I used to, so I've befriended pinot noir. Basically, I'm just *sad* about the way life works. Like, *Here, Cari—here's a man who will be your best friend, then lover, then temporary enemy, then ghost of a stranger. Have fun!* Hopefully Hunter's perspective is true, and the reason behind this madness is something greater than stupid heartbreak and decapitated self-esteem.

Kelsey suggested a spa weekend with acupuncture to help me "deal." Noah told me not to sweat it, that Abel and I would be best pals again in no time—"Guys don't take this stuff seriously like women do"—despite all the times I insisted things will never again be as they were. Ruth suggested I take a few days to collect myself. Her other employees were more than happy to step in for me while I get my writing done. Katerine, from her cozy vacation spot in Toronto, suggested I see a therapist. And, like the dawn waking the sky, I remembered that my mother is a therapist.

Yet, I still can't bring myself to call her.

On Christmas Eve-Eve, I go ice-skating with Hunter. *He* asked: something about not being able to stand the thought of me becoming a hermit and how being alone for the holidays isn't good for my mental health, yada-yada-yada. Ruth mentioned something similar yesterday, but I just offered her a weak thumbs-up and trudged out to the cash register to take a gajillion orders.

On the bright side, I am nearly done with the poetry collection.

It's good for a first draft, even though I feel like my insides have been stripped from my body, spit on, twisted, and inserted at all the wrong angles. Heartbreak will do that to you.

"—dream research," Hunter is saying. We glide smoothly around the rink to Rudolph's theme song. "I've been analyzing the literature, and surprisingly there is nothing on dream relevance. Just some meta-analyses of Freud's—"

"Aren't you studying to be a neuroscientist?"

He looks over at me. "I told you this is for my friend Max."

Oh. Did he say that?

We skate to the middle of the rink, past several cozy couples and one overly excited child who ends up on his bottom. Hunter puts a hand on my shoulder. "Cari. Where are you right now?"

An article on Google called "Get Over a Breakup Faster" informed me that mindfulness and gratitude can work wonders. I have yet to see the effects, even right now with Hunter.

"In my head," I mumble.

We have stopped skating and are just standing in the middle of the ice while too-cool teenagers slide past us.

"What can I do?" Hunter says.

"*You* don't have to do anything. You've helped tremendously already. The collection is nearly done, my editor is eagerly awaiting it, and life is good."

He flashes a stop-bullshitting-me look.

I try to put words together. "I feel stuck in my head," I explain. "Abel and I haven't talked yet, but I feel it looming over me like a... sickness. He's not on his phone. I've tried to give him space, but it's making me anxious."

"It is the holidays. He needs to be with his family. You will talk eventually."

I wring my hands. "I am so nervous, Hunter."

"Hey." He takes my hand, and I let him. Hunter was made with extra love, support, and kindness packed into his bones. He's so sweet his teeth must ache. We all need Hunters in our lives. "You need to trust that things will be okay."

"Trust in the universe?"

"If that's what you choose."

"What do you do?"

He doesn't answer, just tugs at his shirt and pulls out a chain with a cross on it. It's simple, silver and large.

"Why have I never seen this?"

"You didn't ask," he says with a small smile. "Plus, I don't really talk about my faith with just anyone."

Everyone around me believes in God. Maybe that should tell me something.

"Trust that everything will be all right," Hunter says. "I'm worried about you."

I feel stupid. Out of control. The tears come back. I was experimenting in emotional suppression even though extensive amounts of research say that is *very* unhealthy. But this is why I wanted to suppress my emotions: crying fits in an ice-skating rink are embarrassing. Hunter moves closer, blocking the head-on sight of me hiccupping. He lets me cry, lets me wipe at my eyes and make a small scene here in public. He acts like we're not in public. He just wraps his arms around me and offers a comforting squeeze.

I wish I could unzip my skin like a coat, let what's left of my soul spill out and catch a ride on the breeze. No thoughts, no feelings, just be. The weight of this moment is too much. In fact, the weight of every moment is too much. Who knew that choosing to protect your own mental health would hurt like this.

I get my act together because I have to. A mom just gave me the sympathy look, and I'm not trying to have a side conversation with her later about grief and possible casseroles.

Hunter lowers his arms. "You okay?"

I rub my eyes "I'm sorry I can't be better company."

"No, Cari. I'd rather see the real you than anything else."

"Why are you so nice?" Like, seriously.

He chuckles and nudges me along for us to continue skating. "My parents raised me well."

"I think I love you."

His skates swivel a little bit. "You think?"

"I *know* I do. You are the kindest person I've ever met, Hunter Gatelin."

His smile is small and sweet. "I love you, too, Carrington."

Christmas Eve.

In my defense, I have *The Grinch* playing on TV, but my attention is focused on my laptop. I am furiously typing up each poem on a Word document, determined to have the project in to Pamela, my editor at Polly&Pippy, by midnight. It's not that I want to be done with the collection. It's that I want to drop dead and sleep for two years without the weight of deadline reminders in my email.

I'm proud of this collection. It feels *whole* in ways my previous angle didn't. And though it is a knife in my liver to type up poems like "Countdown" and "Why Him?," I know that Hunter *is* right. Someone in the world is stepping away from a loved one for a time, and it scares them. They need this collection to understand they aren't alone.

Around 9 p.m., I finish typing up my hundred-twentieth poem. The last one. When I add the final period, something leaves my chest. It feels heavy and light, cold and hot. Wonderfully bittersweet. I save the document and email it to Pamela, CCing Christie.

Unsurprisingly, I start to cry.

I cry for Abel and myself, for all the people in the world who struggle with a mental illness and for their loved ones who try their hardest to hang on every single day. Love is not about someone's ultra-good-looking exterior or their taste in '80s music or their bubbly personality. Love is showing kindness even in the darkest of moments. Exercising patience and yes, gratitude. Offering forgiveness—to them and yourself.

I cry so hard my heart could burst. Sure, writing is cathartic. Finishing a creative project feels like winning a championship. But it isn't a magic spell. I really feel the emptiness of my apartment now. I feel the lack of Christmas lights and joy. I feel incredibly lonely. All of my friends are either back in their cherished childhood homes with their families or out at a bar, drinking and posing in Santa hats. I do usually go home for Christmas, but in recent years, I have stalled the road trip for as long as possible to avoid Mom.

Except, now that I think about it, I miss the way Mom used to tuck me in when I was little. I miss our impromptu bake sessions and the way she held me when I accidentally smashed my finger in our screen door.

In this early-adulthood phase of my life, I have tried so hard to separate my own image from hers, all because I've thought that she hates me for forgoing a graduate degree. But has my own poetry collection taught me nothing? I need to forgive her. I need to forgive myself. Contrary to my stubborn belief, I am not a rock sculpture. I am not immune to loneliness or regret or sadness. And okay, I'm pretty sure this grief has twisted itself around my life in all the worst ways. Learning to live without Abel is like trying to live without an arm or a leg.

I need someone.

I need my mom.

I reach for my phone before that annoying voice in my head can tell me I'm being a whiny baby loser. My breath shakes as the dial rings. Then:

"Sweetheart?"

That single word pushes tears out of my eyes.

"Mom," I say. "I want to come home."

A few thick beats of silence pass. Then she says, in a soft, warm voice, "Cari, you don't have to call. You've always been welcome home."

51

I wake up in my childhood bed. Hazy sunshine pours in through the cream-colored blinds, smearing across the deep-blue carpet, stretching all the way to my vanity desk, highlighting the cups of pens and piles of YA books there.

Christmas Day.

I got home to Newport around 3 a.m. last night. One groggy glance at the clock tells me that it is now well past noon. I half expect Tucker to skip into my room and yank the covers off my shivering body, like he did when we were young, but it is blissfully quiet. My bones feel like syrup. My bed feels like quicksand. My head is a deflated balloon.

Sobbing while driving should be a category in the *Guinness Book of World Records*: How many tears can leave your eyes in a six-hour span while you simultaneously dodge idiot drivers? New record: Carrington Daughtler. My eyes are *still* puffy from crying. The worst part is that I can't even pinpoint a single reason for being so worked up: I just am. About *everything*. I vaguely recall trembling in the snow before Mom opened the door and pulled me in for the longest hug in the world. I remember Dad snoring his lungs out in his recliner; the Christmas tree glimmering with a sea of presents underneath; Mom's comment that Tucker and Lauren took the guest room. I don't remember falling into bed.

I groan and rub my eyes.

Something sizzling and meaty calls my nostrils' attention. Dad's miniature sausage patties: a Christmas regular for our family brunch. Good. My stomach is eating itself. I roll out of bed and miraculously don't belly flop on the floor.

The meaty aroma grows stronger and mixes with fresh berries and pancake batter as I tiptoe downstairs. The living room is empty. Our fake, fat Christmas tree stands tall in the corner, sporting candy canes, tinsel, and strings of cranberries and popcorn. The presents underneath remain unopened. The commotion stems from the kitchen—utensils clanging against bowls, hushed laughter. I try to shoot for an inconspicuous entrance. Silly me.

"Merry Christmas, Tiny Carrot!" Dad abandons his spot in front of the sink and bounds toward me. His hugs are the best, especially right now.

"There she is." Tucker raises his Avengers mug at me with a lazy grin.

Lauren is next in line for a hug. And then there's Mom, stepping back from the griddle, resting her spatula on a towel, untying her apron.

We didn't talk last night. I was too lost in my emotions, so she gently suggested I just go to bed. Now, I feel that the space between us is thick with what we haven't said.

"Good morning, sweetheart," she says, wrapping her arms around me.

She smells like cinnamon and lavender. Her white-blonde hair is tied in a loose bun at the nape of her neck. I am overwhelmed by how much I've missed the mere presence of her. The bitch part of my brain is still fighting, whining for me to pull away and yank up my guard, but after days of emotional exhaustion, though, I am done playing that game.

I let my mother hug me. I hug her back.

The thing I love about Christmas Day family brunch is that all snarky comments or prying questions are withheld for the sake of the holiday. No one asks me why I got in at 3 a.m. or why the bags under my eyes are more like sacks. My family members have never been gossip hounds to begin with, but the side comments can be brutal at times. Thank goodness for Christmas and the heaping of blueberry oatmeal on our plates. They are a nice distraction.

"Did you get me one of those custom-made *Star Wars* picture frames, honey?" Dad asks, mouth full of ketchup-slathered scrambled eggs.

Mom sips her orange juice. "Did you get me the end pillows I want?"

"You'll just have to see."

I chow down on three blueberry pancakes, finish my oatmeal, and eat a spoonful of miniature sausage patties all while Tucker describes the best and worst students in his high school civics class.

"I never understood why you chose civics anyway," Lauren says, trying to keep a straight face. "That's boring."

Tucker pretends to choke on his coffee. "There is nothing boring about the structures of government."

They bicker in a way that shows they are clearly head over heels in love.

The topics switch from this to that; the pancakes disappear. Dad fights Tucker for the last handful of sausage. Mom pours me more orange juice. Lauren talks about the uptick in school nurse visits and student absences: Covid, the stomach flu, the usual. She's happy to have a holiday break.

When we have eaten enough to burst, we move into the living room to open presents. Normally, this part of the day would occur at nine in the morning. But the older Tucker and I got, the more we valued sleeping in. Presents are distributed. Mom did indeed get Dad one of those custom *Star Wars* picture frames with our best family photo inside. Dad did indeed get Mom her end pillows. They share a sloppy kiss that Tucker and I complain through.

"Okay, okay. I want everyone's attention for this one," Tucker says. He hands Lauren a good-sized present. "Award for the best present goes to me."

Lauren tears at the wrapping paper, cuts through the tape. Inside is another box.

"You're one of *those* people," I mutter, not quite under my breath. Tucker smirks at me.

Inside this slightly smaller box is, who could have guessed, another box—this time wrapped in silver paper. Dad hums the *Jeopardy!* theme song. We all giggle. When the boxes get down to candy pack sizes, Mom says, "Good grief, Tucker."

"Is this the last one?" Lauren asks, holding up the smallest box yet with a green-and-red curly bow.

"Open it and see," Tucker says.

It is the last box. I know because Lauren's jaw drops.

"What is it?" Dad asks.

Lauren whips out two print-out tickets. Taylor Swift: the Eras Tour. Goodness gracious, even the school nurse is a Swiftie. Lauren leaps into Tucker's arms. I will hand it to my brother. If he can set aside his aversion to bubblegum pop music long enough to have his eardrums torn out for three hours at a Taylor Swift concert, he is going to make a great husband someday.

In the midst of Lauren's screams and Dad's congratulations, Mom slips another present into my lap. I look up at her. The smile on her face is kind, and dare I say, proud? I tear at the wrapping paper and something sentimental punches my heart. Inside, its turquoise cover shining, is a brand-new journal.

52

———

I have done countless interviews for my poetry, signed hundreds of copies, walked out on makeshift stages in libraries and bookstores to do fan Q&As. I am a successful, published badass. Yet, my tummy still flips at the thought of talking to my mother and addressing all the ugly thoughts in my head.

Since Dad, Tucker, and Lauren are absorbed in *Home Alone*, I climb the stairs at a tortoise pace and knock on my parents' bedroom door. Mom answers, one hand clumping her wet hair in a white towel, and the other hand adjusting the hem of her dress.

Let's do this another time, my conscience suggests. *Ohhhhh no you don't*, my logic replies.

"What's up, sweetheart?" Mom walks back to the bathroom and the hair dryer clicks on.

"I, uh..." A very *loud* hairdryer. I wait five minutes for her to turn it off. "I need..." Nothing else comes after those two words. Gosh. I didn't realize how hard this would be. The words clog my throat and refuse to pass. Mom waits, her expression growing increasingly concerned. I understand why: when have I ever sat on her bed like this and failed to speak? "I..." *Vomit the words, Carrington, for fuck's sake!* "I need to talk to you."

Mom nods, like she expected this. "Okay."

When she sits beside me on the bed, my stomach begins to burn. Maybe it's acid reflux. Maybe it's a hernia. Maybe my appendix has burst. Maybe—

"Carrington?"

Ugh. I take a deep breath and try for calm. What I give is a jumbled mess. "Abel got manic; I made it worse. I *know* bipolar symptoms, but I didn't want to see what was going on, because I was obsessed with Abel. Well, *obsessed* isn't the right word. More like, infatuated. But can you honestly blame me? I was all like, 'What is love?' That's what this new collection is about, which I just submitted yesterday, by the way. But I learned that I wasn't in the relationship for the right reasons, and I couldn't shoulder his mania." My hands twist at the bedsheets. "God, that makes me sound horrible. I actually took a quiz on some dumb website called like, "How Much of an Idiot Are You?" I got an eighty-four. An *eighty-four*. I still have to talk to Abel, but I bet he's—"

You know you're off the rails when even a clinical psychologist looks at you funny. Even if she is my mom. Kudos to her though, she recovers quickly. She takes a steadying breath, but something about her expression makes me think she does that more for me than her.

"So, Abel went through a manic episode."

I nod.

"Is this the first one you've experienced?"

"I mean, I knew he struggled with mania a few times in college, but I'd never experienced one up close and personal."

"And now you are experiencing...what?"

"Regret. Fear. Isolation. Sadness." My voice drops with each word. By the end, I'm whispering.

Mom presses her lips together, and I almost beg her not to diagnose me with Lost Love Syndrome or something like that. *Please don't,* my mind yelps. *Please don't go down a list of possible symptoms and ask me how I'm sleeping at night or what I'm eating or how much exercise I'm getting in.*

In a stunning turn of events, Mom doesn't do any of those things. She simply pulls me into a hug. I am so surprised I almost ask where the alien species stashed my mom's real body. With my arms still around her, I ask, "Is this some sort of preamble to the list of psychotherapies you're about to recommend me?"

"Can't a mother just hug her daughter?"

My mouth opens and closes several times as I consider answers like, *Maybe normal moms can.* She lets go and sits back on the bed.

"Sometimes all a person needs is someone to sit with. No conversation."

It is odd how that statement penetrates my thick skull so easily.

"I can see that you're hurting," she says. "You never call home, not even to ask me or your father about restoring a water filter or taking the subway in New York City."

I can't help laughing. It's more like an exhale.

"Why don't you?" she asks.

"What?"

"Call home more?"

Put on your big girl pants, Carrington.

"'Cause I don't want you to...tell me I'm doing the wrong thing."

She blinks. A puzzled line furrows the skin between her eyebrows.

Pull the pants up higher, Carrington.

"You always send me links to graduate applications, and it's frustrating." My heart is racing. "I chose writing, Mom. It was hard enough navigating a big city at twenty-two years old without those passive-aggressive messages."

She looks genuinely baffled. "What are you talking about?"

Anger fills my lungs. How can she say she doesn't know what I'm talking about? "Your text messages about me going back to school to get a PhD! I can't be a clinical psychologist, Mom. I don't have the patience or the perseverance to get through that program." My fists come down on the bed. "Ever since I left for Manhattan, I've felt like you aren't on my side. Like, I could publish this new collection, and you wouldn't even read it. You'd just send me an application to fill out for some grad program in...Wichita, Kansas or wherever!"

"Carrington."

"It's the writing, Mom." My face is on fire and my palms are sweating, but I push on. "It's always been the writing. And I'm sorry if you can't forgive me, but this is how I help the world. I write *about* life! You help people *through* life. Why do I have to do exactly what you do?"

"Carrington."

"I am just as smart as you in other ways. You don't have to have a PhD to—"

"*Carrington.*" She sets a firm hand on my arm. My mouth closes itself.

There's an odd look in her eyes, like she can't decide whether to cry or smile. "Sweetheart. Those applications weren't to apply for a clinical program in psychology. They were to apply for doctoral programs in creative writing and the humanities."

I stare at her. Is this a hallucination?

"I figured if you love writing so much, you could study it at a grad level. You never really got that chance in undergrad." She pats my arm. "I didn't realize I was causing you so much frustration. I'm sorry."

The craziest part is that she sounds sincere. I transform into a human broken record. "But—but—but when I told you I got signed to Polly&Pippy, you were pissed."

"Shocked," she corrects. "Not pissed. I was surprised and, I admit, a little hurt that you didn't want to continue our family tradition and go on to be a clinical psychologist, but I got over it. Your dream is *your* dream."

"Well, then, you were pissed at me when I left for Manhattan," I point out.

"Carrington." She laughs. "None of that had to do with you. Being an adult is difficult. Bills are difficult. Difficult patients are difficult. Plus, I was worried about you and not trying to show it or get in your way. I'm sorry. I didn't mean to seem angry."

"You were pissed when I dyed my hair."

"And I still am." She crosses her arms. "Pink is an unnatural color." She sounds as if she means it, but her smile says otherwise.

My mouth could literally be on the floor. All this time...it was just a misunderstanding. I feel silly. Actually, stupid. Actually, weightless. My mom doesn't hate me. She has been on my side this whole time. I feel like I want to climb the roof and go sledding.

I do something incredibly uncharacteristic, which, if filmed, would leave its audience feeling the cringe in their spines: I reach out to hug my mother. Unprompted. She hugs me back, tightly, just like she did when I was little girl and the cookies we'd baked together were sitting in the oven.

"Now that I think about it," I say, my voice thick with fresh tears, "a PhD in creative writing and literature doesn't sound that bad."

She laughs, pats my back. "I don't think so either. But it's up to you, Carrington. This is *your* life, and if grad school isn't for you, that's perfectly fine with me. You're right. Having a Ph.D. doesn't make you smarter than everyone else. It just gives you a cool title."

My mom and I are laughing! *Together*. There must be a heaven. Haiti must have three inches of snow.

"Have you talked to Abel?"

Anddd I'm back on the concrete. "Not yet."

She folds her hand over mine. "What's your plan?"

I let go of a very long sigh. "I...I can't do it. Ever since I met him, I've been obsessed with how I act around him. Kind of like, I can't quite be my real self. If I am, he'll get tired of me and move on."

"You said 'obsessed' wasn't the right word."

I roll my eyes. "That was a lie. I am obsessed to my bones. But that's not healthy. I've been so caught up in this perfect fairy tale that when he got sick again, the whole thing just cracked. I couldn't stand seeing him like that. He called me a fucking waste of time, and I took that straight to the heart. Hardly ate for days. I hated myself. *Still* hate myself. I can't talk to him because I'm so afraid of losing him."

Mom is quiet for a long time. I wonder if she's about to tell me to let go and move on. Finally, she asks, "Do you love him?"

"Yeah. A lot." I touch the necklace he gave me, the one with my birthstone. I haven't taken it off. "That's why this hurts so bad."

"Well, if you love him, that might help you find the courage to let him go."

That hurts worse than an ice bath. Not that I've ever had an ice bath, but still. I start crying yet again, shocker. Mom's hand settles back on my shoulder.

"If you love him," she says, "do you want him to be happy?"

I swallow the tears down. "Of course."

"I'm not suggesting he wasn't happy with you, sweetheart. I have no doubt in my mind that he *was* happy. But...the longer you let these things go on, the worse it can become. It's okay if the mania was too much for you." Her face is calm, encouraging. "Letting go does not mean you are a bad person or that he will end up alone. It's also important to consider that he may not be the right one for *you*. That self-loathing can lead to many problems if you're not careful."

"I know." It's the only thing I can bring myself to say.

Life is beautiful, and twisted, and amazing, and unfair, and fucked up. My eyes shift to the metal cross hanging on the wall between the TV and bookshelf. It has pink roses on it, but to me it doesn't seem any less convicting. *There better be a good reason I have to let go,* I say to Jesus in my mind. I don't feel angry when I think it. Just sad. But I know. I know it's time to choose me.

For the first time in my life, I am going to choose *me*, not the fantasy idea of someone. Abel is and always will be an angel with a broken wing. He doesn't deserve his illness, and in spite of it, he's still the light of the world in his own lovely, unique way. It's my fault I chose to hold him on the highest pedestal; that wasn't fair to him or me. I will love him forever, but his forever isn't mine to hold.

"He's home with his family," I hear myself say.

"Why not go visit him tomorrow?"

That suggestion should give me extreme anxiety, but instead, it sucks the weight off my chest. Yes, I want to talk. Weeks of crying and self-loathing has made me tired. Dare I say, wiser. More aware. More prepared to take a deep breath and finally face the truth.

53

MELANIE OPENS THE DOOR, WHICH BOTH SHOOTS ME INTO THE present moment and drags me down Nostalgia Lane. I haven't seen her since I attended Abel's graduation party after college. Only two years later, she's grown half a foot and has transitioned out of the Artists Only Wear Black phase. Her jeans are rolled up at the ankles, and her white shirt shows each member of the Friends cast.

Her eyebrows draw together. "Carrington?"

I smile and nod because words? What are words right now?

Dimples dig into her cheeks as she returns my smile. "Are you here to see Abel?"

"If that's all right."

"Sure, but it's not up to me."

That's right. Of Abel's sisters, Melanie has the dry sense of humor. Not that this statement is particularly funny, but she is one of those people that could have me in tears by simply breathing.

She opens the door wider, and I step into the Harpen home. More specifically, I step back in time to before *Left or Right* and Polly&Pippy and Manhattan. Before, before, before.

I have always loved this house. The vast foyer—its gleaming laminate, open newel staircase and balcony overlooking a sleek, glass chandelier—splits in three directions. To the left is Mr. Harpen's self-titled man-cave: sliding bamboo doors, a leather couch facing an Elmwood and stone fireplace, and flat-screen. A pool table with a red velvet baize sits against the back wall, along with a minifridge. To the right of the foyer is the spacious living room, with family pictures and tiny plants galore. The Core Four played countless card games in there, back in the day, two of us (usually Abel and me) seated on the couch, and Noah and Kelsey crouched on the carpet at the coffee table. Peeking into the room now makes my head spin with memories.

I head straight down the foyer, toward the sunlit family room. Mr. Harpen is not in the kitchen like I half expected him to be. In fact, it's oddly quiet for a house that, from what I remember, is typically bursting with noise. I spot Mrs. Harpen curled up on one of the couches with a book. She glances over at me.

"Hi, Carrington. He's in the basement."

I didn't text Abel before coming over today, for fear he would reject me or say he wasn't interested in talking. Therefore, it is kind of funny how the sight of me roaming around the house doesn't even surprise his own mother. Then again, if Abel tells me to go away today, I will.

"Thank you," I tell Alana.

My heart hammers as I head for the basement, which is gorgeous in its own way. On one side sits a large cherry wood desk, peppered with paperwork and manila folders. Highlighters of every color. Framed pictures of Abel and his sisters. On the other side is a home gym with thousands of dollars in equipment. A Marcy Smith machine coupled with rowing machines, a treadmill, a pyramid of dumbbells and weight plates, and a Peloton.

I find him doing push-ups on a foam mat. "Wanted Dead or Alive" by Bon Jovi cranks out from the speaker. He is perfectly on beat. Eyes scrunched shut, Abel lip syncs and air-guitars to his feet.

"Abel," I say, in the pause after the song ends.

He jumps, spins to face me. "Oh, Cari."

I offer my kindest smile. Truth be told, I'm quaking in my boots. "Hi."

Van Halen's "Panama" comes on next, but Abel reaches for his phone and cuts the music. He grabs a white towel and drags it over his face before turning toward me, and a familiar ache pulses through my bones. I want to kiss him, even when he's sweating buckets. But that's not why I'm here. Not anymore.

With the music off, an awkward silence creeps in between us.

"How are you?" he asks, kind as ever. No *What are you doing in my house?*

"I'm all right. I'm sorry. I didn't mean to interrupt your workout. Your mom said you were—"

"Nah, that's okay." He waves his hand. "I was pretty much done anyway. What's up?"

You saw me naked, told me you loved me, called me a fucking waste of time, disappeared to the hospital. All I get is a what's up. None of this feels right.

"I..."

Deep, *deep* breath.

Mom said that the greatest things come from courage. Poetry collections. Job interviews. A renewed sense of peace, in my case. What sucks is that courage feels scary in moments like these.

"I wanted to talk to you about...us."

Abel's blue eyes darken, not into anger but sadness. Or maybe dread. A steak knife lodges itself in my stomach.

"Sure," he says after a moment. "Let's sit."

We walk, stiff-backed, to the small couch opposite the desk, and I feel sick. Courageous but sick.

"So..." Abel says, a signal for me to talk.

I draw another deep breath and let my eyes rest on the wood floor, which feels safest right now.

"First of all, I'm happy to see that you're okay." More than happy. *Exhilarated.* Bouncing off the walls. "I was...worried sick about you while you were gone. I felt that I...sort of lost control of that worry and let myself spiral a bit. What you said to me before the cops came..." This hurts like hell. I chance a peek at him and see the frown that has settled on his lips and eyes. He looks *incredibly* sad. Correction: this hurts *worse* than hell.

"God, Cari." He drops his head into his hands. "I'm sorry. I'm so, so sorry. I say awful things when I'm manic, and I don't know why I say them. I don't mean them! They just come out. That's not an excuse though," he hurries to add when I blink back tears. "I wish I had more control over..."

I interrupt, quietly. "That's not what I'm most worried about."

A long talk with my clinical psychologist mother had helped me realize for good that I am *not* a fucking waste of time. That those words were simply said to hurt me because at the time, Abel wasn't himself. *Accept the hurt. Recognize I won't hurt forever. Move forward.* Mom's gold-standard advice.

"What I'm most worried about," I continue, "is that...not too long before you went to the hospital, you told me you love me. I'd been waiting six years to hear you say that, but...did you only say it because you were manic?"

There it is. The question of the century spoken out into the atmosphere. I might vomit on this shiny wood floor.

Abel exhales. His eyes tick around the room. The longer the silence stretches on, the more the truth crushes my heart.

And then: "Yes. I think so."

It doesn't sound easy for him to say it. He sounds ashamed as if his very soul is bruised. Two tears leak from my eyes and drip onto my jeans.

"I *did* fall in love with you, Cari," he says, reaching out to touch me and thinking better of it. "When I left your apartment on Halloween night, I knew I was in love with you. But I was nervous for this very reason—that I would go through a manic cycle and my love for you would get twisted. And that I would say or do something that would crush you.

"When I was in the hospital, the time away made me realize that

I was loving you for the wrong reasons. I was with you to run away from my bipolar disorder. After my mom survived her suicide attempt, I went off my meds because…I thought with you, everything would be okay." His voice is gentle but rough-edged with pain. "I had been feeling better. You gave me a lot of strength I didn't know I had. But…when the mania came back, I realized that was all a fantasy. And now I know." This time, he reaches for my cheek so he can turn my face to look straight into my eyes. "We never would have worked, Carrington. Not in the long run."

A fucking uppercut to my gut. It *burns*. I almost wrap an arm around my torso to hold myself together. I can't help it; the tears spill faster. Abel doesn't look any better. His eyes darken two shades bluer as tears appear.

We never would have worked. That is the truth I came here to finalize and at the same time wanted desperately to debunk. But no. With his unrealistic expectation that I could save him from his illness and with my unhealthy codependency, we never would have worked. It's so simple and so painful.

I exhale. Nod. Cry harder.

The last time I was in this basement, I was helping him dig through the storage closet for Easter decorations, and we were laughing about something utterly ridiculous. I don't even remember what now because it doesn't matter. I was with him. What more could I have wanted?

We never would have worked.

"I know." My voice shakes when I force the words out.

His mouth quivers the tiniest bit. "Cari, I know that you are capable of giving so much love, and I know that you will make some guy *extremely* happy someday. You deserve to be in a wholesome, healthy relationship. I know that one day, you will be. And when I hear about it, it's going to make me the happiest person alive."

More tears dribble down my chin. "Abel." It stings to say his name. "You are such an angel. I don't want you to let anything hold you back because *I* know that you can make a woman feel incredibly special. I know you have so much love in your heart. One day..." It tears a hole in my heart to say, "you will find a woman who can give just as much love as you put out. I know that you will make her *so* happy. And I...I will be happy for you."

I *will* be because I love him.

He pulls me into his strong, sweaty arms, and I go willingly. Our shoulders shake as we cry into each other's shirts.

"Do you think we can still be friends?" he asks.

"Not right now," I hear myself say. "I...I need time."

He nods, releases me slowly. "One day, I hope we can be."

First, I need to figure out who Carrington Daughtler is. Carrington Daughtler Without Abel Harpen. The real Carrington Daughtler. Then...maybe, months or years from now, when my heart is fuller, and the wound of this loss is stitched up and healed, we can return to each other. After all, the universe is a pretty screwed up jokester. "Something tells me we will be," I say.

He looks at me so fondly. It's almost impossible to stand up off the couch. Somehow, I do.

Abel inhales through his nose, the tears still raw in his eyes. "Goodbye for now, Cari."

I am nauseated, nervous, lightheaded. It is only by the thinnest shred of courage that I say, "Goodbye for now, Abel."

54

"I cannot stress this enough," Christie exclaims. Her face is nearly smooshed against the camera. The amount of energy she has might make Zoom glitch and crash. "I LOVE THIS POETRY COLLECTION. The—the *metaphors* and the *vulnerability*. I got shivers, Carrington." I open my mouth to thank her, but she continues. "My favorites are 'Sweet Relief,' 'Climbing Trees,' 'Risk,' 'Why Him?'" She brushes aside her dark bangs. "Oh, what the hell. I loved all of them. You've got a lot of strength in this first draft, and I know Pamela is going to help you take these poems to the next level. I'm thinking a late 2024 release?" I open my mouth to answer, and she still keeps going. "The release tour is going to be *epic*. I'm booking you interviews with *Good Morning America, The Today Show*, and, keep your fingers crossed, Jimmy Fallon! You'd have to come back to New York though."

I wait five seconds to see if there is anything else she would like to add. My agent is an enthusiastic interrupter. She's waiting, business smile stretched cheek to cheek.

"Yes," I say. "If my book tour kicks off in New York City, I will be there."

"Beautiful." She slaps the table. "This collection's going to be bigger than sliced bread."

"That's so funny. That's the exact goal I had in mind when I sat down to write it."

She chuckles and flips open her calendar. "Pamela is already editing, so let's shoot for another Zoom meeting in early March. That'll give you time to make revisions and re-submit."

"Yes, ma'am."

I love Christie. She makes the writing process feel like a delightful trip to the zoo, with large amounts of sunscreen, water, and Advil—just in case.

As soon as Christie finishes marking her calendar and gushing about how excited she *truly* is, I sign off Zoom and call my mother. In the five days since we've talked (or rather, cleared the air), I've made this a new habit. Reconnecting with your mom is like reconnecting with old music or that lipstick shade you swore off but secretly loved. I called Mom after leaving Abel's house the other day, and she got to virtually witness the adult version of sobbing, snotty, emotional me. It was a pretty productive conversation, between her repeated assurances that I would be all right and my nearly unintelligible "okayyys." She reminded me of healthy coping mechanisms, or, as I like to call them, healthy distractions. When I got back to my apartment that night, I cleaned *everything*.

Now, I am sitting on my newly vacuumed couch with my phone on speaker, excitedly informing Mom that I am going to be the next Robert Frost. She tells me that is an excellent goal, which makes me laugh. It is still mind-boggling to me that we could have been having conversations like these since I finished writing *Left or Right*. The sheer power of communication, man. Nothing like it.

Mom tells me she has to do a grocery run for champagne and brownie mix. Tonight is New Year's Eve, and in recent years, my parents have opened their house up to our kooky, elderly neighbors.

"I hardly ever see them leave their houses," she says. I can hear keys jingling and a car beeping over her voice. "It's important to be kind neighbors."

It is the same explanation she gives every year, and I can never tell if she means it or if she is just trying to explain her actions to herself. Nevertheless, I always hear the best stories. In 2019, Mr. Brexton tried to sweet-talk Mrs. Gutierrez, which ended in a very loud explanation that she'd said, "I'm cleaning *windows*" over the phone, not, "I'm a *widow*." Mr. Gutierrez was supposedly in Arizona for the weekend, helping his brother move. Needless to say, the Apples to Apples game that evening was very passive-aggressive. In 2021, Miss Debra (also known as "I AM NOT A CONTROL FREAK, HAHAHAHA") nitpicked every piece of decor in the living room, from the dust on the mantel to the fabric of the sofa. That was the year Dad nearly bit his tongue off trying to keep quiet. In 2022, Mr. and Mrs. Ingram had one too many and ultimately crashed on the pull-out couch.

It's important to be kind neighbors, Mom argues.

Yeah, if she says so.

After I hang up with Mom, I call Tucker. His voicemail goes off, and I leave a message.

"Hey, Bro. Just checking in. What are you and Lauren up to tonight? Don't let her get into a Taylor Swift coma. I hear they happen to die-hard fans. Anyway, don't get too wasted. I know you won't, but just for my sake, count your shots. Give me a call back soon or whatever. Happy New Year. Love you."

Okay, here is the real reason for all my phone calls: I have no plans tonight. First time in seven years. Snapchat, the virtual headquarters for FOMO, has already shown me that Noah is on the Jersey shore, sipping Coronas with his flavor of the week—a redhead bundled up in a mink coat, sporting cute freckles and swollen lips. Katerine, still vacationing in Toronto, is pictured holding Ben's hand over a velvet tablecloth, the blue sky visible through spotless glass behind her. Kelsey is the type of person to upload videos of herself doing everything under the sun, but when she comments that she's hanging out with Raquel Torres tonight, my heart squeezes. That's both great and terrible. Great because maybe the two of them are hooking up. Terrible because they didn't invite me. But I guess I understand.

Abel has been MIA from Snapchat since his hospitalization, but he has always been private about his life. He told me once that he doesn't see the value in posting because his life is *his*, not a tabloid someone can slide up and comment on. My chest aches. I miss him so much my pores hurt. But I work my ass off to stay busy.

I go to the grocery store. I clean. I sleep. Watch funny videos, read sweetie-pie romance novels, call my parents, contemplate life. Sometimes the ache isn't unbearable. Other times, like tonight, it feels similar to a venomous snake bite. Tonight—when society *demands* you go out in your skimpiest dress and down all the flutes of champagne you can.

I exit Snapchat and google ways to avoid FOMO. (If superpowers existed, mine would be Excessive Fear of Missing Out. Helpful: never.) Google advises me to limit social media and reconnect with *me*. I can't tell if that means emotionally, spiritually, or physically, and all the effort put into figuring it out bores me. So I shut my phone in a kitchen drawer and reach for the gratitude journal I bought off Amazon two days ago. Some neuroscientist recommended it on a podcast I listen to called, *Happy for Free!* The journal cost me $23.99, but whatever.

Today, I am grateful for green tea, the color turquoise, and Emily Henry's *People We Meet on Vacation*. I jot these down in the journal. The idea is to create a growing list so that when you feel sad, you can look back and see all that there is to be grateful for. See? I don't need a ruby-red party dress or shots of tequila. I can have my *own* New Year's Eve party right here in the comfort of my apartment.

The FOMO hits bad. I get diarrhea. Thankfully, though, it's just one trip to the bathroom. To soothe my troubled tummy, I crack a can of chicken noodle soup and grab some saltine crackers.

Mom tells me to regard my thoughts like passing clouds. Temporary, fluffy clouds. But when I think about Abel and work my way down memory lane, through past New Year's parties and all the laughter, I can't help but feel like a part of me is wasting away now. That I will never laugh like that again because I will never *be in* that situation again. I can't relive the past. Things are changing, ready or not.

By 5 p.m. I have successfully completed three self-affirmation activities, read a good portion of an early 2000s syrupy romance novel, and powered through a forty-minute yoga video off YouTube. Nobody messaged me the entire forty minutes (unsurprising), so I keep my phone beside me on the couch as I turn on my greatest comfort show: *Parks and Recreation*. Two episodes into my self-proclaimed New Year's marathon, my phone rings.

Hunter.

"Hello?" I ask, trying not to sound obsessively grateful for human contact.

"Hey. How are you?"

"Good. Just watching Ron sprint away from Tammy Two."

"So, watching *Parks and Rec*."

My heart swells at the fact that he understands the reference. "*Parks and Rec*, indeed."

"Well, I know it's no Ron-Tammy drama, but would you be interested in going out for some wings?"

"Like, tonight?"

He chuckles. "Uh, yeah."

It's no old-school Cards Against Humanity with the Core Four, but it might just be the next best thing. Plus, who am I kidding? I'm desperate.

"Pick me up at seven," I tell him, and run to find my sparkliest party dress.

WHEN HUNTER SAID "WINGS," I pictured a smoky bar with the party in Times Square broadcasted on every flatscreen. I didn't think he meant a cutesy diner forty-eight minutes north in Aberdeen. That goes to say, the sequined red dress that hardly reaches my thighs is practically sinful. Not to mention the heels. And the makeup.

"I told you, you didn't need to dress up," Hunter says, and the smirk in his tone makes my eye twitch. "But I am happy to see that you still remember how to leave your apartment and live your life."

"For your information, I just submitted my much-awaited poetry collection. Table for two, please," I tell the waitress. She bites her cheek after regarding my outfit, and I attempt to pull the skirt down my thighs—to no avail.

"I know," Hunter says. We move down the aisles of rose-colored booths. "That's why we're here to celebrate."

Across from our booth, an elderly couple talks about the advertisements on the placemat. I catch the woman saying, "Weekly sewing club" and immediately scan the menu for alcohol. To my horror, they don't serve any.

"We'll take two strawberry milkshakes, please," Hunter tells the waitress.

"Actually, do you have any vodka possibly packed away back there?"

The waitress taps her ballpoint pen on her pad and stares me down with sharp caramel-colored eyes. "Two strawberry milkshakes coming up."

"I think we accidentally traveled back to the '70s," I whisper, once our waitress is gone. "I'll make a distraction. You run and get the car."

Hunter shrugs out of his David Outwear leather jacket. "Relax. I have family in Aberdeen. My parents and I used to come down from Worcester a lot over the summer, before my grandma passed. Trust me, the wings and milkshakes here are to *die* for."

"And yet, no alcohol."

"Life's more than alcohol, Cari." He smiles. "But it's your night. We are here to celebrate *Chasing Never's* first submission."

Chasing Never, the title of my new collection. A title that I adore.

A realization strikes me, and I grin at him. "You didn't have any plans tonight, did you?"

"Why would you ask that?"

"No one cares about the first submission, Hunter. If it was my final draft, sure." I play with the corner of the placemat. "Where are all your guy friends tonight?"

"At ridiculous parties."

"Not in a party mood?"

"Not in a drink till dawn mood," he corrects. His green eyes move to mine. "Plus, you're fun to hang out with."

"I get that a lot." I don't, but he laughs anyway.

Our milkshakes appear, and Hunter clinks his frosted glass to mine. "To first-draft submissions and going against the New Year's norm."

Okay, yes, this is the best milkshake my tastebuds have ever had the pleasure of getting acquainted with. Hunter sees it on my face. He smiles knowingly and nods.

"Any new research I should know about?" I ask.

"Nope, just working hard and practically living in my advisor's office."

"Right on."

He tells me about how his advisor's weird obsession with spiders —particularly the brown recluse—creeps him out, but he will never say anything because she has scored him more opportunities than he has fingers to count. For that reason, he can stomach long meetings in her office with all the spider posters and spider textbooks. ("Which makes me wonder why she didn't just get a PhD in biology," he says.)

"I talked to Abel," I blurt out. Technically, I didn't *mean* to interrupt. It's just a fatal flaw of mine.

Hunter's shoulders slump a little bit. "And?"

"We are—" I make a poof gesture with my hands, "—no more."

"I'm sorry, Cari." He really means it. His eyes are warm with empathy.

"We can go back to talking about creepy-crawly things now. I just had to get that off my chest."

He shakes his head. "Thank you for telling me. I'm sure that was a hard conversation."

"Yeah. Harder than Harry when Sally faked an orgasm in the diner."

Hunter opens his mouth, closes it, and bursts out laughing. I laugh, too. It feels *great* to laugh.

"There was no reason to make that conversation sexual, but... okay," Hunter says.

We laugh harder, even score a glance from the elderly couple across from us. When our waitress asks for our orders, Hunter can hardly keep a straight face. I giggle uncontrollably and slap the table after she walks away. Truthfully, it wasn't *that* funny, but days of being holed up in my apartment has made me slap-happy and laughter-deprived. So now I'm a giggling mess.

"This must be a good sign," I say, once I catch my breath.

"How's that?" Hunter's face is beet red. I love it.

"Because when I make jokes about a situation, you can tell I'm starting to feel better."

"Are you?"

I sip my milkshake, testing the waters of my fragile emotions. "Maybe a sliver."

"A sliver is better than nothing."

"Abso-freakin'-lutely. I guess my only question is...what happens now?" I pick at my cuticles. "Christie said *Chasing Never* will be released in late 2024, and I've gotta go back to New York for the book tour. What do I do until then?"

"Do what you always do."

Our wings arrive: two plates of glistening, barbecue-slicked heaven. They remind me of the chicken wing Ferris wheel Abel ordered the night he swept me out onto the dance floor in front of total strangers. I swallow the memory down.

"What do I always do?" I ask.

"Write," Hunter says. "Work out. Hang out with your friends. Continue to exist but find the difference between being alive and *living*. Plus," he continues, biting into a wing. "I know that if you and Abel ever see each other again, you guys will be fine."

"How can you be so sure?"

He shrugs. "Because you're both mature adults."

"No, I mean, how can you be sure that I'll ever see him again?"

"Because in this group, there's no *not* seeing people. I've only met Kelsey once, but..."

I laugh, and again, it feels really good.

"Just do you," he says.

Just do me.

I like that. There are mountains I still have to climb, worries I still have to confront. What's beautiful, though, is that they are *my* mountains, *my* worries. This is *my* journey. It is a choice, I realize: I can either hide under the fluffy blanket on my couch forever or I can stretch, stand up, and move forward with life. Besides, crying gets exhausting after a while.

I smile and tear a piece of meat off its bone. And, yes, these wings *are* to die for.

"I'm glad you called me tonight, Hunter. I like hanging out with you. Thank you for this mini celebration."

"It is the least I could do for my famous friend."

As we sit here in the booth, cracking joke after joke, it occurs to me that Hunter has moved into the apartment building in my heart. When, exactly, I couldn't tell you. But he's there. This tall genius of a man with the summer-green eyes and lopsided smile and drop-of-a-hat empathy is ingrained *deep* in my heart. And hours later, after we've had our fill of wings and counted down to midnight with the rest of the rowdy elders, I promise myself that whatever 2024 brings my way, I will survive it.

55

My favorite part of winter is the end.

I don't care what the podcast *Happy for Free!* preaches; there is nothing calming about slush, skeletal trees, or drool-gray skies. I had to invest in an SAD lamp to get me through the thick of January, and even then, there were weeks when the pottery class and local book club I'd joined still felt like massive chores. In fact, I reevaluated my whole existence the night MaryAnn, a mother of six in my book club, commented that Colleen Hoover was just a *tad* overrated for her taste but that *It Ends with Us* is still a must-read. When we read my debut, *Left or Right*, the women rated it three out of five stars: "*Amazing, but I find it hard to believe that someone can actually get low enough to contemplate suicide.*" (Tara Anthony, nonbeliever in mental illness but *avid* believer in horoscopes.) That was only early February.

Luckily, Ruth kept me sane with stories of her time with Amber and Mia. Apparently, Amber's new beau Grady is America's Male Sweetheart. Ruth showed me pictures as we waited between customers at the bakery. Amber has toothpick-straight brown hair, streaked with highlights, and her daughter Mia is a spitting image of her. Grady has that chiseled jawline and a soft midsection that suggests he only works out when he wants. He makes the look work. All the pictures of Ruth standing behind her smiling granddaughter or holding her daughter's hand for the first time in years made my whole body feel grateful, not just my heart.

Ruth was particularly proud to hear that I had since reconnected with my mother as well.

"I told you everything would be fine, Cari," she said, swatting my arm.

"You're right. Next time, I will listen to you, Miss Boss."

That same disgustingly cold afternoon, while we were whipping up fresh cupcakes, she asked me about Abel. Was he enjoying his new car? Were things heating up between us? I hadn't told her about his manic phase or the hospital or our conversation because a part of me still winced at the memory. Instead, I explained that things just didn't work out, shrugged, and went back to stirring.

"Eh, they can't all be winners," she said. I appreciated that response.

So, I guess winter wasn't all bad. The best part was that it skipped by. A few badly molded cups, awkward conversations with whiny female bibliophiles, and phone calls home later, I started noticing the sun peeking out more.

And now, as I blow out the candles on the store-bought ice cream cake in my apartment, I feel like I can breathe again.

"HAPPY BIRTHDAY!" Kelsey screams in my ear. She traps me in a suffocating hug.

"Twenty-five and proud," Raquel announces, raising her glass.

Katerine blows me a kiss from across the table.

I've needed this for months: a night with my girls. Granted, my birthday is March 16, so the earth is still a thawing icebox, but it helps to think that spring is now literally days away. That groundhog doesn't know what he's talking about.

"Can you get some plates, babe?" Kelsey asks Raquel.

The two of them went official January 20. I can't be Kelsey's friend and forget that date, not with the way she posts on Snapchat.

They are a glass of brandy and chocolate mousse as a couple. I don't like to take credit for their connection, but I *was* the one who invited Raquel to Friendsgiving, so personally, I think they should tag me in their appreciation posts on Instagram. But whatever. All that matters is that I have never seen Kelsey this happy. And from the looks of it, Raquel doesn't appear to be such a love cynic anymore. When Raquel pecks Kelsey on the lips before heading to the kitchen, I don't even tell them to get a room.

Katerine leans across the table. "I'm glad to see you smiling." She drove three and a half hours to be here for my birthday, occasionally texting me at a stoplight to explain how the car in front, beside, or behind her was being an asshole but that she was *so* excited to see me.

"Well, *you're* here," I say. "Of course, I'm smiling."

"I know the last few months have been rough."

Yes. She was one of my Go-to-When-Panicking contacts these last couple weeks, mostly for hour-long FaceTime calls that were 80 percent me venting about the next round of revisions for *Chasing Never* and the anxiety that my readers will hate it. 20 percent of those calls was Katerine telling me to "get out of my effing head."

"I have you to thank for my sanity," I tell her.

"I have you to thank for the opportunity to hone my unlicensed therapist skills," she says and reaches over to squeeze my hand.

Raquel returns with a stack of paper plates and the tray of home-made margaritas we whipped up not ten minutes ago. We didn't plan the details of this party too closely, considering we bought the cake on our way home from a restaurant and decided on the stairwell up to my apartment to make margaritas. The two don't necessarily mix, but then, twenty-five wasn't a birthday I was jonesing to have perfect. The party wasn't even my idea. Kelsey made a group chat three weeks ago.

"I want to make a toast," Raquel says after passing around the glasses.

"Oh, good grief," I mutter.

She laughs and raises her glass toward me. Kelsey and Katerine follow suit. "To the kindest, most creative, baddest bitch alive." I feel my face turn a pink-lemonade shade. "May twenty-five be a year of growth, love, and good vibes."

"And another best-selling poetry collection," Kelsey chimes in.

"And a kick-ass book tour," Katerine adds.

I remember being thirteen years old, with a wardrobe of Aeropostale T-shirts and light-wash capris, neon-pink hair pieces, and a mouth full of braces, wondering if I would *ever* have friends that felt like family or extensions of myself. My middle school friendships were mostly built off similar classes and lunch periods. My "best friends" by Christmas became acquaintances by the end of June. That theme continued through high school. It took twelve years, but I finally know what true friendship is. It is right here with Kelsey, Raquel, and Katerine—the people who have seen me at my worst and stayed.

"I need a slice of cake before I cry," I say. "Thank you guys so much."

The homemade margarita tastes like fresh starts and gratitude, with the ice cream cake as a sweet burst of excitement. Excitement for the release of *Chasing Never* and summer and life.

I talked about this with Mom today, how I am finally starting to see the shoreline beyond my past and my mistakes. Since Abel's hospitalization, I have been up to my chin, treading water in an ocean of regret and guilt. Like, how much time I wasted thinking my own mother hated me. Or letting go of Abel when I was fearful the decision would come across as weak and selfish, when in reality, we never would have worked anyway. Finally, after weeks of filling in that damn gratitude journal, listening to *Happy for Free!*, and reconnecting with my mom, I'm starting to realize that a miscommunication or an unstable relationship does not make me a failure. They make me human. That doesn't necessarily take away the shame. There are still nights when I cry my eyes out. I miss Abel. I miss home. Hell, I miss the days when Kai and I would walk through Times Square and snap pictures of the colorful screens and buildings just to create an aesthetic Instagram post. Mostly though, I miss *me*.

When I vented all of this to Mom this morning (phone on speaker as I scrambled eggs) she'd said, "There's always a shoreline, sweetheart, no matter how far away it appears."

"You know," Kelsey says now, "when I turn twenty-five next month, we're having a blowout party." She has a frosting mustache.

"Should I contact Doja Cat's agent now or wait till April?" I ask.

"Now's good," she replies. "A month in advance is always best for those things."

Sure, the shoreline is close, but there is still something massive in the way. A whale carcass maybe: Kelsey's twenty-fifth birthday, when she will undoubtedly invite Abel. Though maybe I'll get lucky, and Mr. Flakey Flakerson will resort back to his old ways of not showing. That would certainly spare me some anxiety and embarrassing sweat stains. But a part of me is also desperate to see him. We still follow each other on Instagram, and his lack of recent posting has my prideful brain thinking it's because he has been home moping since December. Highly doubtful, but it was the perfect lie to shake me out of a close depression in the middle of winter. (I also know full well that if he *were* to post, it would be a gunshot to the lung. (Yes, I would still look. Letting go is hard)). But to see him in person...to look into those blue eyes and play the whole "he's just a friend" game...am I even capable of that yet? Everyone has that one person that, if paths were to unexpectedly cross again, all their confidence would drain in two seconds flat. Like, *Hi, I'm the shit...until I see you again. Then, I'm nobody when I want so badly to be somebody.*

Abel is my Oh, Shit Person.

But Mom's right. I *can* swim around a whale carcass. I *can* make it to the shoreline. I *can* see Abel and keep it platonic. I can love him and still let go. Two things can exist at once. After all, if life were so black and white, what would inspire my poetry?

56

I know I am ready to face Abel the moment Tucker sends a thumbs-up in response to one of the three pictures I texted him with the caption:

> Which outfit makes me seem sophisticated and successful?

The first benefit of having a brother: receiving a brutally honest answer. He could have said all the dresses make me look like a desperate contestant on *America's Next Top Model*, but he liked the image of my knee-length black dress with the flowy mesh sleeves. The second benefit of having a brother: receiving a man's input when it matters. I know Tucker has better things to do, like finishing the draft of his students' next quiz and supporting Lauren as she plans every detail of their outing to see Taylor Swift. But he sacrificed five seconds to reply to my text. That is why I love him.

Appearing sophisticated and successful is important tonight because in the last month, I have tried very hard to celebrate "the little things." Opening up in my book club (explaining to Tara that mental illness actually *does* exist and watching her nod slowly, either in agreement or to shut me up). Not accidentally creating a deformed cup in pottery class. Making my mom laugh over the phone after an emotionally tough day with her clients. Looking at myself in the mirror and seeing an okay person. Or, on my better days, an *awesome* person—capable of giving and receiving love. That is why tonight, I want to look like I live in that mindset.

Tonight I am going to see Abel for the first time in four months.

Kelsey's twenty-fifth birthday is at the Cheesecake Factory. If there is one thing Kelsey Witchett loves, it is eating cheesecake in a golden-lit restaurant surrounded by her friends and family. I'd texted her weeks ago, asking who had RSVP'd, feigning nonchalant curiosity. She had responded with a list of the usual suspects: Raquel, Noah, Abel, Hunter, the entire Witchett family, Felix and Piper (Kelsey's friends at the boutique where she works). Abel's name was sandwiched in there, which I knew Kelsey did on purpose. In the past, she would have put his name first or last and in all caps with a couple of smirking emojis to make me blush.

She never asks about my split with Abel. In fact, she knows very little except for the basics I'd briefly explained over text back in December, to which she replied,

> I'm sure that was very difficult. Proud of you guys for talking through it and coming to a decision. I'm here if you need me. I'll text you if Abel calls me crying.

That text never came. But I know Kelsey would never put me in a situation that makes me uncomfortable. After sending the list of party people, she told me to stay as long as I want and leave whenever. Code for: *I won't take offense if you want to jet.*

I refuse to jet. Abel may be my Oh, Shit Person, but he is not the end-all and be-all. Hunter's famous words.

After curling my hair, adding some glitter to my eyelids, and slipping into the dress Tucker okayed, I set off. My fingers shake slightly on the steering wheel, but I expect nothing less of myself. At least Hunter will be there to help calm the anxiety. There is also Plan B: fake God-awful period cramps, but who needs Plan B? Plan B is for wussies. That's not me anymore.

It takes me three years to find a parking space. The glowing Cheesecake Factory sign against the indigo night sky might as well say, *Can You Do this, Carrington?* I slide into a space between two massive Chevy trucks and strut my stuff to the front door. I *can* do this.

Kelsey's grandmother, Nana Hannah, is smoking a cigarette outside the entrance. For seventy-eight, she looks fantastic: a halo of silver-gold hair, naturally beautiful age lines, rosy lipstick, sparkling eggplant-purple shirt and black slacks.

"Nana Hannah," I sing and gently wrap my arms around her. "Do you remember me?"

"I've got the mind of an elephant, child." She pats my arm and nods to the entrance. "The circus is in there."

I burst out laughing. "Am I late?"

"Oh please. It's not a party till *I* walk back in, Carrington."

I *love* this woman.

Once she is finished with her cigarette, I escort her back inside. It is not hard to find the party, with Nana Hannah towing me toward the massive row of pushed-together tables and howling laughter, but also because the second I pass through the doors I am searching.

There he is.

Seated between a suddenly grown-up Bryson Witchett and an animated, talkative Noah. His head is angled toward Noah, a smile tugging at his lips, faint blush painting his cheeks. Dressed in a gray button-up, his golden forearms on full display. Blue, blue eyes—vibrant even from a few tables away.

Kelsey leaps in front of me, cutting off my view. The first thing I notice before she squeezes me in a hug is that her white eyeliner matches the white flowers in her orange sundress.

"Happy birthday," I cry. "I got you a box."

"A *box?*" She releases me and presses a hand over her heart. "That's all I've ever wanted."

I actually got her a pair of custom-made earrings that say, "Boss Bitch." They ate a chunk out of my paycheck, but I know Kelsey will wear them until they disintegrate. She takes the wrapped box from my hands and motions for me to come join the commotion. The pro here is that the only seat left is next to Hunter. The con: it's right across from Abel.

A chorus of "Cari!" and "How the heck are ya?" rain down as I take my seat. Hunter smiles at me. There is a knowing look in his eyes: a look that whispers encouragement. I inhale, nod, and face front.

"Cari!" Noah exclaims. "I'm glad you're here. I was just telling everyone how I pranked my boss on April Fool's Day."

"Pranked is a strong word," Abel teases.

His blue eyes slide to mine. They are kind, but they leave a sting in my chest.

"I would call spilling fake vomit on the floor during a meeting a prank, yes," Noah argues.

"Where do you get fake vomit?" Hunter asks.

"Dude, how are you still employed?" Bryson, Kelsey's younger brother, asks from the other side of Abel.

"You're all missing the point!" Noah says, waving his hands emphatically. "Jamal was *freaking* out."

My eyes are Gorilla Glued to Abel. I expected him to be...sadder? More...at a loss for words, over my outfit at least. But he's just laughing and shaking his head at Noah, occasionally glancing around the table, occasionally glancing at *me.* Where are the secret puppy dog eyes and symbolic pout that GetBackatYourEx.com promised? Where is the regretful lip-biting? He isn't exhibiting any of these signals!

Panic kicks in. I reach for the ice water Hunter ordered me before I arrived and down half of it.

He's over me. He never liked me. He never loved me. I was just a piece in his game! I clear my throat and focus very hard on browsing the menu in front of me. Zero in on a mouth-watering picture of spicy rigatoni. Read each ingredient slowly under my breath.

"The intrusive thoughts," Mom had said over the phone, "can't stand up against logic."

Where is the logic in any of these thoughts? I ask myself as my eyes skip down to the next item on the menu. Abel himself told me that he loved me, but that we wouldn't have truly worked as a couple because of our repressed, unhealthy desires. He wanted to outrun bipolar disorder. I wanted to show him I could be a perfect girlfriend. Those two do not mix well. I use this information and spin it back on my intrusive thoughts. *He's not necessarily over me; he's healing, too. He will always like me. He did love me. We were pieces in* each other's *game.*

When my breath is under control, I look up at Abel and find him looking at me, too. It takes a second to realize he is gauging my reaction to something Noah has just said. Everyone around us is laughing. When I see Abel's lips split into a glowing smile, see the lone dimple appear in his cheek, watch his eyes scrunch shut and his shoulders shake as he laughs...an epiphany settles over me.

Abel is happy right now. His laugh is booming, contagious—his smile even more so. He spent weeks in a lonely manic state, days in a lonely hospital, hours trapped in his own brain. He has exhausted himself, tackling schoolwork, therapy appointments, comforting his own mother after her suicide attempt. Abel has been to hell more times than anyone I know.

But right now...he is laughing, so hard his face has turned pink.

Is this not what I wanted all along? His happiness outweighs my panic. In fact, it *eases* my panic. It sure as hell holds a middle finger up to GetBackatYourEx.com.

Life is more than manifesting or casting spells for someone's downfall. We are all human. We all want to heal. We all want to love. We all want to *be* loved. Mostly, we are all searching for happiness.

I realize, as Abel throws a witty remark back at Noah and bursts out laughing again, that I can let him go. That even with the terri-fying lows, there will still be moments of joy. Hunter is right. Abel is a soldier. He will be just fine.

And so will I.

Suddenly, I don't care about my dress or appearing sophisticated and successful. All I care about is joining in on the laughter and allowing the moment to be as it is.

"You can't get fired for making a grown man scream like a little girl!" Noah shouts.

"You can if it's your boss, man!" Hunter says.

Nearly the whole table is laughing now.

"I'd scream, too," the girl beside me says. "I can't stand vomit."

Her raven hair falls to her collarbone in soft, barely there waves. I notice the semicolon tattoo on her wrist.

"Suicide prevention," I say, gesturing to the tattoo. "That's awesome."

She startles and looks over at me. Never in my life have I seen eyes with the perfect mix of brown and gray, and framed by thick lashes at that. She is gorgeous.

"Oh, yeah," she says, holding up her arm. A blush warms her porcelain cheeks. "I got it after my sister took her life."

"Shit." Embarrassment heats my cheeks. "I'm sorry."

"It's all right. Thank you." Her full, glossy lips pull into a sad smile. "It was five years ago. My mom struggles with terrible depression, too, so I'm no stranger to mental illness."

"Do you...um...have it?" I'm twenty-five. Still don't know where the line is.

"No. I used to wonder about that a lot, why it...skipped me. My dad left when my sister and I were really young, and I had to watch my family crumble. I used to think I should struggle the way they were, too. But then it hit me." Her smile is adorable. "I'm meant to be a supporter."

"Meaning...."

"I belong to a couple mental health committees in the area, advocating for increased resources and education, stuff like that. Our goal is to end the stigma."

"Wait. How do you know Kelsey?" I ask.

"Oh, I work with her. I'm Piper." She holds up her hand.

Color me dumbfounded. A fashionista-slash-mental-health-advocate? This breaks the record for how fast I love people after meeting them. Up until now, number one on that list had been Abel.

"Hi." I shake Piper's hand. "I'm Carrington."

Her eyes narrow the tiniest bit. "Wait, are you by chance Carrington Daughtler? The poet?"

"Guilty as charged."

She slaps the table. "I *thought* I recognized you from your website, but I didn't want to say anything because I didn't want to be *that* girl. I am a *huge* fan. I've read *Left or Right* three times."

She might just be sweeter than the caramel-apple cheesecake I plan to order for dessert.

"Are you talking about Cari?" Abel chimes in. "Yeah, she's wicked talented."

"*Right?*" Piper agrees.

They continue to gush over my work, but that isn't what has me smiling. What has me smiling is that a person like Piper exists in this world.

"I love you forever," Kelsey tells me, as I hug her goodbye.

"I love you forever and then some," I say. "Welcome to twenty-five. Took ya long enough."

She sticks her tongue out and gives me a playful push toward the door. Hunter tells Kelsey happy birthday and then follows me out into the cool April night air. We stop under the glow of the Cheesecake Factory sign.

He shovels a hand through his hair and fixes those green eyes on me. "You okay?"

"You know what? I actually am."

As the night stretched on, Abel and Piper bonded over music, movies, and, naturally, the fact that mental health awareness is not yet where it should be. But at the same time, Noah went on and on about how his mom had sued their dog's groomer, and Hunter showed me pictures from his family vacation to the Grand Canyon last summer, and Kelsey made a spectacle blowing out her candles and opening presents. There was more to the night than just Abel—and his new connection to Piper. There is the fact that I *love* Piper. The fact that Noah made me laugh so hard I choked on a rigatoni noodle and Hunter had to pat my back until I hacked it up.

"Good. I'm glad." Hunter's lopsided smile looks roguishly handsome in this lighting, but I choose to chalk that up to the cheesecake. "What now?"

"Zoom meetings with my team." I step out of the way of a family walking eagerly toward the main entrance. "Pamela emailed me back with the second round of rewrites. She said we're nearly there."

"That's incredible." When Hunter hugs me, I hug him back.

It feels good to know that he has supported me all this way. That even though I feel a twinge of jealousy over Piper and Abel's new connection, I also know that we will all experience happiness in our time, in our own ways, and that it's unfair to deprive anyone of that experience. The thought gives me all the peace I need.

"You're invited to my book tour," I tell Hunter, teasing.

"Oh, yeah? Do I get special access to newsletters?"

"Better. You get to hang out with me before and after I sign books."

"*No way.*"

"Way."

"What can I do to repay you?"

"Nothing," I say. "You helped me write the damn thing."

"I helped you *conceptualize* the damn thing."

I laugh. *My friend soulmate, how I adore him.* "Just remember to do me a favor when you meet me on tour."

"What's that?"

"Stay a while."

His green eyes soften. A smile paints its way across his lips. "Absolutely."

57

Contrary to what non-writers might think, I don't submit the final draft of *Chasing Never* in the lobby of a grand hotel with classical music booming through my AirPods and a glass of champagne in my hand. I submit it on the toilet while chewing a handful of Swedish Fish. Once the document is sent, confetti doesn't shoot out of invisible cannons. I stand up, flush my business, wash my hands, and call my mother.

"I'm so proud of you, sweetheart."

Hearing her say that, it means more to me than all the fan praise I could ever receive.

Dad chimes in with a "Congratulations, Tiny Carrot!"

"Go out and enjoy a fun day," Mom advises.

"I have to go in to work, actually. Ruth said she has a surprise for me." Knowing her, it'll probably be a batch of purple-frosted cupcakes and a congratulatory card. "Did I mention how much I love her?"

"Many times," I hear Dad answer.

I laugh and put them on speaker so I can do a social media post about submitting my final draft. As I refresh the page, a picture pops of up of Abel. He looks ungodly handsome, standing in front of a brick building with Ray-Ban sunglasses and a white T-shirt with cargo shorts. The first picture is stoic, the second silly, the third happy. His smile is still beautiful. I click on the post and see Piper tagged as the photographer.

It is only a pinch. A flu shot. A bee sting.

"Tell Ruth I'd love to meet her sometime," Mom says.

One deep breath. Two. I heart Abel's picture and scroll on.

"I will. She's *awesome*, like, a top-notch boss. Did I tell you about that time I yelled at a customer?"

My stomach sounds like someone dropped a pack of Mentos into the depths of Mount Vesuvius. I am *that* hungry. I can barely concentrate on Noah's dramatic retelling of the first time he had sex with his current girlfriend, Olga. She's a Russian woman he met last month on a vacation to Saint Petersburg, because why not? She is sitting beside him with her long, golden legs crossed at the ankles, swirling the red wine in her glass and nodding frantically to every little detail.

We are at Kelsey's townhouse in Philadelphia for a midsummer cookout, and the heat is not helping my hangry tummy. Even with my floppy sun hat on, the July sun is assaulting the top of my head. My arms are going to be a lobster shade if I sit here much longer (always wear your sunscreen, kids!).

"Be honest, Olga," Kelsey calls from her beach towel. "How small is Noah's dick?"

Raquel tugs her sunglasses down her nose and snorts.

Olga cocks her head. "Mmm...he's average."

The girls explode, howling like hyenas, and I press a hand to my mouth because I'm laughing, too.

"You can all piss off," Noah says.

The sliding glass door opens, and Abel steps out behind Piper, their paper plates filled with veggies, slices of cheese, and watermelon. They aren't dating, but with the way they walk shoulder-to-shoulder and smile at each other like no one else is here, they have to be right on the edge. The "super close friends" label can only go so far.

Sometimes I still feel the sting. I still miss my silly text chains with Abel. I still miss our banter. I even miss watching Hallmark movies and downing two bags of popcorn with him. In a way, I will always feel the sting. That's called being human. What matters now is what I do with the sting.

I channel it into my writing.

Chasing Never hit number one on the *New York Times* Bestsellers List the week it released, late last November. The following week, I got a text from Abel that said simply,

> This collection is my favorite. Thank you.

The serotonin fountains in my brain flooded that day.

I spent the entirety of December on tour, signing books, taking pictures with fans, and chatting about the importance of mental health awareness in the community. Christie lived up to her promise, too. I did *Good Morning America*, *The Today Show*, and *Jimmy Fallon* all in one week. While those experiences were incredible (I took *several* selfies with Hoda and Jimmy), the highlight of my tour was speaking with my readers, listening to their stories. As it turns out, I have a *lot* of readers who struggle with mental conditions of all kinds, from mild anxiety to debilitating schizophrenia. The conversations weren't about those labels, though. My readers told me about how they'd lost loved ones or were finally in a healthy relationship for the first time ever. There we were, in the stacks of a bookstore, chatting about what it means to truly love someone. No two meanings were identical.

I realized later, at a café in Manhattan surrounded by my wonderful agent and team, that there is not *supposed* to be one meaning. Love is not something that can be contained to one type of mind, body, or soul. Hell, it even transcends human knowledge at times. Love is a gray matter, stuck somewhere between the black and the white, in a dimension we may never understand.

What I *do* know for certain is that today, my love for Abel is different from the drooling, infatuated perspective I used to have. I see him as a human being now, not some trophy of perfection that I could compete to win in *American Ninja Warrior*. My love for him has deepened. I have stared his flaws in the face, and I have kissed his smiling lips. All those days of silently yearning for him in college, all those nights hearing him speak about life and his own struggles—all of it has led to this: I recognize myself in him. And as I have grown in my love for Abel Harpen, I have grown to love myself.

Besides, I think I may be more attracted to the sidekicks than to the Prince Charmings.

"One hot dog, extra ketchup!" Hunter calls from behind the grill.

I jump up from the plastic chair and march straight over, so bonkers-ravenous that I don't even see the second hand shooting out to grab the hot dog—*my* hot dog—until our hands lock on the same plate.

"Oh, sorry," Abel says.

Our gazes connect, and we start dying laughing.

"Are you trying to steal my food again, Cari Carrington?"

"It's what I'm known for."

"One hot dog, extra ketchup," Hunter says, setting another plate on the nearby table.

"Go on," Abel insists. "Take this one. I'll let you off the hook." He smiles at me—that beautiful, timeless, wholesome smile that will forever make my heart double Dutch jump rope.

As he moves past me to pick up the other hot dog, my eyes flicker toward Piper. She is seated at the end of the picnic table, strands of dark hair pulled free from her French braid. She glows when she laughs, like the sun bends to her will and gives her full spotlight—not in an arrogant way, but in a way that says, "Look. Here is a precious human being, finding her own happiness in this unique moment." When she speaks, everyone leans forward slightly, like they can't wait to gobble up whatever remark she is about to make. Never in a snarky tone, but in a playful one that suggests nothing but love. When she told me she read *Chasing Never* in one day and went on and on about how talented I am, I didn't get a big head. I got a big heart, swollen adoration for the incredible human being I was speaking to. You could zoom all the way into Piper's bone marrow; you will not find one ounce of malice. That is why I know Abel will be safe and sound in her hands. She catches my eye and gestures to the seat next to her.

"Sit here," she mouths with that darling-sweet smile.

She saved me a seat. Angel.

"One second," I reply.

Poor Hunter has been hard at work with these hot dogs, his own skin grilling in the heat from Hell's fireplace. His baby-blue T-shirt has zero sweat stains though, so he must have some killer genes. Or his body has given up on homeostasis.

"I'm here to rescue you," I say. "Take a break and come join the party."

He laughs. "Oh, where would I be without you, Cari?"

"Living in a box under a bridge, surviving off discarded bags of chips and scraps in the trash."

"That sounds brutal. You have ketchup on your chin, by the way."

I wipe my hand across my face. He sets a plate of extra hot dogs and hamburgers on the table and turns off the grill. A breeze sweeps through the area, rustling his hair, giving it that nice windswept look.

"If I'm living in a box in this scenario, where are you?" he asks.

I consider my answer. "Probably in the box across the street with a journal, writing a new collection entitled *Thinking Outside the Box*."

He chuckles. "Have you? Started writing anything new?"

I grin. "As a matter of fact, I have. And this one's for me."

The way his face lights up gives my nervous system an exhilarating electric shock.

"Well," he says. "We will need to celebrate. I'm thinking something big. Maybe forty people. We have to invite your grandma boss, too."

"Ruth will be the first person on that invite list," I confirm. "But I have a better idea."

Hunter's eyes lock with mine. "Let's hear it."

"Buy me a drink."

He cocks his head. "What?"

Heat kisses my cheeks, but courage lights my heart on fire. "Buy me a drink. At a bar. Just the two of us."

The light starts in his eyes as a tiny flicker, and then it melts down to his mouth and jawline, through his shoulders and hands. His shell cracks, and the real Hunter emerges—someone lighthearted, childlike, and ecstatic. Someone I cannot wait to meet.

He clears his throat, smiles cheek to cheek. "I would love to, Carrington."

ACKNOWLEDGMENTS

Gray Matter is my favorite book I have ever written to date. It encompasses so much that I am passionate about mental health, psychology, and love. If you know me, you know these topics are always in the spotlight of my heart. There are many people I want to thank for making this dream come true.

First and foremost, my incredibly kind and intelligent publisher, Deborah Kevin. Thank you for including me in the writing network and cohort and for providing me with so many opportunities with some outstanding people. I do not think I will ever be able to fully repay you for helping make this project come to life. Additionally, I want to thank Kris Faatz for taking the time to edit *Gray Matter* and really helping me shape my beloved characters into who I knew they could be.

And where would this book be without my parents' undying support? Mom, Dad, THANK YOU for always believing in me and supporting my decision to be an author and pursue my own passions in the mental health field. I am so blessed and lucky to have you both in my life. I do not know where I would be if it weren't for you. I hope you enjoyed this book! May it hold you over until my next project is complete. I also want to thank my sister Skylar for her support and interest in all that I do. She is an amazing role model for me, and I'm very grateful to have her as my big sis.

My grandparents are also at the heart of this novel: Shirley, John, Alvin, and Margaret—some of my biggest supporters. I LOVE YOU

ALL SO MUCH. I hope you enjoyed this book as much as I enjoyed writing it.

These acknowledgments would not be complete without some honorable mentions: Cross Lawrence (for always having my back and helping me brainstorm new ideas), Gavin Franz (for always making me laugh), and Chuck Thrush (for his kindness and support).

And to you, reader, for making my job as a writer so rewarding. I love connecting with you through the power of stories. You make my life so amazing. THANK YOU FOR READING. Onto the next adventure!

ABOUT THE AUTHOR

Photo by: *Photo credit: Helen Kruml*

Avery Volz knew she wanted to be an author when she received her first journal at the tender age of eight. Today, she studies psychology at Penn State York and juggles three clubs, sixteen credits, and research—all in addition writing! A mental health advocate, she loves writing about characters who struggle with their mental health to raise awareness and squash the stigma. She is also a world-renowned hip-hop dancer, dog-lover, and avid reader. She currently lives in Pennsylvania. *Gray Matter* is her third novel. Learn more at https://www.averyvolz.com/

 instagram.com/averyvolzistyping

linkedin.com/in/avery-volz

ABOUT THE PUBLISHER

Founded in 2019, Highlander Press is a vibrant, mid-sized publishing house dedicated to transforming the world through the power of words. We are deeply committed to diversity and bringing big ideas to the forefront. At Highlander Press, we help authors navigate the journey from initial concept through writing, editing, and publishing, culminating in the release of a book that not only fulfills a lifelong dream but also solidifies their expertise and boosts their confidence.

Our unique approach centers on forging strong, collaborative relationships with women-owned businesses across the publishing spectrum, including graphic design, marketing, launching, copyright management, and publicity. We believe in the power of community and operate by the mantra, "a rising tide lifts all boats." This philosophy not only enhances our business model but also ensures that our authors receive unparalleled support and opportunities to succeed.

Join us in making a mark in the literary world, where your voice is heard, and your message has the power to change lives. Visit us at highlanderpressbooks.com to start your publishing journey.

www.ingramcontent.com/pod-product-compliance
Lightning Source LLC
Chambersburg PA
CBHW021226190726
48289CB00005B/1199